HEART

OF

THE

WYRD
WOOD

Praise for RJ Barker

Praise for the Forsaken Trilogy

"This is a splendid fantasy work, full of RJ's trademark invention. Highly recommended."
—Adrian Tchaikovsky, Arthur C. Clarke Award–winning author of *Children of Time*

"A triple-threat of world-building, character and plot, *Gods of the Wyrdwood* represents the work of an experienced novelist at the top of his game. This is *Avatar* meets *Dune*— on shrooms."
—*SFX*

"A sweeping story of destiny and redemption. Weighty, deliberate, tender and brutal, this is a big, wonderful book and an utterly involving read."
—*Daily Mail*

"At times lyrical and others stark in its depiction of battle, *Gods of the Wyrdwood* has all the delicious worldbuilding of a '90s fantasy you'd want to cut your teeth on but with characters and situations that resonate with modernity."
—Linden A. Lewis, author of *The First Sister*

Praise for the Tide Child Trilogy

"A vividly realized high-seas epic that pulls you deep into its world and keeps you tangled there until the very last word."
—Evan Winter, author of *The Rage of Dragons*

"I absolutely loved it. A whole lot of swashbuckling awesomeness by RJ Barker. He has crafted a fascinating world and a twisty plot, both rooted in characters I came to care about. A definite winner for me."
—John Gwynne, author of *The Shadow of the Gods*

"An epic tale of duty and obligation and honor, and what bravery really means. I can't recommend it enough."

—Peter McLean, author of *Priest of Bones*

"A unique and memorable world—harsh and brutal and full of sharply realized, powerful female characters. Barker has managed to craft a story inspired by *Moby Dick*, *Game of Thrones*, and pirate lore, and readers will be drawn in and fascinated."

—*Booklist* (starred review)

Praise for the Wounded Kingdom

"Often poignant and always intriguing, *Age of Assassins* reveals its mysteries with the style of a magic show and the artful grace of a gifted storyteller."

—Nicholas Eames, author of *Kings of the Wyld*

"Outstanding. Beautifully written, perfectly paced, and assured. Kept me reading well into the early hours of the morning. A wonderful first book—a wonderful book, period—that should be at the very top of your to-read list."

—James Islington, author of
The Shadow of What Was Lost

By RJ Barker

THE WOUNDED KINGDOM

Age of Assassins
Blood of Assassins
King of Assassins

THE TIDE CHILD TRILOGY

The Bone Ships
Call of the Bone Ships
The Bone Ship's Wake

THE FORSAKEN TRILOGY

Gods of the Wyrdwood
Warlords of Wyrdwood
Heart of the Wyrdwood

HEART
OF
THE
WYRD
WOOD

The Forsaken Trilogy:
Book Three

RJ BARKER

orbitbooks.net

Orbit
Hachette Book Group
1290 Avenue of the Americas
New York, NY 10104
orbitbooks.net

First Edition: June 2025
Simultaneously published in Great Britain by Orbit

Orbit is an imprint of Hachette Book Group.
The Orbit name and logo are registered trademarks of Little, Brown Book Group Limited.

The publisher is not responsible for websites (or their content) that are not owned by the publisher.

The Hachette Speakers Bureau provides a wide range of authors for speaking events. To find out more, go to hachettespeakersbureau.com or email HachetteSpeakers@hbgusa.com.

Orbit books may be purchased in bulk for business, educational, or promotional use. For information, please contact your local bookseller or the Hachette Book Group Special Markets Department at special.markets@hbgusa.com.

Library of Congress Control Number: 2025930567

ISBNs: 9780316402088 (trade paperback), 9780316402187 (ebook)

Printed in the United States of America

LSC-C

Printing 1, 2025

For my editor, Jenni Hill, who has
taught me so much stuff

What Has Gone Before

After their victory at the village of Harn, the warrior Cahan and the villagers must relocate to the Wyrdwood and found a new village to avoid reprisals. Cahan, needing the strength of his cowl to stop a force of Rai following them but refusing to take a life to feed it, finds he can access his power through the bluevein sickness in the ground. However, this turns out to be a dark gift that threatens to overwhelm him.

The villagers reach Wyrdwood safely and ally with the Forestals. Cahan agrees to assist them partly to get away from Venn, who suspects something is wrong with him. Before he leaves, his burgeoning love affair with Furin, the Leoric of Harn, is consummated. However, when he leaves, he is unaware that the damaged Rai, Sorha, bent on revenge, has followed them. His cowl is unable to sense her, thus she has managed to avoid being found.

In New Harn the villagers rediscover themselves, chiefly the former butcher Ont who dedicates his life to Ranya, the God brought to them by monk Udinny who sacrificed herself to save the people of the village. As well as his new calling, he forges a surprising friendship with the Forestal Ania.

Udinny, monk of Ranya, is not as dead as everyone presumes. She is surprised to find herself reborn in the land of death where she is gifted weapons by her god. Before her is a broken land and she is tasked with fixing it; she does her best but it is a huge undertaking and one she is not sure she is up to.

An enemy trunk commander, Dassit, has found herself on the wrong side of her Rai and is sent on a suicide mission to defend an indefensible town. In the prison there she finds a Forestal, Tanhir, and a strange old man, Fandrai, who the Forestal says is a priest of murder. Their presence is a mystery, and one Dassit uses to distract herself from the oncoming army sure to swamp her forces.

While Cahan is away, Sorha leads the Rai in an attack on an unprepared New Harn in Wyrdwood. At the same time Dassit and her forces are overrun and Cahan and the Forestals in the Wyrdwood find themselves ambushed. Though all seems lost, each group is saved when the Forestals reveal they have access, through the taffistones dotted all over Crua, to a network that allows instantaneous travel across the land and all are brought back to Woodhome, the Forestal city high up in the branches of a cloudtree in the southern Wyrdwood. There Cahan learns that Sorha has taken Furin prisoner and intends to execute her in the Slowlands, a place where death can take centuries. The enemy have agreed to exchange Furin for Cahan. Against the advice of Tall Sera, the Forestal leader, Cahan plans a rescue.

They manage to rescue Furin but pay a terrible price. The monk Ont is burned and loses his sight and senses, Fandrai is returned to Woodhome in a coma and Cahan's undying warriors, the Reborn, are taken by the enemy. Worse, Cahan is overtaken by something terrible and almost kills everyone. Only the Rai Sorha stops him, when her cowl-blocking aura interferes though she is still bent on vengeance. Cahan and Sorha fight on a bridge but both fall into the depths of Crua when Saradis, Priestess of the new God, is told by her god to destroy the bridge. They are presumed lost.

Udinny moves through the unlife world of Crua trying to understand how it works, and though she is doing her best to fix the damage done it is becoming apparent that the task is too demanding. Also, she discovers she is not alone. Something is hunting her.

Back in Woodhome the Forestal Ania slowly helps Ont find a purpose despite his terrible wounds, while the warrior Dassit and her second, Vir, wonder about their place in this new world. The trion Venn is taken under the care of the Lens, the trions of the Forestals, to learn more about who and what they are. All the while Furin mourns both the loss of Cahan and her son, Issofur, who was called to the forest a long time ago and is gradually becoming less and less human.

In the depths of Crua, Cahan and Sorha are forced to work together. He needs her as she blocks the power of his cowl and the thing that is trying to take him over. She needs him as she has been terribly hurt in the fall. Together they find a hidden world and a massive, ruined city. There they encounter something terrible, a huge tentacled creature, and it is hunting Cahan. Only Sorha's power hides him from it.

Udinny, unseen in the otherworld, does her best to interface with the city and lead Cahan and Sorha to safety but they ignore her subtle warning and instead go in the opposite direction.

Sorha and Cahan encounter the feared Osere, the demons of the below world. However, these blind underground dwellers are not monsters at all and have been guarding what they call the "gods" in their underground land of Osereud for generations. But one of these "gods" has been corrupting their people with bluevein, and now it has escaped.

The Osere wish to teach Cahan and Sorha about the "gods" and their journey to learn more becomes a running battle in which Cahan, Sorha and the Osere become more firmly bonded. Despite this, they are not yet strong enough to fight a god and the creature takes Cahan, using his strength to raise a temple from Osereud into the land above where Saradis waits, sure she has won and sure all Crua will burn for her god.

However, all is not lost. Wyrdwood is waking. Ont, Ania and Dassit are drawn north by a voice they cannot deny, though Dassit is betrayed by her second, Vir, who defects to the forces of the new god. Udinny is returned to life in the body of Fandrai, and Venn, the cowled trion, is waking to their power while Sorha, together with the Osere, is rising to the lands above, determined to free Cahan from the clutches of a dark and corrupted god.

1
Cahan

I am with you.

He had been fighting the battle as long as he could remember. There was nothing left but the fight – the battle was his life and would continue to exist as long as he did.

The walls of Harn were strong, they surrounded him and provided an illusion of safety. A subtle green glow marked their outlines and where there had been breaks they had been filled and patched. In places fire had scorched them and newer, wetter wood laid down to stop them being so easily burned again. The people had worked hard, and remembering how they had come together made him smile. It had been a hard path to cut, there had been trials, fights and disagreements. They had struggled but in the end they had come together. That had made them strong and with that strength they held the enemy at bay.

But the people's strength was not eternal; the battles wore them away just as they wore him away. At the end of each fight the dead were taken back to longhouses and round-houses. Cahan never followed them in. Someone had to stand guard. Someone had to be here, alert at all times because the Rai attacked without warning and without mercy.

And the central longhouse, Furin's longhouse, it frightened him because something waited in there. A gift, but
the thought of it was too terrible to approach.

Miracles were worked in the longhouse, wounds that
should have killed did not. Cahan watched villagers dragged
away on the point of death, and yet they returned after
time in the longhouse of Harn.

Until they did, he would stand watch.

He was alone for so long he could barely even remember
their faces when they were not in front of him. Furin: that
name burned. He missed Furin so much, her warmth and
her cleverness.

But she was here.

But he missed her.

Sometimes his thoughts were clouded, fuzzy, and he
could not stay with them for long, his attention sliding off
them.

He longed for the next battle, to be among the people
again, to see his friends, and even though he knew it would
bring them fear and pain and terror, at least he would not
be alone. He grunted, tried to push that thought aside,
that selfishness, to be ready to sacrifice others so he felt a
little better was a poor way to be. But he could not stop
the feeling; this loneliness was like ice within him, moving
slowly through the core of his body and outwards, slowing
his feet and hands, a lethal thing. Cahan closed his eyes,
shutting out the green glow of Harn, though he could
never truly block it.

He needed to be doing, to be keeping his mind busy
until the next attack. He walked through the square, past
wavering stalls empty of anything to sell, past the shrine
to Ranya, the only thing free of the green shimmer, a
gilding of yellow gold upon the eight-pointed star of Iftal
above it. He walked past the longhouse and ascended the
wall, looking out over the clearing to the vast trees of
Harnwood. The nearest were green, in full leaf, and he

could smell the loam and petrichor, the clean scents of the wood, and as he watched he felt Segur nestle in around his shoulders.

"Hello, old friend," he said softly, "we hold them at bay still." As if in answer Segur pushed closer into his neck. A brief moment of respite, of happiness in the closeness of the garaur but it could not last. The line of trees, in the leaf of the least season, was thinner than it had been. He could see where Harsh was biting, the cold blue glow of the cold blue months to come had stripped the trees bare. There the Rai waited, there they amassed for the next attack. As if they could hear his thoughts he heard the chanting start. Words in the language of the Rai, one that Cahan could no longer understand, ugly words, twisted and unpleasant on the ear. "They are coming," he said and felt Segur begin to fade, heard the pushing aside of doors, the swish of curtains, the creak of armour as the people of Harn began to amass before the walls. The enemy would attack here, they always attacked here. They used no clever tactics, made no attempt to come at him from the rear but they had no need to, they had the numbers.

Soon comes the fire.

Waiting, watching, the feeling in his stomach as if a terrible hunger came upon him – *when had he last eaten?* A pain in his chest as though he were pierced by a spear.

Fire, the blue glow out of it in the forest, a great ball rising soundlessly into the air, reaching its apogee and falling towards the village. Cahan watched, felt no fear as he knew what would happen. The same as always happened. The Rai's fire met the village shield made by the Forestals, splashing over a dome far above, cold blue of harsh meeting the warm green of least. He did not remember them putting it there, but he remembered it was a thing they could do. He turned; in the village he saw the Forestals arranged in a wedge shape, touching one another. The camouflage of their clothes gave their bodies fuzzy edges, made their faces hard to make out. He raised a hand to them, and the leader returned his salute.

He gave the forest his attention once more.

The Rai broke through the treeline, striding ahead of their troops in armour that writhed on their bodies, grew long tentacles to hold weapons. Behind marched their troops, blank-eyed conscripts who fought unthinkingly, with no concern for their own safety, thrusting mindlessly with their spears in such a way that they were easy to cut down. Behind him he heard the bows being drawn and he pulled on his own, without memory of stringing it or nocking an arrow; these things came automatically to him.

"Loose!"

Arrows, streaks across the sky, falling on the Rai army, felling soldier after soldier, cutting down Rai. The screaming of the wounded filled his ears, a sound more of anger than pain. Arrows flew again and again but the Rai's forces kept coming. They would not retreat and Cahan knew it: they would make the walls. The fight would be on the walls.

"Loose!"

He watched the Rai, not the soldiers, watched their writhing armour because with every flight of arrows it writhed less, the tentacles grew smaller or vanished entirely, as if the loss of troops diminished them.

"Loose!"

Let them diminish.

More troops staggered and fell, and a few of the Rai even went down. Then they were at the wall and Cahan stood with the defenders. He did not remember calling them, but they had done this enough times that they did not need to be called. They fought through memory. Beside Cahan stood a huge man, on his other side was Furin and they wore the same clothing as the Forestals, all blurred outlines – even their faces could not be made out. Troops crawling over the wall, the way they moved wrong, upsetting, as if they had no bones. His axes rising and falling, killing.

Sword and shields up and out on either side of him. Udinny! Hacking at the enemy.

But Udinny was . . .

"Leave the Rai to me!" he shouted and launched himself at the first one to breach the wall. It swayed and moved, quick as water, blue fire dancing across its weapons. The arrows in its body slowed it a little, as did the loss of its troops. It hissed at him, its tongue long and black, eyes ice-blue. Cahan buried an axe in its head and it fell, dissolving into nothing. The next came at him, throwing fire, and Cahan ran through the flames untouched to behead it, his axes barely stopped by its flesh.

The people of Harn screamed and died around him as they had so many times before. The Rai came on and the fight lasted for ever, it lasted hardly a moment. Then the Rai and their forces were gone and he was tired. So very tired and, despite the villagers around him, cheering once more at their victory he felt so very, very alone. He jumped from the wall. The villagers were either dragging wounded to the longhouse or beginning to fade, to vanish into the houses which glowed a faint green. It was over, but it was never over. Not long until once more they put themselves in front of the magic and the spears of the Rai's forces, to be cut down and rise again, and Cahan found himself overcome.

"Why do you do this," he asked, a sob in his voice, "why do you do this for me?"

As if they all heard his voice, as if they all felt his despair, they turned to him. Furin, face as muddied as all the others, but he was sure it was her. The Leoric reached out a hand to touch his shoulder, a brief moment of comfort, echoed by every villager in the square, a ghost movement. She spoke and when she did it was with the voice of every one of these faded and worn people.

You need me.

2

Udinny

I am Udinny Mac-Hereward, monk of Ranya and chosen of my god, sent from death to life to re-weave the golden web, to resurrect the lands of Crua as I was resurrected myself.

And I am in a spot of bother.

Truthfully, there are things going on in my life that you would scarcely believe were you not me, and living through them. Even though I am me and I am living through them, I am not sure I believe them myself. I am a man now, for a start, an old man, which is less comfortable than I would like. Bits move that should not, and bits that should do not. I very much miss the body I was never sure I really had when I was dead. It did not ache and was quick to obey my every thought.

Still, I did not have time for complaint, more immediately pressing was the woman who was trying to kill me.

I had seen her before, while I had regained my strength, or at least the strength of this body. In the healing room she had been a dark presence in the shadows, behind Issofur, Furin's boy, who was as much rootling as boy now. Her eyes never left me, whereas Issofur was very easily distracted. I was left with the definite feeling this woman wanted to talk to me, needed to talk to me. That I was somehow important to her in a way I could not fathom. More than once I tried to speak to her, of her, but the Forestals who tended me would tell me nothing. In fact, they would tell me nothing of anything. I know the body I inhabited was once a man called Fandrai, and that there was something of him they did not like. Rather than answer me they had me drink teas and take herbs for my health that fogged my memory. Within it was something I found disturbing and could not quite touch. My mind was constantly distracted either by drugs or by being forced to exercise in the longhouse I was kept in. Endless hours of walking up and down to strengthen muscles weakened by my time asleep.

The Forestal woman was patient: she waited and waited until finally even Issofur left my side and the healing room was empty. I was asleep when she came. She woke me with a gentle shake of my shoulder.

"Fandrai," she said. I did not wake immediately, I was in a golden dream where towers rose from barren grasslands and armies of grass marched against armies of gasmaws. It was not a comforting dream, but it was close to being back in the world of Ranya and I enjoyed that. "Fandrai", eyes slowly opening to see the Forestal woman above me, a knife in her hand. "I wanted you to see me before you died. To know it was me." There was something haunted in the woman's eyes, some old ghost that she clearly thought she could banish with my death, or his death.

"I am not this Fandrai. I am Udinny, monk of Ranya."

"A fine fiction," she said, "but you fool no one." With that she lifted the knife . . . and was hit from the side by a bleating crownhead, knocked off the bed. I rolled the other way. Pushing myself up on aching legs and looking for something to defend myself with. The woman was back up in moments, cursing the crownhead, which had vanished into the shadows.

"I am not who you seek," I told her, and all I could find to defend myself with was a wide bowl that had once held sweet-smelling herbs.

"You look like him." She advanced on me, pushing long hair out of her face, "You sound like him."

"I am not even sure I am a him."

"You are going to die." She came on, knife in her hand and its dark wood drank up my attention.

"Is this a good idea? Your people have been nursing me," I said, raising the wooden bowl before me like a shield.

"Tall Sera has denied me long enough and I can fall little further in his grace." She smiled, but it was not a friendly smile. "I will be avenged."

The name Tall Sera was one I knew, though my memory of it was vague, I knew it from Udinny before and many things from that time I saw as if through smoke. A Forestal? A Forestal leader, was that where I was? The woman intent on my next death was definitely one of them, from the green cloak and clothes to dappled face make-up, all these were Forestal things.

"I am in the Forestal city," I said. Now that I had said it, well, it was obvious from the way the building I was in was constructed from living wood; who else could make such buildings? "I did not expect it to be so warm." The woman faltered, as if wrong-footed by words. Then she advanced once more.

"Just because your wits are a little addled, Fandrai, does not mean I will let my family's vengeance lie forgotten in a clearing."

"I genuinely do not—" It hit me, a memory. I knew who this woman was. Tanhir. She had led a crusade against my grove, against my people. I felt aggrieved, but I also understood. I saw her cut down those I knew. I felt her nearness as I ran throughout Crua to escape her. No, not only to escape her. To right some terrible wrong I knew was in the world. Death was a sickening. Cahan!

Back in the living, growing hut I felt my foot hit something, felt myself falling backwards. I hit my head, falling through the pain into another memory, hazy and strange, me and not me. Surrounded by my acolytes, following bandits through the Jinnwood, they had taken and killed those at a small farm. They were ripe for harvest, a gift to Hirsal Who-Is-In-The-Shadows. Their bows would not save them. My people also had bows, smaller, made of horn, and though they lacked range my people did not need range. It was not our way. We stalked, we surrounded, we clothed ourselves in darkness and the thick black mud of the places that saw little light. Places where pools of water were thick with rotting vegetation and acted as dark mirrors where you could see your soul reflected back at you.

Waiting, waiting until they crossed out of the darkness of the forest into the light of a clearing, their laughter filling the gaps between the trees. Stepping out before them, my arms raised.

"Welcome, friends." The group stopping, eight of them, bows unstrung, a couple putting their hands to the blades and axes they carried but they sensed no threat in this one old man. Somewhere, a gasmaw hummed. The scent of bruised grasses filled the air. "I am Fandrai, follower of Hirsal Who-Is-In-The-Shadows, and I welcome you as you have entered the shadow of my god."

"We recognise only the Boughry, may they look away from us, now leave, old man." Laughter.

"Hirsal calls you to him." My hands fell. The arrows sang in the air. This close none could escape and the small group fell. Going among the groaning bodies, watching the shadows of Hirsal as they cut throats. No need to let them suffer, that was not the way of Hirsal. Wrapping bodies in floatvine and taking them through Jinnwood to the swarden grounds. Offering each body to the grasses with a blessing, closing their eyes and wishing them peace and forgiveness through serving the Wyrdwood.

In the room, the woman on top of me, my hand on her wrist, trying to stop her pushing her blade into my chest.

"You were not there," the words gasped from my mouth as I struggled with her. "You were not there."

"So you admit *you* were!" She renewed her efforts to drive down the knife. "I was behind them," I heard so much pain in her voice, "in the rearguard. I saw it all but could do nothing." An emotional agony, "I raised them, I raised them and you made them monsters."

"You murdered," I said, a clear image, a half-built house in a clearing, the screams of those living there as arrows came from the wood. No chance to defend themselves.

"Incomers," she hissed, "with no right to the forest." She pulled her hand loose. Raised the knife and at the moment it would have come down something hit her. Not the crownhead this time. Something small and furred, Segur! Following it more bodies, rootlings, or at least one rootling. The other Issofur, who was not quite rootling, not yet.

Tanhir jumped to her feet, back to the door. The garaur and the rootlings between her and me. I could see she did not care; she would fight them all to reach me. She raised her knife.

Then arms around her. A man's voice.

"You will not do this, Tanhir."

The woman screamed, a sound half-frustration and half-pain. She struggled against the man holding her, trying to fight him off but he was big, found no difficulty in disarming her, in taking the blade and then pushing her away so she sprawled across the floor. Behind the man was another woman, hidden in shadow. "Again and again, Tanhir, you have defied me. You brought outcomers here, and they have shown our enemy the taffistones at the worst possible time. And now, when we are presented with something indescribable, something that could well be the will of the Boughry, you defy me again."

"Tall Sera," she was sobbing, begging, "he is a murderer, he took from me, he took who knows how many of our people and . . ."

"Silence!" it was a roar. "Take her," he said, "I will deal with her later." Two Forestals came in behind and pulled Tanhir up. She was sobbing. I felt for her. Her pain naked on her face, but I was also very glad she had not been allowed to kill me. Tall Sera looked down on me. "She is right," he said, "you took many of ours, or Fandrai did. Now you claim to be this Udinny, who I know not only to be a young woman, but also dead. Though the account given of her death is strange indeed."

"Not as strange as it was to be dead," I told him. Did he smile? I was not sure. He did not really look like the smiling type.

"You could be a message from the forest gods, or you could be a very clever lie, and I have no real way of telling which."

"Well . . ."

"Fortunately," he said, "she does." He pointed behind him and a woman stepped from the shadows. My heart leaped with joy.

"Furin!" I said, "I see Issofur is . . ." I struggled for the right word, I wanted to say well, but the child was quite plainly changed, ". . . healthy. Even if the forest has changed him, Cahan said it might. All that time ago." I nodded at the growling child and she looked his way but she did not smile.

"I do not know how, Tall Sera," she said, "but I think that is definitely the monk Udinny. No one else I have ever met talks so much when they should be silent."

3

Saradis

Tilt was hers.

No, not hers, it was Zorir's, but she ruled for her god.

Saradis walked down the great hall, flags hung but they were in need of replacement, drifts of dust and dirt gathered in the corners of the great hall. The statues of the balancing men of Tarl-an-Gig had fallen, no need for that fiction now, and the wickerwork of the stars of Iftal was coming undone, like all would be undone. Saradis did not care, she barely even saw it. No one would judge her for this, no one dared. No, that was not true; maybe they did, those who still could but they were not important to her. None of this was important to her, it would all burn so what use was there in taking care of it? Let it fester and decay.

She no longer wore the clothes a Skua-Rai, no restricting bodices of twigs, no layers of fabric to show her wealth and power, no complicated braids in her hair. She needed to impress no one, she was the chosen of a god and none would question that now.

Rai still stood an honour guard along the great hall; no, they were no longer Rai. They were the collared now, her servants, loyal only to her and to her god. She had never commanded they stand guard in the great hall, they simply did so. Maybe it was some residual memory of what they had been, or felt they should do. She would ask Laha, though whether the answer would make sense would be a coin toss. Laha was the channel of Zorir, a way for her to communicate directly with her god. She still communed in her own way, was still rewarded by the all-encompassing pleasure of Zorir's presence – if anything it was stronger now. But day to day it was easier to go through Laha. She wondered where he was – probably with the bodies of the Reborn; they fascinated him. He liked to kill them and wait for them to rise again, then kill them once more.

She did not question it; he worked for Zorir just as she did.

Saradis walked up to the nearest collared, her armour was dull and the blue growths in the flesh of her neck were bright. Thick filaments pulsed as the collard's heart beat, growing out from the collar and vanishing below the armour.

"Report to me on the preparations in Seerstem." The collared shuddered and when they spoke they did at one remove from being interested, the voice dead and flat. She knew from experience that the lips of the collared nearest them would also move, mimicking whatever was said by this one.

"The army gathers in Seerstem. The southern armies move to counter us, but they do not have enough troops." Saradis nodded. She knew this already but the novelty of being able to communicate across vast distances instantaneously was still fresh. How great Zorir was. Not long now until the last push. Mydalspire had fallen to them, Seerspire would probably surrender. Only Jinneng and Jinnspire remained. Them and the forest bandits.

She left the collared, its message delivered but its mouth still moving as though there was more to say. In the beginning she had wondered if some remnant of the Rai's personality was left once the collar went on, but she had soon stopped caring. After all, did it really matter? At the doors to the courtyard waited Vir, the man who had once served the red, once been in the Forestal city. She had not collared the soldier, despite he was from the south. He hated and she recognised it. He had brought her important information and shared it freely – out of a need for vengeance. Again, something she understood. Besides, she had learned quickly that it did not do to collar everyone. The collared were good at taking direction and fearless against the enemies of Zorir, but not so good at thinking. They were soldiers, not leaders. Some very particular Rai she had kept uncollared, some soldiers she had promoted.

All feared her.

She liked that.

As she approached Vir he stood straighter, awaiting her attention. His armour was glossy, black heartwood with willwood thorns that crawled across the breastplate. A gift from her. Its last owner would not miss it.

"Tree Commander," she said. She had invented the rank for him. He was resourceful, fearless and experienced, not the only one in her army by any means, but the only one who absolutely owed her his life. And the only one filled with such a need for revenge. He looked a little taller when she spoke to him. "How go our plans to deal with Forestals?"

"Not great," he said. She still struggled with the familiarity he often showed, but hid her frustration. After all, she would not have to put up with it for too long and then she would be reborn in a more perfect world, and have no need to cope. "Your Rai can't get into the taffistone network." She walked on and he walked with her. Before her rose the great taffistone of Tilt, in front of that the sacrifice stones, each of them ringed by a thick, blue root that ran back to the great temple, though the great taffistone remained free of them. "I've had stonemasons from the town trying to crack the big one," Vir pointed at the great stone, "so we can force in some slivers, see if that weakens the rest and lets us in. But no luck so far."

"Do the Rai think this will work?"

"They don't like to commit." Vir grinned at that. He enjoyed ordering Rai about even more than she enjoyed telling them they must answer to him. "We lost one this morning."

"Really?" She stopped walking while she was still in the shadow of the great stone. "How?"

"The stone opened, Jammas Bar-Clay threw himself in and the stone closed, cut him in half. The others are a little less enthusiastic now."

"Surely they should be more enthusiastic, if they forced an opening."

"Feeling among the others," said Vir, looping his thumb through his belt, "was that it was a trap. They were let in, then closed off. If anything, that means we have less control than we hoped." Saradis let out a breath.

"That is not what Zorir wants to hear." She knew, deep down, that the network was important, not just for tactical reasons, but to her god.

"Nor me," said Vir. "I want to exterminate those forest vermin. They're unnatural, ain't right. You should give some thought to my suggestion." She looked up. A formation of gasmaw flew overhead and she smiled: was it a sign?

"I do not want to waste my mawriders in the forest."

"You said that, I agree, I mean the other one. Take another skyraft."

"They are little use if we cannot fly them."

"We can if you collar the crew."

"A raft cannot go into Wyrdwood."

"With respect, Skua-Rai," he said, and she turned to him. The change to serious usually meant he had a good point to make. "I do not believe it is true." She stared at him. "I think they do not take the skyrafts over the forests 'cos they are worried about damaging them. But we're not, are we? Crash the Iftal-cursed thing down on their tree city. That would cripple them from the start. Use mawriders as scouts to find it." She scratched at the side of her head; what he said had some merit. It would turn the rest of the rafters against her, but did that really matter, now she was so close?

"Very well," she said. "I will think on it. Anything else to report?"

"Lost four more collared in the lower city." Before she could say anything he continued talking. "Rumour is, the Osere are loose down there, dark creatures preying on the servants of the god." Saradis laughed to herself.

"You do not look convinced, Tree Commander."

"I think there's a few turncoats. The god is probably not what most expected. Some will always refuse to see the truth." She nodded. Odd, she thought, how this man could find the Forestals and their way of life so deeply unpleasant he betrayed a woman he had fought with all his life, but did not even blink at her God and all the change it brought.

"Feed a few of the townspeople to the collared and our Rai. Tell them we want these Osere, or there will be more punishments." Vir nodded.

"I'll get on that, Skua-Rai." She walked away, out of the shadow of the stone and into the glory of Zorir. As with every time she did this she had to ready herself. Had to calm her breathing lest the majesty of it steal her breath away and leave her faint, here, in front of all she ruled.

In front of Zorir.

The eight-sided pyramid that housed the god reached almost halfway up the central spire of Tilt. Atop was Zorir, her god did not move, the central roundel of its body and the eight tentacles that emanated from it held it on what she thought of as a throne on the top of the pyramid. Just below Zorir hung the proof of her god's power, her enemy, Cahan Du-Nahere, vanquished. Nothing more than a limp corpse beneath what he should have been serving. She liked to think of him as a corpse, though she was sure he was not. He did not spoil for a start. Although the idea of him in torment, shackled to Zorir, appealed to her, she did not like the idea that he still lived. Where there was life there was hope, wasn't that what people said?

Nearer the pyramid the ever-present stink of the city was dispelled by the pleasant ozone of Zorir's power, and if there was a background smell slightly reminiscent of a sickroom, what of it? From the top of the pyramid, from the god themselves, ran thick blue roots, twisting around the pyramid, splitting and reforming. At the bottom they ran over the ground and into the city; one particularly large one ran to the sacrifice stones, curling around them and crawling over them, only stopping before the largest as if something held it off. A fork of the same root passed over the main thoroughfare between the spire and the pyramid; the people had built a walkway over it as Saradis would allow no one to touch the roots. Her footsteps echoed hollowly off the wood as she walked. More collared lined the road to the pyramid and just before the black rock of it was a figure. How small the figure looked, only serving to outline the huge size of the building which had risen from below to gift them Zorir.

It was to the figure that Saradis made her way: Laha, his naked body wreathed in blue lines, roots of his own. He watched her approach but did not greet her or speak or react to her in any way she thought of as human. He was not Laha any more, she knew that. Or maybe he was, maybe he was the purest possible form of Laha, his devotion complete – though it was no longer to her. Laha belonged to Zorir, and somewhere inside she was jealous, but she would not give in to that. She did not want to be like Laha, he was a slave, not chosen in the way she was.

She liked the city a lot more under Zorir. It was quieter. The Rai did not bother her, or look at her with barely hidden scorn. The people rarely came up here, they stayed in the low city, awed, frightened and easy to control.

How they should be.

She came to a stop before Laha and the man turned to her.

"Bored with the Reborn?" she said. He stared at her, his eyes the same blue as Zorir's great roots.

"The trion is needed," said Laha. The words breathy, she wondered if this was actually Zorir she spoke to, or if Laha only interpreted. He had been almost himself when he had first returned from the dead, but that had changed.

"They will be found, as you know we believe they are in the Forestal's city, and it must also be found."

"The taffistones," said Laha.

"We have been unable to break in. It may be that the trion is needed for that." Laha stared at her, his blue eyes unreadable. Was he disappointed, angry? Impossible to tell.

"The trion is needed," said Laha again.

"Yes, our armies amass in the south, we will take Seerspire and Jinnspire, collar their Rai. Then even without the taffistones we will have full access to the southern Wyrdwood, we will find Woodhome, kill or collar the Forestals and bring Zorir the trion."

"The trion is needed," said Laha.

"Yes," said Saradis. "As I said, it should not be long, not compared to how long Zorir has already waited."

"Time is passing. The fire must come. The sleepers awaken." She did not understand that, but she did not understand a lot of the things that Laha said now. He did not always talk of fire, sometimes it was of "the release", or "the journey" which she thought meant the star path. That would be the end of all this, the paradise where she would be close to her god. Closer. "Bring the trion."

"I will do all I can," she said, "to speed the capture of the trion for you."

"Do all you can," said Laha. She nodded and turned away, filled her lungs with the ozone smell of Zorir and made to return to the spire. One more piece, that was all that was needed. They had Cahan, now only the trion was needed.

She would find them. She would give her god what they wanted.

She would bring the fire.

4

Sorha

The room was small and dark, a cellar beneath a tumble-down old house right up against the farthest wall of Tilt. It stank of old fruit and the riper, more uncomfortable, scent of too many bodies in one room. She turned over, trying not to disturb those sleeping around her and reached out, her hand moving through the thin covers until she found the hilt of her sword. How odd it was, to be back in the place she had once called home and feel less safe than she ever had.

Her name was Sorha and she had been Rai. She no longer thought of herself as that woman. Sorha the Rai had existed in another world, this world, but she had died and fallen into the depths of Crua to be taken by the Osere. She had found herself in a strange relationship in the darkness with a man she had done nothing but hate, not a friendship, that would be to overstate it, and to understate it. Not a dependence either, though it had started as that: his dependence on her to hold in check what grew inside him, her dependence on him to nurse her broken body.

Then they had only each other among an alien people,

the Osere, blind and frightening with ways different to those either of them were used to. A people with stories and traditions so far from what she knew that, at first, they had felt like a barrier between them. Then the Osere had shown them their land of Osereud, and that the world was not what they thought it was, was far more complicated and strange than they could ever have believed.

Sorha was reborn in the darkness.

Cahan was gone, and those people, the Osere, were now her only friends.

She wondered what would have happened if the Osere had not captured them. If they had not come across the – she still did not have the words for it – the thing, the creature? The god? She laughed quietly to herself. She would have killed him, there was little doubt about that. Once she was strong enough, sure enough of that dark place they had found themselves in, then her hatred would have festered, risen up and she would have slit his throat in the night.

Maybe she should have.

He would probably tell her that, she could hear his gruff voice saying that would have been the best decision. Preferable to what did happen. To being taken by the thing. Maybe it would, but that god his monk friend had been so fond of, the one who could not stop smiling even when Sorha beat her. How long ago was that?

It felt like a lifetime.

Well, the monk would not have agreed death was better. Would have said something about walking the path, but making it your own journey. She did not really understand, but Sorha knew she was on the path now and had no intention of leaving it. As far as she could see there was only one direction to go in. There had been since Cahan had been taken. Since that thing had risen up from Osereud below to the overworld.

Overworld, a translation of one of their words, the Osere's. She communicated in their language without thinking now, in a manner anyway, speaking half-Osere and half her own language. Frina, their leader did the same. The others she struggled with a little more but she still managed, and understood more every day. They were her people now. She was not sure how that had happened.

Adversity made the strangest bonds.

So did understanding.

They had entered Tilt during the night, she was not sure how long after the rising it was. Days definitely, maybe longer. Before that they had been climbing up a series of endless stairs around the column that had lifted the pyramid. She remembered thinking it would never stop, the ache in her legs. The way the Osere struggled to explain what they believed was happening. Slow conversations, with hand gestures whenever they stopped. Trying to sleep with a rope around her middle, tethered to the stair so that she did not roll off in the pitch darkness. And slowly, as they ascended, she began to understand more and more of what was said. Whispered conversations of "the time" and "the others" but she could not grab quite enough meaning for context. Did they worry for the people left behind, or the world left behind, but she had begun to think it was something else. Meaning had begun to filter through, though at first she thought she was failing to understand. What they said seemed too strange, too unlike everything she had been brought up to believe.

Though that was foolish, she had found herself comrade to the Osere who all her life she had been told were creatures of darkness – which they were in a way – and only the cursed found themselves among them.

Maybe that was true also.

"What do they talk of, Frina," she had asked eventually. "They do not want to go above, I understand that. You will be at a significant disadvantage. That is not your world." It was true; without sight she felt sure the Osere would quickly be cut down. Even the meanest warrior possessed what to Sorha appeared to be an unassailable advantage. Frina shook her head.

"They do not fear, the overworld is promised us."

"Then what is it they say, why do they want to go back?" said Sorha, and what followed, it was strange beyond her imagination, and yet it was familiar and fitted with the stories she knew. Like missing pieces in a puzzle, fed to her in broken words and hand gestures, half of it she barely understood.

The imprisoned gods had not all fought the people, some had sided with them; how else could the people have won against gods? In the end it had not been a victory; Iftal had broken, power had been removed from the gods and given to the people. The gods, the ones who fought with the people, sacrificed their ability to commune with the world to stop their enemies using it. Even so, it was not a defeat, more of a détente. An agreement was made, the gods would sleep, and Crua would be given over to the people. There was more to it, and Sorha was sure that she missed subtleties of language and story, but she understood the argument now. The constant back and forth of the Osere. Some believed this was the time to go to the overworld, others believed that they should go back to Osereud and wake the sleepers. The ones Sorha thought of as the "good" gods. Though she was unsure of the whole idea, these were gods; how could they hold the same morals as people? Did good and bad even apply?

On the other hand, she had seen the power of one of them, and the one thing all the Osere were in agreement of was that now one of them had broken the ancient agreement, more would wake. It was not even an argument, but a dialogue. Sorha was not used to this; for her entire life it had simply been the will of the strongest, or the most wily, that was done. The Osere worked differently, passing ideas between themselves in search of some equitable solution.

As Sorha listened it became clearer that the main problem

was not whether they should wake the gods – they had come to the conclusion they should – but on how, and if it was possible. There were also questions of how many Osere remained below, and how many had been taken and changed into Betrayers. In the end, of the thirty or so Osere, only ten and Frina continued upwards with Sorha. The rest returned underground and there was a poignant ceremony of touching and saying goodbye that, even though Sorha was not really part of, they tried to involve her in. They had watched them go until they vanished, cloaked in their make-up of shadows. The only sign they were still there was when there was a flash of bright colour from below as they walked past some light source that lit them up in glorious pinks and purples and yellows, greens and blues. It happened twice more, then they were gone, round the circle of the column.

They found their way into the overland at night for which Sorha was thankful. Tiltspire was quiet in a way she had never experienced before. Part of her thought the thing on the pyramid would know they were there but it looked inert, dead even. Its pyramid did not: bright blue streams of light ran from it, flowing across and round the building, spilling from the bottom and into the streets of Tiltspire. Sorha wanted to run up the side of the pyramid, grab Cahan and run away with him. Take advantage of the fact the thing appeared to be sleeping. A tug on her arm from Frina stopped her.

"It will wake." She wondered how the Osere knew what she was looking at, what she was thinking. "Must think, plan."

"How do you know what I am looking at."

"What else you look at." She had nodded, amused at that, then led them carefully away from the pyramid.

The blue streams, more like roots up close, ran every-where in Tiltspire. The Osere had some sense of them she lacked, steering her away from them, hissing and clicking to find their way through the empty streets of Tiltspire. Sorha led them towards the outer walls and the poorer areas. The further away they were from the temple the less of the roots they saw.

They found bodies in the street, and occasionally they heard the sounds of fighting. Many of the corpses had been fresh, looking to Sorha as if they had been used by the Rai. She stripped them when she found them, handing out cloaks and hats to the Osere so they could cover themselves and try to blend in a little.

She found Rai corpses as well. Each with a single wound to the neck and no other. Around them other Rai corpses, burned and left. It looked like the Rai had been fighting each other. She would expect such corpses to be stripped of armour but they were not. When she looked more closely the burned Rai had strange rings around their necks.

"Betrayers," said Frina softly and Sorha had wondered if she was right. Sorha had bade the Osere wait and followed the trail of corpses to the point the Osere were no longer in the sphere where her power dulled down the effect of cowls – she had never entirely blocked them the way she did Rai, though she did not know why. Behind her, she heard a quiet exclamation and turned. Frina stood, her head turning from side to side; something in her posture spoke of shock, or amazement. When Sorha returned, the Osere was first to speak.

"I see in this world," she said, "narrow street, like sound pictures but different."

"Colours?" said Sorha, before thinking that was foolish, that the Osere had no frame of reference for colour. "Like different tastes in what is before you?" Frina shook her head.

"No. Shapes," she said, "I feel shapes."

"We will think more on this," said Sorha, "but first we must hide. I think the Rai version of Betrayers have this city now." Frina nodded, and Sorha had led them until they found the abandoned house they were in now. Since then they had been planning, they had made forays from the house, sneaking round the silent city. Sorha needed information and for that they needed one of the Rai. But Rai were hard to find. Twice they had taken what they thought were Rai and found them to be the Betrayers. Different to the Osere version, these had a blue collar of root material around their neck and a sliver of stone from which it grew. They would say nothing; in fact, when they entered the sphere of Sorha's influence they became frantic, fighting with a rote savagery that had no skill to it. It made them easier to overpower but, as the Osere put it, what they once were was gone. They could give no information.

Sorha thought of taking a soldier, but it was unlikely a soldier would know much. She needed Rai.

"Frina," she said softly. The Osere turned her head towards Sorha. "I must go out, do not leave, or let any of your people leave here."

"They are curious," said Frina, "to try out sight they have when you leave. They think it a gift from Iftal, a reward for standing fast."

"Then let them do it in here," hissed Sorha, "if the people of Tiltspire catch one of you they will not be kind. My people are not kind to what they do not understand." Frina nodded.

"I will do my best."

With that Sorha left, creeping out into the night but she could not shake the feeling that a promise to do your best, well, it was not the same as a promise not to do a thing.

5

Dassit

She felt lost in Wyrdwood.

Consumed by it.

Dwarfed by the vast trees.

In Woodhome she had been within the tree, walking along its branches through the villages and houses perched there. She had not understood the colossus she moved within, she was too close to it to grasp the terrifying size. She had existed within it and her mind never had to examine just how immense the tree must be to hold a city of thousands above the forest floor. She had walked through the town and if she had to go up and down in gasmaw-powered lifts, if she watched the wall of the cloudtree pass, she still did not think about its size.

But since they had left, to accompany Ont, she had been given no choice. It had been easier when they were chased, when she was thinking about the horror of the creatures that confronted them. When the creatures of the forest turned up, surrounded them, led them on, she had been able to concentrate on them. When they vanished one night, left them alone and she was sure they had been led into a trap, she had been ready. She had a spear in her hand, a blade at her hip. She understood that kind of danger.

But there had been no trap.

There was only the silence of the forest, the strangeness of it, the sheer size of it. Ania was immune, she barely even looked at the trunks of the cloudtrees as they moved around them. Ont was blind, though he no longer moved like a blind man. He moved like a man with purpose, as though the leaf litter, which shifted and twisted beneath her feet, was solid ground. He walked like a confident man, as if he knew exactly where he was going and what was needed. Somewhere, deep within, she was glad for him. She had seen how battle wounds could destroy someone and the wounds the big man had suffered had been severe, some of the worst she had seen. His skin was still raw and weeping in places from the cowlfire.

At the same time, she resented him and it made her angry with herself, that she could resent this man who had lost so much simply because he was capable of feeling comfortable in the place where she felt like nothing, like a speck on the back of the world. In the distance she saw another cloudtree, a wall of wood, a reminder of her own insignificance. Around the base of it grew the dark-leaved bushes that were everywhere, looking like tiny dots though Dassit knew they would tower over her.

"It makes you feel like nothing, doesn't it?"

She turned. The Forestal Ania walked by her side while Ont walked on ahead, striding as if he had no worries in the entire world. For a moment she couldn't speak, she was too surprised that the Forestal would understand how she felt.

"I thought you would be immune." The Forestal shook her head, stared at the floor as her feet sank into the carpet of needles, using her bowstaff to steady herself.

"You never become immune," her voice was soft. "Sometimes you forget to look," she raised her head, "it becomes like the walls of a familiar home, then one day something is moved and it is unfamiliar. You see it all again. Know that your life is small and your time here almost meaningless." Dassit nodded; she had never considered the Forestal the type of person to think of such things.

"How do you cope, I feel . . ." she looked for the right word.

"Exhausted," said Ania softly. "It makes you feel exhausted." Dassit nodded, for just a heartbeat she could not answer. What Ania said was correct, exhausted and more, hollow, meaningless.

"How . . ." she began, found her voice betrayed her and she had to start again. "How do you get past it?" Ania laughed, but there was no humour there; it was as dry and as dead as the leaf litter.

"Don't ask me that, ask him," she pointed at Ont as he walked forward. "What he has overcome is greater than any cloudtree." Dassit nodded, what Ania said did not help but Ont gave her something to focus on. Concentrate on what they had come to do, even though she did not really know what it was any more than heading north. She would focus on that, on him and on whatever it was that drew him onwards, and her and Ania in his wake. As she watched Ont, something drew her eye onto the bushes.

"Why do you think all those," again, lost for words, "creatures came, and then just vanished, Ania?"

The Forestal shrugged. "Who knows why the forest does anything. If I were to guess I would say it was to make sure we did not turn around and go back."

"But—"

"Movement," the Forestal cut her off, stopped and pointed ahead. Then she pulled a string from her pouch and strung her bow, a simple quick and practised movement. It dispelled any sense of worry from the woman. Dassit saw it fall away as she readied her weapon, took out an arrow and held it in the same hand she held the bow. Dassit grasped her spear more tightly, breathed deeply.

"What is it?" she said.

"I do not know, but follow my lead." Together they ran after Ont, Ania telling him to slow down. He did, though not by much. He had been overcome by something, a confidence, a surety and he was pulled onwards in the grip of its mania. She felt it, too. Whenever they stopped to take some much-needed rest it grew. She thought that for Ont it was almost impossible to ignore: he could not sleep, he paced back and forth. For her it was different, a nagging annoyance, the growing feeling she had forgotten some important detail and when she tried to examine it further she found only one thing. A word, a feeling, a desire: *north*.

It filled her in quiet still moments, so any action was good. She was frightened, that some new forest thing was out there, waiting, but it was better than the feelings the trees engendered in her, that terrible smallness.

When they were nearer, when the bushes were large enough to dwarf her, when the cloudtree was nothing so much as a wall of wood that she could not raise her head to look at – and if she did it became a battle not to throw herself to the floor and cower before the feeling the tree was coming down, Ania raised a hand to stop her.

"Ont, slow," said Ania. "There is something up ahead." He turned, the mask of wood and grass that covered his burned face looking somewhere between them.

"The forest does not wish us harm," he said, the words ragged, his breathing difficult.

"Maybe not," said Ania, "but it does not wish us well either." He continued on and she ran after him, Dassit following. Ania grabbed the big man's arm and pulled him to a stop. "We all hear it, Ont, we all feel the need to go north. But run straight into a littercrawler nest, or something worse, and we will never get there." He shook her off. "Ont, something is moving in the bushes. Even if you care nothing for yourself, think of Dassit and me." That slowed him. He came to a stop.

"Sorry," he said, and his huge shoulders slumped. "The call, it fills me." He rubbed at the side of his head, knocking the grass mask askew. "My head aches. My heart yearns for the north."

"We will not stop," said Ania, "but we go carefully." Ont nodded and Ania waved Dassit forward.

It felt good to Dassit. She transferred her spear to her left hand, took a throwing spear from the quiver at her hip and held it in her right. Doing was good, she needed to be doing.

Both she and Ania kept low, the Forestal half stringing an arrow. They saw nothing in the bushes, no sign of movement, and Dassit began to doubt herself. Still, they moved closer, Dassit watching for any movement in the bushes that she could read as something unnatural, at odds with how it should be.

Night fell.

Though it never really fell in Wyrdwood.

It sprang on you. One moment it was the sepia gloom of Wyrdwood. Then it was night, pitch dark until the explosion of bioluminescence banished it, a natural light show that was as surprising as it was beautiful. Wheels of light, clouds of it, explosions of every imaginable colour.

And something moved in the bush.

Dassit drew back her spear arm to throw. Ania grabbed her.

"No," a whisper. "Not until we know what is there."

"But if . . ."

"Act against the forest, it will react." Dassit swallowed, let her muscles relax. Another rustle of leaves, black in the wash of changing light. Then more.

"There is either many of them or there is something huge," whispered Dassit.

"We hold. If we are to be overwhelmed attacking will not help."

"It would make me feel better to at least strike a blow." Every muscle within her wound up, wanting release.

"There!" said Ania, still holding tight, "rootlings." Dassit felt herself relax. She had become used to the rootlings of Woodhome, familiar, friendly and mischievous. They had already met rootlings, hundreds of them, and come to no harm. She began to lower her spear. "Not yet," said Ania, "back up slowly, forest rootlings are not always predictable." They stepped back, slowly, and more and more rootlings appeared. Dassit could not quite decide why, but there was something different about them. Something familiar about one of them. She was sure that she saw the boy from Woodhome, Furin's child, Issofur, darting among the group but as quickly as he was there he was gone.

More and more rootlings appeared as Dassit and Ania backed up. The rootlings did nothing but stand, the crowd of them growing and with them grew a sense of threat, of menace, of the quiet, growing power of Wyrdwood.

"Will they attack?" said Dassit softly.

"I hope not." The rootlings started to make a noise, a low chattering that spread through the crowd, growing then ebbing like the bluster of winds.

"What do we do?" said Dassit as she and Ania stepped back again. When they did the rootlings stepped forward, keeping the distance between them the same. It was quietly threatening; keeping their attention entirely on the mass of forest creatures, among them Dassit saw traces of what they had been, garaur, raniri, crownhead. Step by step they were moved back, and back, and back with the rootlings shadowing their every move. If they stopped, so did the rootlings. When they moved, so did the rootlings. Unless they moved forward, then the rootlings stayed still, a low growl and sense of threat growing until Dassit and Ania stepped back once more.

"What is happening?" said Dassit. "What are they doing?"

"I do not know," said the Forestal.

Almost as if they heard, their behaviour changed: the great mass of rootlings broke off, ran, vanishing into the bushes before them or loping off into the distance. Dassit and Ania stood utterly still. Waiting. Watching. Then Ania straightened up, placed her arrow back in the quiver at her hip. "I have never seen such behaviour from them," said the Forestal. "But Ont is more in tune with the forest than I have ever been, maybe he can . . ." As she spoke she turned and her words died away, because Ont, who they travelled north to protect, was gone.

6

Venn

Venn sat before the foci of the trion in Woodhome.

In a way, this was a judgement upon Venn, though the trion was not worried, not really. Once they would have been terrified, been cowed by this small council of important people, not now. Venn felt pity for Brione: they had been the leader of the foci and their support for Venn had weakened them. Now Sendir led them and it was Sendir who led this meeting, Sendir who had called it.

They sat around the same steaming pot in the longhouse of the trion they had sat around when they first met Venn. None had spoken yet. They were letting the atmosphere close in on Venn, and once it would have. Once Venn would have shivered and feared and worried about what these people thought of them and what would happen to them and how they would continue, where they would continue.

They were not that person any more.

The lessons they had gone through with the foci had helped them grow, helped them see what was within them and ways to use it, though that had only been a start. Since then, what was within them, the cowl, it had grown and kept growing.

"You are called before us," Sendir spoke, their voice like the grinding together of tree branches in the cold winds of Harsh, "to answer to your crimes."

"Crimes?" said Brione. Once their words would have held power, but Venn could feel how the currents in the room no longer favoured them, how Brione had been forced to stand back from the group as they were the one who had brought Venn into the foci. "A harsh word, Sendir, and a crime brings with it punishment, is that what you wish?" A moment's silence: only the bubbling of the pot, the fragrancy of it, summer flowers and crushed leaves.

"Crimes," said Sendir again, "some of us," she glanced at Brione, "may wish to frame this as defiance, or foolishness, but I say it is crimes. We brought this outsider into our world, we made them and theirs welcome and what have they brought us?" Sendir looked around the dimly lit house and if Venn had hoped one of the other trion would speak up for them they were to be disappointed, but they had not and so they were not. "Betrayal, that is what they have brought," Sendir sat back, the top of their nose was all that was illuminated beneath the hood threaded with twigs, "betrayal and ruin." Again, the trion let their words sink in, let the room settle around the weight of what was said.

"And what," said Brione, "is it you suggest is done? Do you suggest we remove Venn's cowl?" Silence then; Venn could feel how that had landed among them. How it had created an awkwardness because they all knew, or at least suspected, that they could not. That no matter what power they may have within them, or grouped together with other Forestals to amplify their strength, none of them knew if they could stand against Venn.

"I would suggest we at least try," said Sendir. "Let's not forget, their cowl is a twisted thing, born not of the forest but of the Rai's blooming rooms." A momentary shiver ran through Venn's body, a tensing of muscles as if they expected to grabbed, to be held down and have violence visited upon them.

Nothing happened.

"If the cowl cannot be removed," they continued, "then the trion must be removed."

"Only a fool would banish them," said Brione, "the Rai in Tiltspire want their power, we know they search for them."

"And that will bring them here," said Sendir, "to Woodhome."

"So what?" said Brione. "You would cast Venn out into the world, make them easier for the Rai to find?" Sendir shook their head.

"We made the mistake of not chopping the head off the gasmaw before, and look where that has got us." They looked around the assembled trion. "We hear an old god has risen in Tilt, an old darkness has returned. We can feel it in the taffistone network, looking for a way through. It already has the strength of Cahan Du-Nahere. If it takes this trion, a true conduit through to Crua, that will be it for all of us." They looked directly at Brione. "This god has banished all others, it seeks to be everything. We work for all, not for one. This trion is too dangerous and, though it pains me," it did not, thought Venn, sound like it pained them too much, "the only way to be sure, is for Venn to give up their cowl."

"Or?" said Brione.

"They must."

The heaviness of silence, the oppression of it. Sendir's eyes burning in the darkness. Brione, looking down, hiding their acquiescence with their hood; because they were acquiescing, Venn knew it. They were frightened and Venn understood. Venn had been frightened for longer than they could remember. Terrified when Forestals had come through the stone with reports of the creature in

Tilt, the black pyramid with the corpse of Cahan Du-Nahere hanging like a straw doll left out to soak beneath the geysers.

But Venn did not believe Cahan was dead, even if all others did. They looked around, a smile played over their lips and they scratched at the side of their mouth where a little of the green and grey make-up of the Forestals was flaking away.

"You talk with fear in your mouths," they said, and were amazed at how calm they sounded. "You talk with surety but you are simply frightened."

"So you will not give up your cowl?" This voice was not from the foci of the trion, but from the back of the room, from a figure hidden in the shadows.

"No, Tall Sera," said Venn, "I will not." Forestals came out from the shadows, if he was surprised that Venn knew he was there then the Forestals' leader did not show it. He held his bow in one hand, an arrow also. "And none here could take it from me."

"You know what our other choice is, Venn?" he sounded resigned, sad.

"Death, of course. But you talk as if there are only two choices."

"I see no others, neither do the foci or they would have spoken up." Venn stood and all eyes were on them.

"You," Venn turned to Sendir, "cannot take my cowl. True, it was born of the blooming rooms. But I have been touched by Cahan Du-Nahere, the power of the Boughry has run through me and I am chosen of Ranya." They did not know where these words came from, but they felt right. "If my death is the only way you see forward, then you can have it, but I pity your people. And you, Tall Sera, I thought a man of more imagination." Tall Sera drew a long breath.

"Maybe, when I stand before you with a bow, it is not the time to defy me, Trion."

"Nothing has changed since the last time I defied you, Forestal."

"That is not true," said Tall Sera, "and you know it, what has happened in Tilt is . . ."

"Frightening," said Venn, "terrifying even, and they have my friend."

"He is to blame for it." Venn shook their head.

"I doubt he went willingly."

"That is the point we make," said Sendir. "A trion is a key to power, we cannot risk you being taken." Venn turned, looking at each one of them and wondering when they had grown stronger than those around them, when fear had become something they could push away.

"I was one of many trion, they pushed us into the blooming rooms, and many died." The scent of death in their nose, the memory of screams in their ears, "They are still doing it and you know that, you have heard of trion vanishing from the villages, the largers and spire cities." Something cracked in the heated rocks below the pot, sending sparks into the air.

"There is no guarantee they will find another like you," said Sendir.

"And none they won't," said Venn. "If they do at least you have me to stand in their way, and if you are truthful you know they will come for you whether I am here or not."

"How will you stand against them? How will they even find us?" said Sendir, a half-cough, half-laugh. "The man who ran, Vir, he does not know any more than Woodhome is in the southern Wyrdwood. They will not find us."

"Sendir, there is much I do not know." Venn turned to Tall Sera, "But consider this. Cahan hangs below this creature, this Osere god. I am here, Ont walks out into the wood to go north, called by a voice only he, Dassit and Ania, who you trust more than any other, can hear." Did that land, or did Tall Sera only feel Ania had betrayed him for an outsider? Venn did not know, could not know. "And Udinny, the monk of Ranya who died in the defence of Harn so long ago, has returned from death."

"So you say," said Sendir but she did not sound as sure of herself. All eyes were on Venn.

"Those who walk the path of Ranya," said Venn, "are still walking it. This is a time of gods. I am here for a reason, as is Udinny, as is Cahan. That is why Ont and Ania and Dassit walk the forest." Venn looked around, meeting the gaze of each and every one in the tree house.

"You forget," said Sendir eventually, "we are Forestals of the Wyrdwood, we do not follow your town and plains gods. We live under the gaze of the Boughry and our only prayer is that they do not look at us too closely. Your weak and gentle god of pathways has no place here, you have no place here." Sendir stared at Venn, turned to look at Tall Sera. "If they will not give up their cowl," they said, "you know what must be done." Tall Sera let out another long breath, a sigh, then transferred his bow from left to right hand so he could draw it and Venn knew the time had come, that they must try for something they had been unsure of, but if ever was the time now was it.

"Sendir of the foci," said Venn, and as they spoke they let their consciousness reach out, felt themselves as the tree, as the power running through it, felt its connection to the forest floor and through the tree they found Ranya's web, more ragged and frail than ever but still vital, still spanning the entire world of Crua. They did not raise their voice but all heard it as louder. "You forget that I am not only chosen of Ranya, but that in the village of Harn I was a living embodiment of the Boughry." Reaching out and reaching again, further and further, into the cold north where they found the burning light – a frightening power, though not as frightening as it once had been to Venn. They understood more, the interlinkedness of all things that lived and were not touched upon by the corruption of the Osere God risen in Tilt. Venn opened themselves to the power there, let them know what they knew, let them in, let them take control and the words they spoke became a struggle to release from their mouth. "You pray to avoid the Boughry," said Venn and their voice was a well of darkness, a whirling purple and black that filled the minds of all around them, "but they are already here."

Rootlings, rushing around the tree, loping towards the longhouse, hundreds of them; further out thousands more stopped what they were doing and turned towards Woodhome. A skinfetch twisted towards the tree city and hissed. Swarden paused in the building of strange towers. Shyun put down their bows and blowpipes and stared towards Woodhome with black, three-lobed eyes. Venn's mind became a light, a shimmering, spinning, shifting forest light obscured by figures, powerful and broken at the same time. Aware and unaware of what they were, what Venn was. Venn let go, watched themselves as if from above. They were taller now, attended by the shades of the Boughry, and before them Tall Sera and the foci were cowering. If Venn expected some speech, some words, some guidance, there was none. Only the sudden and inescapable knowledge that something terrible and powerful looked this way.

Then they were back. In the room with the fragrant broth and the foci and Tall Sera. None looked at Venn. None spoke, not at first. Eventually Tall Sera took a breath.

"What would you have us do?" said the Forestal leader. At first Venn did not understand. Then, when the words had filtered through, they shook their head, feeling hair as long and thick as it had ever been tickling their neck.

"I do not want to lead you," Venn said, "you work together to look after yourselves and your community. Something terrible and dark has been growing in the soil, and now it is taking our world. I only want you to care for others the way you do yourselves."

"And is that what the Boughry want?" Sendir said. They did not sound as if they agreed, or had any wish to back down, and Venn knew you could not force a friendship. Venn shrugged.

"They came, didn't they?"

7

Udinny

I am not sure these people like me very much.

In fact, that is a lie. I am very sure these people do not like me at all, but I am trying not to take it personally. It is not actually me they do not like. If they were given time to get to know Udinny Pathfinder, monk of Ranya, traveller in the land of death and beyond, then I am sure they would like me very much. I am a very likeable person.

It is the body I inhabit that they do not like, that of Fandrai, monk of Hirsal Who-Is-In-The-Shadows.

Not that I can blame them. As I share this body I see occasional memories left over from the man who lived in it before, and those memories are not pleasant. They are shifting, twisting things that shimmer like the Wyrdwood grasslands where swarden rise from the corpses of transgressors and . . .

There it is again.

These memories are not comfortable, they are like a hand that grabs your innards and squeezes, like cold water flowing down your back or like a sense of your own doom come upon you. Though the sense of doom could also be from the distinct feeling I am not alone in this body. Something else shares it and it watches.

It watches the world.

It watches me.

Or the sense of doom could be from the shackles around my hands and neck, and that I am being led through quite the largest tree I have ever seen to stand before a court of Forestals who will determine my fate. With me, and similarly shackled, is the woman who tried to kill me. I find it difficult to blame her for what she did, considering what happened to those she loved, but I have always been a very reasonable sort like that.

In theory, I could escape at almost any time, for I am Cowl-Rai. Oh, not like Cahan, I am not about to make this great cloudtree walk, or rip apart my jailers with a thought, nor am I about to call up fire and burn them where they stand or drown them in the water of their own body, but I have power. Or, more strictly, what I share this body with has the possibility of power, the memory of it. Tied to it is a great fear, the fear of the one who owned this body before. He was intimate with death, so close to it as to be practically a sibling, but his fear lives within the cowl. I know what he did not, of the great corruption that took Cahan Du-Nahere and that, if these people are to be believed, has had him raise a great darkness in Tiltspire.

I have to admit that does not sound like the sort of thing the Cahan I knew would do, and in the far-below Crua I know he fought against the creature that seeks to usurp Ranya from her web of light. However, I am not sure these people believe a word I say. They are quite a dour lot from what I have seen, though that is little enough. Just row upon row of Forestals, faces masked by dappled make-up, watching silently as I am led through the tree city.

That my captors bring me to stand beneath three great statues of the Boughry, made of wood and grass, which loom forbiddingly over a wooden square on a wide branch, does not particularly fill me with hope. All around Forestals gather in groups and singles and pairs, children run laughing through the trees and to the side stands their leader, Tall Sera, and with him a group of trion and a figure who brings a smile to my face and at last a real sense of hope: Venn. They look so different to who I knew before I died. More serious. More grown up. More hair.

Venn is somehow larger now, not in stature but in themselves. They carry themselves as if they are surer of the world and their place in it. Behind them stands Furin and she is the opposite: she is reduced and I want to hold her, to offer her some comfort in my arms. She has plainly lost so much.

"People of Woodhome!" Tall Sera stood forward, "we come here before the statues of the Woodhewn Nobles of Wyrdwood", he gestured towards the statues of the Boughry which menace the square, "to cast judgement upon Tanhir of our people for going against my word." The woman does not look at him as he speaks. "And upon Fandrai, priest of Hirsal, who murdered many of ours." He looked around; the gathered Forestals became still, and I felt their gaze upon me. It was rather unpleasant to be the focus of so much unfriendliness, but I did not believe that Ranya had led me all this way just to be executed because she dropped me in the wrong body. Tall Sera gave a glance towards Venn, not a friendly one. If anything, I saw fear on his face which I did not really understand. "Tanhir, step forward." The woman's eyes were red from tears, though she struck me more as one soaked in fury than in sorrow. She cast a look my way as sharp as any knife. "Tanhir," said Tall Sera, "you have been told many times that you lost your people to the followers of Fandrai, and that in turn you took his followers, and this was allowed by us."

"But it was he who—"

"Quiet," Tall Sera's voice a roar. "For generations, the

followers of Hirsal have taken those who murdered, they were part of the forest as much as a spearmaw or a litter-crawler. Your justice was allowed after the fact, it was not sanctioned before and would not have been. As such, you were forbidden from pursuing Fandrai, so what he is to the forest could be rebuilt."

"He took my children," her words were raw, bitter and broken.

"Who in this forest has not had children taken?" said Tall Sera. "And we have heard how you took the children of others."

"Outsiders," she spat the word, "intruders."

"Nonetheless, Fandrai acted within the bounds of forest law. As such, he is free to go."

"No!" The word was pain, an agony. "You cannot."

"And you, Tanhir, have disobeyed. First you preyed upon outsiders, then you brought others here."

"And each time I owed a debt," the words were so quiet, so soft they could barely be heard.

"And our people will end up paying it. You are to be sent from Woodhome, and memory of it taken from you."

"No, please," such desperation in her voice, "my children, memory of them is all I have left!" Two Forestals walked forward and took hold of Tanhir's arms, while another undid my wrists and left me free. "Give me to the monk!" It was a cry of grief, of unbearable pain. "Give me to the monk, have him take my life and let me walk with the swarden. Better to be dead than to forget. If you let me live, I will find some way to remember. I will come for the monk again." Whether that was possible or not I had no idea, but I have heard few people sound so determined. All eyes turned to me. I had vague images of a place, of more than one, where I could bury a corpse and wait. I knew how it would feel to make her bones part of the forest, but what would allow it, the cowl within me, shied away from me. It knew this body was not mine, it distrusted me.

"Would you take her to join the swarden ranks, Fandrai?" said Tall Sera.

"I cannot," he looked disappointed. "I am not Fandrai, though I inhabit his body. I am Udinny, sent here by my lady of the lost, Ranya." He did not react. I knew little about the Forestals; maybe people coming back from the dead to inhabit a different body was common among them.

"I think that makes little difference to Tanhir," said Tall Sera, looking down at the weeping Forestal. Plainly the woman meant me ill, whether I was Fandrai or not, but still her pain was too much for me.

"I would not take her life anyway," I said, even though I could not. "I am not a follower of Hirsal."

"Then she will kill you, and the taking of her memories is the only option." He sounded profoundly sad for her, for those lost, for his people.

"I told you, Tall Sera," she hissed, "I will find a way to avenge myself, memories or not." He stared at her and she looked up at him. "Someone will tell me what I have forgotten, you know it is true. If you want that thing," she glanced over at me, "to live, then you must take my life." For a moment the Forestal leader looked lost, and I wondered what I did not know about these two.

"We could bind her." This from one of the trion behind Tall Sera. "If she truly wishes to keep her memories then we could bind them to the body of Fandrai, or whoever they say they are." The other trion were staring at the one who had spoken. Tall Sera turned to them. "Is this possible, Brione?" The trion took a long time to answer.

"In theory," they said.

"And what of you, Tanhir, this seems to me to be a punishment worthy of disobeying me. To make you guard who you hate most."

"This is not, right," I said. "This poor woman—"

"Quiet!" said Tall Sera. "Whether you are Fandrai or not, you are not one of us and you do not make decisions here."

I nodded, though it felt a little rude considering he barely knew me. Maybe I would have been an excellent Forestal. In fact, I think I would though I was not about to raise the matter at this moment. "Tanhir," said Tall Sera, and there was definitely something in his voice — sadness, affection? "Will you be bound to Fandrai, to keep your memories?"

"And what then?" She looked around the clearing in the tree. "What then? I stay here to be pitied or hated by those I once loved?" Tall Sera shook his head.

"You will be sent from Woodhome, with Fandrai." He looked behind him at the small group of trion. "Exiled to the Wyrdwood, there to find some good to do for your people. You may never come back. Your actions in chasing Fandrai when you were forbidden to, and through that bringing others to our home, has brought great sorrow on us. But maybe you can do your people some good out in the forest." Tanhir bowed her head.

"What a choice," said Tanhir softly, "lose what remains of those I love and avenge them, or keep what I have and be bound to the one who took them from me."

"At least you have a choice," said one of the trion, "you gave us no choice, when you brought outsiders here."

"I was not the only one to bring them. Or to go against you, Tall Sera," the Forestal woman pointed at Furin, "what of her!"

"Only you, Tanhir, repeatedly disobeyed for the same reason, only you did not learn."

Tanhir stood, looking around. "You need an example," she said, "I understand that. Bind me to what I hate most then, and set us free in the forest if you think that will save you. But what is done is done, the Rai are coming. They assault the taffistone network. They know we have a city in the Wyrdwood and they will come for us, you all know it. One day you will need every bow there is, you will beg to free me from the binding, and give me Fandrai in exchange for my bow when they do."

"I do not," I said softly, "think you are helping your case."

"Do not speak to me, murderer," she said.

"But I feel I should speak," I said. "After all, if you are bonded to me in some way, then I presume I am bonded to you?"

"You have no voice here, your murders may have been of the forest, but it does not mean we accept you among us," said Tall Sera.

"I have murdered no one. In fact, I have actually been very dead myself for quite a long time." I felt the weight of the Forestal's gaze upon me. "My name is Udinny Mac-Hereward, and also Udinny Pathfinder, a name bestowed upon me by my god, Ranya." I looked around, I did not feel these people looked quite as awed as they should by the fact I was chosen by a god. "If you do not believe what I say, ask Furin, or Venn." I pointed at them. "They will confirm I am Udinny, though I am a man now and once I was a woman and, believe me, that is an even greater change than coming back from death."

"We should not be surprised that outsiders would support another outsider." I did not see the speaker, they were among the crowd of Forestals.

"And what good did you being dead do for us, Udinny Pathfinder?" asked Tall Sera, although they said my name in a mocking way. I did not choose to answer so.

"I fought a great darkness."

"And lost, I take it, as one has risen in Tiltspire!"

"I hindered it. I fixed a lot of what was broken. I fought."

"But you did not stop," said Tall Sera.

"No," I bowed my head, "the beast was too strong for me alone, that is why Ranya sends me back." I looked around. "And as she sends me here, it makes me believe that you, the Forestals, have a part to play in the defeat of what ails our world."

"We have no interest in those outside the forest," shouted a Forestal.

"What have they ever brought us but grief!" An ugliness grew in the air, a certainty of violence, and Tall Sera stepped forward.

"Stop! A decision has been made. Any who attempt to enact their own justice will follow these two into Wyrdwood." He stood, and I think I knew then why these people followed him. He had a quiet authority that left no doubt he would do as he said. "Justice has been done, Tanhir, Fandrai or Udinny whatever you call yourselves, go with the foci of the trion." The Forestal trions stepped forward and took us gently by the arms, led us into the longhouse behind them. With us came Tall Sera, Venn, Furin and more trion. There were two tables in the room, pushed together and outfitted with what looked like shackles.

"Tanhir," said Tall Sera, "will you lie on the table yourself or must we force you?" She gave him a look, one that spoke of a long familiarity, and slid onto the table. Trion undid the shackles on her hands only to bind her once more to the table.

"Udinny," I turned to find Venn, behind them stood Furin. "I look forward to catching up with you."

"I think that unlikely, unless they are throwing you out too." The trion smiled at me, shook their head.

"They are keeping Furin and I, though we have had to move to Tall Sera's rooms and . . ." I leaned in close to Venn.

"These Forestals are not very friendly, are they?"

"They are scared," said Furin. "When we first came they were welcoming, treated us just like them. Now they know the world sees them and that they are not safe in their secret city, they want someone to blame." As she spoke Tall Sera stepped forward and spoke to Tanhir. As I was being laid on the table by her I heard what was said.

"Tanhir," he whispered, "there are things you should know. We are in great danger, and there are few warriors past your ability. I want you to be our scout. The Rai will come, and we need to know about them in advance. We need to know what is happening outside of Wyrdwood."

"You bind me to the murderer of my children and expect favours." Tall Sera nodded.

"It is likely true Udinny is sent by a god," I wished I could have seen her face when he told her that, "and I cannot risk you angering them. We have enough enemies."

"But it does not stop you exiling them?"

A pause, while Tall Sera considered what she said and whether it was wise to exile me along with her.

"I have to go," I said. As soon as I knew Tall Sera was considering not sending me out of his tree city, I knew I had to go. It was simply one of those feelings I knew to be correct, and I had become more and more used to following what I felt rather than fighting it. "You should send me, with Tanhir. I do not understand why, but I know I must be away from here."

Tall Sera moved so he could stare down at me. I lay on a table, head-to-head with Tanhir, and thought the Forestal leader had incredibly wise eyes, full of compassion.

"If that is what you feel," he said, "then I will share with you what I share with Tanhir," his eyes flicked to her. "There are few warriors among us with her experience, or skill. She is strong in her cowl, enough to reach into the network by herself. So know this, the taffisnetwork cannot be trusted, it is all we can do right now to keep it closed from what assails it. But I need information about the outside world. About the army moving on Jinnspire as it is likely to come for us next."

"You want us to go?" said Tanhir.

"Yes. Scout, and scout carefully. I have sent others out and none have returned. I have heard whispers, people saying the forest has turned against us. There is a small group waiting on the Jinneng plains. I want you to lead them. Find out what you can. Make sure someone gets back."

"You expect this, but you will still bind me to the murderer." She sounded resigned.

"I must, but tell me, are you for your people or only vengeance? Because I fear what is coming is greater than we know." Tanhir took a while, breathing heavily, then I felt her shuffle as if she relaxed onto the wooden table.

"Do it then." One of the foci came forward. I felt another behind me and lay back.

"Wait!" I said.

"What?" asked Tall Sera.

"There was a crownhead in the room with me when I awoke and had my unfortunate misunderstanding with Tanhir. Could you exile it as well?"

Tall Sera gave me a very strange look.

8

Saradis

Saradis knew that she should kill Nahac.

The woman no longer had a use. Saradis had no need now for a Cowl-Rai to bring the Rai to heel. The collar did that for her. Those who were collared were her servants, those who were not lived in fear of her forcing a collar upon them. It worked well; there had been attempts on her life of course, but there always had been and the collared and Laha were fanatical about her safety. Laha had used those attempts to make himself truly feared.

Nahac though, what use was she? Most of the time she was catatonic, like now, rocking backwards and forwards in the cage. Very occasionally she would wake and be herself once more. Then Saradis would come up here and speak with her. Often, Nahac would talk as if she were in another time, in the past. They had one pleasant afternoon discussing how they would take the Storspire, how many forces they already had in there, how many of the Rai were ready to come over. She was nervous. To her it was only the third time they had taken a spire city and the first time that the forces of Chyi had truly understood they were under threat. No one had really cared about Harn falling

– the proof of a regime that had grown fat and lazy, Nahac had said at the time. That they were so complacent as to think, "oh, it is only the far north". She was right, of course.

Nahac had been equal parts nervous energy and fear and wonder at how much she had accomplished without any power. Saradis saw the darkness within her, the doubt, the worry. The guilt over her brother, and the anger as well. The second engineered by Saradis, too well, she had thought for a long time, but it had all turned out well for her. They were here now. At the end.

Nahac had been easy to manipulate, though she was the one who had believed she was the one doing the manipulating. Thinking Saradis had forsaken her god and Nahac gloried in the pretence of Tarl-an-Gig, in inventing the god's mythos, its rules and its stories. In making Saradis bow to a figment of her imagination. In a way, Nahac had given Saradis the last push, the last realisation when she had, in her anger, moved against the monastery of Zorir.

The time in the wild had truly put Saradis in contact with her god in a way she had never been before.

She had been shocked, when she went to offer her services to the new Cowl-Rai, to find Nahac. After that she had been in a filthy cell, for a long time. Then brought up, more for Nahac's amusement than anything else. Forced to become a monk of Tarl-an-Gig. But she slowly worked her way in, making herself first useful, then indispensable, debasing herself before Nahac when it was needed, begging for her life, for her place.

Being made to feel like nothing.

Saradis knew she was not nothing and eventually Nahac saw it too. Of course she did; Saradis knew exactly what to say to her, what she wanted, what she craved. So many times Saradis had gone to her knees, weeping about how she had betrayed her god, chosen the wrong child. That it should always have been Nahac, not Cahan, who was raised to be Cowl-Rai. It helped that she had almost believed it, had thought to herself many times as she watched the weakling struggle to harden himself up for Zorir, how much better it would have been if the sister had the cowl within her. Of course, that had not been Saradis' choice, the boy had the cowl within him and the girl did not.

It had taken Saradis many years to work out what linked Cowl-Rai. While other Skua-Rai were out looking she was studying. Finding the truth hidden behind parable and myth. Cowl-Rai never came from the blooming rooms.

They came from the Wyrdwood.

Nahac was not the one then. She was not the one now. Saradis shrugged and walked nearer to the bars, staring down at Nahac's inert form.

Remarkable, how this girl had found her way to what Saradis already believed, "what if there was only one God?" How much easier would it be for Zorir to burn the world if all of it were united by them, the name did not matter to the people, call them Zorir, call them Tarl-an-Gig. Certainly, Nahac never really cared, she believed in no gods.

Only in power. In proving she was worthy.

There had been that one night. A week before they attacked Storspire when rumours had flown that the Cowl-Rai of Chyi was on the move. Strange, how hazy the past was in her mind. Zorir's voice had been quiet for a long time, but it must have been back with her by then.

If that was not the case, how could she have known to make the offer of power?

Nahac had not taken it, not then. She had laughed it away despite her fear of the Cowl-Rai of Chyi.

"I have no need of power, I have got this far without it."

Later though, she had not been as sure. As more Rai surrounded them and it began to be talked about how the Cowl-Rai never showed her power. The Hetton and the dullers had come first, by accident. A Rai made an attempt on Saradis' life, sneaking into her room, angry with how much power she had and wanting to put someone they could control in the position of Skua-Rai. She had found their body in her room in the morning, slumped in front of the taffistone Nahac had mocked her for bringing to her quarters. The Rai was still alive but inert, unconscious. She had shown the body to Nahac who in turn had dragged another Rai, one she thought a co-conspirator, up to look at the body. That was when they found out the way a duller affected the Rai. The way it frightened them.

Experiments had followed: any Rai judged not to be truly loyal had become either dullers or Hetton. Nahac liked the dullers for their tactical purposes, but Saradis liked the Hetton: they were unswerving, loyal and unthinking.

Still, Rai liked nothing more than to foment trouble, and they did not stay scared of dullers and Hetton for long. Nahac had seen Laha, Saradis had made sure of it, how he healed, how he was quick beyond other humans, how the shards of the stone sparkled in his skin.

"Do it to me," she had said eventually. Saradis had said no, despite it being her plan. Overcome with a sudden fear of failure, what if it killed her? What then? What happened if the Cowl-Rai died? Everything would be for nothing.

Was it then that Zorir had spoken to her?

She did not think so, but she remembered it in a different way to the other times. A sense of clarity, of seeing Nahac's face, of where to place the stones. Of necessity and power and the price of it. Veins of blue that brought both strength and destruction. She remembered a sense of shame, that this gift was given to Nahac and not to her. Remembered strapping Nahac down, the time it took to hammer the stone into her skull, the agony she went through, how Saradis made it last longer than it should have, hurt more than it should have. Only understanding later that she had not been passed over, she had been chosen and for that reason must be kept clean of the bluevein.

Nahac had used the power, tentacles of black that destroyed any who came near her; she had walked the battlefield a queen of death and for the first time Saradis had worried she might not be the one who mattered. That Zorir had moved on.

But after the battle had come sickness, and madness and the cage, built of Nahac's own orders, of bluevein-throttled wood.

She smiled at these memories. At the same time they worried her. They were not clear. She thought she knew when things had happened, but she also had a nagging feeling she was wrong. Times and dates and places were not as clear in her mind as they had been once. Maybe the stones in Nahac's skull had been before the dullers and the Hetton? Or had the dullers and Hetton been much sooner than she thought? Did Nahac already have bluestones when Saradis met her? She felt like she did. Saradis took a breath.

When and where did not matter. Only that it was.

"Nahac," said Saradis. Nothing. "Nahac!" she said it again, louder, and the woman moved her head, the hair so greasy it stuck to her skin like nettle webs catching on the boards of the floor. Her eyes flickered open. Bloodshot, empty and dark.

"Kill. Me."

So little said, so much pain within it.

"No." Did she enjoy saying that? Yes. She had never liked Nahac. The woman had been a necessity, a tool that she had needed. "Have you looked out of your window today?" Nahac blinked and Saradis smiled. "I brought you your brother as I promised. You have not forgotten?" Nahac's eyes narrowed.

"I was meant to protect him." The words slid from her mouth. Saradis felt nothing but contempt at her self-pity.

Once she had wanted her brother in front of her, kneeling. Now she wanted his forgiveness.

"You did not protect him very well." She stood a little nearer the cage. "But do not feel too guilty, your real work was for Zorir, it was always Zorir. You may have failed Cahan, but you did not fail Zorir."

A knock on the door. Saradis turned. She did not want anyone coming in and seeing what the Cowl-Rai had become. It would make her look weak, and the remaining Rai would feel foolish and that could make them dangerous, even with the threat of the collar hanging over them. She opened the door a little, pushed her way out to find one of the Rai waiting, the collared either side of him.

"The Cowl-Rai is not to be disturbed," she said, "or even looked upon. Their power will destroy you if you do." The Rai bowed their head. "Why do you disturb my time with them?"

"A prisoner has been taken in the city," said the Rai.

"And? Prisoners are taken all the time."

"This one is strange." That made her curious. Rai were not known for their curiosity.

"More of the Reborn?" That would make Laha happy. He enjoyed experimenting on the undying warriors in the dungeon.

"No," said the Rai.

"Then explain what you mean by strange, Rai." She no longer bothered with names, let them know how little they mattered to her.

"Freakish," said the Rai, "they do not cake their skin in white clay but purples and greys."

"I hardly think that—"

"And they have no eyes," the Rai spoke quickly, almost in panic at the fact she was so dismissive of him.

"Blinded, for some crime? Why should this interest me?"

"No, Skua-Rai, they have no eyes at all. Their head is rounded as if they were born without them, and they do not speak our language." Saradis looked down on the Rai, blinked, then began to turn away.

"I have no interest in some freak." Something drew her eyes to the collared; they were staring at the Rai, and, did Saradis imagine it, or was the blue of their body and eyes just momentarily more intense?

"Osere," said the collared. It felt like being stabbed, to hear that ancient name from the mouth of the collared. They barely ever spoke, only silently carried out their orders. To have them speak of the most cursed, the demons of the underneath. It shook her but she could not show it.

Saradis took a deep breath. This was good, surely? If the Osere were rising then the end must be close?

"Have the creature put in the cages below the spire," she said to the Rai. "Do it at night, I do not want it seen by anyone." The Rai nodded and she watched them leave, while wondering what secrets she could learn from one of the Osere, the Betrayers of the old gods.

9

Sorha

The city outside the walls was quiet and Sorha did not like it.

How many times had she walked through Tiltspire, both inwall and outwall, and wished people would move out of her way? How many times had she hated the teeming populace? Pushed away sellers as they tried to interest her in their wares, shoved past people as they walked too slowly for her or cursed the stink of night-soil carts as they passed slowly through the city in the darkness. But now, walking through the outer streets of Tiltspire, she would have welcomed even the stinking night-soil carts.

It was not right.

The houses of outwall Tiltspire aped the ones of the inner city, great teetering wooden things with pointed eaves and upper floors overhanging the streets, though unlike the inwall houses, these were built shoddily and given to collapsing. That was the way of things. That they were all dark and quiet was not. No lights, no sounds of raucous men and women drinking, fighting or betting. All the things she was used to in the lower city were gone.

Sorha moved from house to house listening as she did;

many of the houses did not have doors, they only had curtains over the entrance. She stopped before, one, two, three, listening for any sound from the inside but hearing nothing. She was unwilling to go in but she did not know why. She had never cared about the privacy of others, never been bothered at all about what they might think or want.

But Sorha had changed. Sometimes she thought it made her weaker, this being bothered about people and what they might think. The whole concept of intruding on another would have been alien to her once. She let out a long breath through her teeth, breathing back in the smells of the city, mud, wet with rain fresh from the geysers, sewage and rotting refuse. Part of her had presumed those who had lived here were dead. Foment and revolution always bred in the poorest parts of the city, and with Saradis' new god risen the people would be frightened, and frightened people were dangerous. She would not put it above the Skua-Rai to simply clear the outwall slums, especially as the Osere were very sure that the Betrayers did not need life the way Rai did.

But there was no scent of death.

She told herself not to be foolish and went into the next house. It was the same as many houses here; multiple rooms housing many people. No sign of life but their possessions were here, a change of clothes, simple grass toys for children. Chests with locks or elaborately tied knots – so the owners would at least know if they had been stolen. She did not open the chests; they were private and she did not feel it her place.

She wondered if the outwall people had simply left, seen the thing that had risen in the centre of Tiltspire and run. She would not blame them; the presence of the thing when it had attacked in the Osereud had filled her with a fear like none she had ever known.

She found food, which she thought odd: if the people had left why had they not taken food? In one of the upper rooms she found a cloak, old but well looked after. The outer layer was of crownhead the skin, the inner woven of crownhead wool, patched and repaired, but warm and waterproof. The sort of thing anyone would take on a journey.

But they had not.

She took the cloak. Her armour made her stand out and any plan she may have had of being able to use it, to be Rai in among the people of Tilt with all the advantages it gave her, was not to be. She did not think the Rai were the power here now. Then she went from room to room, house to house, finding enough clothes to cover the Osere, any guilt she may have had of stealing rapidly ebbing as it became more and more apparent that the whole of the outwall was empty and the people were not coming back.

If she wanted to capture one of the Rai for information she would have to go inside the wall. She tied the cloaks for the Osere into a bundle and left it just inside the curtain of a building, making a mental note of where it was. That done, Sorha headed towards one of the gate roads. As she approached she began to hear the echo of voices down the street. Quiet voices, then the bleating of crownheads and eventually she saw rafters, bringing in food and wood on heavily laden rafts towed by crownheads. The light above was just starting to break the darkness and the shadows of the rafters seemed like friendly, familiar things, though they did not speak to each other or laugh the way she was used to merchants coming to Tiltspire doing. To her left the gate in the wall, manned by troops and beyond that the soaring spires of the city and the dark pyramid within. She stood between two carts; the one in front had a load of meat, blood dripped from beneath its covering. The one behind had firewood and was held aloft by four gasmaws.

"Early to be on your way in there," said the wood rafter, nodding at the city. He had the look of a man who had once lived well but did not any longer. His face drawn, his make-up and clan markings applied sloppily.

"Yes," she said. "I am visiting family."

"Most of 'em are leaving, not coming in," said the rafter.

"Why?"

"All well and good worshipping a god," said the man, then he looked around as if worried others might be listening in, "but living under one, that makes people uncomfortable."

"Is that why the outwall is empty?" she said. "People gone to avoid the gaze of a god?"

"Something like that," he said. "Though it don't have eyes, as far as I know. Just sits up there." He turned away. She wanted to keep him talking but they were nearing the gate now and she did not want the soldiers there paying too much attention to her. They never had before; the gate guards were famously slack but who knew how that worked now. Maybe it would be better if she was talking with someone, as if they knew each other.

"You seem to be doing well," she said, pointing at the load of wood on his raft.

"Barely made my quota, probably won't next time." He looked miserable.

"Quota?"

"You have been away," he said. "We don't do markets any more, all quotas. For the war in the south, see. The spire pays us, and we have to deliver."

"And if you don't?"

He shrugged. "They always need soldiers," he said, "or at least that's what they say they need."

At the gate they were waved through; no one even looked at her and she got the feeling the guards weren't so much slack as uninterested, hopeless, even. When she was through the gates she left the rafters to continue on toward the marketplace while she went deeper into the city. The houses were stone here and there were people, plenty of them, but there was something wrong. Not obviously, or outwardly; more she could feel a sense of oppression throughout the entire city, as if the people walked with a weight on their shoulders. The Betrayers were everywhere, in Rai armour but they were not Rai. The glowing blue around their necks marking them out. It was walking down a street lined with them that Sorha first heard the name the people of Tiltspire gave them – the collared, for the thick vein of blue flesh around their necks.

That bluevein was everywhere in the town, like the roots of a tree, running through gutters, up the sides of houses, around the streets. Sometimes it was thick roots, other times it was a barely discernible filigree, a web hanging over streets like flags. It made the city look like it was flaking away, slowly dissipating.

Walking through the streets she understood what the wood trader had said about living under a god; she could feel the thing on the pyramid. Its presence was like heat, like a baleful sun on her skin and she found herself trying to stay in the shadow, to keep buildings between the creature on the black pyramid and her. The nearer she came to the spires the more she felt like it might sense her, might know her as someone who had fought it.

Still, she knew she must go closer to the pyramid. She had seen no Rai, only these collared which stood as statues on every street, watching. Sorha found herself weaving through backstreets, almost getting lost in an attempt not to walk close to them, though they appeared to pay her no attention, or anyone any attention. They did not move or act. Only watched.

Once she saw them move: they pulled a man from a group of townspeople and, though he screamed and begged for help, those with him were plainly too scared to do anything. If there was a reason for him being taken then Sorha could not fathom it, and the man only repeatedly cried out, "I have done nothing! Nothing", as one of the collared dragged him away. It used only one hand and she made a mental note of that: their strength was prodigious and all the man's struggling had little effect.

It made her even more determined to avoid them. She slipped down dark alleys, along the sides of houses through places that were more midden than street.

She turned a street corner and found herself at the base of the pyramid. Huge, thick roots of bluevein ran around it, from it and out into the city. Others ran up towards the spire, twining around the huge array of taffistones. She wanted to run, the thing at the top of the pyramid was nothing but horror, its presence brought back shifting, terrifying memories of being hunted through the dark by something immeasurably more powerful than her.

Then she saw Cahan.

Hanging below the creature, arms and legs slack as a corpse though she was sure he was not dead; the strangest thing, but it was almost as if she could feel him. Dead but not dead, as much sense as that made.

Voices: she stepped back into the shadows. Five Rai at the bottom of the pyramid. She had been a fool to come this far into the city and think she could take one of the Rai out with her. They were plainly scared, banding together. Even with her ability to dampen their powers taking on more than one at a time would attract attention.

She would have to return to the Osere. They would have to think of something else.

Sorha made her way back through the city, a shadow. What she was had no effect on the collared; they did not appear to be aware of her but nonetheless she made sure to weave her way through the city avoiding the larger streets where the collared were most numerous. Rather than heading for the gate she made her way to the wall. The streets further from the centre were quieter, less people, though there were signs the houses were occupied. She had hoped to break into an empty one and get out through the roof, but it did not look like an option.

Instead, she walked down the street looking for a gap between tightly packed houses, a place where they were not built up against each other. Eventually finding one, slipping down it then climbing with one hand and one foot on each of the walls. Once at the top, she walked across the roofs, heading towards the tallest. From there she climbed up a floatvine that had attached itself to the main wall. At the top she sat, getting her breath back and looking over Tiltspire as the light above ranged across the buildings.

This was not the world she knew any more. The truth was her world had changed the moment Cahan Du-Nahere took her cowl from her. She had begun to change, and she thought for the better. Though the birth of this better person had been hard.

The change in the city was different, going the opposite way to her, getting worse. Far beyond the spires she could see a skyraft coming in. Nearer, enclosed by the outer spires of the black pyramid, the silhouette of the creature atop it. She could not see Cahan from here.

"I will come back for you, Cahan Du-Nahere," she said quietly, wondering why she felt it was necessary. She let herself over the other side of the wall, moving along roofs until she found one that was old and damaged enough to allow her to get into the building. Then down and down. Walking until she had her bearings. She picked up the clothes she had hidden, and from there back to where the Osere hid in their stinking cellar.

"I have brought clothes," a mix of their language and hers. The Osere even quieter than usual. She looked around.

Not enough of them.

"Where is Frina?" A moment of silence, then one of the Osere let out a long stream of language, a lot of which Sorha did not understand, but at the end came three words that complicated everything.

"They have her."

10

Venn

Venn's mind ached.

It was not something they had ever considered a possibility, an ache inside their mind. They knew headaches and this was not that. It was a kind of bone tiredness of whatever it was that made them who they were. A numbness in the centre of their head and they did not know any way to get rid of it outside of sleep and, right now, they could not sleep.

The taffistone needed them.

They had been unwilling to join the foci in shoring up the stone's defences at first. Venn did not feel welcome and the foci were riven with their own tensions, and since the rising of the god in Tiltspire it had become worse. The dissent among the foci had spread to the Forestals and Venn no longer felt Woodhome was the place it had been. The people still laughed and shared what they had but there were underlying stresses, occasionally raised voices would be heard in the canopy. More than once Venn had been stopped, Forestals blocking their way, and although there was no actual violence, the threat was there.

It was the same with the foci, though worse. Brione had convinced them to let Venn join in the defence of the taffistones, through the simple reasoning that none were as powerful as Venn, though they had not asked Venn first. Brione had explained to Venn they could hold longer and better with them than they could without them. That Venn was needed.

When Venn acquiesced Brione spent long hours explaining to them what it would feel like, that this would be different to anything Venn had felt before. When Venn asked for more they could not explain it. All Brione could say was "You will be in between."

When Venn asked what that was Brione struggled. Tried to say it was like the moment of travelling between stones when you were neither there nor here, but for Venn that travel felt instantaneous, like walking from inside a hut to outside. Was there something else, a moment of falling? Maybe, they were not sure.

"Also," added Brione, "you must guard your thoughts. Hold them."

"What?"

"The network is everywhere and everywhen. It is everything, and everything is there."

"Are you saying I will lose myself?"

"It is a danger, it does happen," said Brione, "but more dangerous is the others in there with you. If you are not guarded they will see everything you are. If they mean you harm then they can do it there and none will ever know."

"So how do I guard myself?"

Brione shrugged. "It is different for us all."

"What do you do?"

"I imagine a door, and I shut it." Venn blinked as Brione walked away into the luminous night of Woodhome, trying to decide if that was helpful or not. It did not matter, Venn had no time. They had agreed and their decision meant they were to be thrown into the fray straight away, the rest of the foci were tired. Venn was needed.

The foci of the lens sat around the taffistone in the centre of the square, each cross-legged, hands out and holding the hand of the one next to them. At first Venn thought it a circle, but then realised it was not, it was a spiral. The final one of the foci, Sendir, sat with their hand on the stone. Around the square were statues of the Boughry, Venn had noticed more and more of them appearing in Woodhome, as if their looming, foreboding presence could somehow chase away the danger the Forestals knew was coming.

Venn sat down by the last trion in the spiral and took their hand. They felt cold, though the air was anything but.

They wondered what it was going to be like. Knew there was only one way to find out. They opened themselves, the same way they had been taught to when they were working with Forestals, using their own power to magnify what came to them, a line of cowls all working together.

Everything.

A vast, glowing world. A landscape that stretched out eternally, and yet mirrored Crua. The forests were great frozen waves at either end of the land. The Slowlands a soft fade into infinity. Power everywhere, moving with a low hum that filled Venn up and made them exult, as if they were meant to be here. It touched something inside them.

The attack came swiftly and without warning.

It was like a million hooks, like a hundred thousand biting insects falling upon their mind and trying to drill their way in, blocking out the beautiful golden landscape. Venn had no protection, but their attacker could not protect themselves either; to make the attack they had to let down whatever they protected themselves with. Venn felt the core of them, jealousy, but mostly fear. Fear of what Venn was, fear Venn would take something from them, fear Venn was more than they could ever be, fear everything they had ever known was coming to an end. In this place fear was a powerful weapon, something primal and pure and Venn felt how it could be used to burn out their mind. He saw the intent, felt the mind behind it. Sendir.

So pure in their hatred.

So very frightened.

Venn imagined a door. Closed it.

Felt Sendir recoil, felt their shock and a new sort of fear as they understood Venn's strength in this place. If Sendir and the rest of the foci were candles, then Venn was the light above, an impossible heat, something not to be touched or even looked straight at. They felt the foci around them, cowering, scared, and Venn forced their light down, dimmer and dimmer and dimmer until they were little more than a flickering candle.

What are you?

Venn did not know who asked it, maybe the foci asked together. Maybe it was Sendir, or Brione, or one of the other trion, but it did not matter. Venn did not know the answer.

Their mind reached out, finding the frays and tears in the golden landscape, sensing the damage, the invasion.

Bluevein, Venn said it to themselves, and as if by naming it the ravagement became clearer, a gnawing at the threads of the web, a probing of sharp and unpleasant intentions, a creeping desire: *let me in.* Venn felt where the foci had worked, the thickening of the glow around the damaged areas, the desperate desire to stop not only access to the taffistone network but to undo what the bluevein had done. They were failing. Their strength was nothing compared to what was doing this. That it would get through, eventually, was without question, and what held it back was not the foci but something else, something larger, something . . . *a great golden star . . .*

Ranya!

Venn knew it without knowing it, and in the saying of the god's name they felt an attention upon them, benign, inquisitive and thankful.

Friend of Udinny. A voice that was not a voice, something that surrounded Venn and cradled them. *Walker of the path.*

Venn understood the words, while feeling they were more than words and much was not understood. The soft touch of Ranya faded away leaving them with the definite sense of somewhere they must be, as if Venn had been lent a little of their knowledge. With it, a desire to open their mind once more, to share the light of Ranya.

How could they? Sendir had, moments ago, tried to kill them, and might again.

No. A deep sense of calm fell upon them.

The Forestals shared – it was what they were – and Sendir's refusal to accept Venn, that was because they were frightened of them, frightened because of their power and because Venn was not a Forestal. Sendir had wanted them here so they could remove Cahan Du-Nahere's power, and now Cahan was gone Venn was a threat.

After pushing Sendir from their mind, they would appear to be even more of a threat.

Venn opened their mind a little, feeling for others. Finding them. They were aware of what had happened, they did not approve of the attack but the power Venn had shown frightened them. Past the fear Venn felt how tired they were, how the lights of their minds burned dimmer with every moment. The fight they were involved in, the shoring up of the golden web within the stones, was still happening, but they knew they were losing. They had put up their walls not only against the bluevein but against Venn, even Brione.

Venn knew they were needed.

The foci needed Venn to stand any chance of success.

But they were frightened. Of them, of what attacked the network, of so much. For a moment Venn considered tearing down the walls of the foci, forcing their will upon them and knew they could do it. But those thoughts felt odd, cold, wrong. Not their way. Never had been.

Venn opened their mind, the door they had put up to stop Sendir opened.

They waited.

Nothing.

Then the first tentative reaching out. They expected it to be Brione but it was not. It was a trion Venn did not know – *Sarvin* – nothing more than a brush of their mind against Venn's. When nothing happened, they made a stronger contact. Venn did not try to push them away but let them in. Let them see who Venn was. Then, another touched them, and another and another until they were all connected, even Sendir, though they were last and took the longest to fully melt into the entanglement of minds. Venn let them roll through them, let them know who they were, the pain they had suffered, what their mother had put them through. How Cahan had protected them. They felt the foci soften towards them. Realise they were not a threat, would never be a threat to them. Venn let the light from deep within them leak out, only the smallest amount, thin golden tendrils that found each member of the foci attached to the taffistone. With it, they linked each member of the foci, not to each other, that already existed, but to Ranya, and very slowly they all began to grow a little brighter and the defences of the network became stronger.

Each day from then on Venn spent time doing this with different members of the foci, and that was why there was an ache deep in the trion's mind. The world within the stones was beginning to feel more real than the world without it. When Venn walked through Woodhome they made themselves see the realness of it. The huge branches that housed villages and largers. The lifts taking people up into the canopy of the cloudtree. They let the pulse of life, the gentle continuation of the Forestals' lives, the occasional strong burst of power as a group banded together to achieve some task with their cowls, wash over them until the ache began to subside.

Venn stopped, leaning on a rail over the sheer drop, thinking of the people in Woodhome and the thing that was assailing the taffisnetwork.

All this is doomed, they thought. Closed their eyes, took in a huge breath of the fragrant forest air: acidic cloudtree sap, earthy cooking smells and the soft promise of rain.

They returned to the tree house they shared with Furin. As always she sat in the corner, a pot on the pile of hot stones that she would stir every so often. Behind her was where Issofur used to play, but he was rarely there now. When he had been there he no longer spoke the same language, he spoke what he called "tree words". Venn wondered if Udinny would understand it, then wondered where Udinny was now. A warmth by Venn's ankles and they looked down to see Segur; more and more the garaur was a wild thing, just like the boy. More likely to be found out among the rootlings and playing in the forest, but it always came back to here and to Furin.

The Leoric — Venn still thought of her as that — was lost in herself.

"Furin," said Venn, "the broth smells good."

"They have different herbs here, I have been experimenting." She would always talk about the food, but if Venn strayed to other subjects she would quieten and eventually stop talking altogether, or turn and say that Issofur needed her. Though the truth was the boy had needed no one for a long time, he was happier here in the forest than any of them. Not quite human, not quite rootling, the Forestals called him Woodling and revered him for it. It caused Furin only pain. Venn walked further in, sat with Furin. Ever since Ont had left she had been diminishing. No, that was not true, she had been strong then. It was when news of the creature in Tiltspire, and that Cahan hung below it, came. That had broken something in her, left her brittle. She had hung on for Issofur, but now? Venn took a cupful of broth and tasted it.

"It is good."

"Not right, not yet." She looked up, a desperation in her eyes. "Do you think they would let me go back to Harn?"

"Why would you want that?"

"It was home. The only real home I have ever known."

"Harn is gone, Furin." Venn said the words softly, as if explaining something to a child. "There is nothing there for you." Furin nodded.

"It calls to me," she said, "I know that sounds strange, considering what happened. But I met Cahan there." She looked away. "Sometimes I wish I had not."

"The Rai would still have come to Harn," said Venn. "That was no one's fault. Treefall ensured it."

She nodded. "But if I had not met him, he would not have come to the Slowlands for me." She bit back a sob. "Would not have fallen. I would not have had to lose Issofur by fingersbreadths, watching him become wild. I would be at peace now."

"None of those things are your fault."

"It was easier," she said, and as she spoke her voice was full of pain and loss, "easier when I did not know. When Cahan fell I could still imagine he lived. When Issofur was in the forest, I could imagine he was playing there. But now we know the truth. The forest took my child, and that thing in Tiltspire, it keeps Cahan like a trophy. It says to us, here is your strongest and I have killed him." She looked up. "It is my fault, Venn, and ever since the Slowlands my mind does not rest. It takes me back to Tilt, to the cells that woman, Sorha, kept me in, and the creatures that watched over me. I cannot—"

"Cahan is not dead, I feel sure I would know if he was."

"But the creature."

"I think it needs him." They had not thought about it, Venn was simply sure of this as they spoke the words. Maybe it had been within what Ranya said, maybe it was simply a misplaced faith in the strength of the forester.

"We need to save him," said Furin. "If the creature needs him, and we take him away then surely that is good?" She stood, pacing back and forth. "We should gather troops, what remains of those from Harn, they will come. They will do it for Cahan. For me, and—" Venn put out a hand, stopped her by taking her forearm.

"Those from Harn, they are still haunted by battle and they need time to heal. And to walk in to Tiltspire?" Venn shook their head, "we do not have a big enough army even if we had all the Forestals with us."

"The Reborn," she said. "They are there. If we can find them then . . ."

"They would promise to kill all those in our way to bring back Cahan Du-Nahere," said Venn. "And lead us into death thinking we were all immortal." Furin blinked, looked away, and Venn could almost feel the desperation bleeding out of her skin.

"I will talk to Tall Sera," she said.

"He will tell you the same."

"Then I will escape here, and go alone."

"And what of Issofur." Again, that stricken look on Furin's face.

"He does not need me, he has the forest now."

"Forest needs you," they both turned. It was the boy, Issofur, not seen for many days and now here. Neither had heard him come in and he stood before them, his skin lightly furred, posture slightly stooped, teeth too sharp and eyes too bright as he looked up at them. "The forest needs you here for when they come." The boy laughed, dancing in a circle with his arms out, "and they will come."

11

Udinny

There was a knife at my throat and Tanhir was holding it.

This was becoming a regular occurrence. Around us were the other Forestals that Tall Sera had sent out before her. When he had sent us through the taffistone he had said, quietly and making sure no other could hear, that he could not promise we would arrive where he intended, or arrive anywhere at all, but the transition from Woodhome to here had been no different from any other. As we had met with a group of Forestals then I presume this must have been where he intended for us to go. Not in Jinnwood, or the southern Wyrdwood, but near a larger called Astenak on the plains of Jinneng.

"Is it worth it yet?" I said. Tanhir stared down at me, the weight of her body on mine, the cold blade of the hardwood knife at my throat. For a moment I thought her madness and her grief would overwhelm her. Then she shook her head.

"Not yet," she said. Then she pushed herself up and off me. Sitting on her haunches and never taking her eyes from me. "Refugees will be coming this way," she said. "Now that Mydal has fallen."

"And the armies of the Rai will follow."

We had entered the larger that first night, in darkness and to find it mostly empty. The Forestals, only ten, quickly spread out, vanishing into darkness. Tanhir had grabbed me, pulled me away from the gates and down an alley between two houses.

"Stay quiet," she had said when I had no wish to be anything else. The town was empty, and we were guided through it by a series of whistles and calls, while the harsh hand of Tanhir dragged me forward. "Where is everyone?" she said, to herself not to me. I was not one she aimed any conversation at. We met with another of the Forestals.

"Artiz," said Tanhir, "is the entire larger empty?"

"Can't speak for the entire thing," said the Forestal, "but mostly it seems abandoned, and in a hurry, too."

"Then search the houses, take anything that may be useful."

"Tanhir," a whisper, another Forestal crouching in a doorway. "I need to show you something." She let go of me and followed the Forestal. I followed them and we moved through the larger, towards the walls. Now I saw traces of people, the odd face in a window, or body scuttling back into a dilapidated house. Quick to vanish, and if we could see some I presumed there would be more who were better at hiding. The Forestal led us down a stinking alley and to a stair which led to the top of the town wall. At the top the Forestal crouched, keeping their silhouette as small as possible to anyone outside the larger. I followed, crouching behind Tanhir.

"Look over there," said the Forestal. "You will see why this place is empty." I looked over. A few thousand paces away I could see lights, hundreds and hundreds of lights and columns of smoke rising from them.

"An army," said Tanhir.

"Red or blue, do you think?" said the Forestal.

"Makes little difference to us," said Tanhir, "though I suspect the blue from the way this larger has emptied."

"Why are they so quiet?" Tanhir ignored me, at first. But I could feel my words eating at her. This near, in the quiet of the night, we should have heard something from the army. We should have heard them even before we entered the village. Armies are noisy things, soldiers joke and laugh and fight.

"They have probably been ordered to silence," she said eventually, I think more because the Forestal wanted an answer herself than because I had asked, but it was a poor answer. Even an army ordered to be quiet was rarely this silent. "Stay here and watch them, Yiamo," she said. "I'll come back before the light is risen but I want to know if they move."

We spent the night going through the larger, looking for anything that might be useful. We disturbed the odd resident but they all ran, none stood up to us. The Forestals captured one of them, a half-starved old woman who could barely speak for fear of them.

"Get off," she shouted, "are you Osere from below? Come to take what ain't yours?"

"Quiet, woman," said Tanhir, enough threat in her voice to frighten the woman into silence. "We mean you no harm, what happened here? Where is everyone?" The woman looked around, taking in the Forestals, but said nothing. The white paint on her face was cracked and flaking. Tanhir began to draw her blade, to underline her threat and I pushed in front of her. Offered the old woman some bread I had found.

"You must be hungry," I said.

"So I am, old man." She grabbed the bread and started to gnaw on it with the three teeth left in her mouth. It felt very odd that she called me old man. This body was not mine and I was not used to it or how people saw me through it. In my mind I was still small and female and relatively young. Being reminded I was not was like finding I had a third arm or an extra head. I turned to find Tanhir glowering at me. "You get further with kindness, I have found." I expected some cutting reply but instead she looked puzzled. Maybe my words were entirely at odds with what she believed I was.

The cutting of the throats with the knife of ritual. The preparation of the grass sheaves.

A vision so strong and acute I almost passed out. I looked at my hands, expecting to see blood but there was none.

"You look like you ate some bad meat, monk," said the old woman, still chewing on the bread.

"What is your name, old woman?" She narrowed her eyes at me.

"I'll tell you, but they better not listen," she nodded at the Forestals. "Don't want 'em coming after me."

"I am sure they will not." She shrugged at my reply.

"Name is Geheberd."

"And what happened here, Geheberd? Could you tell me where everyone has gone?"

"Chyi's army came through, more than an eightday ago. Took everything they could get on their way north, said they would free Mydalspire." She pointed the way the army had gone. "Few days ago they came back, must have had a right beating as there were a lot less of 'em." She laughed. "They took anything they'd missed last time and anyone who looked strong enough to a hold a spear, there were some right complaints but after the Rai sucked a few of 'em dry of life that stopped. Whole lot let off for Jinnspire."

"What of the army outside the walls now?" She stared at me. If I expected fear or shock there was none.

"What of 'em? They leave me alone, I'll leave them alone." I found myself laughing and she joined me in that laughter, though I felt quite sure she was not right. Something in her was broken.

"You can go now, if you wish, old mother."

"I do," she said. I let go of her and she vanished into the darkness.

"Well," said Tanhir, "at least we know who is outside the gates now, if there was any doubt."

"Should we leave?" said one of her troops. Tanhir shook her head.

"They might send foragers in once the light is fully risen, but we can hide from them easily enough."

We slept a fitful night, constantly waking, thinking we heard people in the village. In the morning I ascended the walls with Tanhir. The army was gone.

"Is that usual?" I said.

"No," said Tanhir. I think it was the first time she'd spoken to me not to give an order or to threaten murder.

"They would usually loot, even if only a little," said the other Forestal.

"They could be in a hurry, chasing the retreating forces?" said another Forestal.

"According to the woman, they've been here for days," I said.

"We should go and check what is left of their camp," said Tanhir. "See if there is anything of use."

"Tall Sera wants reports on what is going on out here. What if we lose them?" I said and from the reaction you would think I had made the finest joke that had ever been made.

"An army that big will leave tracks even you could follow, monk. And it will be slow." She glanced towards the southern horizon, clothed in the gauzy mists of morning. "Besides, I know where they are going. Jinnspire. Following the other army." She led us back, through the larger and out onto the flat pains of Jinneng. The crops around the village had been cut and burned, making the ground difficult to walk over. When we reached the remains of the camp there was all the usual rubbish of a big army, broken spears, weapons, and tents that were beyond repair. Stinking latrine pits and still smouldering cookfires.

Then there were the corpses. Not a vast amount, no more than a hundred, and they were well spaced out – but not buried, which was curious. I knelt by one, a woman. She looked like she had been hurt in battle. There was a large wound to her arm, but not one that I thought should kill her. I put out a hand.

"Don't!" I turned. Tanhir. "Look on the ground, where the corpse touches it." I looked. Thin strings of blue linked the corpse and the soil, and now I was closer I could see the same just under the skin of the corpse. I had thought them veins but they were not. I stood and moved around the corpse. Looking at it from the other side I saw a piece of wood had been hammered into the neck of the corpse. It looked like the woody stem of a tree or shrub, though twisted and sickly looking. From it protruded hundreds of small and pale mushrooms.

"Fungus like that sent the mushroom growers of Woodhome mad," said Tanhir.

"It looks like bluevein," I said. "Are they seeding the ground here with it? But why?" I stood, walked over to the nearest corpse. This one showed no signs of battle, no wounds apart from the wood thrust into their neck. "This is fertile land, to infect it with bluevein is madness. It is plain the forces of Chyi are in retreat, beaten, the land will be needed for food." Tanhir was staring at me. Saying nothing. I walked over to another body. "They look to have killed healthy troops for this."

"Maybe they were prisoners?" said one of the Forestals, poking a corpse with the end of a bow.

"No," I said, my mind a whirl, "this woman has the clanpaint of Harn county, another over there had Mantuss."

"Maybe they were deserters, and this is a punishment?" said another Forestal.

"Maybe."

"We should follow the army," said Tanhir, "that is what we are here for after all, is it not, to scout and report?"

"Look!" I said, pointing at the next corpse.

"Another body, what of it."

"It is Rai." That brought her over, as if what I said could not be. She stood above the body, staring down at it.

"Maybe this one fought with the others, you know what Rai are like."

"That is always possible."

"Something strange is happening, Tanhir," said one of her archers.

"It is," said Tanhir, then she looked around. "I wish we had one of the foci with us, but we will have to do. Form up, we'll burn these bodies before the land is infected by the bluevein, then we follow their tracks, see what happens."

I turned away, looking towards the south where the army had gone. For a split second I thought I saw a child in the distance beckoning me on, but when I blinked and looked again there was nothing.

12

Dassit

Dassit was no tracker, but Ania was. The most Dassit had to offer was shouting out Ont's name until Ania put a hand on her arm, shook her head.

"Best to be as quiet as we can be in Wyrdwood." Dassit nodded and Ania had crouched, looking at the ground. Then she began to move around the forest floor in a spiral.

"What are you doing?"

"Ont's footprints have been obscured, by us and even more so by the rootlings." Ania looked up. "I am looking for where I can find them again."

"Can I help?"

"Yes," said Ania, still working through her spiral, "by staying still."

"Ont needs us to protect him. Why would he leave us?" Ania muttered something about "Osere cursed rootlings."

Dassit felt lost, confused, stood there in the far northern Wyrdwood bathed in the coruscating colours of night, the web of life turning and shifting around her. In the distance she saw the suffused glow of a copse of huge mushrooms, yellow and blue and green.

"Who was the child he was with?"

"Probably a rootling," said Ania. Dassit thought on that. She felt like she would have known if it was a rootling, but she wasn't sure enough to argue about it.

"Do you think the voice called him away then?" Ania did not so much reply as grunt. "But why? When it called on us to follow him? To protect him?" Something that glowed a deep red shot past her face. "It makes no sense for it to split us up."

"It is a mistake to try and understand the forest."

"Why?"

"Because it is a forest and you are not." Dassit had no answer to that, it was the sort of reply she hated, one that felt like it made sense while it explained nothing. She wrapped her cloak more tightly around herself. Ania stopped moving. "Here," she said, "he went north."

"What a surprise," said Dassit and shifted the shield she had on her back and the quiver of throwing spears so they were more comfortable to carry. "At least we should catch him quickly."

"We should," said Ania, "you say he was with a root-ling?"

"Maybe, why?"

"There's no tracks, only his." She shrugged as if it didn't matter but Dassit felt a cold shiver pass down her spine.

They walked, passing through the mushroom copse she had seen from a distance. Close up they were so bright it felt like day beneath them, and they rained a constant stream of spores from black gills. The spores made Dassit's skin itch where they touched her.

"Don't scratch," said Ania, "if it gets into your blood it is worse." Dassit stopped scratching and covered her mouth with her cloak, though she noticed Ania did not bother. They left the mushroom copse and Dassit wished she could find a wetvine to wash away the spores. The sounds of the forest were getting louder; usually that meant the light was coming, the sepia tint of day within Wyrdwood. Dassit was sure they had not been walking long enough for it to be day, not yet. Ania stopped, raising a hand in signal for Dassit to do the same. Then she took her bow from her back and strung it.

"What is it?"

"Gasmaws," said Ania.

"But they are harmless, if we keep out of the way."

"Not night creatures, Dassit. Not right they are here," she looked around. "Ready yourself." Dassit took her shield from her back, planted her fighting spear in the ground and took a throwing spear from her quiver.

"Cover as much skin as you can," said Ania. In the forest something let out a whoop, a strange echoing sound that felt like it surrounded them, washed over them. It was answered by another, then another. The third call was different, higher pitched, more grating on the ear. "Two gasmaws and a spearmaw," said Ania.

"Is it hunting them?" Dassit moved so she had her back to Ania: together they could see everything around them though the constantly shifting colours made it difficult to pick anything out.

"It should be." The whooping and whistling ebbing and flowing. "But I have never known spearmaws be out at night either."

"That is not comforting." She looked out into the darkness. Did she see something? Glowing lines of icy blue darting among the colours?

"I do not want you comforted, Dassit. I want you ready." Dassit's eyes darting round, not settling anywhere, looking for movement within movement, the kaleidoscope of the night making it hard to pick anything out.

"I am ready," she said. She felt her breathing slow. "I have never fought a maw before." It felt somehow shameful, to admit as a seasoned warrior she had gaps in her knowledge, in her ability to defend herself.

"It will try and use its poison tentacles, they are longer

than the rest." The words came quick, no recrimination, only an efficient passage of information from one warrior to another. "Your armour should protect you from its hooks and suckers. It will try and wrap you up."

"To crush me?"

"They are not strong enough for that, they want to get their beaks on you. Do not let them, they will bite right through your armour."

"How do you kill it?"

"Thankfully," she said, slowly turning with her bow at the ready, "gasmaws die easily, they are soft. Aim for the head or the gasbag, sever the tentacles. If it gets close go in through the eyes."

"And the spearmaw?"

"Let me deal with it."

"I will tell it that, should it attack me." Dassit heard the growl in her voice, the fear she felt bubbling up as irritation. A laugh from Ania.

"The underside is armoured, my arrows can puncture it, your spear cannot." Something out there, something fast and sleek. "Up close, though, you should be able to get through it. It also has poison, but the stabbing tentacles it will shoot out are a real danger. Keep your shield up."

"If we are poisoned?"

"Unpleasant but not fatal for the gasmaw."

"And if the spearmaw poisons me?"

"Try not to let it." Dassit found her eyes would not be still, she could not focus. The constant moving colours of the forest were excellent camouflage for whatever was out there.

"Can you use your cowl on them, Ania?"

"I am not Rai." If there was any quicker way of shutting that down Dassit could not imagine it. She was about to reply when Ania loosed an arrow, the deep song of the bow as it bounced back from tension. Something came at them from the darkness, sleek and dangerous. A spearmaw, a predator of the forest. It veered off and in the heartbeat Dassit's attention was stolen by it a gasmaw charged at her, not coming straight on, but straight down from above. Only a fluke, or maybe a warrior's constant awareness of what was around them, saved her. She raised her shield, stepped back and the gasmaw deflected off her shield, leaving Dassit's arm numb from the impact. The beast had misjudged its speed, or perhaps cared nothing for its own survival, and it smashed into the ground. Dassit thrust her throwing spear into the gasbag behind its head and the air filled with the unpleasant smell of the gas which kept it afloat. Ania was loosing arrows. Dassit felt panic, for a heartbeat as the Forestal aimed at her, then arrows were whistling past her head. Dassit turned and a second gasmaw crashed into the ground, its head and beak pierced with long arrows.

"This is wrong," said Ania. "They do not work together, and they are not given to throwing away their lives."

"Look," said Dassit, pointing at the gasmaw that had attacked her. Lines of blue ran through its flesh, not the symmetrical lines of luminescence that were usual to night creatures. These were a chaos of blue. Glowing splashes and lines that circled back on themselves, or fractured again and again over the creature's body until they either vanished or grew into lumpy, hard-looking protuberances.

"Bluevein," said Ania, "it is in the animals now."

"Where is the spearmaw?"

"I hit it, right between the eyes," said Ania. "It will be dying somewhere." As she spoke the whooping and howling started again. "More of them," the Forestal looked around, "we need to keep moving, find Ont."

"Before they do?" said Dassit, taking up her fighting spear.

"Let us hope so." They moved, following the trail Ania picked out while around them the hooting and echoing calls picked up, the sound swooping and drifting through the cold air of Wyrdwood. There were no further attacks, not then. They came across the body of the spearmaw. Even infected with bluevein the thing had a beauty that Dassit found herself admiring. It was a creature she had heard of but never seen, far sleeker than the gasmaws, a predator designed to cut through the air in silence. The spear tentacles ended in long, thin, sharp points with hooks on the ends. She reached out, wanting to feel the smooth carapace, get an idea for how thick the armour was.

"Don't touch it," said Ania, "it's still poisonous, even dead. And who knows – if the bluevein can get into it, maybe it can get into us." She drew her hand back and they carried on into the darkness, through the wheels of colourful light, always trying to stay aware for movements that did not fit, that were not part of the pattern of the forest.

The next attack came as they passed through a small copse of bushes – small on the scale of Wyrdwood, huge on the scale of the people – they moved into the shelter of the trees, the air thick with small, biting, flying creatures. Ania slowed.

"Stay aware, maws often anchor in the heights of these bushes."

She had been aware, moving slowly, trying to ignore the constant nip of creatures puncturing her skin, searching for blood. Eyes up, eyes to the left, to the right, searching. Still, she did not see it until it was almost too late, the tentacles reaching out for her from the leaves. She thrust her heavy spear up, feeling the wide blade meet the slight resistance of the maw, cutting through its gelid flesh. It let out a whimper as it died, falling from the branches. At the same time Ania was loosing arrows, one, two three. Each one answered with a hiss or a hoot of pain from the maws.

"Run," shouted Ania, "there's too many!"

Dassit felt it, a weight of flesh around them as something closed around her. Lashing out with her spear, she cut a way out. Then, holding up her shield before her, wishing she had some way of seeing in the night, that her vision could push through the gaudy colours the way her spear punched through gasmaws. She followed Ania's voice, getting hit, again and again, by attacking gasmaws but managing to keep to her feet. Running. Breath coming in gasps, the ice in the air biting deep within her lungs, making it hard to breath. Everywhere the creatures. Diving. Appearing from the darkness, buffeting them. Ania's arrows hissing through the air. Dassit wondered how she knew where to send them. How she aimed. All Dassit could do was keep her shield and spear up, thrusting whenever she thought she saw a shape, trying to fight the beasts off. Somewhere inside, she felt Ont must be dead. He could not have survived an attack by these creatures. He could not run, could not fight. Could not see.

In that moment, that distraction of thinking of another, they had her. The impact was from the front, right onto her shield but harder than any other before. It knocked her to the floor, wrenched on her arm. Then the creature was gone as quickly as it had come, but it had taken her shield with it. The next maw hit her and she had only her spear, thrusting it out before her, both hands on the haft. Writhing tentacles surrounded her, the earthy, unpleasant smell of the maw in her nose and before her, her spear embedded in it, the beak, clack, clack, clacking with desperate hunger. She could hear the wood of her spear splintering, the beak biting down, sawing its way through. Behind it the long body of the creature. A spearmaw, not a gasmaw. An agony, her shoulder pierced by one of its spears. She would have cried out, screamed, but she needed all her energy to hold off that clacking beak, pushing back on the haft of her spear even as it began to shatter. The maw's other spear coming in and she rolled. The beast puncturing the ground. Its spear lashing out again and again, looking for her body, her head. She tried to push herself backwards with her feet. Shoulder throbbing. She wanted to scream, to cry out in pain, but was afraid the noise would bring more of them. Her strength ebbing. Pain. Where was Ania, where were the arrows?

Her spear cracked, the creature pushed forward. Saliva falling on her face, thick and stinging where it clung to her skin. She was making a noise, a low, awful sound as much disgust as fear. The spear could not hold. The beak cutting through, little by little. Soon the spear would be gone and then it would be on her. What would it feel like? To die? Would she even know it was happening? Or would the spearmaw crush her skull in a moment?

She was giving up, knew it.

Only moments now. If the spear did not break her wounded arm would give in. Only a moment before she gave in.

Why prolong it?

A roar.

The creature rolled off her. Spears in its side, lots of them. Small. The spearmaw tried to lift off but fell to the floor, tentacles writhing and twisting. It rolled, snapping off the spears but more came. From the corner of her she saw gasmaws, falling from the air punctured by the same tiny spears. Running around the clearing were creatures, small and with three eyes that ran across their skulls. They threw spears with unerring accuracy. Maws fell, and despite the pain, and the exhaustion, she found herself wondering if the spears were poisoned as the fallen maws did not die. The one that attacked her was still writhing, its agony obvious, its spear tentacles thrusting into the ground as it dragged itself away.

Then the rootlings arrived. A tide of them crashing through the forest, falling on the gasmaws and the spear-maws, heedless of the danger, or of the losses among their own. They smothered the creatures with their bodies, biting and scratching and killing.

Then it was done.

Silence. Gasmaws, and small furred bodies lying around the clearing. Hundreds of rootlings standing about, as if confused, in among them the small creatures with spears. Dassit pushed herself up with her good arm. Her other was wrecked, she knew it was a wound that would be life-changing. The bones in her shoulder were shattered, grinding together as she moved. A pain like no other she had experienced. She found Ania lying on her side, struggled over to her. There was a deep cut across the Forestal's face.

"Ania?" Slowly lowering herself while hundreds of eyes watched her. "Ania!" she dropped her spear. Was the Forestal breathing? "Ania!" louder. The Forestal moved, her head rolling over, eyes opening.

"Poisoned," she said.

"Gasmaw or spearmaw?"

"Spear."

"What can I do?"

"Herbs," she coughed, "hold it back."

What do they look like?"

"Ha," she laughed, coughed, "wouldn't you like to know." Dassit felt something behind her, turned. One of the strange three-eyed creatures stood there, and in its hand it had leaves and mushrooms. It made a sound like wind passing over tree branches as it held them out. Dassit took them. Held them above Ania so she could see them.

"These?"

"Yeah," coughed again, "don't know the mushroom though, where . . ."

"These creatures, the ones that saved us," she pointed at the one stood behind her. Ania narrowed her eyes, trying to focus.

"Shyun," she said, "shyun know the forest, feed them to me – Osere!" the last word a cry of pure agony and Ania curled up around her stomach. Then Dassit was pushing her back, trying to ignore the grinding in her shoulder, ripping the leaves and mushrooms into small bits. Pushing them into Ania's mouth and watching her chew, watching her force them down. Not knowing how much to give her, continuing until there was nothing left.

"Is it working?" said Dassit. Ania looked up at her.

"Don't know," she said then her eyes closed, and no matter how much Dassit called, they did not open.

13

Saradis

Saradis watched as the skyraft moored itself to the central spire.

She had worried that it would not come, that the huge craft built and added to over generations would sail past Tilt. She knew from her spies that the Archeos of the raft families were nervous of the newly risen god. Well, she thought as she watched ropes thrown and tightened, they should be, but it did not suit her purposes for them to be too nervous.

Not yet.

They would find nothing different on this visit to Tiltspire, she had made sure of it. The collared she had moved well away from the spire, only Rai and her troops would meet the raft. They would help them set up exactly the way they normally did. She would play her part.

Saradis had always hated the formality of it, meeting the Archeos of the raft, taking a ritual drink with them in their cabin and discussing trade; what goods the raft brought, what goods it needed, the number of gasmaws to be supplied. It had always struck her as wasted time, something she could easily have passed off to an underling. She resented the raft family for making her come to them, leveraging the power of trade and using the fact that she needed the raft to move armies.

Today she did not resent the meeting.

She was looking forward to it. With her stood two Rai, lowly, unimportant and lacking in power. Barely worthy of the title Rai and she did not know their names. They were props, nothing more. A semblance of normality.

When the raft was finally secured enough to let down the lifts Saradis smiled to herself. For so long she had despised these people with their strange cultures and made-up gods. She heard voices from far above as a lift began to drop from the belly of the skyraft. She could have met them at the tip of the spire where it docked, but she had not been ascending the spire recently. Since Zorir had come the spire had changed; it had always been unsettling but now it was worse. She should have expected it of course; the spire was a place of gods, the people may have changed it over time but it was right and proper that her god should take it back. Right and proper that she should not be comfortable there. She did not need comfort now. When the fire burned everything out, when all was remade, she would be comfortable. Waiting along the Star Path was paradise and she would rule the people there, and when the people were reborn they would thank her for her work. They would understand the sacrifices made in this life. Until then her work would remain a thankless task, but no one had ever said that to be the chosen of a god would be easy.

The lift clanked to a stop and two rafters, stripped to the waist and talking in their own cant, opened the doors and welcomed her on, formal, stiff and unfriendly. She stood between them as the wicker doors shut. The lift groaned, began to ascend while she tried not to look down between the woven sticks that were the only thing keeping them all from falling. Instead, she looked forward, getting a much better view of Zorir's pyramid, and of Zorir in its majesty, than she could from below. Lines of blue fell from her god like a waterfall, flowing out and into the town. She loved the way they twisted and curled, touching on everything as if curious, readying themselves for the great drawing of power.

Strange how she had thought that this would be the end of it, the rising of the god, but it was really only a start. More was needed. Laha had tried to explain, though he was hard to understand now. He talked in ways that often made no sense, but she had the definite feeling that it was to do with other spires, other cities. The trion was needed, she knew that, so it was good that Nahac had been so obsessed with them. They were already halfway found. Plans were underway, which was why she stood in this lift. The mechanism of the fire though, she did not understand. It had something to do with the taffistones. With something hidden far beneath. A way to communicate with Crua, or maybe drink from it. It was not clear, none of it, and that made her uncomfortable, to not know.

But she had faith, she had always had faith. She would serve knowing it would all be explained in the end; after all, her faith had stood her in good stead. All had worked out, even when she thought she had failed it had simply been part of Zorir's plan. "Trust," she said under her breath. One of the rafters glanced at her, then they went back to talking among themselves in their own language, and though she did not understand it there was no question about their feelings. They did not like Zorir, or what had happened to Tiltspire. Foolish, frightened little people.

Well, they would learn their place.

The lift shuddered to a halt and the rafters opened the doors. There was more of a breeze up here but it could not stifle the heat from the huge fireboxes on the deck, though the fires had been out for a good time now.

Before her stood the Archeos of the Maglan family raft,

a huge man, wrapped in layer upon layer of material as if the heat was meaningless to him, though the sweat on his face told a different story. His clothes were thick with jewellery, precious ceramics and shining heartwood.

"Archeos Maglan," she said with a small bow of her head. If he cared she was not dressed as was customary for these occasions, no stiff robes, cages of twigs or elaborately braided hair, he gave no sign of it.

"Skua-Rai Saradis," his voice was odd, the words of the people polluted by over-familiarity with his own language. "Tiltspire has changed since our last visit."

"The god has come, you should rejoice. Iftal will be reborn. The people of Crua will be one under Zorir."

"Good for them," said the Archeos, though he did not look like he was pleased. "The people of Crua are restless, they change gods often, you should remember that."

"They have never had a true god, not one they can see." The Archeos bowed his head.

"Well, not since they overthrew the old gods, at least." Before she could reply, he put out a hand, motioning towards his cabin. "Let us get away from the heat of the braziers. Would you enjoy a drink?" His words were traditional, and stopped any reply she may have. Part of her wanted to set the Archeos straight, to have him look down at Zorir and know the greatness of her god, but she let his rudeness pass. Living in the clouds made these people think they were apart from the rest of Crua, but it would not save them from the fire.

"Yes," she said. "Of course I will drink with you." He led her over the deck, past the huge stone braziers that made sweat stand out on her skin. Inside his cabin it was little cooler, shutters had been opened to let a breeze through and a bottle waited on a table that was cleverly built so the legs slotted into the deck below, securing it in case the raft hit strong winds.

"I must tell you, Skua-Rai," he said as he poured liquid

from the bottle, "the Archeos of the skyrafts, they are worried about this god, this new way you have brought."

"They should not be," she said.

"Well, they are. You attacked a raft not that long ago. It has not been forgotten." He held out the stone cup, clasping his own in his other hand. "There is talk among the Archeos of no longer calling at Tiltspire." She stared at him, but did not take the offered drink. "Lack of trade would strangle your city, we require assurances that our lives can continue as they always have, no matter what should happen on the ground."

"A mistake was made with that raft, the Archeos insulted our Cowl-Rai. That could not be allowed." Maglan stared at her and then nodded.

"And yet now their raft is dead, laying on the plains of Tilt as you had no one to fly it." He blinked, sweat ran down his face but it was from heat not fear. She still did not take the drink. "I trust everyone has learned their lesson." Something about him enraged her, so sure in his power, so sure that Zorir could not touch him and his people up here. She put a hand in her pocket, found what she was looking for, a single sliver of stone cut through with blue crystal. She had not been sure what she would do right up to the moment she had come into his cabin. The collaring did not always take. Even among the Rai it killed about a third, but among those who were not Rai it killed about half straight away. The rest did not last more than half a season.

It would be enough, she thought, if he lived a few days. She stepped closer, took the cup he offered.

"I was admiring your necklaces," she said. He touched them with his free hand, smiled.

"They are very valuable, a mark of my expertise in trade." She stepped even closer.

"Then let me also give you a gift. To add to your riches."

Her movement was swift, unexpected. She dropped her

cup, brought the shard up and buried it in his neck. The Archeos never even had time to shout. His mouth opened. If he wanted to speak he could not. The shard acted quickly. Saradis stepped back and his mouth closed. Opened again.

He made a noise, not a word, not loud. A noise like begging, like pain.

"It will not hurt long," she said, "you will either die or you will be owned by Zorir. It is best to relax." What would she do if he died? She was not sure, her troops were ready but she doubted they would be quick enough to save her if the crew realised what had happened. She would have to walk out, pretending all was normal, making some excuse as to why the Archeos did not follow her as was expected. She was excited, thrilled even, she had not truly been in danger for many years.

A line of blue was already forming around the neck of the man, she could just see it, hidden beneath his neck-laces, his face becoming slack, the sweat drying.

She took a deep breath, pleased, he was going to live, well, live long enough to be useful to her. He was still holding his cup. "Give me your cup," she said. His hand shook, some liquid spilled, he was fighting. "To fight it, is to know pain. But give in and you will know the glory of Zorir." He was not giving up, not yet. "Now, give me your cup." Slowly, shakingly, his hand reached out towards her, holding the cup out. She took it from him, lifted it to her lips and then stopped. Something in his look, in his eye, some odd joy even as they clouded over. "Is this safe for me to drink?" He was fighting again, his teeth locked together to hold in the words. "Answer me, is it safe to drink, Archeos?" He did not speak, he sweated. Then shook his head, a swift and involuntary movement and she saw the joy die in his eyes. "You would have poisoned yourself to get to me?"

"Immune," the word creaked out of his mouth.

"Well, it appears I was correct to act first, I had worried

I might be making a mistake. I had even considered offering your raft an alliance." She poured the rest of the drink onto the floor. "I am going to use your raft, take it into Wyrdwood and attack the Forestals with it."

"No," another word bitten out. He must have a formidable will.

"I am afraid that I will, Archeos Maglan, and you are going to help me."

14

Cahan

I *am with you.*

He could hear them in the forest, they were coming and he was tired.

It would be easy to lie down, give in and accept the inevitability of it. Bathed in the green glow of Harn he felt like he should, as if this was all futile, that he was fighting a battle he had already lost, doing something pointless. A madman, repeating the same actions every day in the hope something was different.

It was never different.

Do not listen.

I am here.

He walked to the wall, the villagers appearing around him, more with every step. Each one faceless, green shadows in the darkness. He knew them. But the names were hard to grasp, he had to force himself to think, to concentrate. There, Irva, a forager who knew Woodedge. She had died in New Harn, on the spear of a Hetton, and he had seen her die. But she was here with him now. Soon she would die again on the wall of Harn, cut down by one of the Rai. By her was Milun, who Cahan thought was safe in Woodhome but here he would die behind the walls, skewered by a thrown spear. Every single one of them was doomed, and every single one of them would rise again and fight again. His mind stopped. He felt as though there was a gap. As though there was a piece of knowledge that mattered and was somehow blocked, the same way the paths out of the village were blocked.

He had tried to leave more than once.

He was not a coward, but he was also not a fool. When he had realised they carried out the same actions every night he had called the villagers, and they had come, appearing out of the glowing houses to stand before him.

"We must leave," he said. Faceless faces turned to him, a wall of blankness, of forms that vaguely resembled people he knew. Though not all of them, he felt sure of that. When he had stood in Harn, there had been others with him. They had been important but now he could not grasp their names.

Name them.

That voice. Name who?

When he only glimpsed the villagers they had more detail, more quirks. They were more real seen from the corner of his eye than when he looked directly at them. They did not speak, of course, they never spoke, never made a noise apart from at the end when they cried out in death. "You will all come with me," he had told them. "We will all go. Leave this place."

No answer, no agreement and no disagreement. He took it to mean that they would follow. Surely if they were not coming then they would say? Segur had been by his leg and he had taken comfort from the garaur.

"You will come, old friend?" and he had not meant it as a question but it had been.

When they left, opening the damaged gates of Harn, the village had followed and he had felt something that was almost joy, but joy as if experienced through a veil, a grey and diaphanous thing, something known about intellectually but hardly felt.

As they had headed towards Woodedge something began to change. He was not conscious of it at first, or maybe he was – a nagging sensation in the back of his mind – but within a hundred steps it was not something he could ignore. The villagers were fading, they were not turning around and leaving, they were not abandoning him or fleeing in fear. They still walked but with every step they became less. When they had started they were people, or almost people. They were known shapes but with every step they were becoming shades, shadows of shadows. By the time he reached the first saplings of Woodedge there was only Segur left and even they vanished as he stepped among the trees. Found a path. Followed it and it led him round in a circle until he once more found himself looking at the walls of Harn.

Standing on them were the barely visible shades of the villagers, waiting for him to return, to make them real.

Again and again and every time the same.

He walked out of Harn, holding his axes, palms and fingers hurting. Tension like it was cracking his bones, knuckles grinding. Expecting the Rai, the camp of enemy warriors. Never finding them, always finding himself back at Harn, back where he had started.

He had always been finding himself back where he started.

Eventually, he stopped trying. This place was not Harn, it was not Woodedge.

He did not know where it was. When he tried to remember how he had got here, he could not.

So he returned to Harn, and as he did the ghosts became shadows, the shadows became figures and when he was back within the walls of Harn he was surrounded by faceless, but more solid, villagers once more.

"I am meant to be here, but why?"

A wave of loneliness passed over him. He searched for familiarity among the villagers, warmth, but they did not speak, or help, or project any warmth at all. They only were. They gave no comfort to him, there was no comfort to be had here and, deep, deep within him, he was sure that beyond the blue glow of the surrounding Rai's forces, there was only pain. Pain like he had never known. It was a frightening thing to know.

Sometimes he knew that as an immutable truth. Sometimes he did not.

The sky lit up. A blue glow rising into the air, a ball of fire.

The Forestals appeared. All touching and the fireball bounced off their shield, though instead of exploding or spreading it vanished, as if absorbed. Then came the chanting, and another ball of cold flame. Within it he felt the pain he was sure was out there, waiting for him.

"Archers!"

They came, coalescing out of the air behind him as he stood on the wall, watching the Rai approach in their crawling armour, their reaching tentacles and many blades. He felt no fear. He had his axes. He had his people and this whole fight had fallen into some détente, as if the enemy were no longer really trying. He had been sure at one point he would be overwhelmed, beaten, that he could not stand, that Harn would fall and him with it.

Not so sure now.

It made him no less tired, he felt no less like this was futile, that there was nothing else, that he should lie down and simply give up.

Do not listen.

He feared that even if he let himself die, lie down and give up, then he would only wake again. Here. Unable to escape, stuck in the circle going round and round and round in an eternal battle. Was this what it was like to be . . .

To be what?

To be who?

Again, the feeling that something was missing. Someone was missing from this place but he could not concentrate on it, could not pick through what was in his mind because they were coming. The forces of the enemy. The assault on Harn was beginning again.

"Archers!" he shouted, "loose!"

15
Sorha

The story took a while to put together, the Osere speaking what they could in the language of the people, Sorha understanding what she could in the language of the Osere.

Frina had not been able to stay in the basement, the inactivity had slowly been wearing her away until she had decided she must do something. Together with another Osere, Batruna, who sat dejectedly in a corner of the basement, they had gone into the town where they had been unlucky and run into a patrol of guards, falling into the ways of the Osere without thinking: rather than run they had stood entirely still. Frina had been nearest the guards, realised her mistake as they laid hands on her, shouted out to Batruna to run, he had. Losing his pursuers in the darkness of the city streets.

Then he had turned and followed them. Wept when they beat Frina. Tracked them by sound while they took her back to where they were stationed. Listened while messages were sent back and forth then returned to the basement loaded with guilt for his failure.

"No," said Sorha eventually, going to where Batruna

waited, his body twisted with misery, "this was not your fault. This is war, it brings us pain and misery but all is not lost." He said something to her but of them all he spoke the least of her language and it required another Osere to help her understand. "You think you should have died to save her?" Haltingly, back and forth, explaining he could not have helped, he would have been taken too, then they would know nothing about what had happened to them. He thought Frina was dead, or as good as, but she could not quite understand why, not yet. The words went back and forth again, twisting and changing from something she could only just catch to something she knew. Confusing, at first, talk of teeth which made no sense to her. Only when another spoke of "taking her to the Betrayers" did it make a little more sense and she cursed herself for her stupidity. The spire, of course, the Osere could not see, they described the world in reference to what could be felt, so that the name of a spire should gradually have morphed into the idea of a great tooth during their years below made sense.

It also made her heart sink. She retreated to a corner, taking a little area to herself and wondering if all really was lost. If she was taken to the spire no doubt Saradis would want to see Frina, and they would make her talk. Saradis had people who were very good at that. The best that could be hoped for would be that Frina would manage to keep up the pretence she did not understand the language of the people.

Sorha had been where Frina would be taken, the cells below Tiltspire.

She stood.

"Have they taken her yet, or do they hold her in the town?" Words flying back and forth.

"She is taken."

"Well, then, we must take her back." What came upon her was a madness and she knew it. She would risk her life and any that would come with her for one person, but in some way she could barely understand in herself it felt right. In the back of her mind the ghost of who she had been screamed at her, told her to run, to save herself, but that ghost was old, faint and powerless now.

"Batruna. How many guards were in the town where she was held?" The back and forth. Five. Would five be enough? It would have to be. "Then I need five to come with me. The rest of you can wait here." She should not have brought them up here, even for Cahan. She knew that now, they were too vulnerable. "The five that come must be those I can speak with the easiest, but I will not force you." Five rose, immediately, as if this had already been planned. She nodded, laughed at herself on realising they could not see her. "Thank you," she said, "but I must say this. It is clear to me now having seen the pyramid of the god that I cannot save Cahan." Speaking those words was like a knife within her, she did not like failure and she owed him. But the pyramid was heavily guarded by the collared, and she did not even know if he lived. If it was only her life maybe she would have thrown it away on an attempt. But what had happened to Frina had made her realise she could not throw away the Osere's, they had served for generations. They deserved better. "It may be I try to save Frina, because I cannot save Cahan, but the truth is it may still be a madness that can only fail." Buris put out a hand, sharing a touch with her in the way of the Osere. Then another spoke.

"Generations, we have guarded, but the prisoner is loose. We too make up for failing."

"You do not have to die," she said. Buris stood nearer, touched her face, something she still found hard to accept but she did not flinch.

"We will try not to," she almost laughed at how earnest the Osere sounded. She nodded.

"All will come part way," said another Osere. "Then some

of us will return beneath." The words came haltingly. "Not all gods hate."

"You mean you'll wake others?"

"If they can," said Buris. Sorha nodded.

"Very well, first we go to the guard station. We need their uniforms." Buris nodded. In the back of the room one of the Osere chattered, met with more chatter and all around they started to take off the packs they wore and pass them forward to the Osere going with Sorha. "What is happening?"

"Mushrooms," said Buris, removing a wrapped package from one of the packs, "a poison. Rare. Enough for one weapon. Your weapon." He held out the pouch. She reached out and he pulled it away. "Do not touch."

"Why?"

"Your power," Buris tapped her chest, "twisted, will poison you."

"My cowl is dead, Cahan Du-Nahere killed it." Buris shook his head.

"Different, not dead. But its seed, twisted."

"I don't understand."

"The killing," he said. "The taking." The Osere had opened the gate in the stone. They clearly had access to some form of cowl, and they had done it with her there. She felt at once ashamed that they knew she was not right, and proud that they trusted her despite that.

"You have cowls? But I do not repulse you?" he nodded.

"We feel you, we are weaker. But we share, we not project."

"Do I stop you feeling the world?" He shook his head.

"We not project." She nodded, but thought they must reach out in some way. It explained how they found their way in the darkness, not a sight, but maybe a sense of direction, of place. "The poison," he tapped her sword and she took it out, then the Osere felt for the blade edge, scattering dust along it, "will hurt the Betrayers, weaken the twisted." As he dropped the dust onto her blade she was struck by the oddest feeling, of things falling into place, almost as if they had been planned from the very start.

She took a deep breath. Her greatest fear on going into Tiltspire was not the troops, or the collared or even the Rai, it was the Hetton she was sure would be there. They were kept below and as far as she knew she did not have any effect on them. They were formidable, terrifying and hard to kill. But if this poison affected the Betrayers, maybe it would affect them.

"Let's move," she said.

Batruna led all of them through the silent streets of the outwall city and to the guardhouse. There the rest of the Osere left, going back to the basement to wait for night when they could slip through the city and back down the pyramid to their dark world below. The rest waited while Buris crept close to the guardhouse. Sorha watched, wondering whether they only listened, or if a cowl within was doing more for them than they knew. Buris came back holding up both hands to show seven fingers.

Seven, not really a challenge for her and five Osere. They might not consider themselves warriors but they were. She had watched them fight. Moving by sound and maybe more. Batruna was saying something to Buris who in turn came to her.

"There is one of their cowl warriors there, like you were." She nodded.

"A Rai, we must keep them alive if we can. They will have information." Buris nodded, passed on the information and it was time. Sorha's stomach light with the feeling she always got just before action, not quite fear, not quite excitement but somewhere in between. "I will knock on the door," she said, "I wear the armour of Rai, they will not know how to react and my presence will stun the Rai, even if only for a little. I'll kill the guard, push in and you follow." Buris nodded, passed on her words then Sorha was walking up to the door as if she owned the streets, looking like any Rai would. The door opened, a guard, a woman, dirty-looking, harried.

"What do you want . . . oh, Rai." Before she could say any more Sorha stabbed her in the neck with her dagger. Pushed on, sword coming out, two guards sat at a table to her left, three stood to her right, the Rai at the end of the room, and as she thrust her knife, not wanting to use the poisoned sword unless she must, into the neck of another of the guards, the Osere streamed in. They began to kill and she saw the Rai's posture change as their connection to their cowl fell away, the shock, the panic. It was over in moments and only the Rai still stood, hands lifted away from weapons. The Osere surrounded her and the butcher's reek of combat filled the small guardhouse. She was in front of the Rai, sword extended, blood dripping from the dagger in her other hand.

"Do not move!" She shouted it, felt the Osere flinch at the harsh grating of her voice. Careful not to let the tip of her sword touch the Rai's throat, a woman she thought, though it was hard to tell as when the first guard had died she had pulled down her visor. "Lift your visor." The Rai did so: definitely a woman. Young, not long into her power Sorha thought, she did not have the stretched skin of the older Rai. She looked dirty, as if she needed a wash. Odd. Rai very rarely looked unkempt.

"If you have come for the prisoner, they are gone, taken to the spire."

"We know," said Sorha, the growl still in her voice, her posture all threat.

"You are Sorha."

"Usually Rai call me abomination." The Rai licked her lips. Nodded.

"We did not know then."

"Know what?" Her eyes were wide, trying to take in the Osere, to understand them.

"What was to come, what she would do." Saradis, the Rai could only be speaking of Saradis. "What a true abomination was."

"Your name?"

"Huitt, Huitt Dan-Brihun."

"And what is it Saradis does, Huitt Dan-Brihun?"

"Make us slaves with the shards. Puts the collar on us. Only lets a very few favourites take sacrifice." It was strange for Sorha to see fear in this woman. She had never seen a Rai genuinely scared before. "Are you here to overthrow her, because she has a god on her side now. The collared are . . ."

"I only wish to free my friend, the one who was kept here." Was there a moment of calculation on the Rai's face?

"I can help you."

"How?"

"They sent me to question the guards and bring them back to the spire. I was to take them below."

"Below?" The Rai looked away and did Sorha see something on her face then? Terror? Horror? She did not know.

"I can get you in, that is what I am saying. They are expecting me, and they are expecting me to bring these guards." She looked around, marvelling at the Osere. "You might think you can get in otherwise but you cannot, the collared will not allow it. But when they are expecting something they do not check, they simply let it by."

"We could fight our way in." The Rai shook her head.

"Kill one, more come. They know. Some link in the collar." She turned back to Sorha, away from the Osere. "Maybe fighting your way out, you have a very slight chance, but not fighting your way in and then out. You will be buried beneath the collared, if you are lucky enough not to have a shard forced on you."

"Why would you do this for us?"

"To escape. When you leave," she said, "take me with you."

"You expect me to believe that?" Sorha laughed to herself. "You have just told me I am unlikely to escape. That I only have a very slight chance." For a moment the Rai did not speak, then she closed her eyes, tight, as if fighting back tears.

"Even death is better than the collar," she said and, to her surprise, Sorha found herself believing the woman.

16

Venn

"I know you wish to visit Harn once more, Furin," said Venn, "and this is not a visit to Harn, but it is the northern Wyrdwood which was home to you once."

Furin was staring at him from the darkness of the hut, behind her Issofur's toys were strewn over the floor but the boy was nowhere to be seen. Furin saw Venn's eyes stray to the back of the room where the entwined branches of the cloudtree trapped heat and the smell of Furin's broth.

"Issofur is out among the branches, with the rootlings doing whatever it is he does. He barely needs me now." She sounded incredibly sad, she had done for an age and Venn knew that the loss of her child might be the last thing she could take. The trion had become frightened for her, they didn't know when it had happened, it had crept up on them the way spearmaws creep up on their prey. She was like floatweed that was slowly losing its tether to the tree, gradually becoming detached, floating away from everything that kept her bound to the people around her. Sendir, of the foci — their attitude towards Venn had entirely changed since they had began to guard the taffisnetwork – had told Venn to watch Furin, watch her closely.

"She is losing what binds her to this world and that is dangerous in Woodhome." She had looked at the ground then, as if dealing with some ancient history. "It requires only a few steps up here for those who have found the weight of this world too much to carry." A euphemism, a stepping around of what they really meant but Venn understood, so high up despair could take you in a matter of moments. A short walk out into the void and then there was only the air, the illusion of freedom given by falling. The finality of the drop.

"Not home then," said Furin. Venn shook their head.

"No, but familiar, maybe."

"I never felt at home in the northern Wyrdwood." She began to turn away and Venn was at a loss, they could not leave her alone. Worry over Furin was making their time within the network more difficult, making concentrating harder.

"They want me to go, they say they can keep me safe but I would feel safer if you came with me."

"What do you mean?" A flicker of something, not interest so much as worry? Maybe?

"There are still those among the Forestals who think they would be safer if I was dead."

"You think that is why they take you to Wyrdwood?" Venn shook their head, feeling long hair move over their shoulders, hearing the hiss of it on their clothing.

"No," said Venn, "they take me because the taffisnetwork is strange, most Forestals can no longer open it, and those that can do not always turn up where they wish."

"This is the creature in Tilt? The one that has Cahan?" Venn nodded.

"It cannot get into the network, but it has caused damage. It is like the energy for the network is lacking."

"It steals it?" Venn shook their head.

"No, more like something is using it to fight off the creature."

"Ranya," said Furin, and Venn was about to reply, say they did not think so. Explain that though Ranya might be involved this felt more like it was just the way the taffisnetwork existed, as though it were alive to threats. But Venn did not reply. When Furin said Ranya, something in her eyes lit up – only for a moment – but there was no doubt about what Venn saw there: hope.

"Yes," said Venn. "Ranya is involved", which was not entirely untrue. "But they want me to go as the northern Wyrdwood is the farthest point in the network. No one is confident they can make the journey safely."

"No one but you," said Furin. Venn nodded.

"No one but me."

"You think I can protect you from Forestals?" said Furin. "I am no warrior, Venn."

"I think if someone is with me, then no one will dare do anything." A lie: Venn did not think anyone would do anything, Tall Sera had forbidden it and he was coming with them. Furin stared at them, then nodded.

"I miss the cold air of the north," she said. "It might be nice to shiver instead of sweat." Did she almost smile? Almost.

"Well, Furin, they are waiting for us, bring your bow and warm clothes." Furin nodded. Was there a new enthusiasm about her movements or did Venn imagine it? They were not sure, but still Furin was ready quickly, putting on extra layers, placing her bow over her back and holding a thick crownhead wool coat. They made their way to the taffistone in the centre of Woodhome. Venn had gradually realised that Woodhome was a loose sphere and the stone sat right in the middle. Waiting before the stone was Tall Sera and ten Forestals in green cloaks. Behind them three of the foci waited to assist in the transition through the taffisnetwork.

"Venn," said Tall Sera, "you are ready." Venn nodded as they came to stand by them. "I see you have brought a friend."

"Furin needed to get out." The trion watched Tall Sera who looked neither pleased nor displeased.

"Open the stone, Trion," said Tall Sera and the three of the foci put their hands upon the taffistone. Nothing happened until Venn joined them. Let themselves fall. Felt the non-place, found the golden light and heard the echoes of Ranya's voice. Not long ago this had been easy, they simply thought about where they must be and they were there.

Now it was not.

The taffisnetwork had degraded further and Venn had to push into the link. They imagined Crua, saw it as a vast oblong dotted with largers, villages and spire cities. At the ends the shadows of the Wyrdwoods, in among all this the bright golden lights of the taffistones, they clustered around the spires and were much sparser further out. Venn had the oddest feeling there was more, unseen, but put it aside. It did not matter now. Venn found a stone in Wyrdwood, pushed with their mind, felt a line of light moving across this mental map like liquid flowing down a channel, but a viscous liquid, more blood than water. The flow of energy slowing as it pushed through the land, vast areas of shadow that Venn knew would be blue if they looked too hard at them, that sparkling, unpleasant blue that brought with it a smell of stagnant water, sickrooms and salt upon skin.

Venn turned their mind from it, unable to lose the feeling that to look upon it was to draw its attention.

A connection made, a flash of gold and a whisper that Venn was sure was their name. Not a request for attention, more a confirmation of them, of who they were and that they were welcome in this place. Almost sounding like their own voice, echoing back through the network.

The door opened, vaguely aware of people passing through, waiting a heartbeat, a second heartbeat to ensure everyone had time and then they split their attention between this strange other place and their body so they could follow through the stone and out into the freezing morning of the northern Wyrdwood.

Venn knew the smell, the way the cold made the air feel fresher than it ever felt in the south. The way the cloudtree bark would feel rougher in the icy weather, the calls of the animals the same but slightly different. It was home, which was strange given Venn had spent only the smallest part of their life here. Further to the north there was *something*. Not exactly a call, more an acknowledgement, a nod from the rulers of this place to say they knew Venn was here, that Venn was part of this place. Thankfully, the Forestals would take them no further north and the presence of the Boughry quickly passed as if something else, more important, had their attention.

Before Venn the Forestals gathered in a circle, Furin crouched slightly outside. Venn joined the circle, gently taking Furin's arm and moving her in with them.

"I brought you here," said Tall Sera, "because I want to see Treefall. Since the network became harder to navigate we have sent out no raiding parties, but we must start again. The power of Tiltspire will only grow and this is a way for us to hit them. I want to know their strength. Their defences, what they have set up here since we stopped harrying them."

"Do we kill them?" Tall Sera shook his head.

"No, we only look, we take note of their numbers and we plan." Tall Sera looked around the circle. "We will have to establish a hidden camp, without the network it will be harder." A couple of the Forestals nodded; others were clearly contemplating the danger it meant to anyone who stayed.

"Let's go, then, the Treefall quarry is west of here," said a Forestal. Only now did Venn realise they knew none of them, and they all had the look of warriors, hard-bitten and used to killing. Tall Sera had brought his best and most experienced.

They set off, moving through the forest. Venn walked with Furin, feeling that she was different here. More alive somehow. It was as if she had left behind her worries in Woodhome and, though part of Venn wondered how long it would last, mostly they tried to be happy that she seemed to have found some escape from her misery.

The passage through Wyrdwood was easy, moving between cloudtrees without anything bothering them. Even the herds of gasmaws avoided them. They saw no predators, and when they came across the shrines of shyun they looked old, as if this place had been forsaken by them, deserted. It made Venn feel strange, empty, they kept looking around hoping to see the familiar shapes of rootlings which always warmed something inside them.

But there were none.

"Slow," said a Forestal and they dropped to one knee. "There is a rise here, over it we should come across the road they built for carts. It was always guarded when we raided."

At Tall Sera's instruction two Forestals crept forward to look over the ridge. They stayed there for what felt like a long time and then one let out a shrill whistle that cut through the air. Tall Sera brought the rest of them up and they crouched along the ridge, looking down at the road. Or at where it had been.

Now, where wood had been laid to make a track for rafters to bring cargos from Treefall and goods to it, all had changed. There was still a track but it was hard to make out. The forest had reclaimed it, the wood cracked and buckled by small plants and the roots of shrubs.

"It looks disused," said Furin.

"Could it be a trap," said another Forestal.

"An expensive trap," said Tall Sera. "A lot of work thrown away."

"Why would they let it fall into disrepair?" said Furin.

"Should we go down and look?" asked a Forestal

"No, let's follow the path to the tree quarry," said Tall Sera, "but we'll stay at the side of it. Gustin, Riddis, go ahead and keep an ear out for soldiers and Rai."

They moved forward, following the path, and Venn felt that they should start to hear something soon. They were familiar with the sound of chopping wood, the way it rang though the forest, and for Treefall surely it should be the same, but magnified by a thousand.

There was nothing.

The forest was not silent, but it was not full of the noise they expected. Tall Sera had them halt again as the scouts went forward. Barely any time before they returned.

"You should see this," said one of them: Riddis? Tall Sera gave a nod and they followed up a steep incline. Venn found themselves looking down on the tree quarry, where the unthinkably huge body of the cloudtree had fallen, and where the quarry was, or had been, digging into the heart of the tree for the expensive woods within. Where there should be noise and movement there was nothing. No sign of life at all, the scaffolds were falling down in some places, thick with floatvine and vegetation in others.

"It is abandoned," said Tall Sera. "Why would they do that? They have armies to pay, and trade is the lifeblood of the cities." It was Furin who answered, Furin who explained later to Venn that she had the information no other did. How Cahan had told her, late in the night, of what he had been through as a child, of the prophecy of Zorir, of how they had told him he was the fire who would burn the world. Furin had always thought it a metaphor, speaking in the way monks always spoke of gods, but in that moment before the corpse of the tree she realised it was not, not at all.

"They do not need the wood, or the trade, because those things are for the future," she said, her voice flat and dead, "and they do not intend there to be one."

17
Dassit

Ania was breathing, there was that at least.

Her wound did not look too bad. A tentacle had smashed through the light wooden armour Ania wore beneath her cloak. The creature had raked her side leaving a gash that was bleeding freely but not dangerously. It would probably not even need stitches. But the edges of the wounds were puffy and weeping where the poison was in her, and just to touch the Forestal's burning skin told Dassit a battle for the woman's life raged within her.

Dassit thought herself in no better state. Her shoulder was a wreck, the pain, close to unbearable, flowed over her in debilitating waves. She was sure she was poisoned as well. Her skin felt hot, her heart fluttered in her chest in a way that made her feel faint. She took a deep breath, forced herself to stand.

A crash of pain. Her mind throbbing, vision faltering but she would not give up. She staggered round the forest clearing. Found one long stick, then another. A travois, she must make a travois and then she could get Ania on it, then they could go north.

North.

The second she thought the word she knew the direction, realised that before Ont had vanished she had known the way to go. But after she had not. The lodestone in her mind had vanished and it made her angry that it was back now. She felt used.

She needed that anger. It would push away the pain.

As she worked, slowly, painfully, fighting to concentrate through a haze falling upon her and to make a travois one-handed, she was helped by the creatures of the forest. They did not understand what she was doing, not at first. When they did, in their own way they began to help. They were not always successful and when they were it felt more like luck than design. Sometimes they brought her exactly the right stick, or bit of vine, but quite often what they brought was useless: handfuls of earth, a single leaf, a berry. All these handed over to her by the shyun and rootlings and whether she needed them or not she thanked them.

She did not know how long it took to make the travois, then to get Ania on to it and to tie her safely to the bed. Then to balance it with floatvine.

They were attacked in the making, twice she thought. But the shyun were expert hunters, and the rootlings, careless of their lives, threw themselves at incoming gasmaw and spearmaw, making a living wall between the creatures and Dassit as she worked on the travois. It made no sense. The forest had let them be attacked and now it threw away its creatures' lives to protect them, but the world was making less and less sense the more time passed. It did not move the right way. She was poisoned, definitely, and it was starting to work on her. She was feverish, sweat running freely down her skin despite the icy air.

When the travois was ready, Ania safely tied onto it, Dassit tied a rope around her waist and to the travois. As she was about to set off one of the shyun appeared. It spoke and the wind whispered around Dassit. She could see it, delicate silver lines that flowed north and instilled a renewed sense of longing in her. The shyun held out its hand, in it were the same leaves and mushrooms Ania had eaten before she had fallen into unconsciousness.

"I cannot." Her mouth was dry, as if the heat in her body was burning away her saliva. "I must stay awake, go north." The shyun pushed the leaves at her. The sound of the wind became louder, silver lines wrapping themselves around her. "I cannot," she said again. Then more shyun appeared, pointing spears at her, and the rootlings began to growl and she felt threat in the air like a growing shadow. The shyun shook its head, strange mouthparts moving and the eyes across its skull shining.

Dassit saw no choice: she took what the shyun held and, watched by them and the rootlings, she put it in her mouth, chewed and swallowed. The sense of threat vanished, the rootlings chattered happily and the shyun melted away. What she had eaten tasted foul, and the taste lingered, refusing to leave her mouth. She was thirsty and, as if sensing it, or maybe knowing the side effects of the mushrooms, rootlings brought her leaves shaped like cups, each filled with sweet water. Dassit drank gladly and gave the rest to Ania.

She walked and the world changed, became more colourful. The pull she felt towards the north was pink, a line leaving her body. It stretched out behind her, showing where she had been. It made her want to laugh. Trees and shrubs crowded in, rose up and bent over her, twisting and changing shapes, leaves flashing through patterns of different colours as if they had some message for her — though if they did she could not read it.

The rootlings that accompanied her were growing in size until they towered over her, their eyes huge, mouths shrunken and misshapen, and yet it did not look wrong. Nothing looked wrong, strange, yes, but not wrong. She began to laugh. Found herself unable to stop. She thought she may be thirsty again but then again she may be hungry or she may need to jump up and down.

There was no pain. When she realised that she could not stop herself laughing. The rootlings joined in, though they looked different again, too many legs or not enough legs or their faces were too round or too flat – but they still looked entirely right. She wanted to dance with them. Did rootlings dance? She had never paid attention to them before. She thought they probably did dance, they always appeared to be full of joy. When had she danced last?

It had been with Vir. Where was Vir now? He had been a good dancer. Ania was probably a good dancer. If they survived this then she would ask Ania to dance with her. They would dance in the heat of Woodhome, like lovers, would they be lovers? Lovers danced. Maybe they would. Would in Woodhome. Wood wood wood.

Somewhere deep within she was aware the way she was thinking and seeing was not right but she did not care. Was it the poison or the cure that caused this? It did not matter. It was all too funny. She was probably dying, dying in a cold forest far from home with a crowd of animals. It was funny really, all of it was very funny.

She stumbled, tripped, fell.

Did not get up.

"Water."

Yes, she was thirsty but it was a long way off this thirst, the dry throat, the swollen tongue, the searing pain. A long way off.

"Water."

She was speaking without even being aware she was speaking. Her head ached, no, it throbbed like it was growing in size then shrinking in size. It didn't hurt, not exactly, but it was not comfortable either.

"Water."

To say words without knowing her mouth moved. How

odd, but everything was odd. She could smell rootlings. A friendly smell.

"Water."

She sounded far more desperate than she felt. She was thirsty, but not desperately thirsty. Maybe her mouth did not understand what her mind and body did. Maybe it was some side effect of the drugs and . . .

Ania.

Dassit rolled over, almost screamed as she put weight on her ruined shoulder. Had to fight to get back control of her body. The pain was welcome in a way, it flushed away the last of the herbs in her system. The world was the world again. Cold, damp, uncomfortable and full of pain. She pushed herself into a sitting position with her good arm, trying not to move the hurt one. Night. The air full of colour, the shadows of rootlings moving around her. She found Ania's travois, hanging in the air not far from her.

"Water."

"Ania!" It was her voice she had been hearing, not her own.

"Water."

"I am coming, Ania." Onto her knees, breathing hard, the pain and the drugs had sapped her strength but she was not going to give up. One leg up, foot on the floor. She fell forward, catching herself on her good hand. Hissing in pain at the jarring of her damaged shoulder. Other leg up. She was standing, barely. The world spinning around her until she closed her eyes. Put all she had into staying standing. A step, another, and she was above Ania, the Forestal's eyes were open.

"Water."

She didn't have any water. Stupid. Didn't bring it. A rootling appeared with a leaf cup and gave it to her. Dassit dripped water into Ania's mouth. Not sure how long she did it for, how long she stood there aware of her own growing thirst but knowing the Forestal needed it more. Eventually she got her to drink, and Ania closed her eyes.

"I dreamed of Ont," barely more than a whisper.

"Good," said Dassit, "I still take us north."

"In the dream, he was walking through Wyrdwood, like he had not a care."

"Let us hope that is the case," said Dassit though she doubted it. Not that it mattered, Ania was gone once more, slipped out of the now and into a place between sleep and wakefulness, the word "thankyou" escaping her mouth as she did. Within moments of her drifting off, Dassit was once more grasped by a compulsion.

North.

She put the rope around her waist, wondering who had untied it, and set off even though it felt useless. Ont could not have survived an attack by the maws. Maybe she would find his body, maybe she had already passed his corpse and it was rotting in the leaf mulch or had been ripped apart by clacking beaks. It did not matter. The order, the desire to move north, was still there in her mind. If asked she would have described it as faint but at the same time it was impossible to ignore.

North.

So she moved through the forest dragging her wounded companion and flanked by a hoard of rootlings and the odd member of the shyun. The maws had not given up, they still came and there would be a furious commotion at the edges of the pack around her as the forest creatures threw themselves, unheeding of their own safety, against their attackers.

When she stopped again Ania was awake, staring up into the dim light of the Wyrdwood day. Dassit gave her some berries and nuts provided by the rootlings, watching carefully to make sure the Forestal did not choke as she worked to get the food down. Gave her water. Cleaned her body. That done, Ania's mouth moved, slowly, and Dassit leaned in close. Nothing at first. She leaned in closer.

"Thank you."

The words took all the energy Ania had left and she slumped back into unconsciousness. She was feverish again which worried Dassit, the Forestal's brow slick with sweat and her sleep was disturbed. As they moved through the forest Ania moaned and tried to free herself from the vines holding her onto the floating travois.

When night fell Dassit slept, her body so tired it shut down; one moment she was awake and in pain the next she was being gently woken by the chattering of rootlings. Ania was awake too, a rootling dropping water and berries into her mouth, chattering happily as it did. Dassit shooed it away.

"Dassit."

"You are awake, that is good." A weak smile in return.

"You should leave me."

"No."

"The poison, it has done something inside of me. I can feel it."

"Then I will give you more rootling medicine."

"Too late," said Ania, "too late", and her eyes closed. For a heartbeat she thought Ania was dead, then she saw her chest rise and fall again. Nodded to herself and resumed her trek.

North, always north and always north. She did not know how long she had been walking, time had little meaning because all she knew was the compulsion in her mind and the pain in her muscles as she stumbled forward.

She was not sure when she first noticed the smell, unpleasant, sickly. It took her a while to recognise it, though it should not have — a mark of how exhausted and hurt she was. In some ways the smell was an old companion, though never a friend. She knew it from every battlefield hospital she had ever been in. When she stopped to rest she did not want to remove the leaves and torn cloth she had wrapped around her shoulder wound, did not want to look because she knew what she would see. Black around the wound site, her flesh rotting where it had gone bad. She had been worrying about Ania, never thinking about herself. Never realising she was already dead, a walking corpse. Had the wound been on an arm or leg she might have stood a chance, been able to cut it off. A small chance, almost non-existent, but better than no chance at all.

But at her shoulder? No. The only plus for it was that it would be quicker than if it was a wound to her stomach. The poison of the wound would go to her heart, stop it and all she could hope was that the prior agonies would not be too bad. Or that she would be lost to hallucinations and unaware of the pain.

She wanted to sit, to give up. To let death take her and then she could finally relax.

North.

Not a choice.

Onwards, foot after foot, the smell of her festering wound growing. Ania was more and more restless, the heat of her skin burning hotter and hotter. Still, Dassit could not stop. Still, she walked and she walked.

Until she saw him.

Walking through the wood, leaning on a stick, pushing forward. His gait, his sheer size unmistakable.

Ont.

"Ont!" she cried it out, putting what strength she had into his name. Stumbling forward with the little speed she had. He stopped, turned, his face hidden by the wooden and grass mask. He did not come to her, she had to go to him but she knew why. The draw of the north was so powerful now she doubted he could take even a single step backwards. When she finally reached him she could barely speak, three words fell from her mouth.

"You left us," she said.

"I'm sorry," he sounded it, tormented even, "but I had no choice, they made me."

"Who did?" said Dassit.

"Them," he said, and turned, pointing.

In the distance a ground mist, and from it came a light, soft and gentle yet as fierce as the light above on the hottest day of the year. The light rolled and twisted in the air, and silhouetted within it were figures, three of them, impossibly tall and thin, their heads crowned by reaching branches.

"The Boughry," said Ont, "the Woodhewn Nobles of Wyrdwood."

Whether it was weakness or awe Dassit did not know, but she fell to her knees, head bowed, frightened to look up. Then came the voice, she did not know whether it was in her head or in the air. She did not know whether it was spoken in welcome or in threat.

"We have been waiting for you."

Ont stepped forward, holding his arms wide.

"And we have come."

For a moment Dassit was confused. It was Ont they had called, not her, not Ania, they were simply here to guard him but when the Forest Noble spoke again her sureties were blown away like dead leaves in Harsh.

"As we knew you would."

Fear ran through Dassit, the knowledge she was before something unlike anything she had ever witnessed. She could feel power rolling off them. For a moment she wished she had taken longer, that the poison in her wound would take her before the Boughry did because they filled her with a fear like nothing else.

"You are ours now," they said.

18

Udinny

We followed the path of the army, a wide swathe of trampled grasslands heading steadily south toward Jinnspire.

Behind the army was the usual detritus of a large force, broken rafts, old weapons, spoiled food and bodies. Each body, like the first we found, had been used to seed the ground with bluevein, the corpse twisted in death, face locked in a rictus and from it sprung the lines and gnarled curls of the disease.

"Why are they doing this?" said Tanhir. "Why spoil the land they will need?"

In my mind I saw a dark city in the deeps, a writhing figure that fought the city as much as it fought me.

"Ranya's web," I said softly.

"I hardly think your weak city god is a threat to an army." Tanhir had not learned to like me any more than she had before, but at least I had not woken with a knife at my throat that morning, which made a refreshing change.

"Ranya is like the air," I said, "everywhere and always there and you do not even know it. Though sometimes you feel a light touch on the skin and are reminded."

"I only fear the air when the circle winds roar," she said, it was hard not to hear the sneer in her voice but I decided it was best to pretend I did not.

"Oh, I imagine Ranya can roar. In fact I know it. I have held her weapons in my hands." Behind me a crownhead bleated. "Weapons and more," I looked up at Tanhir. "What you must understand, is she does not need to roar. She is connected to all things, even those Forest Nobles you pretend not to worship in your tree city." Tanhir opened her mouth to reply but I did not give her time. "There is a web we cannot see that runs through Crua, touches all things, even you and I. The thing that has risen in Tiltspire, that is the opposite of Ranya. She wants you to walk your path, live your life. It wants to control you, all of us, by taking over her web."

"Why?" this from one of the other Forestals.

"I do not know," I looked up and shrugged. It was strange to shrug with a man's shoulders, they were much bigger than the ones I was used to. "Cahan always said Zorir, that is what he called the god, wanted everything to burn. Maybe it wants us for fuel."

"Then why does it fool around with bluevein, and not just do it?" said Tanhir. Truly, the woman could not utter a word without it sounding like a challenge, though I must admit she had a point in this case. "The armies of the north rule all but Jinnspire, if this thing wanted the world to burn they could start the fires now." I was still staring at the corpse.

"True," I said softly, and thought of the vast network I had seen when I was dead, or not dead. Definitely in some other state of being. The glowing lines of power brought from the cloudtrees and into the land and I felt like there should be some answer there. I closed my eyes, and hoped for Ranya to speak out in the darkness of my mind.

"Have you gone to sleep, monk?"

"No, Tanhir," I said, and even I could not avoid a little

bit of irritation in my voice, "I am trying to commune with my god in the hope of answers."

"And?"

"Nothing, but you are not helping." I stood. "The bluevein though, I think it is a way of tapping into Ranya's web, and from there to the power that runs through Crua."

"Why?" said Tanhir, and did I imagine it or was the sneer a little more absent than it had been?

"Nothing good, I imagine."

"Burn the body, and any others we find like it," she said, and once that was done we set off again.

We saw the first soldiers as the light above was starting to dip toward the horizon. A ragged group of about twenty led by three Rai. In the forest we would never have been seen, we would have vanished as soon as they were on the horizon, but on this plain it was harder. The swathe of flat grass trampled by the army was too wide for us to escape without notice. Instead the Forestals drew their bows, strung them and knelt, arrows ready.

"Let them get nearer," said Tanhir, "so they can't run out of range." She took an arrow from the quiver at her hip.

"Wait," I told her.

"They are Rai," she said, as if this answered everything. Once it would have, but once I had been a woman and in another once I had been quite dead.

"Things change," I said, "and, look, they are heading in the opposite direction to their army."

"They are still Rai," said Tanhir. "Rai do not change."

"Maybe not," I said, "but there is one thing I know about them, that they are driven to survive. Maybe we can use that."

"If we let them get near they will kill us."

"Are you saying their magic is swifter than your bows?" I think if a look could have killed then Tanhir would have slain me on the spot, but it cannot and a harsh look is not even painful.

"Of course not."

"Then let us talk and I will be the one to approach them, then your only risk is my death."

"And with that goes my memories," whispered Tanhir.

"Tall Sera wanted information," said another Forestal. "Why not let the monk approach, even Rai will hesitate at killing a monk. And I am surprised you care, given how much you hate him." Interesting, I thought, that Tanhir had not shared with her people how we were tied together. Now, of course, she was in a bind. Because everything her Forestal said was true, and she must either tell them of her shame and how Tall Sera did not trust her and had tied us together, or she must let me speak to the approaching Rai.

"Very well," said Tanhir, "but I will not have Rai take one of ours, whether I hate them or not. If they even look like they will hurt the monk we shoot them down. She gave me a nod then gestured toward the soldiers. I began to walk.

The Rai, of course, had seen me, seen us all. Their eyesight was better than any normal persons, but they made no violent move toward me. In fact they had their hands raised, to show they would not go for their weapons. For Rai, they also looked worn and tired. Their soldiers no better.

"Tell the Forestals," shouted one of the Rai, the tallest and from their voice a woman, "I am Rai Ustiore and those with me mean you no harm. We wish only to pass and in exchange can give you information you will find useful." I glanced back. The Forestals held their bows at the ready.

"Lay your weapons down," shouted Tanhir. For a moment I saw pride flare in the Rai's eyes, then she nodded. "Do it slowly and do not try and get any closer." They did, the troops laying spears on the ground and then sitting as if they were glad of the rest. The Rai drew swords, laid them down but they did not sit like their troops, they stood, somehow defiant even though they looked dishevelled and small for their kind.

I counted twenty-eight troops and three Rai.

"Useful information first," said Tanhir from behind me, "then we decide if you may pass." The Rai did not speak, not at first. I could almost feel the pride boiling off her, the anger. She looked around at the troops and I heard her take a long breath. She closed her eyes and I wondered what was going through her mind at that moment.

"I know what Forestals do with Rai, we all do," she glanced back at the other two Rai, who looked to be in worse condition than her. "But the troops," she said, "let them go." It was odd, to hear such words from Rai.

"Information," said Tanhir. "Then we will decide what we do with you." For a moment the Rai said nothing, then she bowed her head, pulled off her ornate helmet to show dark hair, shorn close to her skull. She dropped the helmet and it rang when it hit ground baked heartwood hard by the light above.

"They know you follow, and know you are coming."

"And?" said Tanhir.

"They intend to set an ambush."

"Where?"

"I do not know," said the Rai. "They will hide troops in the long grasses, cut you down as you pass or take you." She looked straight at me. "Do not let them take you."

"We have no intention of being fed to cowls," said Tanhir, her voice full of threat.

"Things have changed," said the Rai and her tone, a mixture of anger and confusion, left me in no doubt she told the truth, though why they would not give their Rai the power they needed made no sense.

"So you hope to prey on us instead?" said Tanhir. She shook her head.

"Tassa, Ganri and I, we have not been Rai long. We do not feel the hunger the way the older ones do." She looked around, then past me to the Forestals. "Was our information enough? Can my troops pass?"

"You are a trap," said Tanhir, and I heard her take a breath as she drew her bow.

"Wait!" I turned, raising my hands and stepping in front of the Rai. "What makes you sure it is a trap?"

"Firstly, they are Rai," said Tanhir. "Rai do nothing except for themselves. And for Rai to throw themselves on the mercy of Forestals? No, I do not believe that for a second, they would know no mercy would be found."

"But they are here," I said.

"In itself suspicious," said Tanhir, "they could have gone in any direction, avoided us completely."

"But I chose not to," said the Rai. Tanhir shook her head. "Unlikely."

"For revenge," the Rai spat the words, her face twisted into something dark and hate-filled, the mask of some ancient forest grove god. Tanhir let some of the tension out of her bow.

"That sounds more like Rai," she said.

"What makes you betray your own side?" I asked the Rai.

"Hate," she said, "hate makes me betray them." She looked past me. "I came here knowing I would likely die, knowing how much you enjoy killing Rai."

"Why not go to Jinnspire?" said Tanhir, but she sounded less sure of herself now, "they would have welcomed more Rai to defend the city, surely?" The Rai shook her head.

"After the way we have treated their Rai? They would have skinned us and hung us screaming from the city walls. At least with you I get a clean death."

"I will give you that gift gladly," said Tanhir.

"What did your side do to you, Rai, to make you run to Forestals?" I said.

"Nothing, not yet," she said, "but it was coming, the collar, it was only a matter of time." She looked back again, "This new god is no god of mine, it wants too much."

"Explain," said Tanhir.

"There were five of us," she said, one of the Rai behind her nodded, "all raised at the same time. We have stayed together since then. Yarit, my firstwife, and Basan, they were the strongest. The five of us together were not easy prey for other Rai see, not easily made into a vassal for them. We did not have much but we could hold on to what we had."

"And where are they, the other two? Did they betray you?" said Tanhir. "It is the way of the Rai."

"They did not," she said, "not how you mean. They were called to the command tent a day ago. Told they were strong, chosen." I turned, Tanhir had her head slightly tilted, listening, interested. "Basan, well, Basan never returned. Yarit did but she was changed. They had collared her."

"Is that not a mark of honour now, to be your god's chosen?" I said. Something in the Rai's eyes, something she was suppressing, a mixture of fear and horror.

"That is what they say, but well over half who are given the shard die."

"The shard?" said Tanhir.

"A splinter of stone," said the Rai, raising her voice, "it is forced into the neck, here." She pointed at a place just above her collarbone and the holes I had seen in the body of the Rai made sense. "If it takes, you become collared, if it doesn't you die and are left behind to seed the ground, such was Basan's fate but maybe he was the lucky one."

"Tell us about the collared," said Tanhir. She let her bow fall. "Are these collared not just Rai?" The woman shook her head.

"That is what they tell us, that the risk is worth the power gained. But it is not true." She looked behind her at the other two Rai. Her troops were sitting on the baked ground, exhausted. "What came back, it knew everything Yarit knew, it looked like her, but with a collar which was growing so fast I could watch it happening. But it was not her any more." She took a deep breath, almost a sob. "Everything of Yarit was gone, even taking delight in her power, creating fire for the joy if it, all gone."

"Her joy?" I said, understanding the horror this Rai must feel, a confusing thing in itself, to feel pity for the Rai.

"Her joy, her power. The collar cut her off from it, she would only say she was part of something greater now. Connected to a god, servant to them." I turned to Tanhir. "The more the collar grew, the less of Yarit remained."

"It is like the opposite of Ranya's web, Tanhir," I told her, "where Ranya guides, this web enslaves."

"I left with my people, my troops," said the Rai, raising her voice, "because there are Rai, powerful Rai, who serve this god. They know what the collar does and will sacrifice all below them. They took my firstwife and I want every Rai and every collared dead. You, Forestal," she pointed at Tanhir, "you are the best chance of that, if it costs me my life that is worth it." Tanhir was staring at the Rai, thoughts flitting across her face in a constant battle and I knew what she was thinking, maybe the process of bonding us had us share something, or maybe it was simply because the same thought was in my mind.

"Tanhir, it seems to me that we could make use of these soldiers, and these Rai. If they joined with us."

"Maybe," said Tanhir. "But I find it hard to trust Rai."

"Then trust vengeance," said the Rai, "something of you tells me you understand vengeance." Silence from Tanhir while she considered what was said.

"What if you come across your loved one in battle, Rai?" she said quietly. "Can I trust you to strike, or will you hesitate?"

"I will not come across her in battle," said the Rai and her voice was empty, dead.

"How can you be so sure?"

"Because, she is already gone," she raised her head, met Tanhir's gaze, "when I realised my lover was lost, I did not hesitate to end the thing she had become."

At that Tanhir nodded, let out a small grunt because what the Rai said was true. Tanhir understood vengeance.

19

Saradis

She stood on the deck of the skyraft.

Her skyraft.

It had been pathetically easy once the Archeos was hers. She had stood there, watching and waiting while the stone did its work, while the collar grew around the neck of the Archeos and the fight went out of them. When the collar was fully on she had them stand, carefully arranging their clothes to hide the blue lines across their skin. When she had first seen the collared she had thought the blue was their veins, their blood, but it was not the case. It was independent of the body, growing through it and around the flesh. A parasite, living off what it touched, she had seen how it wormed its way through flesh when she had attended a dissection of one of the failures.

Laha often cut up the bodies, they fascinated him.

She had watched with interest, not only because the process interested her, how Zorir took control of those who it needed, made them more efficient to its great purpose, but because she had begun to suspect it was not Laha she watched. What he had been was there, no doubt of that, the loyalty, the commitment and his ability to fight had not left, but this interest he had in the world around him was new. Before he had only been interested in serving her. Laha was not simply Laha any more, but part of Zorir, an avatar of her god.

She had wondered why him and not her, but she had slowly begun to realise that she knew why. It was because she was special, she was the one that was actually chosen, actually trusted. Zorir knew her worth and had no reason to slave her to a collar.

"What should I do?"

The Archeos asking her, voice flat and dead. This was the problem with the collared, something went out of them. They could never be spies, never fool anyone that had known them for any length of time, but she did not need them fooled for long. Only long enough.

"Call in your commanders, one by one." She smiled, but they did not smile back. The collared never did.

Then it was simple, each commander came in, she slipped a shard into their neck by the simple expedient of hiding behind the door. The first two died and she had to drag the bodies behind the table. The Archeos said nothing as she dragged the first one over the floor, though they watched her with a look of interest on their face. She realised how foolish she was being. Dropped the corpse.

"You do it," she said, "make sure they cannot be seen by those entering." It was enjoyable, to watch this once powerful and haughty man obey her words. It made Saradis happy. Three more officers came in, one more died and two took to the collar, though one looked sickly and she thought them likely to die quickly.

It did not matter, she did not need them for long.

"You three," she told them, "will go out there, explain you have leased the skyraft to us for the foreseeable future and the crew are to obey my people." She turned to the Archeos: "You will tell them that you and your officers are coming down to the surface, that you will be spending time down there to finalise the trade details with the forces of the new god and exclusive rights to Treefall from the northern Wyrdwood." She knew that last would make it seem more believable to the rafters. They might balk at the idea of their raft being leased by her forces, but trade, rafters understood trade. Longed for it, trade was in their blood.

She stood behind the Archeos as they made the announcement, watched their people as the news was passed over. They were uncomfortable, but used to obeying their leader still, she thought she could sweeten this for them. That was the problem with the collared: they were not good at thinking or persuading, they were blunt tools. She stepped forward.

"If I may, Archeos?" she said and stood in front of them. They nodded as she did, giving their assent. "We have agreed a generous settlement for the loan of your craft." She looked around, rafters stripped to the waist and covered in sweat from the heat still boiling off the great stone fire cauldrons, heads wrapped in rags and colourful scarves. "You do not even all have to work, a small group of my troops will do most of it for you." She raised a hand before any could speak, "Not Rai! I will not send any Rai."

"Why should we trust you?" shouted one of the rafters. "You attacked the Hostiene raft."

"A mistake," she said, "a terrible mistake. And it was not to take the raft, that is only what was said by those who were not there." She looked around. "The Archeos of the raft insulted our god to the face of my Rai. They overreacted. As you can see from looking down, our god is not like any others. They are here, they are real." She looked around, mention of Zorir had quietened them, they could not deny its existence. "But as you know, we did not take over the raft, it lies on the plains of Tilt and does not fly. Those who committed the attack on the raft were punished." She looked left and right. "Harshly." The rafters did not speak, only stared. Then one stepped forward, an older woman.

"How do we know your troops will not try and learn our ways, take our raft?"

"That is why no Rai will be sent, only troops. I have agreed with your Archeos, no more than twenty and they will be here only for manual labour." The dissenter narrowed her eyes, but when the Archeos did not say anything she shrugged.

"If that is the way it is to be," she said and Saradis nodded, as if she were being gracious while making sure she remembered the woman's face for later. Then she turned. "If you would lead, Archeos?" They did, as they passed she leaned in close. "When we reach the lift, tell them you will send my troops for your things." They nodded, walked on followed by their remaining officers. At the lift they stopped and the Archeos spoke to the nearest rafter.

"I will have the city's forces come for my things while I am on the ground." The rafter looked a little confused, maybe they were low in the pecking order and unused to the Archeos speaking to them, but they gave a quick bow of their head. Then they were in the lift, already descending. Outside the lift waited Vir with a group of soldiers.

"Skua-Rai," said Vir with a small bow.

"It is done, take these," she pointed back at the Archeos and the officers, "to the undercroft, they won't last long. There are three bodies in the office, they are expecting you to take some things down for their Archeos, so you should be able to get them out in a chest."

"Then we start the real work?" She nodded, smiled at him.

"Then you start the real work, they will not teach you anything, you'll have to pick up as much as you can. When you are moving the bodies, look out for any books that may help. The Archeos of the Hostiene raft burned theirs before we got to them."

"I've heard it can take a lifetime to master a skyraft."

"I don't need a master, Vir, I just need it kept in the air." He grinned at her.

"We will watch and learn, I'll keep an eye out for those disaffected, or who have been slaves for a long time. They will have expertise and may prefer serving us to the rafters."

"Good." She looked up at the raft. "Now, tell me about the prisoner."

"Below the spire in the undercroft, as you said," he sneered, not for her, a betrayal of his inner thoughts. "Twisted thing, it ain't right. We should have killed it." She said nothing, not at first. The man was driven by need for vengeance and disliked anything different. He had accepted the collared, because he could see the direct link to their god and gods he understood, for the same reason he accepted the Hetton and the dullers.

"Remember, Vir, this is a time of wonders, a god has risen. This creature could be some servant of it." He grunted, looked away. "If it is not then I will collar it, as an experiment. Anything can be collared. I will see if it screams and dies like a rootling or if it lives and serves like a human."

"And if it does?"

"Then Zorir will know its secrets, and secrets are always worth knowing."

"Well," he said, "you're the one that knows gods, I suppose. I better get my lot on the lifts," and he walked away. She wondered if he would be trouble, then decided it did not matter.

After all, anything could be collared.

20

Sorha

It was cold in the shadow of the black pyramid.

Sorha felt watched and she felt worried. It was hard not to feel watched as they skirted the great black pyramid with the writhing creature at the top. Maybe, had Sorha been someone else, she would have said she felt frightened but she was not and would not.

You know me, she thought. *I hurt you*. Somewhere inside she hoped this did not create a link between them, that it did not remember, that it did not thirst for vengeance in the same way she did about those that hurt her. But the thought, *I hurt you*, kept coming back and it changed, became *you hurt me*. Some feeling she did not really understand welled up inside her, made it hard to walk, to move.

But she did.

Below the creature hung Cahan, limp as death and what he made her feel was too complex for her to address. Anger and hate definitely, a whole raft full of negative emotions, but also a sense of loyalty. He had needed her, had only saved her because of that but they had been alone beneath Crua, had fought together there and it had changed her. His actions had made her a pariah among her own, and through that she understood what it was to be him, to be lonely and to need somewhere to fit in. His fight for the people of Harn, which she had thought foolish at the time, made sense to her now. He belonged and would have died for them, they would and did die for him.

Who would she die for? Who would be willing to die for her?

Behind her one of the Osere cursed as they tripped over one of the glowing blue ropes that grew from the pyramid and it was only then, and much to her surprise, that Sorha realised there were people she would die for. It had crept up on her. As Rai she would have hated the Osere, thought them freaks and less than her. But here she was, risking everything to go into the very heart of Tiltspire to save one of them.

Before her was the Rai, Huitt, Sorha did not trust them because they were Rai but she also knew they were frightened, and how powerful the sense of self-preservation was to Rai. Around her the Osere were dressed like guards, helmets pulled low over the bulge of their eyeless foreheads. No one had looked twice at them as they moved through the quiet streets of Tiltspire, in fact it had been the opposite, the people of the spire city had done all they could to avoid them. Turning their faces or scurrying up side streets to get away.

She had thought it good at first, but now it troubled her. Not just how scared the people of Tiltspire were of their guards, but at how few of them there were.

The collared, as Huitt had called them, were everywhere, on every street corner. She had given up trying to avoid them. Huitt ignored them, so Sorha did the same. They circled the base of the pyramid and the huge central spire of the city came into view.

"There is an entrance," said Huitt, "beneath the spire that leads directly to the cells in the undercroft. It is guarded but they will let me through."

"Betray us . . ." began Sorha but the Rai interrupted.

"And I die. I know." The Rai turned and shrugged. "You have made it quite clear by the many times you have told me."

"I don't want you to forget." The Rai nodded and led them on through the city, under huge, thick cables of pulsing blue that arched over the pathways, as they approached the spire the cables became even thicker, connecting the pyramid and the spire. They walked along by one, the Rai's and her footsteps echoing against the hardness of the pyramid. From there to a tunnel and their footsteps echoed in the darkness – though not the footsteps of the Osere. They moved in complete silence.

"Along here, there will be two Hetton guarding the entrance." The Rai paused. "Will they recognise you?"

"I do not know if Hetton recognise anyone."

"Then be ready." Sorha put her hand on her blade, but the Hetton let them pass, recognising the armour and presence of one of the Rai. They passed into darker tunnels beneath the spire, along them ran the pulsing blue veins brought to Crua by the god. The Rai before them began to slow.

"Keep going," said Sorha.

"I am unsure where to go from here," said Huitt.

"You said you knew the way." The Rai nodded, Sorha felt the Osere gathering around her.

"I did, but it has changed." Sorha's hand went to her blade.

"You are leading us into a—"

"No," the Rai put a hand on the wall of the tunnel. "There should be a door here but there is not." Sorha stepped closer, the wall was entirely covered in the blue cables, hundreds of them twining and twisting around each other. She put a hand out and at the last moment stopping, not wanting to touch it. These lines that glowed softly led directly back to the black pyramid and the thing that squatted atop it, *you hurt me*. She could not help but feel that if she touched these strange, cold blue and black ropes then it would attract the attention of the god. To be near was to tempt it, to touch the substance of it, and she was in that moment as sure as she could be that these ropes were part of it, would bring its wrath right upon her and she drew her hand back.

Was this fear, this inability to do a thing?

Maybe it was.

She could see, through the tangle, to a light on the other side. She could make out a doorway, overgrown with the blue lines.

"I think there is another way around," said the Rai. "Follow me, tell your friends to keep their heads down if we meet anyone." She did, in that mix of the language of the Osere and the one of her people. "And tell them to make some noise," the Rai added, "it is unnatural how quiet they are, someone may notice." Sorha shrugged. She was not sure she could convey the idea, and even if she could she doubted the Osere could be noisy, it was simply not part of them. "The way we go now, goes through more cells," the Rai stepped forward, "but I have not been this way in a long time, I do not want you to see me hesitating and—"

One of the Osere stepped forward, speaking haltingly to Sorha.

"What is it saying?" said the Rai.

"He is asking," said Sorha, and she found herself itching for a blade in her hand, understood why so many hated the Rai, "whether behind the closed door is our destination and whether you know the way now. If not, Buris says he should lead."

"I hardly think it has been here before," said Huitt, "someone would have noticed."

"Maybe," said Sorha, "but the . . ." she stopped, stumbled, had almost said Osere out loud and she was sure that would be a mistake. "His people are raised in total darkness, they can find their way without seeing."

"How?"

"I do not know, but they have an excellent sense of place and direction." The Rai made a face, one she knew well, haughty and dismissive. They were going to speak but thought twice about it when they looked into Sorha's eyes.

"Very well, I shall let it lead." The Rai stepped back, letting the Osere past and Buris moved through the tunnels as if it was home to him. Stopping occasionally, moving his head from side to side before deciding which branch of a tunnel to take. The deeper they went into the undercroft of the spire the worse Sorha felt. The place became increasingly oppressive.

Then came the smell, a slowly growing and deeply unpleasant smell, one Sorha recognised.

"Are there blooming rooms down here?" she asked the Rai. They shook their head.

"No, they are in one of the outer towers."

"I can smell death."

"This is a prison," said the Rai. "People die." Sorha nodded, but she thought the Rai wrong. Maybe people did die here, but you did not keep the corpses in the jail. It brought disease and even Rai were wary of disease.

The deeper they went, twisting through tunnels, the stronger the smell became.

She followed the Osere as he moved on, at first fast, then stopping as if to sniff the air, hands reaching out to touch nothing like directions hung in the air and could only be felt. When they found what it was they looked for, they followed these paths only they could feel. The smell increased and Sorha began to feel less sure of what was happening. Were the Osere lost? Were they simply seeking darkness and depth because it made them feel safe?

"Where are you taking us?" she whispered in the darkness, the stink of death so strong it had substance.

"Loop, backwards. Find place," the Osere bobbed their head and walked on, pushing through death, bringing them closer, and bit by bit Sorha felt that strange feeling eating at her once more. Fear. What others felt and now she knew it, she marvelled at the strength of those who overcame it.

They turned another corner, not only a smell now but a noise. People in distress, in pain, but not in the first stages of it where they screamed and begged. In the last stages where speech had deserted them, where pain was all they had left and they spoke a language of low moans. Sorha had once gloried in pain, it had been the source of her power as a Rai; the more pain you caused the more power flowed into your cowl, or so they had all believed.

Now though, she did not want to turn the corner, did not want to see what waited for her around the bend, lit by the sickly glow of the blue vines. It had not passed her notice that those blue ropes were thicker here, their light brighter.

She rounded the corner, found something: it explained so much, it horrified her, it made the muscles of her stomach cramp as if she needed to expel her revulsion along with what small amounts of food she had eaten.

The room before her was huge, a long, arching ceiling that stretched away past what could be illuminated by the few torches along the walls, each one flickering the way life flickered at the end.

The air full of death; of the sound of misery and pain. Lines of blue provided light but not illumination.

Moving in the darkness she saw robed figures. She recognised them. Monks of Tarl-an-Gig – monks of Zorir now. It was easier to look at the monks than to see what and who they ministered to, though that was unavoidable. The monks carried water pots, or maybe pots of soup though she could not smell it for the scent of rot.

Truthfully, it was impossible for her to ignore what was being done in the room. What lay across the floor amid the tangle of glowing blue vines. It was people. The smell, the sound, it come from the people and there were not only a few of them. This was not where they kept a few sad prisoners. There were hundreds. Worse, now she was closer she realised she was wrong about what was happening; they did not lie amid the blue vines, the lines were part of them. Their bodies were covered in blue where the vines penetrated them. A man near her opened his mouth and inside there was a faint blue glow, from his ear a strange, round fruiting body grew. He let out a moan, by him another body did the same and it passed through the room, this echo of pain transmitted down the blue lines that joined them together.

"Rai." She turned to find one of the monks standing before her, in one hand they had an empty cup. The monk's face was painted white, with lines of blue over their forehead. "Have you brought more worshippers?"

"Worshippers," said Sorha, too horrified by what was happening to realise the monk thought she knew all about this.

"The god uses them up ever more quickly." There was no pity in the voice of the monk, no empathy. "We are in danger of running out."

"Why not use some of the monks?" she gestured towards those moving between the hundreds of bodies. For a second the monk looked confused.

"We are important to the process, we are needed."

"Of course you are," said Sorha, and she slipped the knife from her belt, moved a little closer and pushed it in between the monk's ribs. A killing blow. Foolish, she knew it the moment she did it, but she had not been able to help herself. It felt like some small way of exorcising the horror of this place. She lowered the dying monk in among the bodies and his mouth moved, forming the word "no" again and again. Around him the vines shifted, sensed him closed, on him and Sorha turned away. The first man she had seen looked up at her, he wanted death, she knew that. Recognised the look of one tortured beyond what they could stand. She had been the cause of that look herself more than once.

"I am sorry," she whispered, looking around to see if any of the other monks had noticed her, but they only continued to move from body to body in the gloom. "If I give you what you wish, then I fear it will alert the creature that causes your agonies." Did he understand? His mouth opened and shut and again that echo of pain moved across the room. "Here," she pushed the knife into his hand, "it is all I can do." She stood. Turned to the nearest Osere. "We must find Frina, quickly." The Osere nodded, led them to the side of the room and into a corridor that sloped gently upwards. On and on, constantly checking behind her that the Rai was still with them. That the Osere were still with them. Round corners, twisting up and round and round.

"How far?" said the Rai and Sorha echoed it in the language of the Osere, listened to the answer.

"Not far now," she said. The Rai nodded to her. They rounded another corner.

"This is it," said Huitt. "The cells." Sorha moved from door to door, each cell empty until she found one that wasn't. But it was not Frina in the cell. Nailed to the walls, still in their armour, were the Reborn who had fought with Cahan Du-Nahere. One had an axe embedded in her chest. The other a knife in her gut. Sorha stared, then she was sure she saw one move. It should be impossible, but these were not creatures that obeyed the laws she knew. As she looked she saw glittering eyes behind a visor.

"When last we met," said Sorha, "we were enemies, things have changed since then." The Reborn said nothing, only stared at her. "I cannot prove it to you, but I can free you." She did, pulling the weapons out of them first. Then the nails. If she expected something miraculous she was not given it. The women simply fell to the floor. "I cannot take you with us," said Sorha, "we lack the strength to carry you. But you are free now."

She left, and heard no movement from them as she moved down the rest of the cages. Slumped in the last one a figure she recognised and was happy to see. "Frina!" They raised their head, blind face directed straight at the sound of her voice.

"Sorha?"

"Yes."

"Should not have come."

"Well," she said, "I have." She took out her blade, sawing at the dried vines that bound the door shut. Pulling it open. "Now quick, it is hard to believe we made it this far, we must leave." Frina stood. "Come on."

As the Osere came toward her Sorha heard her name, turned. A figure stood between the cells further back, a man, his body wreathed in veins of blue, his face sparkling where small stones were embedded in it.

"Laha!" said Rai Huitt, and she turned, looked at Sorha, "run!"

Then a sword point exploded from her chest.

21

Venn

The forest was alive.

It had always been alive, Venn knew that, but as they had grown into their power, as they had become closer and closer to the cowl within them and the way it connected them to Crua, the life around them had become more and more real. It was not something they saw, or even something Venn felt any more. It was them, part of them, Venn was the life, the life was Venn.

All of it.

Some of it more distant, the orits, the maws, the litter-crawlers, they were there but different. Nearer were the raniri, the rootlings and a hundred thousand other animals that ran and flew and pumped warm red blood around their bodies. Then there were the trees and plants – other but the same. Then the fungus, which was part of and the starting point of, Ranya's web which they felt everything through. Even though it was damaged, ragged, worse than it ever had been it was still all encompassing and golden.

Above it all the cloudtrees.

Unlike anything else in Crua, something Venn could not describe or understand except in reference to other things that would make no sense to anyone who was not as deep within the web as Venn. The cloudtrees were movement and light, the same way the Slowlands were a stopping, a heaviness. In some ways the two were the same, while being entirely different. Like day and night were the same but different but one could not exist without another.

Venn did not quite understand, but they knew it on a level they could never put into words. The cloudtrees and the Slowlands were Crua, as much as the land beneath Venn's feet. No, more so, without them their world simply would not be. They were conduits for vast amounts of power, unthinkable energies collected from, they did not understand. Outside? Outside where? They put the thought aside, reached out into the land where they could feel vast pools of energy, great whirling vortexes of it.

They did not understand what for, or why the feeling of it was so much stronger here in the north, at Harn.

They knew one thing, the bluevein was eating at it, weakening it, creating new channels for all of that power, all of that fire.

"Venn." That single syllable pulled them from a reverie, from floating through all the life around them. The bluevein lacked the strength of Ranya's web, it was thin, would never hold the power of Crua for long, but there was purpose there, an attempt to take over the web and . . . *fire*.

"Venn!"

"Yes?" Furin staring at them. The thread lost.

"We are going down to the quarry," she said. "Tall Sera wishes to look around, see if we can find anything that tells us where the Rai have gone."

"You are right, Furin," said Venn. "The creature in Tiltspire will burn us all."

"How do we stop it?" she said and Venn found they had an answer, but it was not a good answer.

"Cahan," they said and as they said it they knew it was

true, as true as the vast cliff of the cloudtree before them. "We need Cahan."

"Then all is lost, because Cahan is dead," she said the words so flatly, so tiredly that for a moment Venn felt her grief, the pain of it, but they did not answer because somewhere within they felt Furin was wrong. If Cahan was dead they would know, that link they had forged in Harn so long ago would tell them. At the same time, they did not want to share this with Furin, give her false hope. They looked at her, the cracked white make-up, the red eyes, the way she held herself as though she was much older than she was.

"Udinny was dead," said Venn. Furin looked at them, then their brow furrowed and she nodded and maybe that was enough hope. Enough to keep Furin going, the knowledge they lived in a time of miracles so it was not impossible that more miracles may happen.

Furin followed the Forestals and Venn followed Furin down the steep slope toward the fallen cloudtree. Like every interaction Venn had with the trees it was confusing. The size of the thing made it appear much nearer than it really was, Venn's mind simply would not accept any living thing could be so massive. Each step nearer forced Venn's mind to reassess its size as they slid and struggled down the steep shale of the slope before it. Then again as they walked from the base of the slope to the fallen tree.

One of the forward scouts held up a hand. Venn crouched; as they did a smell assailed them, one they knew too well though they had never wished to − death.

A sound ringing through the forest, a rhythmic, loud tapping that bounced around the clearing, almost as if a bell were being rung.

"Someone is mining the tree," said a Forestal to Venn's left. They waited, listening to the tapping and when it continued without interruption they continued, moving along the forest floor toward the sound. Following, Venn began to see corpses. A lot of them, some were guards, some clearly tree miners, a few looked like Rai though they had been stripped of any fine armour. Others were Rai who were infected with bluevein, and from their corpses the sickness was working its way into the land. Venn stopped before one of them.

"We should burn this," whispered Venn, pointing at a corpse thick with glowing blue vines, "it is nothing good for the land."

"When we know what the noise is," said the Forestal, "we will come back." Venn nodded.

The cliff of the tree towered above them and the scaffold covering it was in worse condition up close; vines grew on it and in some places they had lifted away pieces so it stood crazily, all that should be straight was bent and twisted by a wish to be reunited with the land below. The cliff of the tree had been scored deeply by miners, though generations of quarrying remained before the tree would be gone from the hollow it had smashed into the land. Venn followed the Forestals through the quarry and toward the sound. There was no threat to it, it was the sound of work, hard work. Venn hurried to where Tall Sera headed the Forestals and was one of the first to see who made the sound. A man and a woman, using axes to hack into the face of the tree. They wore ill-fitting Rai armour, no doubt stolen from corpses, and were oblivious to the men and women with drawn bows behind them until Tall Sera whistled, surprising them. They drew expensive looking darkwood swords, flattened themselves against the back of the tree face. Tall Sera raised a hand, had his warriors lower their bows.

"Lower your swords," said Tall Sera, "it would give me no pleasure to kill you."

"What makes you think you could?" the speaker was a woman, her belligerence from fear.

"Because from the way you hold those blades you are plainly not warriors."

"Just surprised, is all we are," said the man. "We can fight."

"No warrior would back themselves onto a tree with no escape from our arrows," said Tall Sera.

"Lower your sword, Hanasa," said the woman. "They are right, we are no warriors." The man, Hanasa, looked around, his eyes wide and frightened but he did as his fellow asked and lowered the weapon.

"As you are not warriors, would you tell us who you are?" said Tall Sera.

"This is Hanasa," said the woman, "I am Drunas, we are miners of the tree."

"And now you are all that is left?" said Venn. Drunas shrugged.

"There may be others in the Wyrdwood, though I pity them for it."

"Why?" asked Venn.

"It hungers and we all know it, hungers for our blood."

"So you think it safe to cleave to this great corpse?" said Tall Sera. Drunas shook her head.

"Nowhere here is safe. So we thought we may as well try and get rich."

"Better than dying out there," said Hanasa pointing towards Wyrdwood, his voice harsh with smoke from fires, and Venn wondered whether he was wood hardener, weapon maker.

"What happened here?" said Furin. "Who attacked?" Drunas shrugged, sat on a stone.

"No one attacked, the Wyrdwood drove them mad, I think."

"What does that mean?" said Furin.

"It was endless," she said, "everything here hates us, never mattered how many rootlings they strung up, more came and stole our stuff. Orits attacked constantly, I heard that they had to abandon a mine further up the trunk as swarden attacked them." She looked over her shoulder. "Hanasa don't believe that, though."

"More likely they were attacked by gasmaw and just dare not say."

"I think nothing is unlikely in Wyrdwood," said Drunas, "but Hanasa believes only what he can see."

"There is much to be said for that," Tall Sera smiled at her. "The swarden exist, walking skeletons of the Wyrdwood, I have seen them myself." Hanasa stared at him, wondering if Tall Sera joked with him and then deciding he did, that what was said could not be true. "Tell us of the madness that overtook this place."

"They sent special guards," said the miner, "like Rai but not."

"Hetton?" said Furin. Drunas shook her head.

"No, they had some to start with, but they upset everyone. No work got done so they went away."

"Osere curse them walking corpses," said Hanasa and spat. Venn thought it odd that he believed in the walking corpses of Hetton but not the walking skeletons of the swarden.

"We called 'em blue warriors," said Drunas, "on account of how they had blue lines on their skin."

"But they were not Rai?" asked Venn.

"They dressed like Rai, the good armour, but they didn't take care of it."

"A fortune wasted, never oiled it," said Hanasa.

"Not as bad to be around as the Hetton, though," said Drunas.

"Osere, curse 'em," said Hanasa.

"You were telling us how this happened," said Tall Sera, "try not to tax the patience of a man with a forestbow."

"I said, we don't know, I just know the new guards kept turning up."

"They were not Rai?" said Furin.

"They were and they weren't," said Drunas, "they were strong, like Rai are, hard to kill, too. But they didn't throw fire or do any of them fancy tricks, I think that's why things went badly for them."

"What do you mean?" said Tall Sera.

"Some more Rai came, a lot, ten or so. Some of 'em went up to the big tent, and some went to where the troops lived, down there." She pointed back the way we had come.

"Then everyone went mad," said Hanasa, "people aren't meant to live in Wyrdwood."

"Describe the madness," said Tall Sera, impatience scarred his voice.

"Fighting," said Drunas. "Started in the Rai's tent, fire and lots of it. Then the guards started attacking each other. Some were with the new Rai, and some were with the old Rai and the blue warriors, but no one really knew who was who so me and Hanasa we hid, which is good because the new guards, the blue ones, they started killing everybody. Didn't seem to matter who, guards, Rai, miners, even those on their side. Must have killed five or six for every one of 'em got brought down."

"Would have killed everyone if not for the Rai," said Hanasa. Drunas nodded.

"True, whatever happened in the tent, the normal Rai came out on top, they came down here, burning the blue Rai wherever they stood and, I tell you, they didn't like it, not one bit."

"Bloodbath it were," said Hanasa.

"She's right, never seen killing up close and hope to never again."

"No one survived?" said Furin.

"None with the blue markings, or that fought for 'em," said Drunas. "The Rai, were only five or six of them, banded together and burned 'em all. Lost two of theirs doing it."

"Where are they now?" said Tall Sera.

"The Wyrdwood," said Hanasa, "heard 'em talking I did. Said they couldn't go back to the spires. Said the collared held 'em all now and they wouldn't risk it."

"The collared?" said Furin.

"It's what they said," Drunas shrugged but Venn thought they knew what the miner was talking about.

"The Rai with bluevein," they said, "if you look around their necks, it is where the blue is thickest." Venn looked around, "There was a corpse only a few steps back, I will show you." Venn led them back to the corpse they had seen. The collar was plain to see once you looked for it. This one must have been killed by soldiers, the armour hacked apart and the flesh beneath it the same. "How long ago did this happen?" Venn asked.

"Maybe an eightday, maybe more," said Drunas. "Hard to keep track of time in Wyrdwood gloom."

"The flesh is unspoiled," said Furin. "It should be rotted, and thick with insects."

She was right, but it was not.

"The forest rejects it," said Venn, and they knelt to look more closely. "There is something in the neck."

"Don't touch it," said Furin. Venn looked up. "Best to be safe. Cover your hand with some cloth, leather would be better." One of the Forestals stepped forward and held out a square of leather.

"Do you need this back?" said Venn. The Forestal glanced over at Tall Sera, then shook his head. Venn used the leather to cover their hand and dug in the neck of the fallen Rai, trying to find what they had seen, a small shape, too regular to be natural. Eventually they felt it, pushed harder until their fingers closed around it, forcing the leather to grip and pulled it out.

"What is it?" said Furin.

"A sliver of stone," said Venn, moving it so they could

see the long, thin shape better. They were about to say more when the air rang with a powerful voice.

"Put down your bows, outlaws! Or burn where you stand!"

22

Doughry

She understood little, she remembered less.

Dassit Gan-Brinor floats in warm light. She is a child, growing up in the spire city in a single room with her family, five adults, six children. Raucous, noise, laughter and arguments, but there is always love here, always somewhere to run to. Festivals, and monks and long trips to the woodedge where they gather wood, herbs and mushrooms. She is cooking with her thirdfather, enjoying it. Watching her firstmother create things, real, useful things out of wood found in the forest. The lazy heat of a bed shared with her brothers and sisters. Looking after the youngest, Channifer, who never grew as tall as the rest.

The slow and encroaching cold of war with the north, first her parents leaving, then her brothers and her sisters until she and Channifer were left alone. Each brother or sister or parent promising the same. We will go, we will earn, send you money and come back rich.

They never come back.

Finding what work she can but in the larger all are struggling. The monks of Chyi are hard, the monks of the other gods are welcoming until they realise she has nothing to give.

Channifer weakens and she does not know why. She gives him most of the food she buys with the small stack of coins her sister found, hidden by their parents. Her strength continues to ebb but she refuses to take more than her share.

The hollow within her when she works it out. Only the day before he dies, finding three coins when there should only be one. She had been out begging and looking for work, Channifer had secretly been giving himself as sacrifice to Chyi, feeding the Rai to feed her. She rages, demands to know why, holds him tight to her and weeps and begs him not to go but he never speaks again.

Alone, and with no reason to stay, she went to the centre of the small village, where they were always asking for soldiers below the huge spire. The recruiter was a giant of a man and she was very small, very young. The soldier who signed her up, she was so loud, confident and happy, full of promises of excitement and riches for those who joined. She has the distinct impression from him that if she does well, learns what she teaches, fights hard, then she can advance to become Rai and wouldn't that be fine.

And if she dies, then it will be good to see her family on the Star Path once again.

Training is long and hard and too short and not enough. They march for hours, she learns how to hold a spear and shield and stand in line and little else. She asks about her brothers and sisters and mothers and fathers but no one knows them. She learns that it is no happy band of siblings in the army as she had been promised. No group of men and women, bound together through adversity and shared ideals and love for Chyi and the ways of the south. Every guard has their own god and their own ways.

Not all are volunteers. Not all are good people and she quickly finds you need friends. You need a gang as there are those who see only strength, and as such believe those weaker are prey.

The officers encourage it, and she gets used to hearing them say, "The Rai have no need of the weak."

She thinks that foolish, builds a little group around her, some are strong and some are not. She looks out for those who are clever. She meets Vir there, he had been weak then, small, and she and her little group saved him from a beating when someone was trying to take his rations. Small but stubborn, she liked that.

How long is training? There is an air of desperation to it, a sense they are being hurried through. The strongest, most aggressive, are put in charge, not the cleverest, and even then she thought it shortsighted but said nothing. What did she know? She was a new recruit. She thinks it has probably always been this way.

Surint, Who-Lies-in-Darkness.

Algor, Who-Walks-The-South.

Churigar, Who-Wakes-The-Dead.

She heard the echoes of so many names.

The first battle. Pushed to the front with her little group. The strongest stand in the third rank. The fear inside her like nothing else she has ever felt. It holds her, freezes her in place with heartwood rings around her muscles. Around her she hears tears and prayers and the air is full of the scent of sweat and urine and it will only get worse. The enemy are coming. They all look bigger than her, fiercer than she has ever been. Her hand sweats, the spear slippery in her grip, the shield getting heavier by the moment.

"Hold fast," a voice from by her, a man she has never seen before. "They'll come to us, you just push with the shield and thrust with the spear. That's all there is to it."

She never knew his name, she never saw him die.

There is screaming and heat and pressure and pain and part of her thinks that a first battle should be distinct.

Should be clear but it isn't. They are all the same. All familiar. Terror and blood and death. Slowly rising through the ranks, at first by dint of simply surviving. The ones who walked away get painted with success, and those who die are failures.

Dassit wonders if she is dying, failing. She must be. This was what happened, wasn't it? Your entire life passed before your eyes as you were judged for passage along the Star Path.

Strange though, some of the places, faces, battles. They were not her memories.

Yet they were.

Ania grows up in a village.

She is very small.

The village was also small. Near Woodedge in the north or the south she does not know, she is too young for such clarity. Three mothers, four fathers, a trion, six sisters and two brothers. Or less or more. They make things. They make things from wood. They make things from wool. They make things from vines. They are happy but it is all very hazy and she is very young. Sometimes monks come, they make a lot of noise and there is a lot of colour.

There are heavy days, when there is arguing, and shrines are pulled over but she does not know why. She does not know names or monks, or what they wore or even if the air was hot or cold. It is all interchangeable. She remembers angry voices. She remembers blood and screaming. A hand drags her from the village, people around her and then there is only the trees. The trees and her and she is alone and frightened until the trees come alive and men and women with long sticks surround her.

It is hot.

It is cold.

It is night.

It is day.

They are frightening at first, but they speak kindly and whisk her away down a tunnel to a strange place full of huge glowing mushrooms where the air is thick with feathery floating spores that make her laugh and the world twists and changes.

She lives in the air. Lives free with other children, running along branches and every adult is mother or father or trion and she is safe.

They give her a stick, and arrows. She learns to shoot the bow, to put the arrow in the target. To hunt for food but never take too much, she knows the forest as mother and father and trion as much as she knows the Forestals, shyun and rootlings that live within it. This is her place, a safe paradise like others hope to find along the Star Path. She becomes friends with rootlings, she has a pet garaur and when it finally dies she is sad but knows this is the way of life, the cycle. She has a pet crownhead and when it finally dies she is sad but knows this is the way of life, the cycle. She learns to feel the world around her with the cowl beneath her skin. She knows the dangerous dark places. She knows the creatures of the forest and how to avoid them – which you must always try to do – and how to kill them cleanly when there is no other choice. She knows that this city high up in the branches of the tree is safe. Not only for her, but for all those who live in it, those who were born to it and those who were brought to it.

She knows, above all things, you hope the Boughry look away from you.

Inside her lives a terrified young girl who has seen all she knows taken away by figures in the night. She dreams of fire and fire frightens her.

She learns of Rai who control fire and kill for their own amusement and she hates them for it. They are who she remembers, fire and death are inextricably linked in her mind, and fire is the enemy of the great trees who took her in.

This place in the tree, she would die for it. It is a safe place and she will give all she has for it to stay that way for others. She becomes a warrior, a taker of lives so that others may live. She has no mercy for those that threaten what she knows, what she believes is important, those she cares for. She kills and comes to enjoy killing and not to question that. There is Woodhome and the Forestals and there are those that are not, and they are less because they choose to serve the Rai and the Rai kill in fire and she hates fire and she hates Rai.

Then Cahan Du-Nahere, and Harn and a slow change within, a slow understanding that people are all one, good and bad scattered throughout them.

Ania wonders if she is dying now, failing. She must be. This was what happened, wasn't it? Your entire life passed before your eyes as you were judged for passage along the Star Path.

Strange though, some of the places, faces, battles. They were not her memories.

Yet they were.

People say Ont is big but his father is bigger.

Before he is the butcher father is the butcher; he does both hunting and butchering. He sets up the business, Ont only inherits it and by the time he takes it over the village has hunters and Ont never has to travel the forest. His father never misses an opportunity tell him how lucky he is. His firstmother cowers as father wraps the belt around his arm: "the boy knows nothing, never even had to go into the forest to learn how hard life really was." There was never a secondfather or secondmother in Ont's family and when mother dies, fades away to nothing with only pain as a companion – a more constant one that his father ever was, there is never another soft presence in the house. The whole village knows what father is like and none will risk a child in marriage to him.

It is a lonely, cold house to grow up in, the smell of death and rendered bodies ever-present. He has few friends, the children make fun of him and say he smells like the offal buckets that his father keeps to sell to those who barely have two few splinters to rub together. He learns to move quietly in the small hut, he learns to ask for nothing for himself and if he needs something – anything from food to clothing – the question is never "can I have?" and always "how can I earn?".

He grows, big like his father, and he learns that even though he does not have friends his size frightens others, and that draws some to him. They are weak and cruel people that want to shield themselves in the shadow of his size and the money his father has earned. He learns that his weight can be thrown around to get what he desires, and he begins to enjoy it, begins to think his father had been right to raise him in the way of the cold sneer and the quick hand with the leather belt. That every lash and hard word has done exactly what his father intended: it has taught him the truth of a cold, hard world where only the strong get by.

His father gets old, and even though he can physically look down on the old man his father is still bigger than him, still more than him. It is as if the bent body is just a shell, built around something twisted and hard and unbreakable. When the sickness finally takes the old man, eating him away bit by bit in agony, Ont has little but a sneer for him because that is what he has always been taught – though he longed for something a little softer, and somewhere there are buried memories of being very young, of his mother's laughter when the old man was out hunting. Of games and of joy and of a different way.

But his father's shadow buries those memories in darkness. Ont had been well on his way to becoming the man his father had been. Until Cahan, until the Rai came to Harn and he saw in the forester what it was to be truly hard, and that you could also be soft with it. That a man could long for friendship at the same time push it all away.

How foolish it was when seen from outside.

"Is that me?" he thinks. "Do I long for others?"

He does, and in that truth he tears the cloak of shadow away from the memories of the laughing woman, which may be small, but they are bright. His father was bigger than him, but he was dark, and light always drives away darkness. She was light and he yearns for light.

Ont knew he was dying, failing. He must be. This was what happened, wasn't it? Your entire life passed before your eyes as you were judged for passage along the Star Path.

Strange though, some of the places, faces, battles. They were not his memories.

Yet they were.

All of this they experienced, alone and together. They were aware and unaware of the others' existence and the existence of themselves, and versions of themselves that were not them. They lived as if in a dream, and were held within the minds of those who were as eternal as the land of Crua, and as cold and as cruel, but also as full of beauty and life and hope as the land could be. These minds, though terrible, were not sentient in the way of the people, nor alive in the way of the animals. They were of the tree and of Ranya's web, they were of the land and the land was of them and they did not plan in any way understandable to the smaller, quicker minds of men and women. They saw growth and decay, they saw the future and the past as one and what could be and what was and what had been were overlaid like the layers of forest. They longed not to be as they were, they schemed to become as they had been. In the web of possibilities they picked out what they thought best for the land, for the trees and the life that sustained them, and they wove futures. And within the weave they gave gifts of knowledge to be passed on, seeds to be grown. They were the three.

They were the Woodhewn Nobles of Wyrdwood.

23

Saradis

She wanted to see the prisoner but was forced to wait. As she descended from the skyraft a monk was waiting for her, she did not know their name, names no longer mattered.

"Skua-Rai," said the monk.

"I am busy," she said, her eyes drawn to the figure on top of the black pyramid. It made her heart flutter and a smile breezed across her face like a memory of another time. She had done that, she had brought a god back to life and it would not be long now until the world burned. All the pain, all the suffering that was the land of Crua would be undone. The people would walk the Star Path together, to paradise. That was her comfort in moments of weakness, when she doubted, when she was repulsed by the cruelty that she was forced to enact she remembered that. This place. What happened here, the pain, the misery the fear, it was fleeting.

Like hers had been.

Strange, she had not thought of her youth in many, many years. Taken by monks from her home, joining a procession of the chosen, a joyous, colourful thing. Until

they reached the monastery. There they were led underneath the building, kept in the darkness and starved,
given strange bitter liquids to drink that wracked their
bodies. Told the chosen would hear the voices of the god
for the monks. She never did. But she was clever, and
watched the monks when they came to administer water,
how they paid more attention to those who were lost,
driven to the edge of madness by pain and visions. She
had not drunk the strange liquid they gave, she had taken
it into her mouth and spat it out, despite what they had
told her would happen if she did, despite how much she
thirsted. She had watched as people she had known garbled
meaningless nonsense words and were chosen, taken away
from the dark room, brought back later to be chained
once more.

So she had copied them. Found herself brought before
men and women who were richly dressed in shining clothes.
Some were Leorics, or High-Leorics or even Rai, and while
she garbled out nonsense the monks used it to give advice,
and take the price for it from those who came asking.

Then she would be put back, and in the darkness while
her stomach ached and pained her, she thought of one
thing only. Escape. That was when she first heard it, first
heard them.

Zorir.

Knew the truth then, the lies told by the monks, the
reason that Crua was cruel and hard. These monks had
forgotten the gods, the real gods. All this known in one
word.

Slowly, those around her died, until there was only her
and one other left. The weaker she became, the more clearly
she heard the voice of the god, *Zorir.* The more sure she
was.

And one day, when she was weak, when powerful men
and women came to listen to her words, as she listened to
the monks interpret them to mean what they wanted them

to mean. As they extorted coin for greasy promises of success and power. She made her move.

"Lies," it was hard to speak those words, real words, when she had got so used to simply letting her mouth make noises.

The world had stopped. Monks had tried to hurry her away but one of those great warriors, one of the Rai, stopped them.

"I have never heard one of your seers speak the language of the people before," she said. Monks tried to stop her, to dissuade the Rai but they were not interested in the words of monks.

"Rai, you must not—"

"You seek to tell me what to do, monk?"

"Of course, not," the monk, these robed ones who held her life in their hands grovelling before this woman in polished armour. She remembered that well.

"Speak, seer," said the Rai. She did, and not in garbled, strange and looping ways that could be interpreted by the monks. She spoke to those powerful men and women, to the Rai, who she knew were quick and vengeful, and she told them what was happening, how they were being fooled.

"They starve us and drug us until we cannot speak sense. Then they tell you whatever they want you to hear." She looked around. "Some pay to have our words interpreted how they wish, others are here to be manipulated."

"Hmm," said the Rai, and the monk started to speak but stopped. One look from the warrior did that.

She did not think this Rai really cared that this was a trick worked by monks to enrich their monastery, not really. She cared about being made to look like a fool before those who were not Rai, and worse, those who were Rai.

"Tell me, seer," she said, "how old are you?"

"I do not know, I was ten seasons when they took me

from my family. We journeyed for a season at least after that."

"You are clever, I think," said the Rai. "And it never hurts to have a seer on your side."

Many died. She had never seen the Rai's power before, never really understood what it was to hold the life of another in her hand, how those who were frightened would offer all they had in exchange for safety. The monks begged but it was no use, the monks died. At the end, the Rai told her the monastery was hers. She would be Skua-Rai of this place and she thought, from the way they smiled, that this was a grand joke to them, to put a child in charge.

She freed the other seer child, fed them and in doing so gained a servant in Laha who would die for her, and of course, she had done something the Rai never expected. She had prospered. The fact she truly heard her god speak meant little to the Rai. In the early days she was happy to do their bidding, she was young, clever and full of the fervour only truth can bring.

Strange, she had not thought about her youth in many years.

"Skua-Rai," said the monk again.

"What?" she could hear the irritation in her tone, she wanted to see the prisoner, the strange one in her cells. Something about it nagged at the back of her mind in the same place she heard the voice of Zorir.

"The Cowl-Rai asks for you." She suppressed a momentary annoyance. The pretence must be kept up among those who did not yet know, but she did not like it. She was not a servant to the Cowl-Rai, she was master to all but Zorir. A deep breath.

"Of course, I will go to them."

She made her way through the quiet town, going around and under the tendrils of the god which reached out and touched everything, a measure of its magnificence, a blue glow that reached every corner of Tiltspire. A blessing in light. It annoyed her that she had heard people complain about the tendrils of the god being in the way, as if a small inconvenience could make up for the glory that was to come, the great gift they would be given of a new life along the Star Path.

She walked around the pyramid. It felt as if the air here vibrated, as if the god itself touched her when she walked, its presence running across her skin. Every time she approached the pyramid she looked up, at Zorir, at the corpse of Cahan Du-Nahere below it, and she smiled to herself. Victory, but not only victory, proof she had been right from the start: to choose him as the one. She had thought his weakness a fault but it had been important. His weakness, and his concern for others had led him to the god. Zorir had planned it from the start and she, like he, had been the god's tool.

She found Laha, standing before the great stone. Staring at her as she walked.

"Something," he said. As always when he spoke the words were strange, more like a disturbance of the air than a voice. The rocks in his skin shone.

"Something?"

"Wrong." She stared at him for a moment, nodded.

"Can you deal with this, or should I do something?" Laha blinked, the rest of his body entirely still.

"I will."

"Good, I must see to the Cowl-Rai." A momentary pause in the existence of the world, a stutter of time.

"Yes." She nodded and walked away, through the taffi-stones, down the long hall past the collared. As she walked some of the collared left their positions, walking toward Laha. Every one of them expressionless, more like corpses than people. Good: she felt no pity for the Rai. They would have killed her if they could, now those who were not collared served her and feared her in a way they never had before. Two of the collared stood guard of the Cowl-Rai's room and she passed them without comment. They did not need her to speak to them, they were servants in the very purest way. She took a deep breath, readying herself for the smell of the room, of a body unwashed for months.

Instead she smelled soap.

Nahac stood, naked, with her back to the door, washing herself.

"Cowl-Rai?"

"I never really believed, you know," she said.

"You seem well," said Saradis, for months Nahac had been unreachable, Saradis had expected her to starve to death but something had sustained her. "How is the pain?" Nahac passed a cloth over her neck, water running down her back and over a scar caused by a sword.

"Gone, it vanished. I think the god looks away from me."

"Zorir is busy, they have much to do in our world."

"They do not need me." The splatter of water onto the floor.

"Who can know the mind of a god," she said.

"You do not need me any more."

"No," said Saradis. "I do not."

"Then why am I alive?"

"You are the Cowl-Rai," said Saradis and she was very careful to keep her voice flat.

"And you hate me for it." A moment of shock for Saradis. She had always thought she hid it well. "You think I don't know? Think I didn't feel the resentment from the very first moment? That upstart girl," she turned, dropped the cloth on the floor. "The one you rejected, I enjoyed the fact you hated me. That you needed me." She smiled and walked toward the bars. "I was so very angry, all the time."

"That I chose him?" She stared at Saradis.

"I thought so," she said. "But I think I was angry that you took us both away. Life was hard in Woodedge, true, but we were a family, and I was happy."

"Happy? Your father beat you. Your work would have broken your body before you had seen twenty seasons." Saradis smiled to herself. "You offered to come, do you remember that? To look after your little brother, then you blamed him and you hated him and you undermined him."

"I was meant to protect him," she sounded very far away.

"And now look," Saradis pointed out of the window. "You made me Skua-Rai to enjoy standing over me, but that did not work out, did it? In fact, you failed in everything. You never protected your brother. You became Cowl-Rai in name only, and ended up as slave to me, the woman you hated the most." For a moment, Nahac did not move.

"I enjoyed," she said eventually, "every single thing I did to you. When I made you march with troops, eat with them, walk with them like you were nothing. When I had you bow before me, when the Rai laughed at you. Every single thing I did to you, Saradis, I savoured."

"And I put up with it, with you, for my god. Now look where we are."

"Do you hate me as much as I hate you?" said Nahac. Again, Saradis smiled, for someone who had such a knack for tactics, the Cowl-Rai could be incredibly transparent.

"Not as much as you hate yourself. Does looking out the window at your brother bring it all home? He was all you had, and you threw it all away. But you should not be sad, Nahac, you have helped a god to rise." Nahac stared at her, something unrelenting in her face.

"You should kill me, Saradis, because I place all the pain of my life at your feet. When I escape this place, I will kill you." Saradis found herself laughing.

"But you will never escape, and you know it. You designed the cage yourself to make sure." Saradis stepped back toward the door. "It is good though, to watch you feel guilt for mistakes made as a child. But maybe you would feel a little better if you knew the truth." She stopped in the doorway, smiled at Nahac. "I set you against him from the start." From the look on her face, it had never even occurred to Nahac that this could be the case. "To harden him, to strip him of everything. I set you against him."

"I will—"

"Nothing, you will do nothing, Nahac. You are right, you debased me when you could. And I know you seek to anger me in hope I will end your life before the pain and madness returns." She shook her head. "But I will not, you will live, and that is my vengeance." With that she turned, walked away and behind her she heard the madness start. Felt the air crackle with the Cowl-Rai's twisted power and knew it constrained by the cage. Screams as Nahac once more lost herself and Saradis heard the woman begging, "kill me, stop the pain, kill me".

But she would not.

24

Udinny

How curious life is, that I, Udinny, was once a homeless monk of a forgotten god, wandering the lands with my hands out in hope of my next meal and wishing someone would listen to my tales of a kinder, gentler god.

Now I marched with forest outlaws and Rai, the nobles of our land and their soldiers and, most alarmingly of all, I was also a man, which I was not before and never cease to stop thinking about because, of all the odd things that have happened to me, that may be the oddest.

I am not entirely sure I am completely Udinny now. I was definitely not the Udinny who had first met Cahan Du-Nahere. Dying changes you. More worrying was my memories were not only my own, some belonged to the man I had been. Sometimes I remembered death, I remembered the feel of a knife as it cut a throat, the hot rush of blood over my hands and the exultation at feeding my god, the places to plant the corpses where the earth was hungry for flesh, and rewarded the hunger with soldiers of the forest.

Other memories belonged to long-dead versions of me.

We walked through long grasses which hissed gently in

the wind as their heavy heads released streamers of bright yellow, musty smelling pollen. We no longer followed the road made by the Rai army. After the warning of a trap Tanhir had led us round in a half-circle so we came at the army from a different angle. They were not hard to follow, a great cloud of dust marked their place on the horizon. It would be days at most before they reached Jinnspire.

"Do you trust them?" Tanhir's voice pulled me from thoughts of who I was and who I could be.

"The Rai?"

"Who else?"

"Why ask me, not your people?" Something clouded her features and I wished I had not asked, though it was days now since I had woken with a knife at my throat. Our relationship was definitely improving.

"My people are Forestals, they are Rai and their soldiers. I know what answer they will give." I nodded and watched the Rai before us. Tanhir made them walk ahead as she did not want them behind us. One of their soldiers was struggling and his compatriot took his weapons and shield. The struggling man had sacrificed some of their own life for their Rai. I had watched them do it that morning and felt something inside myself as they did, the cowl of the man who had once lived in this body reacted. Though I felt it I could not reach it. I knew its presence the way one knows rootlings are in the forest, it was a hint of existence, but shy and wary of me.

"Trust them? No, they are Rai," I said it softly in the hope the Rai did not hear me. "What they care about is their own survival not ours." Tanhir nodded and her hand reached toward the arrows on her hip, an unconscious reaction. "But they are telling the truth about the army they deserted, they hate them. And they will never say it because they are Rai, but they are frightened."

"So they will fight with us," said Tanhir, "but may turn on us."

"That is the way of it."

The Rai at the front of the procession stopped, raised a hand. Their troops dropped to one knee and Tanhir made a signal so the Forestals did the same. Then she went forward at a crouch and I followed. The three Rai waited, close up they smelled of the oils used to keep their armour in good condition and something else, something I knew well but also did not know. Inside me the cowl shifted, as if looking for a place within to hide.

"Someone is out there," said the leader, Ustiore. The other two were Tassa, a small, thick man with constantly moving dark eyes as if he did not know who or what to trust, and Ganri, a tall gamine woman who barely interacted with the world around her.

"How do you know?" said Tanhir. An odd question. Tanhir had a cowl and she could feel the world around her.

"It is what my cowl does," the Rai shrugged. "Tassa is strong, and controls water well, Ganri can throw fire as far as a Rai three times her age. I can do fire, but am better at feeling the world out." She stared at Tanhir. "You have a cowl," she said, surprised. "How?"

"Most Forestals do," said Tanhir, and I wondered at the ease with which she threw away secrets, "but ours work differently to yours."

"Maybe you can learn from us," said the Rai. Tanhir ignored her.

"What is out there?"

"Soldiers," she said, "and Rai, and some collared, I think. The collared are harder to sense, it is almost as if they are hidden by the world."

"Numbers?" said Tanhir, she was a different woman now, a soldier. She did not sneer or ignore what the Rai said simply because she hated them. They had strengths and those strengths would help keep her people alive so she would use them. I thought better of Tanhir for that, understood her a little more, what drove her and had made her pursue me, or at least this body, across Crua was the same thing, loyalty.

"Less than a hundred," said Ustiore, "more than fifty." The Rai looked back, she had twenty troops, and there were ten Forestals. "We should go around them. There's no vengeance in being killed. This is not the place to strike."

"Fifty is no threat," said Tanhir.

"It is almost two to one," said the Rai.

"You have never fought Forestals, have you?" said Tanhir. The Rai shook her head. "You will see," said Tanhir, lifting her bowstaff, "that this is a great leveller. There is a reason you outlawed them."

"You mean to walk into a trap?" said the Rai. Tanhir shook her head.

"No, I mean you to walk into a trap." The Rai's lip curled into a look of anger. I felt something move within her, power gathering.

"You will let us die."

"If I wanted you dead," said Tanhir, "I would have shot you down from behind while you walked. What is needed is for the trap to be sprung, and for you to trust my archers." The Rai took a deep breath.

"Trust must begin somewhere," she said, then looked to the two Rai with her. Tassa shrugged and Ganri gave her a small nod. "We will spring this trap then, but kill the Rai and the collared first."

"We have fought your sort before," said Tanhir, "we know what to do." The Rai stared at her, then gave a short bow of her head and took her soldiers forward. Tanhir raised a hand, bringing up her Forestals to surround us. "String your bows, be ready. You know who to target."

"What should I do?" I asked.

"Stay out of the way," she said without looking at me. I wondered if she was frightened of losing me and the memories tied to my life, though I will not pretend I was sad to be out of the fighting.

The Rai went forward confidently, as if they did not know about the waiting ambush, as if they could not feel it.

"Why are we doing this, Tanhir?"

"What?" Tanhir turned to me.

"Tall Sera sent us to scout and report, why are we fighting?" She blinked. "We know where they are, we know where they are going. Surely it is after Jinnspire has fallen that they become a danger, should we not keep back until then?" Her eyes, so predatory, and angry, remained locked on me.

"You are not a warrior," she said, the words low and dismissive, "you walk through this world and those in power protect you, you even bring a pet with you," she pointed behind me where a crownhead calmly chewed on grass. I did not remember it being there before. "So I cannot expect you to understand tactics." She glanced toward where the Rai were advancing. "Firstly, I do this to thin the herd; the more fall here the fewer they have later. Maybe it lengthens the battle for Jinnspire by a day, maybe an hour. Either way it hurts them." I watched her, and saw in her face the same hatred for the Rai that Ania had. "And it tests the loyalty of our new allies," she said. "Which sorely needs testing."

I watched the Rai's forces as they walked through hip-high grass toward the sinking sun. In the very distance I thought I could make out the tip of Jinnspire.

"Why send people after us, after them?"

"What?" Tanhir looked confused. "Because they are Rai, they cannot stand it when anyone stands up to them."

I had a feeling within, though it was barely my own. I think I owed it to the memories of the body I was in. A man who had fought and killed and ambushed even the Forestals of Wyrdwood. "Something is wrong, Tanhir."

"Forgive me if I do not take the worries of a monk seriously."

"This makes no sense."

"They want to kill us, we want to kill them. War is often simple, monk."

"Why only fifty?"

"What?"

"In Harn, when we fought the Rai, they came at us in huge numbers. Put their faith in that even though they only fought villagers. They outnumbered us three to one. She said there were no more than fifty." Tanhir blinked again, then shrugged.

"They underestimate us." She turned away, "They always do."

She was sure, and yet I could not help worrying.

"What if there are more than we thought?" I watched the Rai continue forward. "What if they hide themselves."

"Don't be foolish," she said, and she took an arrow from her quiver, "Rai cannot do that, it is a Forestal trick." With her words, a thought drifted into my mind and like a raincloud in the north it gathered strength, gathered darkness and surety as whispers heard in Woodhome became shouts. A chain of possible events, an echo of Tall Sera speaking.

"I have sent others out and none have returned. I have heard whispers, people saying the forest has turned against us."

"They can hide, Tanhir."

"What?" Tanhir looked puzzled, not worried.

"This collar, it makes Rai slaves. What if they have your people, too?"

"Rai do not take Forestals prisoner." A coldness settled within me, like Harsh ripping the leaves from my innocence, a realisation as to what we faced. Of its ruthlessness and its power.

"Tanhir, have you not been listening? They are no longer

Rai." I saw Tanhir understand. I saw her make the connection I had made and she stood, I think to warn the Rai, her alarm so great she could not let even Rai walk into this trap.

As if the enemy listened, as if they knew what I spoke of they appeared from the long grass. Not just fifty. A hundred at least, maybe even more and they were not in front of the Rai, they were to one side. In front of them rose the fifty that were expected, a small squad of Rai and soldiers with spears. But it was the forces to the side that held our attention.

"No," said Tanhir, "it cannot be."

What she saw was rows of archers, Forestal archers. They lifted their bows in unison. The Rai who had come to us saw them, she hesitated for a moment and then I heard her shout.

"Forward!" She was no fool, knew they stood a better chance in a close fight with the fifty in front than against the bows of the corrupted Forestals and if she could get close then they would not loose at her. Tanhir took charge, years of experience coming to the fore.

"The archers!" she shouted to her people. "Target their archers." A moment of hesitation in her people, because they saw what we saw. They recognised their own and could hardly believe it. "They are not us any more, they are taken!" shouted Tanhir. She loosed an arrow. I saw an archer fall, but the rest were already loosing, and the forces of our Rai were dying. Before any more of our Forestals could shoot the Rai's soldiers were in the way. A carefully choreographed move, putting themselves and their shields between the Forestals serving them and Tanhir's archers. Behind them I saw terrible, familiar loose-limbed figures moving forward.

"Hetton are coming," I said, "Tanhir, we need to go." She looked around, back to the approaching soldiers. "Scatter!" she shouted, "make for Woodhome! Tall Sera needs to know they have bows. They have us." Then she grabbed my arm and looked back at the shield wall coming towards us as three Hetton pushed through, loping toward our position. "Come on, monk," she said, "pray that your god can hide us in the grass."

We ran.

25

Sorha

The Rai fell, and behind her stood Laha, the chosen of Saradis, but he was not the man he had been. Blue lines ran across his skin, the stones in his forehead sparkled and his face was curiously dead, no expression of any sort. The scent of sickness filled the air and behind Laha came two Hetton, behind them the strange Rai, the collared, with their blank eyes and the same glowing lines as Laha.

"Run," shouted Sorha, "get us out of here."

"Leave me," the words of Frina, her body hard against Sorha's, needing her strength to walk.

"No." Sorha pulled her on, following the Osere going in the opposite direction to Laha. Knowing she would never be quick enough.

Laha did not run after them, he did not hurry. He walked, and somehow that made it worse because to Sorha that spoke of certainty, spoke of nowhere for them to go.

They lost two Osere straight away, not used to this new world they fell back on what, to them, felt like safety and froze. Became still in a place where to be silent and still was no protection from those who could see. Laha cut them down without breaking stride.

She felt sure this was it. The end.

Then the sound of battle. Of blades scoring armour.

Fighting, but who? Not her people.

The dull thud of bones cracking.

Sorha glanced back.

The Reborn erupted from their cell. One with an axe, one with a sword. Two of the collared died first, heads split open. Then the Reborn turned on the rest. Whirling and dancing their way into them. Sorha, backing away with the weight of Frina heavy against her. One of the Reborn looked at her. They shared a glance, a moment. Then Laha turned, heading back to the fight behind him and motioning towards two Hetton, pointing at Sorha. The grey-skinned Reborn warriors shouted, "Run, friend of Cahan!"

Sorha ran.

Osere, pulling her on into the darkness. She had no idea if the Hetton behind them could see in the dark. If Laha and the collared could. If any of them would survive the fury of the Reborn. She only wanted to get away. She had seen the Hetton fight and she did not want to face them. At the same time knew she would have to. The Osere could never stand against them.

"Take Frina," she pushed her to the closest Osere, two of them took her, pulling her away into the darkness. "Get away however you can." She drew her sword. The Hetton slowed, looked at her, dead fish faces, white eyes, pin teeth and flaking skin. "Come on then," she said, "get it over with, you know you want to."

"Want to," hissed the lead Hetton and began to come forward. Sorha readied herself, she wondered how long the poison on her blade took to take effect, how long it was good for. She wished she had found a better place to die, somewhere outside with the light above warming her skin. Not here in a cold, damp and dark tunnel. The Hetton stepped forward, one had a sword, the other a spear; did she feel eagerness from them, or did she gift that to them when in fact they had no feelings, only purpose.

"Wait!" A voice in the darkness. It stopped the Hetton moving though she could hear their voices, echoing around her down the tunnel. Behind them Laha.

No sign of the Reborn.

"Wait, wait," words like open wounds in the air.

"Let them run," said Laha. She was used to Rai, she expected some joy in his voice, some pleasure in the idea of letting the prey go so he could hunt them down, but there was nothing of joy in Laha's voice, nothing of humanity. He found her, eyes sparkling in the darkness, his body a strange framework of blue lines. He was staring at her. "Like the Reborn said. Run, friend of Cahan."

She did. Quickly catching the Osere, following them into the warren of tunnels, stumbling and tripping. When they came to those places where many tunnels came together the Osere pointed down one tunnel. She glanced back, shadows behind them. Two figures appeared, cut and torn at but miraculously walking: the Reborn. Sorha waited as they ran up to her.

"Do not stop, friend of Cahan, we will guard your rear."

She nodded, then ran ahead of the Osere and headed down the tunnel.

But not far.

Figures in the tunnel, the blank faces and glowing blue skin of collared Rai.

"Back!" she shouted, expecting to walk into Laha and the Rai behind them, to be caught between them, but she was not. They were doing nothing but blocking the way back.

"We can kill them," said one of the Reborn.

"Not the time," said Sorha.

"That way," Buris of the Osere pointed at another tunnel and Sorha led them down it. Clear, nothing in the way. She dropped back. "Frina," she said, taking the weight from one of those holding her.

"Leave me," said the Osere leader, "faster without."

"Speed does not matter. They are herding not chasing."

"Why?" said Frina.

"Nothing good," said one of the Reborn from behind them. "But we protect you now, strange creature."

Sorha glanced back, faint silhouettes in the tunnel behind them. "Have your people use their bows if our pursuers get too near."

"Kill those, ahead," said Frina, "go where we want."

"We like that one," said the Reborn, pointing at Frina. "She is worthy."

"Maybe," said Sorha, she looked back. "But I think that would just bring them all down on us, and the Hetton." She only wanted to get away. Frina said nothing more but Sorha knew what she must be thinking. If they were being led somewhere it would not be to anything good.

But she felt there was only death in these tunnels and she did not want to die. She had not cared once, but no longer. Every beat of her heart was precious, it was not cowardice, not at all. She was not afraid to fight and she knew she would most likely die soon.

She did not want to die here.

Dying down here, it filled her with a new sense, made her heart beat fast, made her breath quicken, and she had no name for it, it was not fear, but was a cousin to it.

"We carry on," said Sorha, and wondered if the Osere with their sensitive hearing could tell how she was feeling, wondered if they knew the name for it but she could not ask.

"Yes," said Frina, and they did. Up tunnels, down tunnels, at every junction there were collared, standing silently in some tunnels, barring entry. At every junction the Reborn offered to fight and Sorha had to say no. They slowly wound their way upwards and as they did, despite the danger and the constant threat, Sorha began to breathe more easily. Upwards, towards the light. She could die in the light. She was tired, breath struggled in and out of her chest with every step.

Until they came out into the light, emerging from the base of the spire behind the great taffistone, before it the rows and rows of smaller stones used for sacrifice. Towering above them all, filling her view, the black pyramid of the new god. It sat atop it, four tentacles writhing in the air. Hanging below the creature was Cahan, slack as the dead though she knew he was not.

How?

She could not answer that, she only knew it was true, that in some way Cahan Du-Nahere was still alive. Was this her chance? Guided up here by the forces of this god? But why?

"Cahan!" she said it, she shouted it, and her voice echoed from the hard surfaces of the spire and the floor and the stones. Around her the Osere angled their heads to listen to the echoes. It was a single moment of peace and of quiet. Sorha entirely forgot the Osere, and the Reborn, the collared, Laha and the Hetton behind them. For just one moment she was there with Cahan and the light kissed her face.

"He is gone," said Frina. "The god has him now, he is gone."

Sorha turned, Laha and the Hetton and the collared emerged from the tunnels. They were curiously silent, as if not even their clothing or armour or footsteps made a sound. They were death walking and she knew it, to her but even more to the Osere. What they could not hear they could not defend against. She stepped forward to stand between the Reborn, her footsteps made no sound, her armour did not creak. Laha stared at her, smiling.

Was this some desire of the god above? Had it brought the Osere who had kept it prisoner for so long here to watch them die?

"Go," she shouted to the Osere. When they did not react

she shouted it again and the Osere nodded. Sorha pointed in the direction that headed away from the spire and into the city. Their only chance, to lose themselves in the streets and alleys of Tiltspire, and she, Sorha, would die here beneath the black pyramid, with her skin touched by the light above. In the moment, when Laha sent the Hetton forward, and she drew her sword and readied for their advance. When the Reborn readied themselves by her, then her breath no longer came short and her heart no longer beat quickly.

"I am ready," she said to herself.

The Hetton came on. Not just the two who had been in the tunnel. Six now, two for her, two for each Reborn. The Hettons' mouths moved but no sound came out. The air felt alive, thick with the scent of stagnant lakes and ponds, the same moist air that you smelled if you stood near the geysers when they went off. She had no eyes for anything but her attackers. The air before the pyramid became unreal, refracting, making giant colourful globes and arcs in the air as the Hetton split, one to the left with a sword, the other to the right with a spear. She backed up through air that felt as if it fought her movements. An awful pressure on her neck, from the corner of her eye she could see the god atop the pyramid, the long tentacles no longer waving. She felt sure it was watching. The pressure she felt, the strange air: symptoms of a god's attention, damp upon her skin.

In the second she was distracted the Hetton attacked. Sword from the left and spear from the right. She stepped back, so as not to be trapped between them. The sword deflected, not by her, a spinning, twisting Reborn in her view for only a moment. The spear was the danger. She had no shield but her forearms and chest were armoured, she could take a sword slash. The spear would pierce her.

Then no more thinking. Only action. The spear came and she knocked it aside, slid her blade down the shaft until it collided with the Hetton's hand and she pulled away, slicing as viciously as she could, hoping she cut through the splintered wood of the creature's gauntlet. An impact from behind, against her helmet and back, pushing her forward. She used the momentum to ram the hilt of her sword into the spear Hetton's face. The space let her step forward and turn, in time to parry the incoming blow of a sword. The Hetton followed it with a dagger, scraping across her breastplate. She lashed out, more to give herself room than from any desire to do damage, and her sword scored the Hetton's face. Behind her the spear Hetton was still down, it began to push itself up and a Reborn danced past it, sweeping low with a spear it had taken from one of its foes. Smashing the Hetton back to the floor before the Reborn danced away to continue her own fight. The spear Hetton's body began shaking and convulsing. Then the sword Hetton took a step forward, raised its blade and froze. At first she did not understand.

Of course, the poison on her blade. The poison was working. The Hetton did not guard themselves the way normal soldiers did, easy to wound, hard to kill. The wound was all that was needed and the Hetton before her gasped and fell to its knees, the flesh around the sword wound corrupting and blackening. She stepped back. Saw Laha, head tipped to one side as if confused. Then he looked at her, smiled and pointed.

From behind him, more Hetton, more collared.

They came forward, came for her.

She wondered how many she could kill.

"Sorha!" The voice faint but familiar, Frina. She turned. The Osere were back, following them were more collared, and Rai soldiers. "You have to escape."

"You escape, I'll hold them here!"

The Osere were running toward the massive taffistone and Sorha understood. What a fool she had been. There was their escape. Towering over them, eternal and forbidding.

A taffistone. Laha, realising what they were doing, trying to shout but the strange air ate his words. She would hold for long enough, get the Osere away.

Then a Reborn was by her side.

"Go, friend of Cahan. We will hold them."

"You can't win," she said.

"We must be here, for Cahan Du-Nahere. You are needed elsewhere."

"But . . ."

"Go," said the Reborn. Sorha held out her sword.

"Take this, it poisons them." The Reborn shook her head.

"You will need it. Go, friend of Cahan." With that she gave her a light push and turned, let out a shout that could be heard even in the strange air and she and her sister ran at Laha and his troops.

Sorha turned, ran for the stone. The bizarre feeling in the air vanished and it was only air again.

"Stop them!" She didn't know who shouted that. Didn't care.

Troops, coming from all directions. The Osere laying their hands on the stone. Frina took Sorha's hand, then the hand of the nearest Osere. This should be it. The stone should open, transport them across Crua.

Nothing.

Nothing but the sound of hundreds of feet on stone as they ran toward them

"What is wrong?" said Sorha, Frina turned to her. "Does your magic not work on the surface?"

"Something stops us."

It took a moment to sink in. Then Sorha nodded, smiled. This was it then.

At least she would die in the light.

26
Venn

They were surrounded by soldiers. Rai stood along the cliff tops, some stood on the rickety scaffolding around the cloudtree and Venn wondered how they had managed to sneak up on the Forestals.

"I wondered when you would show yourselves," said Tall Sera, and Venn thought it from bravado not actual knowledge.

"I said put down your bows," shouted one of the Rai, taller than the others, the helmet of their armour worked into the image of a gasmaw, tentacles writhing around their face.

"No," said Tall Sera, "I do not think we will. If you were going to attack us, Rai, you would have done it, not announced yourself." The Rai stood above them, glowering down, and Venn found they were holding their breath. Behind the Rai their soldiers had formed a shield wall, though Venn knew enough about battle now to know it would not hold if they were forced to move down the steep slope. Though the incline gave them an advantage for their spears, increasing the range and the power with which they would fall. Venn thought, in that moment, that Tall

Sera had been foolish if he really knew the Rai were there, the forest bows were fearsome, and the shields the Forestals could make together would protect them from fire, but not for long enough. Every Forestal making a shield was not loosing arrows, and eventually they would tire, all the Rai had to do here was to hold their position and not run out of weapons.

"Brave words from a man in a such poor tactical position," said the Rai.

"Attack or don't. I become bored." Tall Sera still sounded relaxed, though Venn felt anything but. Silence, or what passed for it in Wyrdwood, the howls and chirps of creatures, the patter of moisture falling from far above.

"You do not know how tempted I am, outlaw." Tall Sera took an arrow from his quiver and held it loosely, ready to shoot.

"You would be first to die, Rai," he said. The Rai nodded, and Venn thought they saw the ghost of a smile play across their face.

"Stand down," said the Rai, the shield wall behind them loosened, and Venn felt sure they heard a collective sigh, a release of pressure. "I do not want to die today," said the Rai.

"Then what do you want?"

"A difficult question," the Rai shouted back, "all my life, I have simply wanted what I wanted and taken it. It had never occurred to me to ask or think of anything else." The Rai glanced back. "I was like the spearmaw, the Rai of the forest that fears no other."

"So something has taught you fear?" shouted back Tall Sera, "cannot say I am sorry, we've been trying to do so for generations."

"But you are not a god, forest outlaw, Iftal knows our gods have been cruel enough, but this new one." He shook his head. "It would make us all slaves, and I will be no one's slave. I think that could make even us allies, outlaw."

"Wyrdwood does not want you, Rai. It never has."

"And I do not want it. Believe me, I wish to lead my Rai and my soldiers out of here and out of Harnwood. Maybe in Woodedge we can hide, live in a form of peace, maybe even trade with you one day."

"Until you need to feed the cowl," shouted back Tall Sera, "and my people become a temptation."

"We are having to change," shouted the Rai, "even though it is hard. The soldiers," he waved behind him, "wanted promises and protections if they are to work with us, and we have given them. We offer the same to you."

"We do not need your offers," shouted Tall Sera, "and we protect ourselves." He held up the forestbow.

"Nevertheless, my offer is there. And information too, on what your enemies plan."

"You give this from the goodness of your heart?" The Rai shook their head.

"No, not at all." He smiled a strange, dead-looking thing. "In fact, the truth is that if I did you would not believe me anyway." Tall Sera, shrugged. "I ask your help and in return I will help you."

"And what does a great Rai, a spearmaw of Tiltspire, need the help of outlaws for?"

"Something hunts us, outlaw. Something dark and terrible."

"Wyrdwood is full of such things."

"I know, I have spent far longer here than many of my kind, know it better than any other Rai, nonetheless, what hunts us . . ." his words died away. "It is not something I have ever come across before. That is why we approach you rather than run or fight. I know you hate the Rai, and cannot blame you, but my soldiers, they are men and women like you. They do not deserve to be carried off screaming into the night." Venn watched, wondering what Tall Sera would say. It was unlikely, given what Rai were, that this one, old and powerful, actually felt pity for their troops. More likely they felt frightened for themselves and thought they knew how to manipulate the Forestal. As ever with Rai, it probably never occurred to them that Tall Sera knew that, and that the Forestals who had never cared for outsiders, had hardened even further recently.

"Very well, Rai," said Tall Sera eventually. "Come down here, sit at a table and join me. Let us talk of what you fear, and what you know of the ways of this new god." For a moment the Rai stared down, and Venn had the unmistakable sense of anger emanating from them, a deep and furious thing. Then it was gone, and the Rai with two others, what looked like a trunk commander and branch leader, made their way down the steep slope to join them at the bottom, looking around at the tree quarry as if they had never seen it before.

"This should have set me up for life, you know, and our lives are long," said the Rai. "Ever since we heard of the fall I had been working to take command. So much coin can be made from Treefall."

"And now?" said Tall Sera, and he pulled out a seat at a small table.

"Now I wish I had been posted to some out of the way larger where no one ever came and nothing ever happened." The Rai sat. Tall Sera sat with them.

"Stop feeling sorry for yourself," said the outlaw leader, "and tell me something useful enough to keep you alive." A brief flash of that anger again.

"Not even interested in my name?"

"Not really, though I suppose it would be useful to know what to call you."

"Well, before I say it, know that if you move to kill me, you burn first." Tall Sera only stared. "I am Rai Sunan Kit-Pellor." Venn saw a momentary tightening of every muscle in Tall Sera's body, a tension in every Forestal around them. "You have probably heard that name on occasion."

"You were an outlaw hunter, out of Storspire. I lost many to you in the north."

"Yes, but I have not been that for a long time, an easier life called to me." He looked around at the Forestals. "But knowing my name, you know the risk I take sitting here, I hope that tells you something of the danger I believe is out there." He nodded toward the forest.

"Give me one reason not to kill you," the words came out tight, as if they were bitter food forced on Tall Sera.

"The collar," said Rai Sunan

"That thing that makes Rai slaves?"

"Not only Rai, outlaw. Any man or woman, it is just that more Rai survive than others. What will matter to you, is that when someone is collared, all they know is shared."

"And this affects me how?"

"Because they have some of your people."

"Your doing, no doubt." Tall Sera's gaze was icy, like coldest morning of Harsh. The Rai shrugged.

"They will know where your Woodhome is by now." Then it was as if Wyrdwood's darkness fell upon the quarry, that sudden and total night, but it was a darkness of feeling, a blackout of fear.

"No, that cannot be, no Forestal would ever betray—"

"The collared are no longer your people, or who they were. They become servants of this new God, Zorir, and instruments of Saradis who serves them." He glanced up at his soldiers. "They also know of your stones, and that you can travel within them and how. Though I hear that was because of a traitor."

"Not one of us," said Tall Sera, "we are Forestals, we do not . . ."

"And you are not listening," said the Rai. "I am old," he looked around and Venn could see their age on them, in the smoothness of their flesh, the paleness of their eyes and the emptiness of their gaze, "old enough to be true to myself about what I am. My drive is to survive, and to survive Rai need power, that is how we stay strong. We seek power or we seek to get close to it and we let nothing stand in our way, not affection nor friendship." Behind him, Venn watched one of the younger Rai, saw something close to confusion on their face while the one next to them, a little older, nodded with some wistful expression passing across their stretched skin. The old Rai looked over at his Rai, at his soldiers, at the Forestals. "Imagine what it takes for someone like me, who has survived for generations by seeing what is strong, what is rising, and betraying whatever cause I have stood with to make sure I continue by being close to it, to walk away from the greatest strength I have ever seen." Forest silence fell again. The patter of moisture from above. The trill of creatures. "You cannot understand Zorir unless you have seen it. The immensity of it, the god's presence fills Tiltspire, ropes of its essence twine through the city. Those collared in its name, they are puppets. Many of my fellows hang on there because they believe it will not be them that is taken next, but it will be, and not one of us is powerful enough to fight a god." He sat a little straighter. "That is why I have come to you, because what is out there, it cannot be fought. Zorir itself has come for us. A god hunts in Wyrdwood."

"The enemy of my enemy is my friend?" said Tall Sera, and he spoke into an almost unnatural stillness.

"There is only one enemy now," said the Rai.

"You think we can fight a god?" this said from behind, one of the Forestals, and they sounded riven, hollowed out by what the Rai had said.

"I think you already are, whether you wish to or not."

"But we cannot—"

"There is nowhere for you to go," said the Rai, his voice harsh. "Not even your city in the trees, some trick of Zorir has allowed them to control gasmaws and spearmaws, the collared ride them and Saradis has taken a skyraft, collared the crew and will ride it into Wyrdwood. She did not know its location then, I imagine she does by now. How will your tree city stand against that?"

"No," a voice from one of the other Forestals.

"We are not taking you to Woodhome," said Tall Sera, "maybe I see some sense in us fighting under the same branch, pooling our resources, but you will not come to our home." The Rai looked around, the ghost of a smile and a nod. Tall Sera turned to his people. "And as for you, Jurnast, who thinks we cannot fight a god, have you paid no attention to Crua? Gods die all the time, even cloudtrees fall."

"Why trust you, Rai?" said another Forestal.

"Because I have lived a long time," said the Rai, "and I want to carry on living. It is that simple." He looked around, shrugged. "And once this is over we will be enemies once more, do not doubt it. But for now, we stand together."

"Tall Sera," said one of the Forestals, "we cannot trust the Rai." Venn did not know what they expected, but it was not for Tall Sera to turn to them.

"And what of you, Venn, what do you think."

"The trion," said Rai Sunan and leaned forward. Bows were raised, the Rai stopped. Lifted their hands. "I am curious only. You are the trion Saradis searches for? The one with a cowl?"

"Go near them and you die," said Furin. The Rai sat back. Licked their lips.

"You could bargain me for much power," Venn said to the Rai, all the time watching their eyes. The Rai nodded.

"Oh yes, Saradis would give almost anything for you, we are told the god wants you." The tension under the cliff of the cloudtree built. "But before anyone gets any ideas," Venn had the distinct impression Rai Sunan spoke not to the Forestals or Venn, but to his own people, "all Saradis really offers is a collar, now or later, all will be made slaves."

"You don't know that," said one of the younger Rai from

behind him. "We have noticed, she only takes those who betray her." Rai Sunan laughed.

"Granahist," he said quietly, "had you lived a little longer you would know that is always what we say of those who cause trouble, or simply get in our way."

"But . . ."

"There is no but, Granahist. There is the possibility of life with these people, or there is Tiltspire and the collar of Zorir." For a moment, Venn saw the flair of rebellion in the younger Rai's eyes. "You have already killed her collared and her Rai, you think she is the forgiving type?" The younger Rai nodded, the spark of rebellion extinguished.

"Venn?" said Tall Sera.

"I think we should trust them, for now." Tall Sera raised a hand, and his Forestals lowered their bows. At the same time silence fell in the forest once more. A different silence, a thing of totality. Venn saw something then they had never seen before. Fear on the face of a Rai, on the face of an old Rai.

"The god is coming," he said. "We should leave here." Venn felt it, and was sure everyone else did. The air becoming heavier, pushing on their skin.

"There is a taffistone, back there," shouted Tall Sera, "Venn, can you open us a way?"

"I think so."

Something screamed in the wood, a sound like nothing they had ever heard. It made muscles freeze and bones ache.

"Run!" shouted the Rai, "we will make fire, it hates fire."

Then they were running, behind them Rai throwing fire at something crawling over the ridge, huge and black and writhing. The fire intensified its screams, beat it back. All Venn could think of was escape, the terror within them a primal thing. Tall Sera shouting as they ran.

"When we reach the stone, we must all be touching to pass through, those who are not will be left behind!"

Another scream, an awful, hateful pressure on the back of Venn's neck as they ran, an awareness of something terrible. They put all they had to running, into reaching the taffistone half buried before a fallen tree. Stumbling, fighting to remain upright, mind full of panic. Then their hand on the cold stone. Waiting as they felt others around them, hands touching them, The familiar presence of Forestals, lending their power, behind them soldiers, women and men. Behind them, the Rai, dark mirrors to the Forestals. Walled off in a way the outlaws never were. Venn pushed their mind into the taffistone. Finding the protectors back in Woodhome there, the constant fight with the presence trying to break into the network. Knew the struggle to use it would be even harder, it had degraded further in the small time they had been away.

Woodhome called, but Venn could not take them there. Tall Sera had forbidden these Rai Woodhome. The rest of the network was hazy, hidden, difficult to sense a connection and Venn called out, unsure if in their mind or with their voice. "Ranya help me."

At the same time, they heard an echo, not a voice but another true and clear and desperate desire for help. With it came a destination, one that Venn had never even considered, *down*, but that was enough, that was all Venn needed, a place to go no matter how unfamiliar it may be. As Venn reached out, they felt a barrier, a veil, that was older than Venn could understand. Had they not been shown where to go they would never have known there was anything there, but when they reached out the veil fell apart, as if it had been waiting for them.

Venn opened the stone.

27

The Three

He was Dassit and he was Ania
    She was Ont and she was Dassit.
She was Ania and she was Ont.

All one knew they shared. Like a garaur or crownhead chosen to be a rootling they bathed in the womb of the forest and they grew and they changed. Were they chosen for some reason? Had this been engineered in some way by the great, forbidding and terrifying forces of the Boughry? They did not know and it never crossed their minds to ask. They simply were, the three had passed from the pain of corporeal life and into another plain, somewhere golden suffused with a soft and cradling brightness. This was the root of all life in Crua, a vast flow of life that had always been and always should be until the end. It came from outside, it was concentrated by cloudtrees and it pooled in the depths of the land. With it came a sense of vast and terrible power. Energies beyond the understanding of the three and many of the things they saw, or experienced, meant nothing to them. Vast cities, huge columns of throbbing power, unthinkable distances to be crossed, lines of numbers and symbols that stretched on to eternity.

A place of ash, burning and suffocating air left behind, a promise of light and rebirth; a destination.

Together they spoke – "The Star Path" though they knew what they said was not to understand, it was only to give a name to a thing so it could be named and through that could be real to them. A concept created in numbers they had no comprehension of could in some way be understood. They saw the path beyond death, and the way to be travelled was long, long beyond their ability to conceptualise, this was not forest paths, or taffistones. This was distances measured in hundreds of thousands of generations.

They saw other lives lived. Some were theirs, some were not.

They saw a golden land of glowing cities, covered over by a layer of energies that kept at bay the great cold of outside. They felt the weight of the Slowlands, and how it held everything down. They saw a great propulsive fire that burned in the north, beyond Wyrdwood. They saw black tentacled lords who sat atop pyramids and directed energies, and working with them, not as supplicants, not as worshippers, but as equals, were the people. They moved through cities, and they husbanded the great cloudtrees and forests and understood that what they were committed to was a great endeavour. The glowing cities, the spires that fountained energy and the huge trees that collected it. All must be kept in harmony if the great striving was to work. The men, the women, the lords, all linked to one another and lending their power, or linking it.

In the centre of it all, Anjiin. In Anjiin lay Iftal, one great spire, and eight around it. These were linked by the three towers of Iftal, pillars of light that rose from the spires of Harn that steered, which sent them to Jinneng which fixed, and Tilt which controlled. And each of these great pillars of light was alive and the three knew they looked upon the manifestation of Iftal in the world, the great god who was the guide and was, in some way, the star path and the journey and the vessel.

Somehow, familiar.

Entirely alien.

So much understood as they saw the land as it had been. The people worked with cowls, coming together to maintain and improve, the lords, the gods – they were not gods and the three knew it but they could no more understand or explain the truth of them than they could speak the language of them so they thought of them as gods – conducted and understood. There was no sickness here, no hunger and no death. Every corner of the land was easily reachable by the taffisnetwork. Those who were hurt or whose bodies became old and useless returned to the great flood of power and were brought back by the gods and the great endeavour continued. The Star Path was walked and time passed and though the three did not understand how, as Crua was always Crua, the Star Path was travelled. The people used their cowls, the priests atop the pyramids linked them and allowed them to speak with the gods. The beasts of the land worked with the people, they rode gasmaws and marants, orits built for them and the littercrawlers and the tiny creatures of the soil recycled all that died into good earth so more could grow.

To the three it appeared a paradise.

Until it was not.

They did not see it, they felt it. A growing impatience that became a rift among the gods. A split among the creatures that sat atop the pyramids and directed the great energies of the land.

A taffistone, sat in darkness,

Crua, like a jewel set in the night. Around it danced gods, blackness on blackness and within Crua the golden sparkle of life: the people, the trees, the raniri and the garaur and the littercrawlers, the gasmaws and the spearmaws and everything that lived upon it. Through it all moved fire, a fire that passed through all life, that gathered it up into a ball that span and twisted and fed on itself and grew and grew until Crua itself became a taffistone and through it was the end of the Star Path, the promised paradise, but all that could pass through this taffistone was the gods, and the people and all else that lived upon the land were gone. Eaten up to provide the energy that would open the great gate within the land.

They saw a war among gods, not a war of killing, not at first. A war of numbers and concepts so far beyond their understanding that it was simply a roaring in their ears, a great disagreement that flowed back and forth and as it did it grew. It passed from disagreement to anger and from anger to fury until the two sides, the larger one committed to the new plan, the new path, the smaller one determined to stop them, found themselves with no resolution left but violence.

The gods warred in Crua. The people were made slaves, the link forged to travel the Star Path used to twist them to fight for their own deaths, and those that the three saw as dark presences were winning, beating back the golden forms of the gods who stood by the people and the life of Crua. Eventually, those remaining saw no way for them to win that was not drastic, not terrifying even to creatures that were as gods. To save life they destroyed what mattered most to them, the glowing golden columns of Iftal in Anjiin fell. What connected all things in Crua was destroyed. The people were free, and most – but not all – joined with the golden gods, the war turned though it was not won. It was fought and fought hard and many died never to return, their experience and knowledge lost forever, until a détente was finally reached. The land was so damaged that the Star Path could no longer be travelled. The gods would sleep, and the people would inherit the land and rebuild.

"But we did not rebuild" said Ont/Ania/Dassit.

"We forgot," said Ania/Dassit/Ont.

"And now a dark god has returned," said Dassit/Ania/Ont.

They saw blue veins growing throughout Crua, slowly linking the living things within it, they saw the god atop the black pyramid in Tiltspire.

Before the three-as-one appeared the Boughry, the terrifying branch-headed gods of the Wyrdwood. Each one of them bathed in glowing and flickering golden light and understanding came to the three-as-one.

"You are remnants of Iftal."

They saw the three cities: Harnspire, Tiltspire and Jinnspire. They felt the presence of Venn, Udinny and Cahan and each of three saw the great taffistone of the city before them and felt the touch of one of the Boughry upon their shoulder. Each heard a voice echo in their mind.

"Carry me." A speech, a compulsion, and instruction and a way. The three felt it and felt despair for they knew the truth of themselves.

"We are broken," they said. "The land of Crua has broken us."

The reply, when it came, was golden and glowing, it was a beseechment and a promise and a threat.

"We will renew."

28

Udinny

The trap was better set than any of us had given the Rai credit for, but how could any of us have known they would have Forestals on their side? For such a thing to happen was to flip the balances of our world, north become south, hot become cold, crownheads herd garaurs and women become men, which is not a thing I am particularly enjoying.

Maybe I should have expected something like this to happen, it seems the season for it.

The terror of having those mighty bows turned against us panicked many of Tanhir's Forestals. Even I, Udinny Pathfinder, who was the chosen warrior of Ranya, our finest god, and a person who had conquered death, felt a fear like few others I had ever known. I knew the power of the forestbow, I knew the distances it could kill at and that there was little defence but to hope the arrow missed.

Arrows whistled through the air. I saw Forestals simply standing, loosing arrows but unable to process that by being still they became targets. Easy prey for those brandishing their own weapons. Tanhir pulled me down into the grass. The sounds of battle all around us, shouting, screaming, the whistle of arrows cutting through the air.

"Why aren't we running, Tanhir?"

"They are poor archers," she hissed.

"But they are Forest—"

"Were," the word hard, cut off my speech and yet I felt a terrible sadness in her. "They were Forestals, what has been done to them means they no longer are." A scream, the hiss of a Hetton and I heard the roar of Rai fire. Tanhir pointed through the grass. "Crawl, that way," she said.

"But that is towards . . ."

"Do as I say if you want to live." I found myself transfixed, like a Histi caught in the rush of a spearmaw, unable to move unable to run. I knew the Hetton were out there, I had seen the terrible power of those creatures, how hard it was to stop even one of them and there had been four, five, maybe even six coming through the ranks of the enemy soldiers. To go toward them filled me with terror, I was not sure how many times I could die and still have Ranya's favour. Even though I am her favourite it is best not to tax a god too much.

"Why that way?" Her eyes widened, and I saw in them the reflection of my face, an old and craggy white-haired and bearded man, I saw her hatred of me.

"Because they are poor archers," she said again, as if that explained everything.

"They seem to be killing plenty of us." For a moment I thought Tanhir may strike me. Then she sighed.

"Crawl, I will explain if you move." She began to crawl and I followed, trying to keep up with her. Occasionally, as she spoke she would make us wait while fighting raged around us. Some of the Rai's forces had got among the archers and the infantry were engaged with them. Further from us I heard more screams, and knew the Hetton hunted. "Forestals," she hissed, her head constantly moving, watching, listening, "we train for one arrow one kill." I nodded. "These taken archers do not, they loose en masse."

"We did that," I told her, "at Harn." She nodded.

"Because you lacked skill," she said it offhandedly, and I felt affronted by that as we had fought hard to save Harn. Though it was also true, we had lacked skill.

"You only loose like that when you cannot be sure of hitting the target."

"Yes," I said, though it was grudging. I do not think she could tell for the hiss of grass we crawled through and the fear in my voice that the Hetton may find us.

"They did it to split us up, and I did not realise until too late."

"Why split us up?"

"Because with the Rai and good archers our forces were still equal when you take the lack of skill into account." She held up a hand, we stopped. Feet ran past us. Fighting. A grunt and a body fell. Feet moving away. "They scattered us, so the Hetton can hunt us down. One on one, we stand no chance. Together we may have done better. Concentrated our arrows." There was a bitterness there, an annoyance that she had not realised sooner.

"Then gather your people," I hissed back. She shook her head.

"No, those who have realised their intention was to scatter us will be hiding, those who have not will be leading the Hetton away." She glanced around, the grasses around us waved, calm, as if death did not stalk through them stinking and hissing. "We must use what space we have, someone must get back to Tall Sera," she said. "He has to know that we can be turned. That we have been."

"And you will sacrifice your people for that?" She nodded.

"I will sacrifice anything," she said, "for Woodhome." She grabbed my hand. "And know, if it comes to it, I will sacrifice you even though it will cost me everything I love." In that I saw the truth of her, how she loved Woodhome, what it stood for. A different way, and in that I felt a kinship – though I do not think she did or ever would for me – for just like Woodhome, I would, and have, died for Ranya who promises us better ways.

"So where do we go? What do we do?"

"We crawl," she said, "we keep quiet and we keep out of the way."

"Woodhome, Tanhir, is weeks away. We must pass the army about to lay siege to Jinnspire, we must pass the city itself, then get through Woodedge, Jinnwood and southern Wyrdwood. All the time they will be hunting us, the Hetton will follow us. They will find our tracks eventually and they do not need to rest." She nodded.

"So we make best speed," she said, "and we do not bypass Jinnspire or their army, we head for it."

"To a city under siege?"

"A city with a taffistone," she said, crawling onwards.

"But the network, Tall Sera said it is blocked."

"It is watched by our trion," said Tanhir, "I hope we can get their attention. And you are right, the Hetton will track us, but maybe we can lose them in among the tracks of their own army." I blinked. Slowed. Was she mad? To go into the army that hunted us?

I stopped.

"Tanhir—"

A searing, burning pain in my chest. Like ice that was at the same time on fire, penetrating my bones. I looked down to see a blade of blackened and cracked wood. It was coated in blood. My blood. Then it was swiftly withdrawn and all I could think at that moment was, "oh, I really do not want to die again."

Tanhir screamed "no!" It was a thing as much pain as fury, in the strike of that blade she saw her memories vanishing, all she had and loved being taken from her. She brought her bow up, an arrow to the string. Drawing it fully taut and loosing at short range. I saw more than my eyes could show me, as if I hovered above. I knew the blade in me was a Hetton blade, I knew the creature behind me raised it for the final blow, to cut down into my body and extinguish what of Udinny was left after the first thrust of that cruel black blade. I tasted the Hetton, its being, a terrible hunger that would never go away. It was like a Rai that had spent all its power. Hollow. Desperate to fill a void within but unlike the Rai it never could, no matter how much life it took it would never be full. It was like a pot with a hole in it. What was poured in drained right out.

The blow never fell.

The crownhead who had followed me, that loyal and beautiful crownhead, leapt up, butting the Hetton and pushing away. The Hetton's blade cut it down in return. Tanhir's first arrow knocked it back again, her second too, and she drew and loosed with such speed and anger that the Hetton never had a chance. She did it with such single-minded fury that she never saw the second Hetton, coming up on her from behind, spear in hand.

How I knew all this. How I saw all this?

Maybe because I was so near to death, in that moment I knew something more of the body I inhabited, the priest of murder. I felt the power of the cowl within and it knew death, it recognised the nearness and for the first time it reached out. It had begun to know me. Had I been an intruder up to this point? An unwelcome occupant? Did it blame me for the loss of the mind it had always known?

I do not know.

All I know is I saw and knew so much all at once.

That in that moment, the cowl within chose to lend Udinny Pathfinder, warrior of Ranya, a little strength and I launched myself from the ground. Hit Tanhir in the centre of her body and we fell, rolling into the long grass and the spear meant to skewer her found only air. With every roll she shouted and screamed and cursed in the name of every forgotten god there ever was. Then we were up, the strength from the cowl leaving me whole and fixed once more, and Tanhir drawing the bow again. Not enough time, the Hetton quick as water over a leaf, was on her and she was forced to spin the staff of her bow, using it to knock away a spear thrust. She was fast, blessed with the cowl of the Forestals, but not as fast as the Hetton. Had she stepped back, she could have fought better, but she did not. She stood over me like a garaur protecting its nest. Refusing to step back, to move, for even though she hated my body, she loved the memories that were tied to it.

It was no way to fight a Hetton, and I think she had given up, decided to let her end come before mine. At least die with her memories intact. Let the burden of taking the news of her people being twisted fall upon other shoulders.

But it was not my day to die, it was not hers. Ranya yet had a path for us to walk. Fire leapt from the tall grasses, curling around the Hetton, consuming it and it screamed in a thin, reedy voice as it batted at its own flesh. From behind it came Rai Tassa and Rai Ustiore, arms outstretched to burn the thing. Tassa had an arrow through his chest and Ustiore's armour was rent and scratched from spear and sword thrusts. As the Hetton died Ustiore let her hand fall, leaving Tassa to finish the thing off.

"We must run," said Ustiore. "North, away."

"We cannot run," said Tanhir, "they will hunt us down."

"No," said Ustiore, the fire from Tassa's hands died away. "Look," she pointed. We followed the direction, saw what she saw. The force that had attacked us had split, following the mixture of soldiers and Forestals, tracking them down like garaur after lone crownheads. "We go now. We stand a chance."

"South," said Tanhir. "We go south."

"There is nothing south but an army," said Ustiore, "only a fool would go south."

"There is Jinnspire."

"A city about to fall."

"We can hide within their army, gather information and then I can get us away from within Jinnspire," said Tanhir.

"Out from Jinnspire?" Ustiore spat the words, "how would we even get in? Those chasing us will reform. You have not seen the army of Zorir, it is vast and full of Hetton and the collared." She looked over at Tassa who said nothing, only returned her stare. "And unless you have forgotten, we are Rai of Tarl-an-Gig, do you know what they will do to us in Jinnspire? What we have done to them? Can you imagine the vengeance they will take? Go south if you must, we go north."

A mistake to split up, I knew it. For so many years Rai had been the enemy but access to their power, and just the fact they were Rai may be what got us through the army about to besiege Jinnspire. On the other hand, they may be right about what would happen to them if we got into the city.

"I think I have a way for you to be safe, Rai," I said.

"What is your plan, monk?" Tanhir pulled me down. The Rai, after a moment, also knelt and we hid in the grass.

"These Rai are still young, it is only their armour that gives them away." The Rai were staring at me, it was second nature for them to wear the clothes of their power, to think nothing of it. To be Rai was all they had ever wished for, all they could think of being. "Keep the armour for now, it may help us get past the army. Then we steal some clothes and you, and we, can become soldiers or traders or what-ever it is that will let us blend in when we enter Jinnspire." Ustiore looked at Tassa and the man shrugged.

"They will be hunting in the grasslands for us, not in their own army," he said.

A pause, then the Rai nodded. "The monk may be right," she said.

"What of Ganri?" said Tassa, he bled from his mouth as he spoke because of the arrow in his chest. In answer Ustiore shook her head and Tassa stared at the ground.

"To Jinnspire then," said Tanhir, "and we make the best speed we can."

And so, once more we walked upon Ranya's path, knowing not where it would lead us, only that we must journey upon it.

29

Sorha

Sorha could no longer see the Reborn as they were surrounded, but she knew they still fought as she could hear them. Though even they would eventually fall under the numbers brought against them.

She was ready to die, here, today, now.

Since the moment she had set off to save Frina she had been ready to die, realistic about the chances of going into Tiltspire, of walking under the shadow of a god to steal what was theirs from them. Only a fool would expect to walk away unharmed, and she was sure those who had come with her knew the same. They were warriors, maybe not warriors by choice like her, no, the Osere's martial prowess had been forced upon them by the first ripples of the creature that squatted above her on its black pyramid. The one whose cold soldiers, stinking Hetton and frightened guards were approaching right now and she, Sorha Mac-Hean, who had spent so much of her long, long life thinking only of herself, thought this was not such a bad way to die.

It would mean something.

"Come taste my blade!" she shouted it, felt a fierce

joy in the challenge, in the way the guards of the spire paused in their advance.

But the collared, and the Hetton? They did not pause.

"Be ready to run," she whispered, hoping the Osere heard her, sure they would hear her. "I will buy you what time I can." Shield and sword, lived by them, ready to die by them. Ready to take as many as she could with her. Going out of the world in blood.

Then a change. Something in the air.

"Sorha!" A single word, a hand on her arm and she was pulled away from the violence of the courtyard and into the taffistone. The world behind her vanishing. Another chance at life gifted to her.

This was not a transit like those before. Not an instantaneous movement from one place to another. This was to be caught in a storm, to fall from a tree and hit every branch on the way down. Colours whirled around her. She felt her mind being ripped away from her body, felt the same of the Osere around her. There were others here. Other voices and personalities, some of which she felt were familiar and some were not familiar at all. They twisted, they spun, they moved. She was delirious, fevered. Something tried to touch her, to run unfamiliar senses over a body she felt oddly detached from. It repulsed her. She pushed it away and it overpowered her. She was flooded with repulsion again. With familiar unwelcome feelings.

She was back, back in the days just after Harn when Cahan du-Nahere had stolen her power, burned out her cowl and she was nothing. What touched her, what intruded upon her found the still smouldering kernel of hate inside, it fanned it, beat at it and enflamed it. Bathed Sorha in fury, in a desire for vengeance and for a moment she gloried in it. Remembered what it was to be Rai, to be filled with fire.

But she was a warrior, and she had fought this battle and knew this for what it was. She recognised this touch, the god, the creature. This was another fight with the enemy, a touch upon her to promise what the worst of her desired. No words, but still the message was the same, "serve me, and I will give you what you want." But the thing that touched her, it did not understand her, and as she swirled around in the colours and the strangeness of the place between here and there in the taffistone she found herself screaming into this voice, "Come taste my blade!" for this was the fight, and she had committed to it. She had been ready to die for Frina, ready to die for the Osere and would not simply give in now, or ever.

Out.

Nausea flowing through her. The colours gone. Replaced by an almost total darkness. A familiar smell in the air, old fire, strange stone. Her hands touching a ground of millions of tiny black beads.

"I am beneath?" she said to herself, then looked around for those she had been with but of course she saw nothing. The blackness was total and would remain so until her eyes accustomed themselves to the weak glow of the mushrooms that grew here, even then she would see little. She needed fire.

"Frina?"

"Here." A warm hand on her arm.

"Are we in Osereud? In your home?"

"Yes, I think it."

"How? The way was blocked, you said the way was blocked."

"It opened," said Frina in a whisper. Sorha bit back a reply, to snap would not help and even if Frina could explain Sorha doubted she understood enough of the Osere language to follow what was said. "Not only us."

"What?"

"Quiet," said Frina.

Sorha looked around, felt a fool as she was as good as blind here, but it was such a part of her she could not do anything else.

"Others came," she could barely hear the Osere leader's voice.

"What others? Where?" Had the enemy followed? The thought of the Hetton down here, stalking through the darkness filled her with fear, she felt sure they would not need to see, there was something of the night about them. Something past normal senses, the same for the collared. "They followed us?"

"No," said Frina, "came with us, from another place." She heard a noise, something she recognised as frustration in the Osere, where the words she needed would not come. "The opener, they came with them."

"Who is there?" a voice out in the darkness. "Show yourself, we are armed!"

It did not sound like the collared, and definitely not the Hetton. Could it be soldiers?

"I said show yourselves!" A voice used to being obeyed, but unable to hide the dismay at where they had found themselves. Someone from Crua no doubt, she knew what they were feeling, remembered first arriving here. How strange it sounded when you shouted, the complete lack of other noise to soak up your words, how it felt like they went on forever.

"Frina," she whispered, "do you know where in your world we are?" All Sorha knew was that they were not at Anjiin. She would have felt the walls of the buildings, heard sound bouncing off them and the last time she had seen Anjiin it had been lit up, strange power flowing from above.

"No, must scout, find markers." Sorha nodded, another useless gesture.

"Show yourselves, cowards!" The voice in the darkness again, and Sorha knew they were scared. Remembered being scared herself when she had come round from the terrible wounds of the fall, lived because Cahan had protected her.

"We are here and mean no harm," she shouted back, felt Frina's hand on her arm tighten and knew it was the nature of the Osere to slip away in the darkness. They wanted to do what was natural to them, not confront these strangers, this new danger. "We came through the stone with you, which tells me you know its use. Are you Forestals?"

"Who asks?" they shouted back and Sorha used the voice to pinpoint where the speaker was, at the same time slowly and silently moving away from the place she had been when she spoke, wary of the skill of the Forestals with their great bows, knowing how fear could make people act rashly.

"I will tell you," she said, "but you must promise me not to act too quickly when you hear what I say." She moved again, noting the speaker did not move.

"Who are you? Where are we?" The fear more apparent in their voice now.

"When I first came here," she said, "I thought I had died."

"Answer my questions," fear moving toward anger, she could feel it growing in the darkness. With anger came danger.

"I will," she said, "but first I ask for trust when trust will be difficult to give."

"How can we trust when you dance around what is said?" She took a deep breath. One of them had to trust or they would be stuck here, but if they knew her, who she was, what she had done in the past, how would they react? There was little choice of course; to move forward someone must make the first move.

"Were you there when Cahan Du-Nahere came to save the woman Furin?"

"I was not, some with me were."

"You know what happened?"

"Yes." She moved again, not wanting to make herself an easy target, more worried that if an arrow was loosed at her it may hit Frina who clung onto her.

"Do you believe in change?" A long pause, the voice in the darkness had clearly not expected such a question in such a place.

"Given what has been happening in Crua, the things I have seen, it is hard not to."

"Then I hope you will let me speak, and not loose the arrow you hold."

"You can see down here?"

"No," she said softly, "I only know what I would do if I had a bow, and how I felt the first time I came here."

"Speak then."

"I was there when Cahan came to the Slowlands. I fought him on the bridge. I fell with him."

"Sorha!" That voice, she knew that voice and on recognising it felt any chance she had of talking to these people vanished. "You are Sorha, the Rai?"

It was the trion, Venn.

"Yes," she said. One word and she felt the focus of attention upon her. At any moment an arrow could come from the darkness and she could not blame them for it.

"She must die," the first voice.

"No." The voice of Venn. A shock to her. "We must listen to her. She knows what happened to Cahan. She came with us through the gate. She knows where we are. More is happening here than we know."

"Cahan is dead," said the first voice.

"Cahan is not dead," she said. "I went to Tiltspire to try and save him but it was not possible."

"You?" said the first speaker, "you hate him, why would you wish to save him?"

"That is why I asked you if you believed in change," she said. "I have changed in ways I can barely understand myself."

"All I have heard of you," said the first voice, "tells me you will lie and lie to save yourself."

"Wait," hissed Venn, and she imagined in the darkness,

a bow being gently pushed to point at the floor. "We should listen."

"She is Rai."

"Like the one who came with us down here?" That surprised her, the Forestals were with Rai? What could that mean? Crua was turning on its head.

"I have been moving, to stop you aiming at me," she said. "Now I will stop. I will put down my weapons and I will lie on the floor." She whispered to Frina, "go, but follow when I go with them. I will let you know when it is safe to approach." No answer, only the warmth of the Osere's hand leaving her arm. She raised her voice again. "Come, bind me, make me your prisoner and listen to what I have to say." She pulled off her sword, knelt on the black ground and then lay on her face. "Come," she said, "I will continue to talk so you may find me." She did, saying nothing of use, talking about the place, how strange it was, how she understood the way they must feel and they homed in on her. Bound her arms behind her back tightly enough to hurt. She heard another voice.

"She is the abomination, she should be killed." Rai, no doubting that.

"No," said Venn, "we need her."

"Why?" this was the first speaker.

"She knows this place," said Venn, "she knows what happened to Cahan." Rough hands pulled her over and made her sit. She felt bodies around her, felt their hate of her and then Venn spoke again, their voice was gentle despite what she had done to them, what she had been prepared to do to them so long ago.

"Tell us, Sorha, why we should trust you? What is this place and why have you brought us here through the taffi-stone." Why? She thought about that, some of the Osere had returned here and they had a purpose, had fate brought her back to assist them in it?

"I fell to this place before with Cahan and was sorely

hurt," she said. "He nursed me back to health in the darkness, he needed me and I needed him. The god, the thing that took him, what I am hid him from it."

"And what did you get out of this?" said Venn. "All you have ever done has been for yourself."

"True," she said softly. "But down here I saw the god, I saw what it had done, still did, to those who live here."

"There are people here?" said the man.

"Yes, and do not judge, this place is called Osereud, the people who live here call themselves the Osere."

"Creatures of darkness," hissed by a voice she did not know.

"No, they are not. They are only people. Different to us, but people. The gods, what we call gods," she said, "they are prisoners down here, the Osere kept them in their prisons until . . ."

" . . . they failed." No pity in that voice.

"Yes, and the price they have paid is terrible. Their people decimated by the bluevein, but we have all contributed to it. Our world is crumbling and we ignored it. Too obsessed with fighting each other while a dark god reached out through the cracks to find new servants."

"You hunted Venn and Cahan across Crua and you expect us to believe you have changed?" said the other voice. She did not think she could convince Forestals simply by talking.

"Believe I have changed or not," she said, "it does not matter, but Venn will tell you that I want to live. That thing up there, it makes people into its puppets and I will not be anyone's puppet." She expected some argument but it did not come and she wondered how much they already knew.

"The thing in Tiltspire," this was a Rai speaking, she could hear it in their voice, "you are saying there is more than one?"

"Yes," she told them, "there are many of them." Again,

she felt they knew something she did not. "But all hope is not lost," said Sorha, "these gods, they fought a war before and some fought with us. They are still down here. That is why the Osere wanted to return. Wyrdwood holds the old gods prisoner, they seek to free those who would help us." She could not help thinking what she said sounded like insanity, that if someone had come to her with this story she would have thought them mad. Killed them out of hand.

"Lower your bows," said the voice of the Forestal, "I would know more of these imprisoned gods."

30

Saradis

The Rai knelt before her, behind it stood four of the collared. In the back of her head she knew the Rai's name, knew their sex but she had pushed such concepts away. They were a servant of Zorir, to be swept away with all the other life when the god was ready, nothing else.

"Escaped?" she said softly. "This creature escaped?"

"Yes, Skua-Rai," they said and they did not look at her, did not dare raise their head and it made her smile as she sat on the uncomfortable throne.

"How?" Did the Rai shake? Did they tense? "Tell me this, Rai. Explain to me how a prisoner escapes from within Tiltspire, the centre of Zorir's power."

"Laha—"

"Do not blame Laha," she bit the words out. "He is a servant of Zorir, you are in charge of the prisons of Tiltspire." Silence as she waited and she savoured it, not that long since the Rai had enjoyed her discomfort.

"No one expected people to break into the prison, Skua-Rai," they said. "Especially not for such a creature. And the Reborn, they came to life, helped them" Again, the silence gathering. "We have recaptured them for you."

"It sounds to me like you guard my prisoners poorly."

"No." Was there panic in the Rai's voice? Was that what propelled the words out of their mouth at such speed? She had never heard Rai panic before, not until the last moments before the stone went in their neck. "We have guards, but none expected that anyone would come for such a creature, all thought the Reborn dead after what Laha did to . . ." lost for words, trying to describe his tortures, ". . . them." She waited, enjoying their discomfort and as much as she wanted to know about the creature she had thought it simply some misshaped product of Wyrdwood, brought to Tiltspire to sell and it had escaped. Plainly it was not. People did not break into the inner sanctum of a god to free some misbegotten Wyrdwood beast. What was special about it?

"The creature, describe it to me." The Rai glanced up at her: did they sense some opportunity? "It would please me to hear this." A nod from the Rai. They let out a long breath.

"It has the appearance of one of the people. It was not furred like a rootling but its skin was covered in some paint-like substance that could not be removed, it screamed when we tried. Most striking was it lacked eyes, where there should be eyes its head bulged."

"Was it intelligent, like one of the people?" she leaned forward, "or an animal, like a rootling?"

"I do not know," the Rai shrugged, "it could not speak to us, only made strange noises. Some of us thought it may be a language."

"And you?"

"I thought it a creature, not intelligent."

"Did you try to communicate?"

"Yes, Skua-Rai, but even when we tortured it the thing only screamed. It made no attempt to learn our words, or even our names."

"Interesting," she said, sitting back. "So you are sure it was not intelligent?"

"Yes." The familiar unearned confidence of the Rai in their voice.

"Tell me, Rai, did it wear clothes?" A long pause, as if they suspected a trap, which of course was right but it was too late to avoid it now.

"Yes, Skua-Rai," they said. "It did."

"How many forest creatures that you have come across wear clothes?" A long pause while she watched the Rai before her.

"Who knows what the forest does," they mumbled the words.

"Did it occur to you," said Saradis, and she let ice seep into her voice, "that the creature was intelligent enough not to communicate?" No answer. Of course it had not occurred to them. She would get no more going that way. "Tell me how it escaped."

"Inside help. One of our own betrayed us. They were helped by the abomination, Sorha, and more of the creatures."

"And they walked right past you," said Saradis, she was almost done with this one.

"No," a cry of desperation, they knew what waited those who failed her. "I discovered they were in the lower levels."

"And you did nothing."

"I . . ." their voice died away.

"Speak," she said. Nothing. The Rai only stared at the floor. "I said speak."

"You have forbidden me to talk of Laha."

"Then I unforbid it," she said. A nod.

"I was putting together a force to capture the incomers."

"And?"

"He stopped me."

"Explain."

"Laha wanted them herded to the courtyard. I do not know why." She thought on that, she would ask Laha, he waited for her now in one of the rooms to the side of the throne. She could feel him there, just like she could feel the presence of the god throbbing on top of the pyramid.

"Very well," she stood. Stared down at the Rai. Collar them? Or would they serve better for this scare, would they feel tied to her by mercy? A risk but it was a risk to set the stone in this Rai here and now. There was always the chance they could call fire, burn her. "Return to your place, Rai."

"Thank you, Skua-Rai," they said and they sounded grateful, pathetic and weak. She watched them leave. Once they were gone she went to Laha. Stopping by one of the collared. "Collar the Rai who just left as soon as you can." They nodded, and closed their eyes, sharing the message with the rest of them.

Laha stood before a chair, still as rock, looking at it as if he no longer understood the function of such a thing.

"Laha," she said, and he turned, his skin alive with blue lights that ran over it in flashing lines, "it seems I have you to blame for this creature escaping."

"They were wanted," said Laha, the words little more than breath.

"By Zorir?" Only a stare in reply, though that in itself she took as assent. "Why steer them towards taffistones now we know how they work?"

"Blocked."

"It plainly was not."

"The needed one intervened." His eyes sparkled as he spoke, and she wondered how much of the Laha she had known remained. Every day there was less of him. Was the man before her just a shell serving Zorir now? A thrill ran through her at the idea that she was talking directly with her god.

"The needed one? Do you mean the trion Venn?" A nod. "Do you know where they are?"

"Below Wyrdwood."

"Below Wyrdwood?" He did not move, eyes unfocused

though the blue lights of his skin were momentarily brighter.

"Below now, to go above." Saradis considered those words for a moment.

"They are below now, but will be in Wyrdwood at another time?"

"Yes," the word long, drawn out.

"I can send people below," she said, "I presume that is where the stair down the edge of the pyramid leads?"

"Do not."

"Very well, then I will continue to prepare for the assault on the Forestal city?"

"Yes."

"What of the others who went below? What will happen to them?" Laha's answer when it came was simple, matter-of-fact.

"They will die."

31

Venn

It was getting harder to move between stones.

Where before it had been instantaneous, this time it was not. Part of Venn thought it might be that two stones were open at the same time, the one in Wyrdwood where they were, and the other, far away. They did not really believe that. Surely whatever had created the network would have allowed for such a thing. No, what was causing the problems was the god risen in Tiltspire. The touch of blue, the corruption of the network as it sought to find a way in and with that knowledge came more. Venn knew the second stone had opened in Tiltspire, that part of the difficulty came from that, the nearness of the god, its strength was concentrated there.

All this understood while they transitioned from one place to another. Venn could have taken control, forced where they went but it would have taken time and they did not have time. The god of this wood was almost upon them. The god in Tiltspire was using the second stone, forcing its way in, the nearness giving it an opening. Then something happened, it was thrown back. The door closed. They were denied.

The place they headed pulled at them, an alien will and yet not one that threatened them, and like a leaf falling from the tree Venn let themselves be pulled, let this strange breeze drag them and all those with them to a new destination. As they fell, Venn left the touch of Zorir behind but felt its intention. The creature in Tiltspire was impatient: if it could not find a way in then it would try to destroy the network.

"Twisting in the strange currents of this between place. They heard laughter, a child's delighted laughter. Furin was torn away from them, pulled toward Woodhome. Venn tried to follow but the way was swiftly shut off. Descending, always descending . . ."

They heard screaming.

Never heard a sound in the between of the stones before.

Then they were out, ejected and falling, not walking from one place to another, thrown out of the place that was not a place.

Am I dead?

The first thought.

Such complete darkness.

"I cannot see!" from close by.

"I am blinded." A different voice.

"No," said Venn, "it is just dark."

"Where are the lights? The forest is always bright in the night."

"Smell the air," Tall Sera, Venn was sure of it, "this is not the forest. Where have you brought us to, Venn?"

"I do not—" something more came through the stone, more people. Venn felt them, knew them as different but the same. This whole place, different but the same. Venn did not understand. Voices, back and forth in the darkness. A name, Frina, not one Venn knew.

"Who is there?" Tall Sera shouting in reply to the voice in the darkness. "Show yourself, we are armed!" The creak of bows being drawn. Venn listening. Those out in the darkness replied and they could barely believe what they heard. Worse, they knew that voice. But how? How could she be here? The monster, the one who had taken Cahan. Who was driven by hate and pain. No, it could not be her. It could not. As the voices bounced back and forward, somehow duller than voices usually were, like the darkness ate them up, absorbed them, Venn became more and more sure it was definitely her. Sorha.

Though not her as well. Different somehow, something in her voice was not the same. An illusion of this place? A trick because she kept moving to stop the Forestals tracking her with bows?

They did not know.

"Who are you? Where are we?" There was fear in Tall Sera's voice now. Venn had never heard him sound frightened.

"When I first came here," said the other voice, "I thought I had died."

"Answer my questions." Tall Sera's fear twisting, becoming anger. Frustration at being in this place where what he relied on all his life, his sight, was denied him. Venn moved toward Tall Sera. Something of the way this maybe-Sorha spoke made them think they knew this place. They were calm, too calm for a first time in a land that plunged you into such total darkness. Venn had an advantage here, their cowl let them feel detail of the world around them, the Forestals the Rai that had moved with them. It was Sorha, they could feel nothing from where her voice came. She was an absence.

What if it was some trick of this alien land, what if it was someone with a similar voice, or a skinfetch? But why would a skinfetch come as someone Venn feared?

"I will," it was her, it was definitely her, "but first I ask for trust, when trust will be difficult to give." She asked for trust? A trick, it had to be trick. She had never shown anything but hate but there was that small voice in Venn's head, telling them she sounded different in a way they could not put their finger on. "Were you there when Cahan Du-Nahere came to save the woman Furin?" she said.

Yes, thought Venn, I know what happened.

"I was not, some with me were," said Tall Sera.

"You know what happened?"

"Yes." She was moving again and Venn was putting all they had into listening to her, really listening, trying to hear past what was said to what was meant, what she felt, what she planned. "Do you believe in change?" A strange question for her to ask. Tall Sera's reply, when it came, was equally unexpected, as if by asking that question she had opened up a train of thought he had been chewing over himself.

"Given what has been happening in Crua, the things I have seen recently, it is hard not to."

"Then I hope you will let me speak, and not loose the arrow you hold."

"You can see down here?"

"No," came the soft reply, "I only know what I would do if I had a bow, and how I felt the first time I came down here."

"Speak then." Venn found themselves desperate to hear, and starting to think that they needed this woman, even if it was Sorha, she had been here before and this talk of change. All was change. Change was the only sure thing on Ranya's path. Did she walk the path?

"I was there when Cahan came to the Slowlands." Her voice slow, hesitant. "I fought him on the bridge. I fell with him."

"Sorha!" Venn surprised themselves with the outburst but needed this final confirmation. "You are Sorha, the Rai?"

"Yes," she said. Venn heard Tall Sera draw, put out a hand, their cowl letting them find the arm of the Forestal. Hold him when he would have loosed the arrow.

"She must die." Tall Sera sounded implacable, but in this place, in this darkness Venn felt something within them that glowed, a hidden knowledge that came from the web of Ranya, the web that touched all things. Not a certainty, so vague it could be they imagined it, but they listened.

"No." Venn felt Tall Sera's muscles tense beneath their hand. "We must listen to her. She knows what happened to Cahan."

"He is dead," said Tall Sera, it was final.

"Cahan is not dead," she said, and at that something soared within Venn. They were right, they had believed that also. "I went to Tilt to try and save him but it was not possible."

"You?" said Tall Sera, "you hate him, why would you wish to save him?"

"That is why I asked you if you believed in change," she said. "I have changed in ways I can barely understand myself."

"All I have heard of you," said Tall Sera, "tells me you will lie and lie to save yourself."

"Wait," hissed Venn, and they pushed down Tall Sera's bow, so the arrow pointed at the floor. "We should listen."

Then it moved quickly, tales of gods and the underground and things that sounded so fantastic Venn could barely believe a word of it. Yet here they were, in the darkness. Sorha let herself be bound and held and all she did while she was bound was beg for the safety of those she was with.

"Do not be scared of them, they are different is all," she said. "But they stand with us, many have died in a war we never knew was happening." Circling back to repeat. "Do not be scared, they are only different."

Venn did not know if Tall Sera believed her. He made no move to release her, only looked down at her in the flickering glow of a torch one of the Forestals had brought with them. Even that light felt somehow dimmed in this strange place. It was as if the darkness absorbed the light.

"Sorha," said Venn, looking down at her. She was smaller than they remembered, though by no means diminished even though she was bound. There was a pride to her that she held tight, as if it were as much part of her as her arms or legs. "Do you know me, Sorha?"

"Venn," she said with a nod. "The cowled trion. It must be hard for you to stand so close to me."

"No," they said, and realised they had never thought of that, they knew it was difficult for a cowl user to be near her, what she was stopped them being them. But it did not affect Venn, had never affected them. The Forestals either. "I am different to the Rai," they said, looked around though they could see nothing outside the circle of torchlight. "The Forestals, too, they do not seem affected by you."

"They have cowls?" she sounded genuinely surprised.

"Yes," said Venn, "they do. And trion. They work differently, with the forest and the world, not against it."

"Like the Osere," said Sorha to herself.

"I do not think Tall Sera believes they exist."

"Why would I make them up?" she said. Then laughed to herself, "Though I suppose I have never given any of you reason to trust me before."

"Where are they?"

"Out there," she nodded into the darkness, "waiting for me to tell them it is safe to come in."

"Can I meet them?"

"Why would you want to?"

"Because we are at an impasse. I do not think Tall Sera believes your stories of Osere and he does not trust you. He thinks this all some form of trick, even the darkness."

"If I was that powerful I would not be kneeling here bound."

"He thinks you work with Saradis and her Cowl-Rai." Venn did not believe Tall Sera thought that, but it made enough sense to use in the moment. "They do not know how much power that gives you." Sorha laughed.

"None, as far I know. Saradis has the power and it comes from her god, the Cowl-Rai is never seen." Venn stayed silent, thinking about that.

"And the god has Cahan, why do you think he is still alive?" Venn found themselves confused, because this was not the Sorha they had known before. That woman was sneering, sure of herself, cruel and hard. This woman was hard, there was no doubt of it, but the sneering was gone, and though Venn could not speak to her cruelty, the hardness they had seen in her before was less, as if her sharp edges had been worn off.

"Because it hunted him," she said. "It was focused entirely on him. What happened, before we fell, it infected him. If it wanted him dead that would have been easy for it. But it wanted him alive. The Osere tell us the gods were cut off from the land, the bluevein, it is a way for them to reconnect but even that does not work well." She looked up at Venn. "It needed Cahan, to start the process of rising from below, to sap his power? I do not know. But as we are not all dancing to its tune yet then he cannot be enough." Something cold slithered down Venn's spine.

"It needs me," they said and Sorha nodded.

"I think so. Saradis wanted you for the Cowl-Rai, but they are all in the thrall of Zorir. Tarl-an-Gig was a fiction."

"I am a conduit," said Venn softly. "That is why it wants me, Cahan may give it power, brute force, but I think I am still a bridge between him and the land. In Harn, Cahan was the power, Udinny the knowledge and I was the conduit. Cahan still has power, it has knowledge. Only the conduit is left."

"Then," said Sorha, "and I do not say this with the intention of scaring you, only because it must be said, you are a danger to all those who stand with you. The creature will not stop until it has you."

"What does it want?"

"I do not know," said Sorha. "Power? Control? Isn't that

what all want, the Rai, your Forestals, what I wanted? It is what drives us to be our worst selves. But if you let the Osere help, there are other gods down here in Osereud, ones that will oppose Zorir, that opposed its kind before."

"Then I would meet these Osere." A voice from behind them. Tall Sera walking into the light.

"You have been listening?" said Venn.

"Hard not to," he said, "sound carries in this place."

"Can I trust you?" said Sorha and at that Tall Sera laughed.

"Should we not ask you that?"

"The Osere helped me when I was down here with Cahan, helped us both. They did not have to. They have been fighting against Zorir, for generations," she said softly. "They have given everything. As far as I know, those few with me are all that exists of their people. I will not risk you slaughtering them because they are different."

"They are what changed you," said Venn softly.

"They have been dying," said Sorha softly, "fighting a war with no expectation of thanks and if they had been successful no one would ever have known about their sacrifice." Again, that humourless laugh. "Something like that can make you re-evaluate yourself."

"Bring them in," said Tall Sera, "I cannot speak for the Rai who came with us, but they are unwilling to come anywhere near you and my people will continue to keep them away."

"A good decision, Tall Sera, you are wise to trust me."

"What makes you say that?"

"I risked my life to save the Osere from Tiltspire," said Sorha, "they are a loyal people and this is their place. They know how to fight in the darkness, how long do you think you would have lasted against them if they came for me?"

Much to Venn's surprise, Tall Sera laughed.

32

Dassit

She felt like she was waking from a hard night's drinking.

Everything hurt, her throat ached and her lips were cracked for want of water. Her shoulder felt like it was on fire, her skin like it was crawling off her body. At the same time she felt curiously disconnected from these sensations. She knew they were agonies and that they were hers, but she also felt one step away from them. Was it a side effect of the maw poison? Was this how it worked? At the end of your life did it give you the gift of no longer caring, stepping your consciousness away from the final agonising moments?

It sounded like something kind, and she thought it unlikely because Crua had never been a kind place, and besides, she had seen crownheads taken by maws, had heard them scream as the creatures spirited them away into the canopy and ate them alive. It did not seem to her that they were given a kind death. So why would she have one?

Another shiver of discomfort running through her and out beyond her which felt like a madness, sounded like a madness and maybe that was the poison? Madness, to lose all you were as you were eaten away by a predatory creature that could not even live off your flesh, would eventually discard your dying, bleeding body as distasteful. That sounded more like the Crua she knew. To die in pain and in madness and Broken Iftal she was thirsty and it was dark and she didn't want to die alone in the dark.

Then open your eyes.

Yes.

She should do that.

A flood of visions in her mind. Of her. Of Ania. Of Ont. A shared history and in her mind she was as much them as she was her. Her father, huge and domineering. Her brother Channifer slowly slipping away. A village burning. A spire city falling to an army. A new life among the trees. Flashes so quick she barely had time to see them, shared lives she did not know and at the same time she did. Thoughts like the fruiting bells of fungi, showing above the ground when so much more was buried far deeper.

Golden cities. Tiltspire and Jinnspire and Harnspire. Washes of numbers she did not understand. The screaming of gods. Visions of a huge glowing star of Iftal floating in darkness.

What was this?

She did not know. The thoughts receded like water soaking into ground and unless you put your hand upon it you would not know it was there. Unless she pushed she did not know her world had changed.

Not that it mattered, because she was dying. Her shoulder was rotting, no one came back from that.

The Boughry.

What had they said, they would renew?

She did not understand what that meant.

Maybe she would die and her body would feed the forest. Was that to be renewed in the minds of creatures such as the Boughry?

Open your eyes.

Was that her voice? Or their voice?

Opening her eyes should be easy. Should be simple but she felt like a baby, the poison had taken something from her and she could no longer make her body obey her. It would be much simpler, easier, to lie down and die, to give up.

No.

Her voice or another's? She did not know. It was determined, incredibly determined. Angry, also sad. Three parts to it. Her and him and her. What was happening.

Open your eyes.

She put all she had into it. That one thought. Open your eyes. Our eyes. Open *my* eyes. Not a thought from outside, a thought from inside, her thought, her will, her body. It would do as she commanded. If she was going to die, then she would watch death coming at her. All her life she had been a soldier, she had watched the enemy come at her, knew it held death on a hundred sharp wooden spears and she had never looked away. She would not look away now.

I will open my eyes.

Slowly, she did, first slits of light, then greens and browns, swimming and changing in her vision. Something wrong, even in this first bleary look at the world. What? The browns and the greens were the wrong way round. Upside down. Was she upside down? She did not feel upside down, no blood rushing to her head, no sense of the world being turned over. She was not upside down. A moment of increased blurriness and the image righted itself. She fought to understand it. Ground, something on the ground, a light brown. Darkness, and green, the huge bushes of Wyrdwood slowly coming into focus. Slowly becoming the world she knew.

No Boughry. Huge mushrooms, slender yellow stalks, red gills. Beautiful, she tried to turn her head to look at them but it would not move. Something else wrong.

On her side. She was on her side.

Odd that she should not have realised such a thing, but something was wrong even with that thought. Too high up to be on her side. Was she lying on something? Thirsty. She tried to move. Couldn't.

What was she looking at? A blur. It took concentration to make her eyes focus on any one thing. She had to make herself see it.

A figure. A huge figure. It looked like a man, a giant man. Bushes and grasses and mushrooms grew around it. A statue? It had clearly been there for a long time. A man but not a man. The face had a carved beard, it only had three fingers not four. Its proportions were not quite right, the legs too short, the arms too long, the head slightly too heavy looking for the thick body.

"What are you?" she thought and it was like an echo, the same thought but not her voice.

Was it looking at her?

She really felt like it was looking at her.

Renewal, to be fed to this forest giant? Was that it?

No, it was a statue. Not real.

One of its hands moved, a twitch, almost as if the thing was sleeping and it dreamed.

Or a trick of the poison in her blood, a hallucination as she approached death.

She so desperately wanted to move, and to drink water and eat something. The thought of food made her stomach twist, hunger. Pain and nausea mixing together.

Food.

The statue twitched again. Unmistakable this time. Its whole arm moved, a jump, like muscles in sleep and then the arm slid to the floor. Her first instinct was to run. But she could not move.

Did it move because she thought of food?

No. How could that be?

Food.

The strangest thing, that in the word in her mind she heard Ont's voice, not hers. One of the things she knew about the scarred man was that the fire had stolen his sense of taste. He was a big man, but she sensed he had once been bigger, his burned skin had hung off him but sometimes he had spoken of food and when he had it had been with the relish of a man who enjoyed eating. He spoke not only of eating but cooking, of meat over fire, of flowing juices.

Food.

A definite sense of pleasure. The statues fingers twitched.

Ont?

Dassit?

That voice was not Ont. It had a different feel, a different timbre. More like –

Ania?

That was Ont.

We can hear each other.

A shared thought. A realisation of three people that were linked,

"Had . . ."

. . . the Boughry

. . . done that?

What was happening?

Something of the Boughry. That was definitely Ont.

We are not alone. And that Ania, she could hear her sneer, something more, a warning. *There are creatures here, huge.*

"I can see one too," she thought it, "like a man, lying on his side."

I also see them, Forest Men. Ont, maybe, she wished it was clearer who was speaking – thinking – at her. *But I see two.*

Ania – *I see only one.*

"I see only one. It moved when I thought of food." Strange, she had thought communication by thought should be clearer. Then it was.

Ont – *Oh, food. I am so hungry.*

The statue moved its hand, the three fingers opening and closing. A thought crept into her mind. An impossible thought, but what of her life recently had made her think anything could be impossible? Three statues. Three of them. Renewal.

"Ont, you can see."

Ont – *What?*

Ania – *He could see before, in the wood.* Dassit could almost see her face as she said that, the shake of her head as she thought it was something obvious, something Dassit and everyone should know.

"How well do you see, Ont?"

Ont – *It was . . . blurred. But now it is almost as clear as before the fire.* Joy in his voice but Dassit did not feel joy, she was frightened. *I can see. I did not even think about it. So much has happened and . . .*

"Did you move your arm, Ont?"

Ont – *I wanted to move.*

Ania – *Your hand?*

Ont – *Yes.*

So Dassit was not the only one thinking it.

The statues. The Forest Men.

Ania – *We are the statues.*

Ont – *How could that be?*

How could many things be? We were brought north for some purpose, the world is no longer a thing we can understand.

Ont – *How can a statue be hungry?*

Ania – *Or thirsty?*

"I am so thirsty."

Ont – *We are all thirsty.*

"Ania, you can see one statue? Ont, you can see two?"

Ania/Ont – *Yes.*

"So we are both looking at Ont. I think. Describe what you see, Ont?"

Ont − *Yes. I see . . .*

His words dissolved into vision. Two statues lying on their sides, heads close to each other. Plants and grasses twined around them, bushes growing over them, moss growing on them. They looked like sleeping people, the one opposite her, that she thought was Ont, had a beard but these did not. The faces were stylised, not like the faces of the people but ghosts of them. The same three-fingered hands, long arms, shorter legs, thick bodies.

Ont − *. . . and some sort of conical hat.*

Fear seized Dassit. Was she locked in this thing forever? Was this the Boughry's twisted idea of renewal? Some strange joke in their unknowable minds, three people locked in huge wooden bodies and left to starve? Her thoughts were running out of control, she could feel fear twining around her mind. This was worse than any battle, worse than the fear of wounds. Madness would come eventually, she only hoped it was before she starved, or would she just be eternally hungry and thirsty, would she—

Ania − *Ont moved.*

The words stalled her panic.

He moved.

Ania − *Ont, move again.*

The hand of the statue, blocky fingers opening and closing.

Ont − *I moved my hand.*

Ania − *I saw it. Now I will try and move. Say which of the statues moves.*

Dassit felt time passing, felt it acutely.

Ania − *It is difficult. Hard. I cannot move.*

Ont − *You will.* He sounded very calm. *Remember when I was first burned, when you helped me walk? The patience. The work. Maybe that is why I can move? I have been through this before with my own body? Maybe we have new bodies, and must learn to use them like children learn?*

Ania — *I cannot move!* Now she sounded on the edge of panic.

Ont — *You can. You will.*

The giant statue before Dassit shuddered, a hand moved up, clumsy, flailing, then smashed into the ground, sending up a fountain of dirt.

Ont — *I am strong.*

She could hear rumbling, the breaking of wood like branches stressed by the wind and the statue before her pushed itself up into a more comfortable sitting position. It sat like a child, legs stretched out and apart, hands flat on the ground, immovable face looking out at them with carved eyes.

Ont — *That was hard. I am tired.*

Ania — *Ont, it took you months to learn to work with your new body, we do not have months, I will starve or go mad or die of thirst or—*

"Ania!"

She shouted in her mind and arrested Ania's train of thought, the same panic that had been Dassit's a moment ago had infected Ania, and it made Dassit wonder, made her think that maybe what they were now was more than just one person.

"When Ont described what he saw, I looked through his eyes, was it the same for you?"

Ania — *Yes.*

"Then I have something I want to try. Ont, explain to us how you regained use of your body after you were burned."

Ont — *I do not know. It was not really conscious, it was just work and pain and —*

His voice faded away, and then came agony, excruciating pain that ran through every nerve in Dassit's body. The pain of a man who thought himself nothing, whose every nerve was burned, who had to learn, step by agonising step, how to move and how to walk and how to live. She wanted to scream but she could not. Ania the same. But part of Dassit was also happy, because with the wave of pain Ont had once suffered, came another wave.

Knowledge.

Knowing.

And now she understood.

Renewal.

33

Cahan

The scent of blood on the air, so strong he could almost taste it.

You cannot taste anything.

He could not remember the last time he had eaten or drunk or done any of the small acts that punctuated the life of every person in Crua. Still, the memory of blood, the taste of it on his tongue, felt real.

The fight was over. The fight would come again. Each time the enemy getting a little closer, the safe space shrinking a little. He had been fighting for ever. This was the first day of battle.

How could both things be true at the same time?

He fell to one knee, almost overcome with pain. The world around him, green and blue and red wavered and fell apart. A heartbeat where there was nothing but pain. Memories washing over him. Black tentacles in the darkness. The agony of strained muscles as he hung from a spike extruded from a black pyramid. The smell of the creature at the top, somehow cold. The strength of its intent, its need burning on his skin.

The horror of it, of being helpless, of knowing he was helpless.

I am with you.

The village preparing for another attack, villagers running to and fro. Some gathering arrows, some fixing damage from the last attack, some readying themselves for the next push. Some scared because they had never been in a fight before. This was the first day. This had been going on forever.

The people seemed thinner. Less real. The green glow around the buildings and the walls brighter. More noticeable.

Was this even real. Was he real? His shoulders ached, his chest ached but there were no wounds. It felt like there should be wounds. Panic surged within him. This was not real. Nothing was real. He couldn't breathe. Something was outside and he could not see it. He was trapped in a lie and he could not escape. He had to escape. He had to get out of here. Past the walls, past the blue glow of the Rai forces.

Maybe if he ran. If he scaled the walls, if he fought through the Rai, if he unleashed the power within him, ripped the life from the enemy to feed his cowl he could escape. Find what was real. Find what was happening.

What was happening?

He could feel the power within him, the same power was all around him. Different to the power out there. It was waiting, massive. If he embraced it, took it on, he could sweep away the armies coming against Harn, he could save all of these people. He would fear nothing, he would be stronger than he had ever been before if he just let it in.

This was familiar. Why?

No matter. His people should not suffer. The Rai would come again. He would reach out to the blue, open the gates for them and take the power.

I am with you.

The village was preparing for another attack, villagers

running to and fro. Some gathering arrows, some fixing damage from the last attack, some readying themselves for the next push. This was the first day. This had been going on forever.

The people seemed thinner, somehow. Less real. The green glow around the buildings and the walls brighter. More noticeable.

Was this even real? His shoulders ached, his chest ached but there were no wounds. It felt like there should be a wound. Panic surged within him. The blue, power was in the blue if he just . . . *I am with you.*

He could hear them in the forest, they were coming again and he was tired.

It would be easy to lie down, give in and accept the inevitability of it. There, in the green glow of Harn, he felt like he should, as if this was all futile, that he was fighting a battle he had already lost, doing something pointless. A madman, repeating the same actions every day in the hope something was different.

It was never different.

He walked to the wall, the villagers appearing around him, strange and faceless though he knew exactly who everyone was. He knew their shapes: there was a forager who knew the Woodedge. She had died in New Harnwood, on the spear of a Hetton and he had seen it. But she was here with him now and she would die on the wall of Harn, cut down by one of the Rai. By her was someone who Cahan thought was safe in Woodhome but here he would die behind the walls, caught on a thrown spear. Every single one of them was doomed, and would rise again and fight again. His mind stopped. He felt as though there was a gap there. As though there was a piece of knowledge that mattered and was somehow blocked, the same way the paths out of the village were blocked. In desperation he had tried to escape one night.

"We must leave," he said. Faceless faces turned to him,

a wall of blankness, of forms that vaguely resembled the people though when he saw them out of the corner of his eye he always knew them. If anything, when he only glimpsed them they had more detail, more quirks. Were more real than when he looked directly at him. They did not speak of course, they never spoke, never made a noise apart from at the end, when they cried out in death. "You will all come with me," he had told them. "We will all go." In the distance the blue, in the blue was power and if he had power then . . .

I am with you.

He fought a battle.

He had been fighting the battle as long as he could remember, there was nothing left but the fight – it was eternal. No, eternal was not its essence, it was not for ever, but it was his life and would continue to exist as long as he did. When the final battle came, when the forces arrayed against him finally overcame his, and that was an inevitability, then the battle and his life would end.

This felt familiar.

It does not matter.

The walls of Harn were strong, they surrounded him and provided an illusion of safety in the Harnwood. A subtle green glow marked their outlines, marked where there had been breaks and they had been filled and patched. Places where fire had scorched them and it had been put out and newer, wetter wood laid down to stop them being so easily burned again. The people had worked hard on them and remembering how they had come together made him smile. It had been a hard path to cut, there had been trials, fights and disagreements, they had struggled but in the end they had come together and that had made them strong and that strength held the enemy at bay.

But were they nearer, now, were there fewer people than there had been? He could not remember names and something about names, that mattered.

We wait.

But the people's strength was not eternal, the battles wore them away just as they wore him away. At the end of each fight the dead were taken back to longhouses and roundhouses to be worked upon within the green glow of the structures. Cahan never followed them in, someone had to stand guard. Someone had to be here, alert at all times because the Rai attacked without warning and without mercy.

And the central longhouse, the Leoric's longhouse – *something felt like it was stolen from him* – it frightened him because something waited in there. A gift, but the thought of it was too terrible to approach.

Someone worked miracles, and although Cahan never saw who he knew it was true, wounds that should have killed did not. Cahan watched villagers dragged away on the point of death, or inert and yet they always returned after time in the longhouse of Harn.

Someone had to be here, alert at all times because the Rai attacked without warning and without mercy.

He looked around, felt like there was something he had forgotten. Something he was missing. People who were missing.

It does not matter.

But it did not matter.

The fight, the fight would start soon. That mattered.

We hold.

I hold with you.

34

Udinny

What a strange and ragged group we were, making our way through the grasslands in a great looping circle back toward the same army that had not long ago tried to kill us and no doubt would do again. Tanhir had collected a uniform from a body we found to dress in, together with white face paint. She did not like the idea of wearing it. Worse, I had painted my lineage on her so I could claim she was my sister if anyone questioned us on it. Something Tanhir hated, but I think that was mostly because I had suggested it rather than because she thought the idea was actually bad. She was not the sort of person who put up with bad ideas, though she was the sort of person who enjoyed bad moods and was currently indulging herself, so was not speaking with me.

The two Rai were also poor companions. Tassa had removed the arrow that had gone right through his chest and was healing quickly in the way of Rai, but his cowl was beginning to hunger. I could see the need to feed it in his face, lines of tension running from the corner of his mouth, a clenching of the jaw and a hunger when he looked at me. Needless to say, he was not interested in conversation.

The leader, Ustiore, must hunger too, but she did not show it as clearly. Nevertheless, she was preoccupied. I think the idea of returning to the army she had just run from terrified her, or maybe it was the loss of her friend. I had never thought Rai had friends before.

I was not too pleased with the idea of slipping into an army that had hunted us myself, but no one had come up with a better idea so we were committed to mine no matter how bad it may be.

I wanted to talk but no one else did. As no other would talk to me on our journey I was forced to talk to myself, and by myself I do not really mean myself, I mean the cowl within me. It had moved to save me, before that I had barely been aware of its existence most of the time, I think – and this will sound foolish as all say the cowl serves the user, but I think it was unsure of me.

Natural, I suppose, if it was aware in some way. I had usurped the body of who it had known all its life, or his life. Now I was here instead, maybe it resented me. In turn I was frightened of it. What did it know but murder in Wyrdwood? That had been its life with Fandrai, and I most definitely was not going to continue that tradition.

Strange though, I did not feel a hunger from it like the Rai clearly felt. Maybe it was more akin to the cowls of the Forestals.

"Tanhir?" She did not reply, but that was not unusual. "Do you speak to your cowl, Tanhir?" She gave me a look that was all the answer I needed. Not only did she not speak to her cowl but she thought the whole idea of it ridiculous. Of course, people think many things are ridiculous, almost every person I met in my first life thought my worship of Ranya, may she guide my steps, a fool's errand.

Maybe I am a fool, but it has got me this far.

"Can you hear me, cowl?" I did not say it out loud of course, one can only take so many withering looks from Tanhir before it begins to grate on you. No answer. So I asked again. This time I thought I felt something. Not language, but contact. Wonder, curiosity, fear, resentment, all at once and not one of these feelings was the same way I would feel them. How do you explain that? To know something, to feel it as utterly alien to you but at the same time it is part of you. I think, without my experience in death, of touching Ranya, I would not have been able to understand the brief touch of the cowl. It was closest to communing with her bright spirit, though infinitely less bright – meaning without words, images without seeing, sound without hearing. "I am Udinny," I thought at it, "I did not ask to be in this body just as you did not ask me to be here. I am not even a man, though I am in a body which belonged to a man. What I am is a servant of Ranya, this is our path now and I ask you to walk it with me." No reply, nothing definite anyway. Maybe a feeling of contemplation. Of time moving, of seasons changing, of the possibility of fruits growing and blooming and the possibility of rot and death. All this so faint I could have imagined it. Still, I was keen to experiment more. After all we shared a body and as it seemed we were tied together we should find a way to work together. Though the same was true of Tanhir and that was not going as well as I could have hoped.

"Udinny!" Now Tanhir was talking to me.

"What?" She stood before a corpse.

"This one looks your size, and seems free of bluevein."

"What on earth are you talking about?"

"You have had us dress as their soldiers, but not yet done so yourself."

"I was a little distracted."

"Well, stop being so, we are near the army of Tarl-an-Gig now."

"How do you . . ." I stopped talking. I knew how she knew the army was near, you did not need a cowl or to reach out with some power. You could smell it. Rotten food and unwashed bodies, death and blood and too many of the people in one place.

"Put on the armour while I go have a look." I did as she asked, the uniform stank, and parts of it I could not use as the soldier had died of some sort of dysentery and there was no way to wash the clothing. Still, not all troops had full armour, and the cheap wood of the breastplate fitted well enough. Tanhir returned. I noticed she wore the armour of a soldier who had died of something less disgusting and had a breastplate and greaves. I put on my helmet, which did not fit well and fell over my eyes.

"We are nearer them than I thought," she said as she knelt down. Then she turned to the Rai. "How likely are you to be recognised?"

"We should be fine if we keep to the edges of the army," she said. "The collared keep to the centre, the remaining Rai, too."

"What about the Hetton?"

"Kept in cages, close to the food animals and the marant stables."

"I am not sure I would want to eat an animal that has been near Hetton," I said, "I cannot help thinking the stink of them would infect anything near."

"That is why they are kept there," said Tassa, "it discourages theft."

"Well," said Tanhir, "we avoid the stable areas, and the centre." She looked around the small group. "Anyone asks, Ustiore, we are your personal guard."

"No," said Ustiore, "better to bind your hands and say you are being taken for other Rai to feed off, as punishment."

"You are not binding me," hissed Tanhir.

"We are not important enough to have our own guard," she said. "It will attract attention."

"Tanhir," I said softly, "what she says makes sense. Look at us, we look like the worst soldiers in the army. No one would question us being given over to feed cowls." Tanhir sneered at me, looked away but she could not deny what was said.

"Very well, but loose binds, mind, and you leave us knives." Ustiore nodded. "What about my bow?" Silence. Ustiore looked the Forestal over.

"I could have a staff. The arrows though, we will have to leave them.

"You could claim them as trophies," said Tanhir.

"No Rai would touch them," she said. "They will quickly draw attention."

"They have archers now," I said, "maybe we can find arrows in the camp?"

Tanhir chewed on the inside of her mouth, then nodded and unstrung her bow. Passed it over to Ustiore. It was a hard thing for a Forestal to do.

"We make our way round the skirts of the army, gather as much information as we can, then we break for Jinnspire." She pointed. Jinnspire rose in the distance, tall and black and as strange to the land as every other spire, a place that was not of the people – though we used the spires happily enough. Well, the lower parts. "We need to get into the city with the minimum of fuss, we have to hope the gates are open and they are still letting in those fleeing the army. We will have to lose this armour," she looked over at the two Rai, "lose all of our armour."

"I need to feed my cowl," said Tassa, the words escaped his mouth in a rush.

"It will attract attention," said Ustiore, "you will have to bear it."

"No," this a bark. "You would understand if you were not so weak in the cowl. I need to feed it." It did not pass me that as he spoke he was looking hungrily from Tanhir to me. "Maybe we would be better—" Tanhir drew her knife.

"One more word, and your hunger ends here." Tassa's

eyes flared, and I thought he would attack Tanhir. Ustiore put a hand on his shoulder.

"A few hours, Tassa," she said, "and maybe we will come across an animal while we pass through the army. You can take that." She locked eyes with him. "Now is not the time to fight, or cause problems with allies." Such heavy emphasis on the word allies, as if she had to hammer home we were no longer fighting each other. "Especially those who have little enough reason to trust us already." Tassa grunted, stepped back, but the way he looked around, the light in his eyes made me wonder if he would obey her. Not someone I wanted to turn my back on, even for a moment.

Be careful here, Udinny, I told myself. Enemies are all around you.

Darkness was falling as we approached the vast army of Tarl-an-Gig, or Zorir, now, I suppose. The light above was falling behind the far away line of the southern Wyrdwood, setting the sky alight and below it the army rested. I have known a few armies, but none as subdued as this one.

"Who is there?" The voice of a picket, set to guard the rear. We expected that of course, but still it tightened up my stomach in a way that was most disagreeable.

"I am Rai Bellesan," said Ustiore, "sent out as part of the force to ambush the Forestals behind us. We got cut off from the others."

"I do not know you, Rai Bellesan," shouted the guard. Something barked out in the night, a lonely sound.

"And I do not know you, soldier, though you clearly take your job seriously. But why would I be coming here if I was an enemy, I would be running as far as I could before such a vast force." A moment of silence. Then a laugh from the darkness.

"Yes, only a fool with a death wish would stand against us, and I have never met a Rai that wanted to die. Come forward."

Ustiore, advanced, and we went with her, with every

step my stomach tightened further, was this another trap?
It could be. Who knew how this army worked now, or
what they knew.

"We must report back," said Ustiore, "point me toward
command if you would, soldier." The guard pointed back
and behind her.

"That way, though we're spread out some as we make
final camp, can't see them until morning, though."

"Why?" asked Ustiore. As she spoke I felt Tassa come
up behind me. The Rai stood far too close but there was
nowhere I could move to and get away from him. I felt his
breath on the back of my neck.

"When we camped before Jinnspire they put us on
curfew. Anyone found walking round after sunrise is taken
away." There was a dullness when she said "taken away",
the voice of a woman who had accepted something she
knew was terrible. "There's plenty of places to sleep among
the camp followers, and if you have a few splinters spare
you can buy food and companionship. But don't stray out
of the tail and into the main camp before the light rises,
not if you enjoy living."

"Thank you," said Ustiore, "we will stay in the tail
until morning." She gave the guard a nod and we walked
on, into the hustle and bustle of the army's supply tail.
The smell of cooking food and woodfire thick in the air.
Usually such places were raucous and noisy but not here.
Not even the tents of the companions were loud, the men
and women outside made a desultory pass at Ustiore as
we walked down the lines of tents but there was no effort
to it. No intention. It was as if everyone was worn out,
worn down. We found food, tough meat and a thin soup,
and ate before finding a tent and bedding down for the
night.

I do not know how hard it was for the others to sleep,
but it was easy for me. I have always found sleep a close
companion and the days walking and fighting had left

me tired beyond belief. As soon as I laid my head down I was out.

Until I was not.

Woken by the warmth of a body on mine. Its weight pinning me down. A hand over my mouth and the face of Tassa above me. A smile on his face, his eyes no longer human, lost entirely to the hunger of his cowl.

"Be quiet," he hissed, "this will not hurt."

I did not believe him, not for a moment.

35

Sorha

She was still bound, but they had let her stand.

At each side of her stood Forestals, blades drawn. Across from her, almost lost in the darkness, were the Rai and the soldiers who had come with the Forestals. Between them both stood the trion, Venn – clearly uncomfortable with both parties, and they were the only kind face here. Remarkable considering what she had done to them.

The Forestals hated her. It was an ancestral hate born from generations of war with the Rai and yet they had come here with the Rai, they had overcome their hatred. The Rai hated her, their hatred of her was a pure thing and she had no doubt that, given the chance, they would kill her. She was a direct threat to them simply by existing.

She laughed quietly to herself. Maybe she misunderstood the Forestals stood either side of her with drawn blades. Maybe they were not here to guard against her, but to protect her from the Rai. She was useful to them as much as she was a hindrance to the Rai.

"Call your friends, then," said Tall Sera, the light of the fire flickering over his face, distorting his features so she could not read his intention.

"I will," she said, "but hurt any of them, and these bonds will not save you."

"We have given our word," said Tall Sera.

"And them," said Sorha, nodding towards the Rai and knowing she did it more to poke the spearmaw with a stick than because she needed to ask.

"I am sure they do not want to be stuck down here," said Tall Sera, "and I have made it clear your friends may be the only thing that can offer them a way out." Sorha nodded. Then she whistled, and called out a few words in the language of the Osere. Waiting, squinting into the dark outside the circle of torchlight. Figures began to appear, not many, not all of them. Frina at their centre. They came in on the Forestal side, to her left, moving slowly into the fire, and as they did she heard muttering, shock, fear. Before anything was said, before the Rai or Tall Sera spoke, Venn stepped forward.

"Welcome, Osere," they said, "I am Venn." In halting, slow footsteps, the Osere made their way over to Venn, their blind heads constantly moving, reacting to the sounds of the people around the fire. They stopped before the trion. Frina touched her chest.

"Frina," she said. Then something in her own language.

"I am sorry," said Venn, "I do not speak your language."

"She wants to touch you," said Sorha.

"Why?" said Venn.

"I don't know, they have cowls, like the Forestals do and—"

"They are abominations, brought here by an abomination!" This from the Rai named Sunan. He stepped forward, lifting a hand as if to call fire.

"Stop!" shouted Tall Sera. Forestals raised their bows. The Osere froze in place. The fire never bloomed on the Rai's hands. His real intention unknown as he was too close to Sorha to call it.

"Do you not know the stories?" said the Rai. "These are

our ancestral enemies, they are darkness brought into being."

"You are my ancestral enemy," said Tall Sera and there was no mistaking the tenor of his voice, the potential for violence in his words, "and yet I have not ordered you filled with arrows."

"They are in league with what hunted us in the forest," said the Rai, and she knew he was scared, which gave her a strange joy.

"Sorha says they are not."

"And she is an abomination."

"To you," said Tall Sera, his voice as cold as the north of Crua, "lower your hand."

"You will regret this," said the Rai. Sorha could not tell if it was a threat or if the Rai believed it a prophecy.

"Or I may not," said Tall Sera, "but right now I am in charge, or," he pointed out into the darkness, "you can go your own way if you wish."

The Rai stepped back. "On your head be it." All this, the Osere took in, head turning from one speaker to another, understanding tone even though they may not understand every word. When there was a silence, a hole in the darkness, Frina spoke again. The same words, aimed at Venn.

"Yes," said Venn, and they nodded. Frina put out a hand, closing it around the bare skin of Venn's arm. The trion went stiff, every muscle in their body tensing. Bows changed their aim from the Rai to the Osere.

"Wait!" shouted Sorha, "just wait. They will not hurt them. They do not hurt anyone outside of the Betrayers. Just wait." The bows quivered but the arrows did not fly and the darkness remained silent. All eyes focused on the Osere and Venn.

"Yes," said Venn softly, "I see now." Frina let go. Venn looked around. "We must go north."

"You spoke with it?" said the Rai.

"Her," said Venn softly, "I spoke with her. Cowl to cowl."

Tall Sera cocked his head, something new to him clearly. "The forest, we have to go to the forest."

"There are forests here?" said Tall Sera.

"In a way," Sorha said.

"How far are they?" asked the Rai, their soldiers gathering around them.

"Distance," said Sorha, "is different down here. We used taffistones before, but I do not know if we can now."

"I can help with that," said Venn softly.

"Then we should move," said Tall Sera, "I do not like it here, I wish to be away as soon as possible."

"Good," said Sorha. A shout from the darkness cut her words off. A word that meant nothing to most around the fire but Sorha understood it, as did Frina. Everything about her changed in that moment.

"Cut me loose," she said.

"Why?"

"The Betrayers," said Sorha, "they are coming."

"Who?" She felt Tall Sera's attention on her.

"They are the collared of the Osere." From the other side of the fire she heard the Rai shout out. "Form a line!" Tall Sera towered over her and she wondered what he would do, what would happen to her. Did he think she had set this up? Frina and the Osere were spreading out.

"No," she shouted, "no lines spread out, lines make you an easy target down here!"

"Ignore the abomination!" shouted the Rai, "shields up!" Tall Sera moved behind her, she heard the drawing of a knife. Felt a moment of fear, and once more hated this new emotion.

"Do as she says," shouted Tall Sera, and he cut her bonds.

"You trust me?" she whispered, trying to look back at him.

"I see your companions doing what you said," then he leaned in closer, "and I need you to keep that Rai in line." He pulled her up and gave her back her sword.

"Stay quiet," she said, "the fact you can see and you have a bow gives you a huge advantage. Watch for the glow. They glow."

A sound. A low mournful howl that twisted through the darkness, giving it a cold and gelid form that crawled across Sorha's skin; made her hand tremble. She gripped her sword tighter. From the soldiers of the Rai came a returning shout. A-HA! And they slammed their spears into their shields. In the weak flicker of torchlight she saw the Osere move away from them.

"He is going to get them all killed."

"Why?" said Tall Sera.

"They hunt by sound." Tall Sera nodded.

"Venn," he hissed, "stay close to me." The trion moved nearer to the Forestal and she could see the worry on their face. Bad enough to be down here and armed, the trion carried nothing but a stick. She could not save Cahan, he was lost to her, but she owed him a debt for saving her life. She would protect the trion. It was what the forester would have done.

What she would do.

The low moan rose again, like the wind, though the creatures down here would never know it. In the distance she saw the glow, weak enough that it could be her imagination. She pointed, Tall Sera nodded at her. Lifted his bow.

Again, the hammer of spears on shields from the Rai. The moan grew in intensity. Sorha felt a touch on her arm and found Frina there. The Osere pointed away from where the noise was coming from. A gentle whisper of words that Sorha barely understood.

"What does she say?" whispered Tall Sera. The drumming of spear on shield rising in volume. The soldiers shouting defiance into the darkness.

"A taffistone," she said, "that way, it is where we need to go but she is not sure it will work."

"I can make it work," said Venn.

"Then we must move," said Tall Sera.

"They will hear," said Sorha. "Silence is the best defence."

"They are many," said Frina. The drumming of spears on shields.

"We need to help the Rai," said Venn, "Sorha says they bring death upon themselves and we may need their numbers." Another noise out in the darkness, weaving in and out of the mournful howl, a roar. It reverberated through the air, shook the ground, made every hair on Sorha's body stand up.

"The thing from the forest," said Venn, "it is here." Tall Sera nodded and even in the dim light of the torch Sorha knew he was frightened.

"We go," said Tall Sera, "if there is an army and one of those tentacled beasts, we must escape. The Rai will be our distraction."

"But they will die," said Venn.

"Better them than us," said Sorha and she took their arm gently in her hand as the air filled with the moans of the Betrayers and the beat of spear on shield and the roar of the creature out in the darkness.

"Cahan sacrificed all for those he cared for," she hissed to Venn, "and I will protect you in his name, so stay close. If the thing out there is anything like the god, it cannot see you if you are with me."

"You talk like it wants me." She almost laughed, then she did, it escaped from her mouth in a bubble of noise and she bit down on it, afraid in that moment that if she started she would not be able to stop. That the sheer madness of everything she had been through would over-power her mind and she would die here, on the spears of those drawn to her laughter in the darkness.

"Ever since I left Harnspire all that time ago, Venn," she said, "it seems like every step I have taken has been because of you." Did the trion recoil a little at that? "I do not resent it, but all through this people have wanted you. Your mother wanted you, Saradis wants you, her god wants you, so whatever is out there," she pointed, shrugged, and noticed how intently Tall Sera was listening, "my bet is it wants you too." The trion looked away from her, to Tall Sera.

"Stay close to her," he said with a shrug. "And when the attack comes, be ready to run."

"We show the way in the darkness." Frina spoke, quick, quiet words as she appeared at Sorha's shoulder.

"The Osere will guide you, make sure your people do not attack them." Whispered orders passed among the Forestals.

Then all sound but the beating of spears on shields vanished.

"Ready yourselves!" shouted the Rai. Sorha looked to Tall Sera, looked to Venn, and gave a nod to each. She felt every muscle tense, her breath come short. The screams started. Coming from where the army was.

"They're behind us!" shouted someone. "Reform, reform!"

"Now," hissed Tall Sera. Then they were running, leaving behind the Rai and their soldiers to their fate. In the darkness the Betrayers were everywhere, but the Forestals had keen eyes and fast bows. The pale blue glow of the Betrayers was enough for a target. Those that got past the bows fell to Sorha's blade and she could not believe it was this easy, this simple, to escape.

Again the roar in the darkness from the direction of the Rai, then a vast gout of flame that destroyed Sorha's night vision. She found herself blind. Unable to make out even the faint glow of the Betrayers for the afterghost of the fire dancing before her eyes. No more arrows flew, the Forestals similarly affected. She dragged Venn to a stop. Hoped they had the sense to stay still. Tried to quiet her breathing while she waited for her eyes to adjust once more, the fear inside her welling up, threatening to overcome her and send her running screaming into the night. Without vision she was useless.

This was the Betrayers' land, and she was in their world now.

36

Saradis

She stood in the centre of the skyraft, the heat from the braziers intense but she did not mind. Let her clothes be stained with sweat and her white face paint run. That heat was the heat of victory, it was her heat. Her strength. The power of Zorir running through her and this craft. Soon the god's fire would burn all of Crua and she would walk the Star Path to stand by them in a paradise.

"Skua-Rai," she turned, Vir waiting for her. He had taken to the raft in a way that made her wonder if he had done it before. Once she would have made him pay for keeping such a secret, hiding knowledge from her, but now it did not matter. They would all pay eventually, and for now his skills were useful, needed. Vengeance would be of no help to Zorir at this moment. "We are almost ready to leave. You should start loading up soldiers and provisions now."

"Should I?" she said, and the man's eyes widened, white make-up cracking at the corners of his eyes as he realised he had given orders to the Skua-Rai of all Crua. Should she teach him a lesson? She bit the desire back. She needed this man. The crew of the skyraft had been useful, but only one out of every five had survived the collaring and now they were fading fast, like ghosts of who they had been. Their weight falling off them, skin loose and grey, teeth falling out and eyes beginning to whiten with blindness. Those without cowls never lasted long once they were collared. She had been surprised when she received news about the captured Forestals, and that they lasted, until she had worked it out. They must have cowls, to use the stones would require it and the reports of them protecting themselves against Rai fire made sense now.

"I did not mean to presume, Skua-Rai," he looked down, not at her, not meeting her gaze, "only I am not used to dealing with . . ."

"It does not matter, as long as you can do your job." She looked out across the sky, at the slow movement of towering clouds as they drifted across the sky. Soon the clouds would swell with the eruption of the geysers along the centre line of Crua. Water would flow, rain would fall in the northern and southern forests. All seemed so normal, she had somehow expected more. All the talk she had heard, all her life of how the Wyrdwood was somehow alive, knowing, yet it did not move against her. It did nothing to fight the coming fire. She had worried that Cahan Du-Nahere had somehow been its vehicle, its avatar, but he hung lifeless from the tower of Zorir. All that held out was Jinnspire, which was in hand, and the Forestals. Thanks to her foresight in taking this skyraft and the power of the collar they would soon be gone. Maybe the forest thought it was too big to die, or maybe it was just trees and nothing else. "How long until you can have this thing knocking on the door of the Forestal city?"

"Well, loading up will take a few days, at least," he sighed in the way of professionals the land over when confronted with a job, "then the winds around Tilt are always weak, and they mostly pull north and we want south. So we'll have to bring it out past the city, then come low and put out the main hawsers. I've been arranging as many crownheads and troops as I can to meet us outside the city and we'll have to pull this thing across Crua until we catch the southern winds. That's hard work, they need to rest often or you kill the crownheads. Then you have to build up the momentum all over again, it's not easy. A slow business. Or that's what they tell me."

"I will provide you with all the people you want to replace the crownheads, there will be no need to rest them. They will do this for the love of their god. They will not stop and they will not sleep." Vir looked away.

"As you say, Skua-Rai," he answered.

"Once you have caught the southern winds, it will be quick then?" He shrugged.

"Depends on the winds, can't control 'em. And I'll have to slow to get height."

"How do you know all this?" She could not help but be suspicious.

"The books, mostly," he said, "and they had a few indentured servants, they were more than happy to serve us, tell me everything they knew. The main points of it aren't that hard."

"So, how high does it need to get?"

"Enough to get the thing over Jinnwood. Some tall trees in Jinnwood and if we snare the sails or the maw nets then it's long work to get them good again."

"They don't need to be good, this thing only has to survive until it gets to the Forestal city." He nodded, did not look at her.

"As you say. But still, if you are going to attack you want a stable platform for it." She did not reply. What he said made sense, foolish to let the attack falter at the last. "And when it comes to getting through Wyrdwood," he shrugged huge shoulders, "well, I have no idea how that works, what the winds will be like under the cloudtrees or if we'll have to pull the thing through." She took a deep breath, looked over the edge of the raft, down at Zorir's tower, at the god waving black tentacles in the air. She felt such urgency it was hard to convey it, hard to stay still even though she knew he made sense. Foolish to rush it, to risk losing the raft for the sake of speed. Zorir had waited generations for its triumph; a few weeks, even a season would mean nothing to her god. Better to do it right. Have the raft in full working order for the assault. The Forestals would be scared when it appeared. The illusion of safety in their forest city shattered. Then she would find the trion, they were in that city, and when that was done she would kill every single Forestal as punishment for all the years of trouble they had caused her. Robbing her convoys, disrupting her plans with their greed.

She may even have some brought back here and have her remaining Rai sacrifice them. She would enjoy that.

37

Dassit

She could move, it was not easy, not simple. She felt like someone had beaten her, someone skilled in such things. The mixture of headache, pain and nausea threatened to overwhelm her whenever she pushed herself too hard. But she must push herself. This was a battle, she was used to battle, to fighting. She would not lay down and give in.

The others felt the same, she could feel it and tell from the way they moved their huge ungainly forms, the creaking wooden bodies, arms and legs as thick as Woodedge trees, faces carved and unmoving – though all different. Ont's face was round with a long beard that looked to be of chains of wood. Ania's was more delicate, thinner, and Dassit had the distinct feeling it had changed in the time they had been forcing these strange Wyrdwood bodies to obey them, in the long painful hours of learning to stand – a feat in itself. Dassit had new respect for children taking their first faltering steps.

She watched Ont push himself up from kneeling with one hand. Of them all he was learning the fastest, he had the most recent experience. For Dassit and Ania it was second-hand knowledge, passed along from him like a memory of long-ago youth, something you know happened but you had changed so wildly in the time since it no longer felt like you.

Watching him she thought Ont's wooden body had changed as well, become more like him. It was taller than Ania's, thicker. He stood, swaying slightly, trunk-like arms by his side and then very slowly lifted the arms, bringing them out to his side as if to balance himself. It let her study the body more. So far no one had managed to stand for more than a few seconds, crawling had been possible but balance was much harder. Now she saw the entire body that Ont inhabited.

Hair and beard, the hair carved long and falling down the back. Something of the shape of it reminded her of the helmets the Rai wore. Now she looked closer, a lot of the huge thing reminded her of the Rai, the shoulder pieces were mushroom bells, grown round and solidified and the closer she looked at it the more she saw within it was all of the plants of Wyrdwood, thick vines bunched and relaxed under sheathes of bark that passed for skin, the face was fruits and berries – though denuded of all their softness. Thick bands around the wrist reminded her of the grasses that grew as hard tubes at the edge of pools, the thick fingers were gnarled like roots and all had the colour of old wood.

Ont – *I am standing.*

Ania – *Good for you.*

He took a step, faltering, slow, swaying, and as he moved she heard the creak of trees in the wind, the rustle of leaves and the patter of geyser rain falling on the canopy. Another slow step and when the wide, round foot came down she was sure she felt the ground tremble beneath her. Or was she trembling? No, she felt his footstep through the ground, and as she was aware of that, she felt where Ania stood, she felt the ground around herself and she felt the bushes and the trees and beyond that Wyrdwood, full of life: raniri and maws going about their business uninterested in her or Ont or Ania. Nearer she felt others, rootlings and shyun, out of sight but watching, full of curiosity about these new creatures in their forest. Beyond that, other presences, vast and powerful, they were here and they were everywhere and a word jumped into her mind, "distributed". That was right, she felt the Boughry and they were here, watching, at the same time they were in the trees and in the maws and the rootlings and shyun and even in her. Separate and distinct within themselves and yet part of it. It was dizzying, she felt like she was losing herself, being diluted.

Ont – *Be careful, Dassit.*

His voice pulled her back, his presence solidified her.

"There is so much out there."

Ont – *Ranya's web.*

Ania – *All the monk's talk of a gentle god, and it turns out they are the Boughry, not gentle at all.*

Ont – *No. They are part of it, but not it. Like we are part of it. Can you not feel it?*

Ont took another step.

Ont – *I am walking.*

Ania – *I know, every time you take a step I feel it.*

"As do I."

Ania – *How can that be? I have a cowl, but you do not and—*

Ont – *Neither do I. Yet I feel you both, where you are in the forest and I feel . . .*

" . . . the forest beyond and what lives in it."

Ont – *These bodies, they are cowls.*

Ania – *Do not be foolish, how can that be?*

"So much has happened, Ania, you think nothing else strange is likely?"

Ont took two more steps and then his huge body came crashing down in a cloud of dirt and dust. Dassit felt laughter, and with it came knowledge, how he had walked, how it had felt, how he had done it and now it was there, in her mind. She put her huge hands on the forest floor, for a moment lost in all the life there, roots and seeds and plants and tiny creatures, the weave of the fungal mat that connected all things together. Then she closed her eyes – a moment of total darkness – opened them again and pushed herself up. Feeling herself swaying, suddenly aware of her terrible hunger and thirst but the body locked it away. As she stood her vision filled with lights, as if it were night and she blinked them away. She had enough distractions just trying to stand, struggling to keep balance as if she was drunk. She did not raise her arms like Ont had, instead she took a step forward, the world tipping and twisting around her. Her foot hit the ground, for a moment she thought she would fall but she held her balance, had raised her arms without thinking. Another step, harder this time, had to concentrate on it and then she fed the momentum into the next step, one two three and she was walking until she was not. Falling heavily to the floor. Unlike Ont she did not laugh. To her it was a humiliation, she had failed.

Ania – *Well done, now share and I will try.*

"I do not know how to."

Ont – *Think, remember and it will happen.*

She was about to say something, tell him how foolish he sounded but she was already sharing, the feeling, the way she had used the speed she was building to continue the walk.

Ont – *No shame, Dassit, we all fail and all learn from failure. You took more steps than me. Ania will take more than you. I will make more than her.*

Ania – *Or so you hope, though I wish I was not so thirsty.*

Ont – *And hungry.*

"Do not remind me." But the hunger and thirst scared her, surely they would need to eat eventually?

She watched Ania stand, sway for a moment then walk. She was markedly more successful than either Ont or Dassit had been and managed ten steps before she fell with a crash into the ground. With the impact came a wave of satisfaction, a joy at going further than any other and with that also came knowledge, experience. The day continued in this way and by the end of them each could walk without having to concentrate on it and information flowed between them as easily as conversation. More and more Dassit became sure that the wooden bodies which housed them were changing to resemble who they had been. Ont's body was becoming taller and thicker, and when she was up close she saw that the wood which made the thing was no longer dead and flaking, in places she could see shoots of green along the lines of the armour, the soft buds of new leaves. She wondered if she was the same. She took a step closer to Ania; the shoots were on her, too, thin vines growing from the joints of elbow and knee.

Ania – *You are growing, Dassit.*

"So are you, and Ont."

It was not speech they shared, they spoke as if in a dream, not even in words, in shapes and feelings and colours and scents. A non-language that was nonetheless as clear as any speech, even more so in many ways. It conveyed where they were, how they felt, even how healthy they were and as soon as she thought of that she knew they were not healthy at all. The bodies within the wooden shells were broken beyond saving. The toll of the forest journey had been a fierce one, but worse than that the wooden bodies themselves were running low on energy. Like someone with a cut slowly bleeding them to death, every movement they made cost them, and as she became aware of the price she knew they were teetering on the edge of bleeding out, starving, dying of thirst.

Ont – *We need strength.*

Ghosts of hunger and thirst echoing through the web between them and bouncing back and forth, they all felt it. They all knew it.

Ania – *You would think if we are here to serve some purpose, they would have given us some instruction.*

Ont – *That is not Ranya's way, she shows us the path but does not define our destination.*

Ania – *Reborn as a wooden giant and yet I must still suffer monkish foolishness.*

"But we have found the way, simply by exploring the world with these bodies."

Ania – *Not much of the world. And if we do not do something we will starve and explore no longer. When this wooden body dies, so do we.*

Dassit said nothing, she did not need to and neither did Ont. When Ania said it they recognised the truth of it. Who they had been was damaged beyond saving, they were these wooden bodies now and these bodies were them. Death of one brought the death of another.

Ont – *Did you hear that?*

Ania – *What?*

Ont – *Laughter. A child.*

As he said, Dassit heard it. The delighted squeal of an amused child. From the corner of her eye, at the base of the cloudtree she caught a glimpse, nothing more, gone as soon as it was there, the image of a child stood with arms outstretched against the base of the cloudtree.

Ont – *Issofur.*

Ania – *Furin's child? But how?*

Ont – *He is of the forest.*

"And he comes here to laugh at us?"

Ont – *Or to guide. Venn once told me when Cahan was weak he asked the trees to give him strength through his cowl. If these bodies are similar to cowls then maybe the trees will help us?*

Ania – *It sounds like foolishness to me.*

"No, he is right, can't you feel it?"

She didn't. As Dassit said that she knew Ania did not feel it the way she did. Ont did. Maybe it was Ania's already existing cowl, a part of her, with all her cynicism contained within that stopped her. Whatever bonded Dassit and Ont to these things was new, open to new ideas.

Ont – *Only way to know is to try.*

He walked toward the wall of the cloudtree trunk, every step of the great wooden body resonating with her as it lumbered forward. With each step she also felt the life of the thing ebbing away. So little left to him. He could not die here, not after his journey had been so long and so painful. Not after they had sacrificed so much. She wanted to stop him, for her to do it and risk what was left of her energy but knew it was too late. Even the journey back from the tree would drain all the life left in his construct.

Construct? Where had that come from? But now she had thought it she knew it was definitely right. That was what they were. Constructs.

She watched.

Ania watched.

Ont walked.

Ania – *Should we join him?*

Ont – *No, wait there. No sense in us all running down if we are wrong.*

"Yes," thought Dassit, and realised she was no longer always thinking of herself as I, but of them as "we" and clearly the same for Ont.

Ont – *I am at the tree. I am going to lean with my back against it.*

Ania – *Why?*

Ont – *It feels right.*

Dassit wished she could see him more clearly. Then she could. He was magnified. His body against the tree clear in her vision.

Ania – *If we don't die, I am going to enjoy being a construct.*

Nothing was happening yet, Ont only leaned against the vast trunk of the cloudtree. His wooden body inert, no longer moving and death closing on him. She felt his breathing coming more slowly, felt heat and claustrophobia. The connection with the construct withdrawing and the man within becoming aware he was a dying body locked in a box. Sharp spikes of pain lancing through their connection. Dassit grit her teeth. Her connection wavered, images danced in front of her eyes like she had eaten the wrong forest mushroom and allowed the spirits of the wood to cloud her vision and enchant her mind.

She heard the laughter of a child again.

Ania – *Look!*

Movement. Not around Ont, but above him. Vines, snaking down the great wooden edifice of the cloudtree, vines of all types. Wetvines, floatvines, bladderweeds and other vines she did not know the names of, had never seen before. The speed they moved at felt impossible. Not the deliberate, slow reaching of natural growth. She felt scared for Ont. What was happening? How could this be happening? Plants did not move with such speed. Or with such purpose.

Then the cloudtree itself moved.

Dassit felt herself open-mouthed with shock, unable to understand what she was seeing. The bark around Ont peeled back and enveloped his construct, leaving it half in and half out of the tree. It was as though the massive thing had grown over him. At the same time, the vines wound around Ont, around the neck and arms. A sigh. She felt a satisfaction and a satiating.

Ont – *The trees.*

His words the gentle rush of a breeze through leaves and at the same time they were a call, to Ania and Dassit. To come to him, to entreat this great forest god for life and they had no doubt, not for one second, that it would grant it to them. It was simply the way of things; this was how it was meant to be when you were part of the construct.

38

Udinny

The weight of a man on me. The smell of his breath, his armour, his body.

I was pinned most effectively, and in the glitter of his eyes I saw a man too far gone for talk or for reason. The desperate desire of his cowl had overridden everything but the hunger within. He had a need and he saw me as the way to take what he wanted.

Cry out, Udinny!

Struggle, Udinny!

These thoughts, a clarion in my mind and yet I could do neither. Something of the man's power froze me, left me helpless as he prepared to take my life to feed his own. His hand, warm on my chest. His breath a whisper in my ear.

"Old man, you have had your life." I was seized with the desire to explain I was not an old man at all, but a young woman trapped within the body of an old man. I do not think it would have swayed him and I was unable to talk anyway. The onset of death had frozen me. "Now you will feed me life, it will take time. And I lied when I said it will not hurt."

I did not want it to hurt. I did not want it to happen at all. Something within me knew this as a true death, no chance of rebirth in the strange darkness of Ranya's world of the dead. No chance of the Star Path for poor Udinny, only extinction; complete and total, to feed one man's thirst for power. From his hand began to spread a heat, a gnawing heat that seeped into my skin and leached away what gave me life. It felt like someone taking rough paper and using it to scrub off my skin layer by layer, and with it came a promise that this would only get worse, that Rai Tassa would work his way through my entire body, stealing the life from it and keeping me aware and agonised and silent as he did. Unable to struggle, unable to scream. A nightmare. The worst death and one many had been through before me at the hands of the Rai.

In vain, as the pain spread through me I hoped one of the others would wake. That Tanhir, linked to me by her memories, would somehow feel what was happening. All I heard from her was the steady rhythmic breath of sleep.

There was only this man, this powerful, murderous man, and I, Udinny Pathfinder, servant of Ranya, who was powerless before him.

No.

Another voice. Not mine. Not Tanhir's. Not of any of those who travelled with us. Not even really a voice, more a communication.

How? Who? What?

But of course, I, foolish Udinny, had forgotten that I was not only Udinny Pathfinder, servant of Ranya. I was Udinny Pathfinder, servant of Ranya who occupied the body of Fandrai, priest of murder, who had once been Cowl-Rai. A Cowl-Rai of death. His cowl had been quiet, reticent, barely there for me, only surfacing in times of real need.

What was this, if not real need?

Slowly, gently, the pain ebbed away, but it did not seem to me that the Rai above me was aware of what was happening. That the slow seep of life from me to him had stopped, and maybe it had not. Maybe the cowl within saw this as a way to be rid of me; would it let my life seep away until Udinny was gone, and only the body was left once more?

It would not.

Tassa's eyes began to lose focus, his mouth moved and I saw a word upon his lips that was never spoken, "What?"

Within me I felt a shivering, a shift of something beneath my skin and it was not power, not what I thought of as cowl. No hunger, no pain. Only a pulse, something mournful and melancholy and despite this sadness, this reticence to act I felt within me it did not help Tassa. He shuddered, shaking as if he had a fever and the skin of his face withered, the flesh beneath slowly hollowing out, his eyes whitening, breath coming in rasps and yet I felt no sensation of filling with power as I had heard Rai speak of. I only felt a sadness at a life extinguished. With a final gasp he collapsed, more a husk than a person, his armour crashed as he hit the floor. Tanhir sat up, as did Rai Ustiore, both with hands on the hilts of their blades. Within me I heard that soft voice-not-voice.

We are safe.

"Tassa!" hissed Ustiore and she was up, blade out, fire dancing around her hands, looking for the threat. Eventually her eyes came to rest on me.

"What have you done?" she said, murder on her face.

"Stop." Low, threatening. Tanhir stood with her knife ready.

"He has killed Tassa."

"I have no love, for Udinny, but they are no murderer." She moved slowly, going into a fighting position.

"The proof you lie, lies in the dust of the floor," said Ustiore.

"If we fight here," whispered Tanhir, "we bring the whole camp down on us."

"Tassa has been with me for . . ."

"He was going to kill me." All eyes on me. "To feed his cowl."

"And you expect me to believe," said Ustiore, "you were able to stop him?"

"Cowl-Rai," said Tanhir softly.

"What?" Ustiore stared at her.

"The body is not Udinny's," she said softly. "Do not ask me to explain how, just know it is true and I was as confused by it as you will be. But before it was Udinny, it was a man called Fandrai, who was Cowl-Rai to a god called Hirsal, a god of murder. They were the leader of a cult that brought the swarden of Wyrdwood into being." A twitch on Ustiore's face, a narrowing of the eyes and then they seemed to lose focus, and I felt that movement beneath my skin again. Ustiore stepped back, eyes wide.

"Chyi's tears," she said. "Will he wake?"

"What?" Her words made little sense to me, but the world had been going mad since I had met Cahan Du-Nahere, maybe I should not have been surprised.

"If what is within you raises the dead, will he wake?" She pointed at the husk of Tassa.

"I do not know." It was an interesting question, one I should spend time thinking about, but I also suspected that the middle of a camp of people who would kill me as soon as they found out who I was may not be the best place for soul-searching, or cowl-searching.

"There is great power in you," she said, "it hides, but it is there."

"I am just a monk."

"Well," said Tanhir, "now you are a monk with a problem, a problem for all of us. If that body is found there will be questions."

"Corpses are common in an army," said Ustiore.

"Not corpses like that, or Rai corpses." She walked over and knelt by Tassa's desiccated body.

"He was a good friend to me," said Ustiore softly and I had no answer to that. I did not really think Rai made friends, only found those who were useful to them.

"We need to get away from here then," I said. Tanhir walked to the flap of the large tent and pushed it aside.

"The light is rising," she said. "The army will be waking, we should be safe to leave now."

"What about him?" I pointed at Tassa. Odd that I felt no guilt. When I had been part of other deaths I had regretted it, even when I had no choice. At the battle at Harn I had prayed Ranya take every soul my arrows freed from the flesh. For Tassa though, I felt nothing, and it was not because he had been intent on my death. Sooner blame a spearmaw for hunting as blame a Rai for killing to preserve themselves. It was simply what they were.

No, I think I felt nothing because I knew this death was not my fault, had not been caused by me. I had no control over the cowl within me, it did not answer to me, or talk to me. It had acted in self-preservation. Now it was safe once again I did not even know it was there.

At that thought, I felt something odd, a warmness. Almost like it was acknowledging me.

What could that mean?

"We should leave," said Tanhir, "come on. Ustiore, you lead, same story as before. We are your prisoners." The Rai nodded.

"We should head as far from here as we can before the body is found," said Ustiore softly. With that we moved. Threading our way through a camp as it woke, people all around us, hundreds of different clanpaints on their faces. Each one studying us. Judging us by what they saw on the white make-up both I and Tanhir wore. We passed through the camp followers and into the army proper, soldiers everywhere though they seemed a miserable lot. There was noise, but not happy noise. There was little talk, little of the laughter I associated with soldiers at work. I heard knocking and sawing, the noise of carpenters working but no conversation with it.

"Siege weapons," said Tanhir softly, pointing in the distance at where I could just make something out.

"No," said Ustiore, "that is not a siege weapon. I have overseen their building before. The shapes are wrong."

"We should find out what they are then," said Tanhir. "We are scouts after all."

"Is that not in the very centre of the camp? Surely that is the last place we want to go."

"We'll skirt it, find somewhere with a view," said Tanhir. Ustiore nodded and we followed her as she led us through the outskirts of the camp. Soldiers were making fires and occasionally we would see one of the collared, stood silently watching as people went about their business. As we passed close to them it was hard not to see how unkempt they were, how their skin flaked and their armour lacked the lustre of Ustiore's.

"They make my skin crawl," said Tanhir once they were beyond the sight of the last collared.

"And mine," said Ustiore. It felt like we had walked for hours, and the size of the army was filling me with pity for poor Jinnspire. We passed another of the collared, and as we did I was sure I caught a flicker, a movement of their eyes.

"It looked at us," I whispered to Tanhir.

"It did not," she said.

"I am sure it did." Ustiore heard us, and turned.

"Did you see this?" she asked Tanhir.

"No," said the Forestal, "but when we pass the next one I will pay more attention." We walked on, through the throngs of the army and everywhere was that odd quietness. The soldiers talked in whispers, went about their work with suspicious eyes. We passed another collared, the blue around its neck pulsing as if it were a living thing, a congealing of the flesh of its neck into a liquid, spongy scarf. This time there was no doubt; it turned its head to watch us as we passed.

"I told you," I said as we passed down an avenue of tents, the crownhead leather of them ripped and unkempt, stitched and fixed many times. The smell of something cooking hung in the air and it turned my stomach. Whatever it was smelled rancid.

"It may be nothing," said Ustiore, but she did not sound convinced.

"We must hope you are correct," said Tanhir. From the end of the tents we began to hear noise, which was odd in this strange and silent army. Ustiore led us between two tents and told us to look busy. Then she stood over us as we pretended to tighten the cords holding up the tent. As we did, soldiers were passing and she grabbed one. Pulling him to one side, fear washed across the man's facc.

"Rai," he said, lowering his eyes.

"What is happening?" He did not look at her.

"A body," he said. "Murdered, in a strange way. The collared have us searching for a Rai and two soldiers. Think they've slipped in from Jinnspire to spy." He did not seem to suspect us, maybe he thought the Rai was not with us, or maybe he did not think at all for the people of this army seemed cowed and fear stifled free thought. He scratched at the side of his mouth, making tracks in the white face paint. "I'm to gather more soldiers so we can search the outskirts of the camp, they've been seen heading that way."

"Well," said Ustiore, "be on your way then." He nodded and set off at a jog.

"That is going to make things far more difficult, if not impossible," said Tanhir. "They will be watching for anyone making a run for Jinnspire. There'll be spears ready, and Rai and collared."

"We must go back," said Ustiore. "I said before this was a fool's idea, to move into an army that already searches for us." She looked from me to Tanhir. "You can head to

Wyrdwood and I . . ." her words died away and she shrugged. "Well, I will try and find somewhere I can live quietly and not be seen." Tanhir replied to the Rai but I was not listening. I was thinking of where we had been and what we had passed and what I knew of this place and was hatching a plan, a most glorious plan that would get us into Jinnspire.

"What are you smiling at," snapped Tanhir, "this is no time for foolishness."

"No," I told her, "you are wrong, this is the time for utmost foolishness, this is the time to indulge in the maddest of ideas."

"No," said Ustiore, "it is not."

"All my life, Rai," I said, "I have been told not to be foolish, and always I have been and, look, I stand here now alive by you."

"No," said Tanhir, "if you are to be believed you stand here now having died twice, once in this life and once in the next."

"Well, yes," I nodded, "that is true. But I still stand here and that is what matters. I, Udinny Pathfinder, servant of Ranya and conqueror of death—"

"Keep your voice down," said Tanhir. I quietened, continuing at a whisper.

". . . conqueror of death," I said softly, "and I have seen the path to take."

"And what is this path?" said Ustiore, she sounded tired, worn out.

"Towards the centre. To whatever they build."

"Are you mad?" said Ustiore.

"That has never been in question," said Tanhir.

"Just listen to me." They stared, incredulous at what I suggested but listened nonetheless. I think mostly because they had no other option. No idea of their own that did not involve a long walk to Wyrdwood.

"Speak then," said Tanhir.

"First, they are expecting us to leave. So we would be fools to head outwards. Instead we head into the camp."

"Why?" said Ustiore.

"To find out what they are building, not just for Tall Sera, but because everyone in Jinnspire will be asking that, they will be afraid of it." They did not look convinced. "Information will give us power there, so they will not kill us out of hand."

"And how do you suggest we get into Jinnspire, if we cannot leave the camp?" said Tanhir.

"The animal pens," I told her.

"The Hetton are there," Ustiore looked at me as if I had gone insane.

"Are you intending to search for a crownhead to replace the one you lost?" said Tanhir. I shook my head.

"Oh no, I believe my crownhead is a creature of Ranya, she will find her way back from death when the time is right."

"You are quite mad," said Ustiore.

"And you are Rai," I said. She stared at me, "So you must know how to fly a marant?" At that, Tanhir smiled and the look on the Rai's face, well, if I could have bottled it and sold it I would never have needed to work again.

39

Saradis

She had never enjoyed flight before, but there was something truly majestic about standing on the deck of a skyraft. The great fires burning, the balloons half full of air to keep the massive construction afloat and if she concentrated she could just hear the keening of the gasmaws, trapped in nets beneath the craft and providing most of its buoyancy. The man Vir had made master of the craft was striding up and down the huge deck, shouting orders – most of which were so alien to her that he may as well have been speaking a different language – and the crew were jumping to his commands. Most of the activity was directed at two great ropes, thick as hundred-year-old trees, that ran around the capstans where the crew had toiled for hours to pull the skyraft closer to the ground.

Of course, they had people to spare, the raft was packed to the wings. A platoon of the collared stood around the raft, watching as they always watched. They never tired, they were hard to kill and if they did not have quite the power of the Rai then that was a price worth paying for the fact that they were utterly loyal. Soldiers were everywhere; she had brought almost every soldier from Tiltspire, the collared there would keep the peace and Laha would make sure of it. Scattered around the decks were her newest weapons, captured and collared Forestals come from the north with their mighty bows. She had once despised and feared those weapons. Well, now her enemy would fear her.

The trion was the reason they went to Woodhome.

She was impatient to get them, bring them back for Zorir. She had cursed the master and Vir when they had made their slow way over the geysers, demanding they lower the raft and have it pulled rather than drifting painfully slowly on what small winds escaped the circle currents. The master had refused, oh, he had been scared to do it, staring at the collared all the time and knowing what had happened to the rest of the crew, the ones that disobeyed. But he had stayed adamant and Vir had backed him. Said the geysers would cook them alive and she had laughed at him but he had remained firm. Only when they passed over the geyser line, the master constantly calling for more height, did she understand.

The geysers of Tilt were not something she thought much about; they were part of the world and taken for granted. They regularly exploded, sending huge streams of water into the sky to be caught by the winds and fed to the forests at the north and south end of the land, falling as rain in between. They had not been over the geysers for long, and once they were past the line they exploded, regular as the light rising.

She had never seen so much water, or realised how much fell back to the land, its weight so great it had scarred the ground around the slight rise of the geyser line. On each side were rivers, flowing like veins across the land until they were absorbed or fell down one of the crevasses that were constantly appearing throughout the land when it shook and shivered.

"Skua-Rai," said Vir, "you should get under the awning." He pointed towards the cabin and the tent of skins over the deck there for shade. She did not generally like being told what to do but he was respectful in his tone, so she moved as he asked. A gentle rain began to fall, and as it did she heard the hiss of pain from the crew on deck and she put out her hand. The rain was scalding, burning her skin where it touched her. She watched, pleased neither Vir nor the master were weak and that they made the crew work even through the scalding rain.

The collared, of course, gave no sign they felt anything.

When the rain had passed she walked over to the rail.

At first she had avoided the edges of the skyraft, the rail only came up to her waist and without even looking she imagined how easy it would be for someone to tip her over. She wondered what it would feel like to fall from so high, like flying, maybe? Or would she know only fear in those few moments of freefall? It frightened her, and that made her more determined to go to the rail. She would be cowed by nothing.

So far down. Even though they were low for a skyraft, barely above the distance of a spire tether, it was still a long way down and the thought there was nothing keeping them up but gasmaws and hot air made her head spin. Below she saw the land laid out like a map, villages and largers and in the distance she could see Mydalspire and imagine the ominous shadow of the Wyrdwood's cloudtrees beyond it. Below her were hundreds, maybe thousands of people. She had sent soldiers on ahead to round them up. Great herds of crownheads moved between them.

The giant ropes that were attached to the skyraft fell over the side. As they neared the ground they split into smaller ropes and those into smaller and smaller ones until they could be held by the people below who worked in teams of hundreds, pulling the raft across the centre of Crua to pick up the southern winds. Usually such things were only done in the far north and south, where the rafts avoided the woods in fear of getting tangled, and then only done when the raftmaster felt real need. As a rule they would just drift across on the loose currents.

But she wanted speed, and she was willing to force those below to pay for it as shown by the scatter of bodies behind them. Maybe they were unconscious, resting or dead. She did not really care.

"Not long now till we are ready to catch the wind, Skua-Rai," said Vir, joining her at the rail. She nodded, taking one more look at the land below, at the people and animals labouring in her name for her god. She smiled.

"Thank you, Tree Commander," she said. She was going no further on the raft, foolish to risk herself in war and she must be in Tiltspire, with Zorir. From there she could control her forces across Crua, those left in the north, those about to take Jinnspire and those on the raft headed for the Forestals. "I will leave you here, ready to make war on those who oppose Zorir." He nodded, not looking at her. She paused, not ready to leave and unsure why. Tiltspire was an empty place now. "The master," she pointed at the man striding over the decks. "He can be trusted to pilot this thing?"

"Yes, Skua-Rai," said the soldier.

"And the assault, will you be in charge of that?"

"Doubt it," he said, "There's a Rai aboard, Rai Sason."

"She is capable?" Vir shrugged.

"Then you will return to Tiltspire with me," she said and she was not sure why. Had she been weaker she would have said she felt alone, but she was not weak.

"If that's what you want," said Vir.

40

Venn

The darkness was absolute.

But not for Venn. If anything, they felt like they were becoming more aware of what was around them. There was less clutter down here in Osereud, less aliveness. The power that ran through Crua was more stark and more explicit in their mind. Lines of energy going hither and thither to collect somewhere far away, a tangle of knots and . . . No. That was wrong. Not a tangle. Above was tangled, where the forests grew wild and free to a design of their own, fighting for life and light. Down here there was order, or at least a memory of order, though it was one that had become fractured and split, drained in places and corrupted in others. It gave Venn a perspective they had lacked above ground. Venn felt sure that life was somehow longing to find an order it had once had. Like crownheads without a herder, they still lived but they ran wild and became ragged and filthy because that was not the life they were meant for, and they were never truly happy. How to explain that to anyone outside themselves, that the land above did not live the life it was meant for?

It sounded like madness.

Maybe it was. Maybe all that had happened to Venn had cracked their mind and they searched for meaning in what was meaningless.

Or maybe this was another step along Ranya's long and winding path.

Then the confusion and the panic. The beating of swords. Running through the darkness. The appearance of the thing. The god. They could not see it, the darkness swallowed it but Venn could feel it. A twisting, reaching bundle of power like the power than ran beneath Crua, but damaged, disconnected and infected with bluevein the same way Cahan had been. It was huge. Much taller than the people, more akin to a gasmaw in feeling: cold but sure and determined. For now its attention was on the soldiers and the Rai. Venn could feel the action there, the raw emotion. They were dragged along by Sorha. He felt her panic, her fear and her determination and if he had doubted her before he did not now. She was going to protect Venn. They knew that as surely as they knew there was air to breathe. A flash in the darkness. She pulled them to a halt.

"Silence." Hissed into the night. Venn obeyed. Sorha was blinking, odd that they could see her face even in the pitch black. Not as an actual face, but as the life moving beneath it. Around them orbited other lives and beneath them ran the strong pulse of Crua's energy.

She is blinded, thought Venn, the flash had blinded her. Venn touched her arm, found skin and brushed against her senses, cleared away the blindness. Felt her awareness on them then they were roughly pushed aside. Sorha's blade licking out and cutting into a body Venn could barely see, barely sense. Around them more fighting. The swish of sword. Thrust of a spear. A grunt of pain. The Osere, protecting the Forestals. Then the hiss of arrows as Tall Sera and his people regained their night vision. Venn experiencing the world as layers, the battle near them. Further out the Rai and the vast creature.

"Run!" Sorha's voice, crystal-clear. In the distance Venn felt the pull of the taffistone and knew they were going the wrong way, they would go past it in the night if they did not change direction. Venn pulled her back on course and she let them. Around them Venn could feel the Osere, gently herding the Forestals toward the taffistone.

In a loose circle around them Venn could also feel the collared, but they were not chasing. It was as if they were waiting for something.

"The battle has stopped," said Sorha. "I can't hear them."

"It's coming," said Venn, "I can feel it."

"Run, harder."

They did, running with all they had, and the urgency stretched out from Sorha and Venn to the Forestals and the Osere. Venn could feel the expenditure of energy as pulses, feet hitting the floor, an exchange of power for every step.

A screech in the darkness, a noise like nothing Venn had ever heard, louder than anything they could imagine. Before them the taffistone, bright in Venn's mind. They would reach it before the creature caught them, Venn was sure. Already some of the Osere were there, hands on the stone, trying but failing to open it. Behind them the creature, closing, its speed phenomenal.

"Let me through!" shouted Venn. "Let me through!" Sorha shouted something in the language of the Osere and they moved aside. "Everyone touch someone, link to the taffistone!" Venn put their hand on it. Felt the place within that would open it. The encroachment of blue in the stone, the slow cracking of the network and they had the distinct feeling that the god, unable to access it, had instead decided to destroy, degrade it. The Forestals strung arrows. "I need to know where to go!"

"Frina," urgent whispers. Venn felt the touch of an Osere, something gentle, and the Osere was in their mind, telling them of a place far to the north where they must go. A huge amount of power there, a concentration of it. A golden place. Venn felt the network and at the same time they felt a huge baleful attention turn on them. A screech of fury in the night. The creature was nearer, angry, determined to stop them.

Venn pushed into the network, found the Forestal trions back in Woodhome. Let them connect, a back and forth, a combining of power and the stone opened. Somewhere in the back of their mind Venn heard Sorha shout.

"Through! Go through." Felt the passage of others but they could not move, they were hypnotised, frozen by the approach of the creature, feeling its entire attention on them. Bluevein in the ground twisting up through the matter of it, twining around their legs and trying to hold them. Then they were grabbed, roughly pulled through and into the taffisnetwork. Buffeted from side to side, aware of the others, shouting, screaming, panicking, frightened. This was not the way of taffis journeys. The god in Tilt was trying to grab them, take them, hold them, own them.

Then they were out, thrown roughly from the stone on the other side. Skidding along the ground until Venn's progress was arrested, painfully, by something round and hard against their back, making them groan.

"Venn, are you hurt?"

"I am fine, I hit something."

"A root."

"What?"

"A cloudtree root." Venn found themselves surprised, though after a moment's thought they knew they should not be. They were in the far north, they were underground. The cloudtrees must have roots, it had just never occurred to them that they would see them. "We are at the edges of the root forest."

"We are as far below the Wyrdwood now as I usually live above." Tall Sera stepped forward and Venn was seeing them again. Really seeing, there was light here. Huge structures, like the fungal towers Venn had seen in the world above, but these glowed with a gentle white light that bathed the travellers and let Venn see how dirty they were, how tired they all looked.

Apart from the Osere, who were glorious. An explosion of colour, brighter than anything they had ever seen before. Even in the darkness, with the aches and pains in their body, with the fear they had felt still making their heart beat fast, it made them smile.

"Yes," said Sorha, "they are beautiful." Frina stepped forward from her small group of Osere, her body and face aglow with pinks and blues and greens and yellows.

"Move," she said, pointing away from the fungal tower and into the root forest. In the distance Venn could see the soft glimmer of another tower.

"Can we not catch our breath?" said Tall Sera, leaning on the staff of his bow. "Tell your strange friend we need rest." Frina's head focused on Tall Sera, then back to Sorha, and she let out a stream of words in her own language. "What did she say," said Tall Sera, looking at Sorha.

"That the god will be coming. It will not stop, it will not rest." Sorha wrapped her arms around herself. "Betrayers walk the forest, they will know we are here."

"God?" said Tall Sera and he laughed, more to himself than out of mirth. Then glanced over at Sorha. "I thought your people said there was only one god now?"

"They are not my people, I do not serve Saradis." She spat, shook her head. "I do not think those creatures are gods at all, but I have no better word for what they are. They are not us, that is all that is certain. And they are strong." Tall Sera nodded, looked around at his Forestals, they were wilting.

"Then at least tell me there is food down here."

"Food?" said Frina. She walked over to the nearest root, running her hands over it and clearly finding something. Then she took an instrument from her bag and began to scrape at the root, gathering from it. As she did Venn saw she was favouring one side and when she turned to bring over what she had collected they saw the sparkle of something wet on her side, soaking her clothes.

"You are hurt," said Venn. Frina held out what she had gathered to Tall Sera and looked over at Venn. Spoke a long sentence and in the middle of it she said – "It does not matter." Tall Sera ate what he was given, grimaced then ate the rest, sending his people to join the other Osere at the roots to gather more of it. "What did she say, Sorha, all of it?" Sorha turned to Venn, her face a mask of misery.

"She said she took a sword strike in the last battle. Her time is over but it does not matter. Her people have failed. This will be her last journey to the root forest." Her voice died away and she wiped at her face. For a moment Venn thought she was pushing away tears but that did not sound like the Sorha they had known. "This will be her final act, her last penance."

"What do you mean?"

"When the gods fought, her people chose the wrong side. They had their sight taken as punishment and now they guard those who once ruled over them."

"Not well enough," said Tall Sera.

"They know that," there was a flash of the old Sorha, the vehemence, the anger. "But they have laboured down here in the darkness for generations and asked nothing. That creature in Tilt, the one like it down here? Their servants have decimated her people, you do not wonder why there are so few left? That is why. And they did it all to protect us knowing no one would ever know or thank them." For a moment, there was violence in the air, and Venn expected Tall Sera to draw a blade, or to order his Forestals to nock arrows at the spite in Sorha's tone. Then he took a deep breath. Nodded.

"I spoke foolishly," he said. "Thank her for her sacrifice if you would." He laughed again. "I am unsettled by this place. I am used to the freedom of the trees and it made me act poorly."

"Will her cowl not fix her," said Venn.

"The cowls of the Osere do not work like that."

"Then they and us are more alike than not," said Tall Sera. "We carry cowls, but are not Rai."

"I can help," said Venn, and they stepped forward. "I can heal her." Frina's head turned to Venn and she spoke again. This time not trying to speak in anything but her own language.

"She says," said Sorha, "that you need your strength, she knows that healing will take it from a Rai."

"No," Venn stepped forward, putting out a hand and Frina shied away, hissing with pain. "It is different for me. I am not like them." The Osere cocked her head, and Sorha spoke in her language. Venn smiled, nodded then felt foolish as the Osere could not see them. Sorha spoke again. In return Frina shook her head, more words in the Osere language tumbling out. She pointed at the ground, then above. Shook her head.

Despairing at communicating, knowing that even Sorha's grasp of the Osere language was likely not good enough to put across what Venn was, what they could do, Venn reached for Frina. Grasped her arm.

"No!" this from Sorha, a panicked shout.

Too late.

The connection was made.

Venn found the flow of power running through Frina, where it leaked from her flesh at the wound and began cycling her strength through themselves. At the same time, felt their cowl exude tiny cilia through their feet and into the ground.

What they found was like puncturing a wetvine under huge pressure. Such power ran through this place, it felt like every root in the forest lit up in Venn's mind. A rush of fire, threatening to burn both Venn and Frina where they stood. Every part of Venn, every hair, every bit of skin suddenly aflame with it. They pushed back, trying to shut it down to something controllable. It was like when they touched Cahan back in Harn, but this was greater, many, many times greater. Venn fought a battle none could see, struggling to extinguish the fire in their mind, a power far above anything they had ever come across before. A certain death to all who touched it.

But their time with the trion of the Forestals had been well spent. The touch of Cahan gave them an experience of power few others would have. The memory of the Boughry provided a familiarity with the land. Venn had discipline and control and knowledge and a will. They used it to stem the flow. Cut it to manageable levels. They healed Frina, and at the same time, without even needing to touch them, they refreshed all those around them, banishing tiredness and hurt.

Then Venn let go, staggered back, breathing hard. At the same time they felt like they could run for hours and hours without pause. Frina's blind head was locked onto them. All around here, the Osere knelt, said a word, said it in awe. Then Frina followed it with a few short sentences.

"What did she say?" said Venn softly.

"I am not sure. She said they did not believe you would ever come, the one that was spoken of."

"What?"

"Their language," Sorha said softly, her voice sounded hoarse, "it does not translate directly, the nearest I can get to what she calls you, it is godtalker."

"What does that mean?" said Venn. Sorha shrugged.

"I do not know, but I can tell you one thing, Venn. For the first time since I have met her, she sounds hopeful."

41

Udinny

There was no question that the camp was looking for us — though I do not believe they actually knew much about who we were aside from there being three of us. One Rai and two soldiers and such groupings were not exactly uncommon in a camp of soldiers and Rai. The searchers were still looking for people heading away from the centre of the camp, and we headed towards it. Even so we had to be careful, with most of the soldiers heading outward, going against the flow was an oddity and such things could attract attention. So we were careful, slow. Stopping to talk with those soldiers who looked like they were busy when troops or groups of Rai or collared who looked like they were searching passed.

The closer we got to the strange construction in the centre, the more soldiers we found involved in carpentry and the more what they were about interested me. This was no ordinary carpentry. And what they made, Ustiore was right, it was no siege weapon.

"Tanhir, do you have any idea what they make here," I said softly as we walked away from another carpenter.

"I am no expert in siege machinery," she replied equally softly. "But I have never seen anything like this."

"I have told you, it is not siege machinery," said Ustiore.

"What is it then?" asked Tanhir.

"I do not know." We continued on our way and every time I passed the carpenters I spied on their work, I watched as they cut and sawed, I paid attention and became more and more confused with every step.

"Udinny, the face you make is likely to bring them down on us," hissed Tanhir, "try and look like this camp is normal to you. If you are so obviously an outsider it will attract attention."

"But I am confused, Tanhir," I told her.

"That is normal for you, I think, so act like it."

I did my best, but the closer we came to the construction the more confused I was. It was large, not massive, but very large and would require many soldiers to drag it along. Gathering floatweed for what appeared to be some sort of platform would also take a large number of soldiers a long time. It seemed a foolish use of resources. There was another thing that struck me as odd, resources. Siege machines were built from the common trees, the fast-growing ones that shot up like weeds in the Woodedge, but the carpenters were working on expensive woods. I saw cloudwood, both outer wood, and heartwood. I saw carvers creating works of art, beautifully cut sets of geometric shapes and intricate knotworks. I saw others bloodied from carving willwood and none of this made sense. Why would an army about to launch a siege on the most heavily defended city in the south be practising art? To improve morale? Hard to imagine as looking around the camp there was not much morale in evidence. The collared ruled this place by fear and I saw only evidence of that, shifty eyes, bowed heads.

We approached what looked like a construction area, large timbers were stood up and being prepared by what I guessed were master carpenters. These were made from the more usual woods of construction but each timber, whether straight or curved, had a thick channel cut into the centre. Where they had been put together I found them disquieting: there were no right angles, no absolutely straight pieces and they did not look to me as though they should fit together, though they did. Looking at them made my head ache and my eyes feel dry. Groups of soldiers were fitting something into the channels in the wood. They had the air of a punishment detail about them, the truly beaten. It looked like every movement they made pained them, like every moment they worked was a draw upon them and I wondered if they were slaves, being worked to death. As we got even closer I knew I was right, though not in the way I had thought. They were not being denied rest or food, in fact I could see food laid out for them, and plenty of it. Standing over them was one of the monks of Tarl-an-Gig, or Zorir now, tall and robed and their face painted in white with swirls and circles in blue. While the soldiers worked they harangued them, talking of the glory of their god, of how they would receive their reward along the Star Path for important work done.

A few steps closer and everything made a little more sense.

Though not much.

The soldiers worked wood thick with bluevein, I could see the glow of it, and they were inlaying it in the channels of the larger pieces of wood. It was this that took its toll. Far from being slaves I had the suspicion they were fanatics, and that in turn gave me an idea of what was being built here. I took a small detour from our route so I could pass by a woman who looked to be a trunk commander.

"Commander," I said, bowing my head, "this is where they are building the platform for the god?" Her eyes widened, and in that single moment I knew not only that I was right, but that I had made a mistake.

"That is not meant to be known," she grabbed my arm, "come with me. I must speak to the monk about you, they will want to know where you got this information."

"No," I squeaked it, "I was told by my Rai to come this way, to find the pens." In my panic I gave away our plans. This was not the finest moment of Udinny Pathfinder, warrior of Ranya.

"And I say again, whoever told you what we build should not have." She pulled me on, hard. All around the eyes of those working were turned on us and I knew I had ruined any chance of escape with my insatiable curiosity. Then Rai Ustiore was there.

"Trunk Commander," she said, holding herself high and haughty like any Rai. "I see you have found my servant. May I speak with you for a moment." She pointed at a nearby tent. The trunk commander paused, unsure what to do. Looked over at the monk but they had not noticed us yet, they were lost in their sermon. Behind them stood two of the collared. I had not noticed them before as they were in the shadow of the platform. "Commander," bit out Ustiore, "do not displease me, I am about the work of Zorir." That decided the trunk commander; she nodded and led me into the tent followed by Ustiore. The moment we were out of sight Ustiore put her hand on the trunk commander's neck, touching her flesh and I saw the moment of horror when the woman realised she had been tricked and then her face froze as Ustiore, with a sigh of pleasure, fed her cowl and burned the life out of the woman.

"Come on," she said, her face glowing like she had been with a lover, "we must move, Udinny, the body will be found soon and they will know we are here."

We moved, hustling ourselves out of the tent and to where Tanhir waited. I could feel displeasure radiating from her.

"If you have killed us with your foolishness," she hissed at me, "I will find you on the Star Path and beat you back to life once more."

"I am sorry, but I know what they build now."

"And was it worth it?" said Tanhir. Ustiore said nothing, I think she was lost in the aftereffects of feeding her cowl.

"Well, I do not really know, they are expecting their god to come. That is what they build, that is why they take such pains to decorate it. They do it from devotion."

"All fear a Cowl-Rai taking the field," said Ustiore softly, a smile on her face, "imagine how frightened they will be when they see a god."

"They will likely just give up the city."

"We cannot let them," I said. "We must hold the army here for as long as possible."

"Why?" said the Rai. I realised I had no answer. I just knew they must be stopped. "If they do give up the city, maybe we can slip out to Wyrdwood."

"With the army right behind us to advance on Woodhome?" said Tanhir. "No, Udinny is right: they must be held here for as long as possible."

Before we could talk more about how poor the situation was for, well, everyone really, a shout went up from behind us.

"Murder! Traitors!"

We were discovered, but I could smell the animal pens, see them rising not far ahead of us in the camp. Between the pens and the building area were more avenues of tents set up on the dusty ground. Soldiers milled around. I could make out the collared among them and a few scattered Rai.

Now was time for us to move. Not to run, as that would draw eyes on us. We must walk, quickly, stay businesslike and hope we could find our target, a marant, before an entire army found us. Formidable as each of us may be, Tanhir the Forestal, Rai Ustiore and Udinny, warrior of Ranya, we could not take on an entire army.

"Here," said Ustiore, handing Tanhir her bowstaff and leading us away from the platform that was being built.

"Little use without arrows," said Tanhir but she took the thing and I think it gave her some comfort. Behind us more shouting, what sounded like the voice of the monk.

"I saw them! A Rai and an old man." It took a moment for me to realise they spoke of me. I still did not think of myself as an old man, I was still Udinny, a relatively young and quite attractive woman, in my mind.

"We need to get out of here," said Ustiore, "follow me." She led us down an avenue of tents and through what was clearly an armoury. There were hundreds of spears, the throwing and thrusting kind on racks and the air was full of woodsmoke from the fires lit to harden their tips. As we passed Ustiore stopped at a rack and took a long spear and a quiver with throwing spears which she put over her shoulder. A soldier, busy at the fire hardening wood, looked up and was about to say something, but seeing she was Rai stopped and bowed their head, looked away.

Behind us the noise was growing. Alarm calls were going up.

"Find them!" being roared out. The soldier looked back along the lines of tents.

"You heard them soldier, traitors are about. I need to arm my fellows here."

"Take what you need, Rai," said the man. It was almost incredible how calm Ustiore sounded when all I wanted to do was run. My arms and legs felt like they were filled with energy, my heart jittering.

"Arm up," said Ustiore. I stepped in and took a spear for myself, a shield and a quiver of throwing spears, though to be honest I knew little of their use and would have been happier with a bow. "Are you making arrows for the archers we have now?" How she managed to sound conversational when all around the calls were going up to track down and find us I do not know, but she did.

"No," he said, "why do you ask?"

"I have never seen arrows," replied Ustiore brightly. I looked around. Groups of armed soldiers were combing through the tents behind us. "But I have heard of the damage they can do. I was curious to see them."

"Carrack is making 'em," said the soldier, "he's down toward the pens, two lanes across." The soldier looked up, the white make-up of his face cracking as he narrowed his eyes. The soot of the fire had blackened around his clan-paint so it could not be read. "Shouldn't you be searching with the rest of them?" For a moment I thought Ustiore would kill him, but the area was busy with armourers and soldiers coming to arm themselves for the search.

"Of course we are," said Ustiore, "but there is nothing to stop me dropping in on this Carrack on the way?"

"No," said the soldier, but he was plainly suspicious. We moved away, pushing through the soldiers around us. The atmosphere of the camp was ratcheting up, no longer an odd, subdued place, but one full of fear. The soldiers not involved in the search were congregating in groups, finding those they knew and who they felt safe with. Aware a hunt was going on but not yet knowing for who. No one wanted to be caught alone. Ustiore steered us past muttering groups of troops. More and more I felt eyes on us.

"They are noticing us," said Tanhir softly to me, "something we are doing must be drawing attention."

"It is me," replied Ustiore, "Rai do not generally come into this area of the camp. I am drawing attention. Get ready to run. It cannot be long now before we are singled out."

"Those searching are behind us," said Tanhir.

"Gossip always runs ahead of action," said the Rai. She turned down another alley, made a sharp right and pushed through groups of soldiers, the smell of oiled bark armour, baking in the heat of the light above, was almost overpowering. Ahead I saw the tent of the man making arrows. He sat beneath an awning propped up on sticks, placing each arrow into a bucket beside him. Quivers hung from a rack. We made our way there, our walk picking up speed, and I felt every eye upon us. Not far from here to the animal pens, though there was a high fence between us and them. The attention we were gathering was becoming a physical force that I could feel pressing down upon me.

"How quickly can you string that bow," said Ustiore softly as we approached the arrow maker.

"Pretty quickly," said Tanhir.

"Be ready," said the Rai. "The minute we touch the arrows, they will know."

"Why are you here?" Ustiore turned. We were within a few paces of the arrow maker, maybe a hundred of the animal pen fence. The woman who had shouted was big, broad and well-muscled. Behind her stood ten or more soldiers and her voice brought the attention of everyone here down on us. "They're looking for a Rai and an old man. Seems you are near enough to fit the bill." In her hand she had a heavy axe.

"We are on our way to the pens," said Ustiore. She still sounded calm. "Do not detain us or you will pay the price, soldier." The woman licked dry lips, looked around her then back at Ustiore.

"A few moments and those searching will be here," she said. "Costs you nothing to wait."

"It may cost you dearly if you dare to delay me," said Ustiore and sneered in the way of Rai.

"Once, maybe," said the woman, "but it's all changed now, ain't it, since the collared came? They hate us all equal and I'm more frightened of what they might do than of you, Rai." She raised the axe and those around her lowered their spears. "So you wait here." The tension was like morning ice over water, brittle, and easy to break.

"I am afraid I cannot do that, soldier," she said. Tanhir looked from her to me, gave me a nod.

"Then we'll make you," said the soldier.

"No," said Ustiore. At the same time Tanhir grabbed two quivers of arrows and we turned and ran for the fence. Ustiore followed us and the soldiers roared as they gave chase, shouts of "They are here! They are here!" filled the air.

"Through the tents!" shouted Ustiore and Tanhir turned, pushing between two tents, jumping over guy ropes. I followed, behind me Ustiore. As we broke out the other side, surprised soldiers staring at us. Ustiore held out her hands and gouts of fire leapt from them, setting the tents alight. Then she turned her fire on all those around us, screams of agony rang out as she created a barrier of fire. "The fence!" she shouted. "Go!"

We were running again. At the bottom of the fence Tanhir stopped, knelt and made a pocket of her hands.

"Up, Udinny," she shouted. I placed my foot on her hands and she pushed me up, so I could get my hands on the top of the rough fence and drag myself up. Ustiore was still throwing fire, making an impenetrable wall. Beyond it I could see the army coming. Soldiers, collared, and Rai who would be able to put out her fires. I put a hand down and pulled up Tanhir.

"Ustiore!" I shouted, "come on!" Someone launched a spear and it stuck in the wall below my leg. With a final blast of power the Rai ran to the wall and Tanhir pulled her up, then we were on the other side. Tanhir stringing her bow. The air full of the panicked lowing of crown-heads as they reacted to the smell of smoke in the air, pushing against the fences that penned them in. A few confused looking animal keepers stood around. Across from us were the Hetton pens, next to them the black forms of duller pods, though not many. They had become less and less common, I presume because those trapped within did not live long, and now people were collared rather than transformed by whatever process was used to make Hetton and dullers. The Hetton in the pens were hissing and spitting, glaring over malevolently at us. Further down from the Hetton and dullers was a single marant tethered by a stake, its huge manta-shaped form at rest but already fitted with goaders and a riding cage. A face appeared on top of the fence.

"They're here! I see them!" Tanhir silenced them with an arrow.

"The marant!" I shouted and ran towards it followed by Tanhir and Ustiore. Behind the marant a group of soldiers came out of a small, roughly made hut. They were quickly arming themselves and running towards us. One split off and headed for the Hetton pens. Soldiers were coming over the fence behind us.

"Tanhir!" I shouted as I ran for the marant, "don't let him reach the Hetton or we are lost!"

"I will take the soldiers," shouted Ustiore.

"No," I shouted back, "you are the only one who can fly a marant, and you will be weakened by the dullers. Tanhir and I will hold the soldiers." The words were out of my mouth before I realised what I was saying. I may be Udinny, warrior of Ranya, but that had been in another place, outside of life. Here I was Udinny in the body of an old man.

"He is right," said Tanhir, and loosed an arrow, taking down the man running for the Hetton, "get to the marant." The rest of the soldiers from the hut were banding together, and moving toward where Ustiore was running for the marant. Tanhir looked at them, strung an arrow then looked toward me, drew and loosed. A moment of fear as the arrow streaked past me and I heard the sound of it hitting, the cry of pain cut short, and turned. Soldiers coming over the fence. From the corner of my eye more movement as soldiers came in the main gate. The air was full of shouting and the sound of bleating crownheads.

Tanhir was backing up, heading toward the marant. Ustiore ran for it but the soldiers coming at her would intercept. She may beat them, even without access to her power, but they would hold her up long enough for the rest of the soldiers to overwhelm us.

Which meant there was only one thing for it.

I, Udinny, warrior of Ranya, must intercept the soldiers

before they stopped Ustiore, and hope I could deal with them before the rest of the soldiers were upon us. Which, I must be honest, felt rather unlikely.

But that did not matter. Ranya shows me the path and I walk it.

I ran as fast as my legs would carry me and while I ran I shouted out a garbled prayer to Ranya, drowned by the bleating of crownheads. Nearer and nearer to my target, six soldiers, armoured and armed, faces grimacing, spears and swords ready, shields held high.

"Ranya guide me," I shouted, readying my spear and my shield.

I heard an answer. Not from outside, but from within. The gossamer touch of the cowl of Fandrai. I do not think it understood what I was about, or the importance of the marant – our connection was not strong, it only knew the body was in danger. In that moment I felt our connection strengthen. With the connection came, not memories, not exactly, but knowledge. Fandrai had been a warrior all his long life, he had fought for his god and to bring the swarden into being, he had trained many others and now in some way, through his cowl, he was with me.

Had I not already experienced similar from the ghosts of myself I would have fought this intrusion, but I had so I did not.

The soldiers were not expecting my attack. Oh, they saw me coming, but they saw an old man in raggedy armour. They thought I would slow and stop, give them time. They thought their numbers would give me thought. Their hesitance was my advantage. By the time they realised I would not stop it was too late. They did not have time to form their shield wall. They still, I imagine, thought their numbers would overwhelm me.

But they did not know they faced Udinny, warrior of Ranya, imbued by the spirit of Fandrai, priest of murder.

A spear came at my head, my eyes. A lesser warrior

would flinch. I went low, thrusting my spear forward and the cowl lent its strength, the hardened wood smashed through the first soldier's armour, and into his gut. I pulled the spear out, the soldier falling to the ground. From my right came a sword. The woman holding it screaming as she brought it down. I let myself drop into a roll. The sword swept through air and my spear came around, hitting the woman on the back of her legs, taking them out from beneath her and she fell on her back as I rolled to my feet. All the speed built up into my roll used to bring the spear down on her.

Two down.

The remaining four stood open-mouthed in shock. I ran one through with the spear before he composed himself. Then ran at the three left. One thrust a spear and I parried, knocking it aside and putting my own spear through his neck. The other two ran and without thinking, as if this body was no longer mine, I threw the spear, taking a runner in the back while the last one zigzagged her way back toward the forces coming through the gate.

The whole process had taken no more than a few seconds.

"Come on!" Behind me, Ustiore was on the marant and I ran to join her. The bleating of the crownheads was frantic, noisy. Tanhir coming as fast as she could but stopping every few paces to loose arrows into the forces coming towards her. They were coming at us, but slowly, her arrows and my dismantling of the guards from the hut had made them much more wary of us. Someone opened the Hetton cages as I climbed onto the back of the marant, it smelled of forest herbs and warmth and was buzzing gently.

"How long until it can take off?"

"Not long, someone must have been planning to leave."

"Tanhir!" I shouted, "hurry!" She ran, leaping onto the back of the animal and it squealed, then Ustiore leaned on the goaders and squealed again. Not quite ready to take off yet.

"Come on!" she said. Tanhir began loosing arrows. The Hetton, ten of them, were sprinting toward us.

"Come on, beast," shouted Ustiore and the creature began to moan, its thrusting jets filling the air with a warm, organic smell. But it did not take off and the Hetton were closing and all appeared to have been for nothing.

With a crash, and a furious bleating, the fences holding the crownheads collapsed, and every crownhead in the camp, and there must have been hundreds, escaped, stampeding out of the pens, led by one particularly brave crownhead who headed straight for the Hetton. Too late, the creatures noticed what was coming, then they were buried in a mass of woolly angry flesh.

"Syerfu," I said to myself. "I knew you would return!"

And with a lurch we were up, rising above the camp as Ustiore steered the marant in a tight circle, to turn us toward Jinnspire.

"We are free!" shouted Tanhir, "we made it!"

And maybe that would have been true, if not for the archers, gathered at the edges of the camp and aiming their forestbows at us.

42
Sorha

Her second time in the root forest and it felt no less strange to her for it. Guided by the soft glow of fungal towers they moved forwards, a motley group she had never expected to find herself among. How far her life had veered off course; it was almost funny in a black sort of way. No rooms low in the spire for her to live out her life in luxury. No, she was in a leafless forest, in a land she had never imagined had existed, surrounded by outlaws and creatures she would once have considered worth nothing more than hunting for sport. They were not creatures to her now, they were people, and people she was prepared to die for.

And had come close, not only above, but in the last few moments. It was not an easy walk through the root forest as she had done before with the Osere. They were hunted, the Betrayers were everywhere. They did not chase, they did not come in large groups. Instead they found places and waited in silence, they coated the gentle blue glow of their infection with black soil, they stood next to roots and were almost invisible until the moment they struck and it was like the darkness came to life. A sudden movement, a scream, a death.

They lost an Osere and two Forestals before Tall Sera called them to a stop.

"We cannot continue like this, how far to where we are going?" She had to translate for Frina, then try to understand what she said with her barebones knowledge of their language and Frina's barebones knowledge of hers. It was hard, not only that the Osere spoke a different language but they thought differently, the lack of sight changed their entire world. They knew the world by scent and noise. They measured distance by steps and north, south, east and west were alien to them. They thought in terms of what was within their immediate sphere, of what they could hear and feel and smell; they measured distance in these spheres of understanding, in the distance the smell of a cut root travelled, in the echo of a footstep. Day and night were meaningless and Sorha struggled to understand a lot of what was said.

Struggled even more to get it across to the Forestals.

"What do you mean, you do not know how long?"

"They do not think like us."

"Will these Betrayers have time to pick us all off? Can you at least tell us that?"

"It is a distance," said Sorha. "The best I can tell you is they understand these roots are cloudtrees, and the roots are the same width as the canopy above. We must walk at least five of them. Usually they would use taffistones but we cannot now." Tall Sera nodded in the gloom of the fungal towers.

"A long walk," he said, "maybe days as we measure it above depending on the terrain." Sorha nodded. She had estimated the same but the Forestals knew the trees better than her so she had not wanted to say. "Those creatures will kill us all."

"Maybe not," said Venn. Their eyes gleamed in the darkness. "I think I can feel them."

"Why did you not say?" Tall Sera snapped. In his voice Sorha heard a brittleness, the sound of a man out of his element, whose usual surety was being stripped from him step by step in this alien and echoing place.

"I was not sure, not until the last one struck and what I feel is very subtle, very small."

"But you do feel it?" said Tall Sera.

"I think so, but all of you," Venn waved a hand, a blur in the darkness, a half-sensed movement, "you muddy it."

"So what do we do then?" said Tall Sera.

"I go ahead," said Venn.

"No," It was instinctual, the word escaping from Sorha's mouth before she knew why. "You are important, Venn, to the Osere. And to those things, they want you."

"Then they are less likely to kill me," Venn said. Behind her Frina was speaking, a stream of urgent words.

"She says the Betrayers are not really clever, they may not know Venn is valuable, or even which one of us Venn is."

"This will save lives," said Venn, and even though Sorha knew they were right, she felt the need to argue. To protect.

"You do not kill," she said. "You know we will kill them if you find them." She almost felt the trion's misery, the battle within them, and found herself feeling bad about it. Another unwelcome and alien feeling she had never had a use for in the past. If this was becoming a better person it was far harder than she had ever thought such things would be. How long had she told herself those who were not Rai were weak? They were anything but.

"They are not alive," said Venn. "Not any more. What is done to them, it takes . . ." They left the word hanging, then added quietly, "everything."

Frina spoke again, words so quick Sorha could only just

understand, and some parts she had to make the Osere repeat.

"Frina will walk with you, she is used to looking for the Betrayers."

"But—"

"It is not for negotiation," said Sorha, "I will walk with you, too." For a moment she thought the trion would argue with her, then they nodded.

"Also," added Venn, "more of her people are out there. I can feel them." A few whispered words from Frina.

"Can she touch you?" said Sorha. A moment of silence. Then a soft reply.

"Yes."

Sorha watched as Frina put her hand on Venn's arm, something almost reverent in the way she did it. There was a moment of something, a communion between them, a whisper through the root forest then Frina took her hand away. Venn turned to Sorha.

"The other Osere, they will find us," said the trion.

The party formed a loose triangular formation, Venn at the front with Frina and Sorha. Behind them the Forestals, and around them the Osere, to make sure no one got lost. Venn had been careful to make sure they did not spread out too much, outside Venn's sense of what and who was where.

It was a tense journey, Sorha could feel an ache starting in her jaw even after only a few steps. She had to concentrate on not clamping down, on not tightening every muscle in her body in line with her mind. She concentrated on Venn, the shadow just before and to the right of her, taking slow steps forward through the root forest. They stopped. Venn pointed further right past where Frina stood and the Osere stopped. She cocked her head and they stood without moving, in total silence.

Or total silence to Sorha.

Not for Frina.

The Osere moved, quick as liquid and bright with colour under the light of the fungus, one sweeping action that brought out the blade she wore at her hip, arcing up and out through the air until it cut into something Sorha could not see. A body fell, crumbling to the ground without making a sound and Frina knelt, wiping off her blade on the corpse before putting it back on her hip and standing. Venn stood absolutely still, one pale hand outstretched and glowing in the soft light of a fungal tower.

They moved on. This was to be the pattern, for the length of their journey. No rest, they did not stop. Not when Tall Sera said they should, when he said his people were tired, that they could not keep going, never knowing if there was someone Venn had missed, if they would be struck down from the darkness.

Eventually Frina spoke, a long string of words that Sorha listened to, had her repeat, and agreed with.

"We can stop," Sorha said, "but the Betrayers will not, and the creature we saw will not. They do not know exactly how quickly it can move, but it is far quicker than we can." Tall Sera blinked in the darkness, a momentary vanishing of the light reflected in his eyes. "Are you willing to risk them finding us?" The Forestal sighed.

"No, we should move then, maybe it would be better to go more quickly."

"It will not," said Sorha, "and you will regret it the first time it is one of yours lying in the dirt." He did not reply, but her words had hit home and they continued onwards, Frina and Sorha cutting down the hiding Betrayers when Venn pointed them out. Once they knew where they were it was not too hard to find them. They covered their blue glow but not well as they could not see to know the parts they missed. Eventually, Tall Sera joined them, his arrows cutting down the Betrayers from a distance and from then those at the front rotated, sometimes Osere, sometimes

Forestals, the better to keep them fresh. Only Venn did not rest.

"Are you all right?" she asked them.

"My head aches. But I am becoming better at this." She nodded, it was true. Venn was spotting the Betrayers far earlier than before, early enough that the Osere had become almost redundant in the process. Mostly they served to guide in other Osere as they were drawn to Venn and Frina's call.

The Forestals and their fearsome bows were doing all the work. Killing silently and from a distance. Gradually, they loosed their arrows less and less. Sorha felt sure they had passed the main concentration of the Betrayers and as if her mind was being read Venn spoke up. "I can sense no more up ahead, I will keep trying, though."

"Maybe we can move even faster now?" said Tall Sera.

"Yes," this from Frina, "faster is good."

Now it was apparent they had outpaced the Betrayers, they did not stop or slow. The Osere would not allow it. Freed from constant watchfulness, Sorha began to see a beauty in the root forest she had not seen before. It was not showy, like the Wyrdwood. Osere aside there were no bright flashes of light or cascades of colour here. All was muted glows and soft colours, from far above there was an almost constant gentle light. It was not there if you looked at it, but she knew it was there when she didn't. Closer to the roots they had colour, a very, very soft green that could only just be seen, and had there been any more light she would never have noticed the gentle pulse of the life running through them. The more she walked, the more she felt it. She had thought this place dead once but it was not.

Then she began to notice the buildings. Though they were not buildings any longer. Ruins, built of the same black material as ancient Anjiin, though whatever this place had been it was gone now. The walls only visible as low, serrated shadows against the barely-there glow of the roots.

"What is this place, Frina?" she said softly.

"E'elm," she said.

"What is E'elm?"

Frina pointed behind them and away. Gave Sorha a measurement that she did not understand.

"City, E'elm," she said. "Here, E'elm Statyon."

"Like an outlying city? A village?"

"Yes, village," said Frina. "Betrayers, destroyed, many lives of Osere."

"What does she mean?" asked Venn.

"I think this was a village or larger, of a city or county the Osere called E'elm which is behind us. But this place was destroyed generations ago by the Betrayers."

"Harn," said Venn.

"What?"

"The creature, the god," said Venn, "it rose from Anjiin to Tilt." Sorha nodded. "We are in the north, so this E'elm, it is probably under Harn if that is how this Osereud place works."

"It could be," said Sorha.

"Then there is a way out?" said Tall Sera.

"If we could make the temple rise like it did under Tiltspire, if there is even a temple there," said Sorha.

"Only god," said Frina. Then she spoke to Sorha in her language.

"What did she say?"

"That only the gods can raise the temples." Frina nodded.

"So we must try the taffistones again," said Tall Sera. "Once we have done whatever your friend wants down here."

Frina pointed at an angle to the way they had been going. Let out a string of words.

"Let me guess," said the Forestal, "she wants us to go that way? What will we find when we do?" Frina spoke again and Sorha took in a sharp breath.

"A god," said Sorha.

"Why would we want to go near one of those monsters?" said Tall Sera and in reply Frina pointed at Venn.

"Godtalker," she said, and Sorha could not suppress the shudder of fear running through her.

43

Venn

They were tired in a way they had never been tired before, not even when the trion of the Forestals had tested them, pushed them beyond what they had believed was their limits. They had thought that was hard, that it was work beyond what their body was capable of but they were wrong. Venn no long.. walked consciously, they walked in a dream where they did not see the world. They saw shapes and power, pulsing lines of energy and their awareness stretched out from them, growing constantly with use until Venn had to fight not to reach too far. Deep within Venn was a sense that if they spread out too far, if they let their awareness stretch too much, they may never come back. There was a certain peace in that thought, that Venn would cease to be and instead they would become a small part of every creature and plant and leaf and vine that ran or walked or grew in Crua. No more fear, no more running, no more of the pain nurtured by their mother that had never gone away.

There was peace within the network of Crua, there was joy in the golden pulse that ran through it. They knew, without thinking or questioning, that what they touched was Ranya. Ranya who was in all things. To most, like the light of the root forest, if you concentrated on Ranya they could barely see them, they were diffused, everywhere and nowhere.

But, as Venn became more aware of Ranya they also knew Crua was sick, broken, limited. So much less than it had been, than it could be. Something was missing. No, that was wrong, something had been taken, leaving a space and it was into that space that the bluevein had crept. No, not crept, been pushed, a gradual and growing sickness. Venn felt it as a null, a place they could not sense, that was how they found the betrayers, how Venn knew where they were.

They also knew they were followed by more of the Betrayers, a large group trailing them but not attempting to catch up. Venn could only think they were waiting, waiting for that creature they had seen before. The god.

A dark god, Venn had no doubt about that.

They headed toward a great and shining light. A place in which the lines of power running through Crua collected. Venn could feel how this whole area somehow drew power to it, and how the power itself changed here. It did not only run through the ground and the roots, it reached up, into the air, petering out like the water of a geyser. The strangest idea, that the power had a memory of what it had been and it was trying to be that again. Of course, foolish: energy had no memory.

Then again, Ranya had memory, and was Ranya energy?

Even when Venn spoke words with their companions they were only partly here.

E'elm, Harn, names flowing back and forth and Venn had no doubt those places were the same, or had once been the same and slipped away from one another with time. This was what the energy strived for but was denied, to be what it had been. Venn wondered, if it remembered could it feel loss? Did it mourn? Or was it simple and unthinking, like the orits and swarden making their towers? Only doing what they had always done.

"Godtalker," said Frina and Venn knew that word was hopelessly inadequate to describe what she meant. They did not understand her language but they felt what came with the word, the hope, the possibility of something better, the fruition of a hundred thousand generations of suffering in the darkness. The prospect of leaving this place, of seeing once more, though Frina did not mean seeing as having eyes. She spoke of seeing in a deeper way, of having an understanding, of a knowing, but knowing what was long lost to Frina's people.

The Osere pointed and even before she did it Venn knew where to go, it frightened them and thrilled them in equal amounts. The concentration of power, the great glowing star in the distance. Sorha was frightened of it, the Forestals wanted to be away from this place. Venn could feel Tall Sera's desire to leave not only because he thought he should be back with his people above but because he was frightened of the darkness, of his inability to see what may come for him and that fear transferred itself to his people.

They walked, Venn lost in a reverie, feeling the roots of the cloudtree close around them as they pulsed, energy from above feeding into the ground, and once they were close, feeding into the thing at the heart of the tree.

Slowly, Venn came out of their fugue, and interfaced completely with the world. The roots here growing thicker and closer together, harder to get through until it would not be too far until they could go no further. Even if that had not been the case Venn knew they would have had to withdraw at that point, the thing ahead was so bright and that brightness was a barrier.

"A cocoon," said Sorha softly. "I have seen this before."

"No," said Frina. "Different."

They saw the first body leant against a tree root, not a

skeleton but it had been dead a long time. The skin stretched tight over old bones.

Once they saw one they saw more.

"Is this a trap?" said Tall Sera and he drew his bow. Frina talked softly to Sorha.

"No trap," said the Rai. "Put your weapon down, Forestal, this is a graveyard." The Forestal did not put his weapon down, not immediately. Not until he looked more closely at one of the bodies and saw it strewn with dried fungus that had long ago lost its glow. Saw that each mummified corpse had faint marks drawn on the bulge of their head, stylised eyes.

They moved on, the roots thicker with every step, harder to get through, the brightness growing in Venn's mind. They found themselves in a corridor where the roots had been carefully bent out of the way and at the end of the corridor was a cage, millions of criss-crossed roots forming an impenetrable barrier. In Venn's mind it was not only the roots, but the light that stopped further progress. The grave corridor was walled with bits of old wood, strange fungal materials, some had colour and some did not. Some looked to have a use, some did not. Bits of armour, maybe tools, clothes? Other things they could not name and did not see a use for. To Venn's eyes it was a riot, no rhyme or reason to it until they reached out a hand and touched some of the pieces and knew themselves wrong. There was pattern and meaning here, they did not understand it as it was not a pattern of colour like they were used to, it was a pattern of texture and shape. A message for the Osere, a communication and a devotion, a place of offerings. Held within it was a sadness so palpable Venn could feel it.

"We come, at the end," said Frina haltingly, thinking hard about each word and reaching out to touch one of the pieces. "To give of ourselves."

"You leave an offering?" said Venn.

"And our body," she said, "for the tree. To feed the god."

"What do you get in return?" said Tall Sera.

"Nothing," said Frina. "We owe this."

"Surely your debt is long since paid," said Sorha softly.

"Do not know. Godtalkers gone long time." Venn nodded.

"But now Venn is here," said Tall Sera. "Has this all been so you can be forgiven?"

"No," said Frina. "This maybe save all." But Venn was barely listening to what was said, the cage of thorns and sticks was calling them. They saw beyond it. It was pulsing, glowing so brightly it should blind them but it no longer felt like a barrier now they were nearer, they felt warmed by the light. It was similar to the touch of the Boughry back in Harn, but that had been a harsh thing, using them whether they wanted or not. This was softer, an invitation. Venn took a deep breath. Stopped themselves doing anything.

This was Crua, the draw of golwyrd felt like safety when it pulled you into a spiked pit to die. The skinfetch came among its prey wearing the faces of those they loved. The Osere's gods betrayed them.

"This is one of those creatures," said Sorha. Frina began to reply, falling back into her own language and Venn did not understand, having to wait for Sorha to translate. "Like in Tilt."

"Well," said Tall Sera, "is it?"

"She does not think so," said Sorha. "This one fought those who wished to enslave the people above."

"So it is safe," said Tall Sera. Sorha did not speak, not immediately. Frina said more and Sorha sighed.

"Venn, Frina believes you have the power to speak with the god within, but she would have me warn you. The Godtalkers of the Osere were first to fall."

"But if this one is on our side . . ."

"The one that took Cahan, the one sitting in Tiltspire, that one was also considered a friend once. That was how it took the Godtalkers."

"Oh," said Venn.

"Frina believes the only way forward is to commune. But she understands that you may not be willing to risk yourself. She does not know if she would."

Venn stared at the light, the glow only they could feel. They felt fear, yes, and they felt calm, as if this was inevitable. Had always been coming.

"Udinny would say Ranya has shown me the path, it would be rude of me not to walk it." They laughed, couldn't help themselves. Their mind filled with an image of the monk. She always brought a sense of joy. "I have come this far. So I will walk to the end." With that, and before they could think or worry or listen to the sudden babble of voices around them, Venn stepped forward and put their hand out, to touch the cage of thorns and as they did it folded back, the roots curling and twisting away, opening to reveal what was within. Surely all saw the golden glow now? All bathed in the warmth?

Venn did not know, could not look away from the pod within the cage, like a blister on the massive taproot of the cloudtree, and within it a creature like the one that had taken Cahan, but to Venn this one looked healthier, its slick black substance not shot through with the sickly glow of bluevein. Venn felt sure they were doing the right thing. They put out both hands, laid them on the blister.

The world.

Gone.

Everything gone.

Venn no longer was.

They were no longer corporeal.

They did not exist and yet they did.

They had no physicality, no weight and no sense of being.

They hung in a nothingness, a darkness thicker than in the land of the Osere.

Though it was also not truly darkness, that was an absence of light and in this place there was no light to be absent of. It was like sleep, thought Venn. Like the moment you cease to exist between falling unconscious and waking. A time when you still existed but were not in any real way there.

Except Venn was there.

Wherever "there" was.

They were conscious, and real and somewhere in the back of their head they knew their mind was creating feelings in a bid to understand this place. They were floating, that was the easiest thing to believe, they floated in a place between life and death and as they thought that the idea solidified. Of course they were; if they were to commune with the god they would need to join it in whatever place it inhabited, and these gods slept.

A sudden and powerful oppression fell upon them. The feeling of having been imprisoned for a time beyond Venn's understanding. Being unconscious, but while they were unconscious some part of them was not, it was waiting, hoping and knowing that it slept. That outside the world moved on and it had no control, it could not even wake itself. Venn felt – at the same time – the incredible sense of peace of the sleeping mind and the exquisite torture of the second mind, the one that could never sleep. With that sense came knowledge. These beings had chosen this, knowing what it would do to them, what part of them would have to go through.

Or at least this one had. Others, Venn felt, no, knew, had not chosen, had been forced.

Connection?

A voice that was not a voice. A word that was not a word but there was an understanding. A question.

Connection?

Yes.

What else was there to say? How else to end this long, long journey to this place but to invite conversation with a being that was entirely alien to Venn? As unlike them as they were to the gasmaws of the forest.

And yet, Venn knew them.

Connection.

Satisfaction, thankfulness.

The feeling of another mind reaching out, touching, examining.

Screaming. Venn knew they were screaming and could not stop. They were crushed under the weight of the other being, crushed by its despair as they became fully aware of how much time had passed. It was too much, too strong, and it would eat them away, scour their mind clean in a sandstorm of horror.

The connection vanished.

Venn was safe, hanging in the nothing place.

An almost image, a shadowy shield, like those used by the soldiers in Crua. With it a question. A feeling. Why did Venn not protect themselves? Another connection, but far more gentle, the other side holding back. Before Venn could reply, say they did not know how to protect themselves, they realised they did not need to.

So much is lost.

So sad, resigned.

Too long.

Translate?

What? Venn did not understand. A flash. An image.

A golden city teeming with people and the creatures Venn thought of as gods. Gods sat upon the tops of temples controlling the flow of power through the city, making it move and change. And a hundred thousand others, gods and people, in the city below were going about tasks Venn could not understand. At the top of each temple, by the god on its throne, stood one of the people. On their face glowing signs and sigils, one hand on the creature and one hand on the pedestal and there was a great peace, a flow of power, a mutual and beneficial exchange. The gods did not control, they could not do it alone. That was not the way of creation.

Yes.

They felt themselves become a portal, a way of communication and something passed through them and into the land. A flow of alien words and they felt sure that buried deep within they heard a name. Or an approximation of it.

emRaNyA?

In reply more words, these they did understand. *Severe degradation.* Following that another string of replies. *Entropy – outside expected parameters. Corruption – unexpected. Purge. Renew. Restart.* Venn knew that in these words was more meaning than they could glean, and even with the distance the god, the entity, was keeping from them what they saw. Still echoes of it, shock, confusion and terror, reached Venn.

A pause.

A moment in this unplace when nothing existed except the connection between them, the entity in the tree and the land of Crua. They felt the land, the sheer size of it, the complexity, and how every single system within it relied on another in a vast circle. No, it was once a circle, now a spiral, a slowly decreasing curve and its journey down had been getting faster and faster until now when they were at, or near, the very end. Then another question, hanging in the air.

Share?

It wanted them to open themselves up again, to share everything they knew and had been through and there was no doubt for Venn that this creature could force them to do this, if it wished. Also that it would not. It asked and would respect Venn's reply. For a moment, Venn thought to refuse, the memory of the shared pain was still strong, but it also began to filter through that the offer to share was not one way, the creature would know of Venn, but Venn would know of it.

How could they ever refuse such a thing?

44

Share

They sat atop the (interfacmple) tower of (Helmarn?)
Below them the city stretched out, behind them the spire hummed with power and all was golden and flowing and every (person??) and (god??) from here to (enJinneerring?) in the south knew their place and their task in the great achievement.

All things touched one another, (RaNyA?) spoke within them all. The gods understood the great machine and the working and the number that kept them on the Star Path, but could not host the material of the (controlwl?) that let them maintain the material of the (Crua??). The people could not understand the working, but could host the cowl without harm.

This was how it was made, how it was to be. The partnership.

The Star Path beckoned and from Harn the gods steered the path and they knew the path and they followed the path. In (EAngjiine?) The power gathered by the cloudtrees flowed and changed and fed (iFTaL?) and from there all things were in turn fed and cared for and all was good for the journey. The gods contained and powered the flow and the numbers through iFTaL and the people, bonded with their cowls, maintained the physicality of the (worldship), taking on all the work that the gods were unable to do, their strange minds contained the necessary theories and shapes and calculations that would allow them to travel . . .

Unimaginable distance
Unimaginable time
The void

Venn was reeling, hit by ideas and images and truths they had no frame of reference for. Words they did not understand. Things they thought they knew curling around concepts that made them feel unimaginably small. They wanted to pull away, to run, but they were held tightly within this sharing, experiencing another's life, and as that came to them they realised they were not experiencing the life of god, it was someone like them. A conduit, separated by a length of time their mind rebelled at, but at the same time, this was them.

Their panic was washed away by another succession of images, of feeling that was so real they were there, even though they were not there.

This was the purpose of (*the*) (Crewua), to protect what had been and what would be and what is. All creatures working together, knowing the great work, understanding its importance and their place within it. The harmony of life, the circle of death and rebirth and the energy that flowed through them. The lesson hard learned of . . .

Desolation
Fire
Ash
Death

. . . and this last chance.

And while the tower guardians saw to the health of the land there were others, in the *beneath* that worked with iFTaL on ways to speed the journey along the path. All was good. All was right. And this continued for . . .

Time . . . time beyond thinking . . .
And would continue for . . .
Time . . . time beyond thinking . . .
Until the great work was complete and the Star Path was travelled in its entirety.

But even gods can become impatient.

And gods did become impatient. In a secret space within iFTaL a theory began to grow. At first, a theoretical, a hypothetical.

Fire and ash.

Nothing more than the dalliance of those minds that held within them the most complex of ideas and numbers. Not meant to be looked at seriously, a side branch of the main trunk of investigation. A curiosity. An *it could be . . .*

That among the minds of some gods became a *we could.*

A inTeraffifacestone that could cross the void.

A leap.

There was within the make-up of the world, a way to take some, but not all, of the life upon it and circumvent the time and the distance and send them along the Star Path.

For every action a reaction.

Fire and ash.

A bright point in the blackness. A spiralling, fire. The world, no longer on the Star Path, empty. Those left behind *fire and ash* blackened and broken. A decision made on who and what was worthy and who and what was not. Venn felt the horror of the great mind they touched, that had believed all life was sacred and worthy and to be protected as it remembered a time when such things were not the case and that was why the world was.

Fire and ash.

Not all chose to remember.

Impatience, the knowledge even gods may die given time. That the journey on the Star Path was not certain, that much could befall them on the way.

The conversation became binary, with no midpoint between the two parties. Go or stay. judge or be judged. War.

Terrible energies unleashed. The gods and those who followed them commanding lances of fire that laid waste to cities. Temples sinking into the ground to protect themselves, the beneath being too precious to both sides to risk in war. The above, not.

War, raging, both sides equally matched until one side began to lie. To offer passage to more than they ever could truly give. To pretend the concepts did not say what they said. An army rising, pushing back and the spectre of fire and ash rising higher and higher.

Until, drastic action was taken.

In ancient Anjiin stood the eight pillars of iFTaL. The control. An agreement existing that they were sacrosanct, to be untouched.

In desperation. Explosions.

The ebb and flow of energy stopped to save all. The link between the gods and the world broken. Only the cowls still worked and they were not enough. Time, already spooling out ahead beyond Venn's understanding grew. The Star Path lengthening as iFTaL was lost.

In that moment both sides saw their madness. How close they had come to recreating what had been before and losing everything. The gods chose, knowing even they could not live for the time required, to sleep. Those who had fought hardest, on both sides, chose to become their guardians. Were changed, for this underground world, no longer lit by the power of iFTaL.

To sleep, to trust RaNyA knew the shapes and the way to rebuild what had been broken. That the people would rebuild iFTaL and the Star Path would once more be put within reach.

All this Venn saw in the beat of a heart, the blink of eye. Knew that gods could be as foolish as the people of

Crua, that they had been. Knew that something, in the time since the war, had gone terribly wrong. That this god did not expect to wake to a broken land, a land of the lost.

And as the god shared with Venn, so Venn shared with the god. What they had been through. The land they had grown up in. Crua as they knew it, where nothing shone, and there was only cold and mud and they felt from the god their disappointment, and confusion, and sorrow.

And anger.

Cold and furious anger at the Rai, at the perversion wrought upon the cowl and as the god sorted through memories and stories of Cowl-Rai then the anger grew, it focused and the god felt nothing but hate for those who would reach for power, kill for power, set aside the great task. It understood struggle, it even understood those who had desired to burn the world for the Star Path, in these places each side had truthfully believed they worked for the good of the many. Even its bitterest enemy had not been trying to simply put themselves in power, this god had little understanding of Rai – though they mentally recoiled in horror at feeding the life of another to a cowl – or Leorics or trunk commanders, all were as alien to it as the concepts it had been showing Venn were to them. The trion felt a growing misery in the god, that it had fought for all. That it had given all it had to stop this land burning. But it had been wrong. Those it had trusted had betrayed it. The Crua had not fixed the land. They had not given themselves to Ranya and begun the rebuilding of the towers of Iftal. They had squandered the life bought for them with the lives of many gods and people. They had forgotten the sacrifice of those who slept and guarded. They had become something it found repugnant. When it saw the creature atop the tower in Tilt, when it felt through Venn, the web of Ranya and the bluevein it felt another level of horror and betrayal. These two creatures were allies of old.

For the first time since they had touched the creature, Venn began to think they may be in real danger.

The god, the creature was doubting. Wondering if it had made a mistake? Was its old compatriot, once fighting against the burning of the world, now working for it, right? Were the Crua the problem? Once the people and the gods had worked together, needed each other. But had the Crua become something poisonous to the world?

Fire cleanses.

The concept, powerful and thought without malice. Simply the way someone sees a problem and proposes a solution. Venn felt the god's belief that not only was Ranya somehow corrupted, broken, but that the people were also. The only way was to burn and level the ground and start again and Venn, caught within the creature's mind, had no escape. No way to run and tell the others.

All they could do was share more with it.

Share Cahan Du-Nahere, how they had made him what he was. How hard he had fought in his determination to be something and someone better. How his downfall had been brought about by a desire to help others. Share what Venn knew of Sorha, once a monster, now changed beyond recognition. No longer seeking power. They shared the Forestals, the way they worked together and hid in the forest in a bid to live their lives in balance with the world around them. They shared how the people of Harn, faced by a force far beyond them to combat, had sacrificed everything they had, given their lives so Cahan Du-Nahere helped by the Boughry and Venn and Udinny who had offered their life up, could raise a forest to save the people. How those people had gone on to change and make themselves into something better. Then they shared memories of shyun, and rootlings, and garaur and raniri and spearmaws and all the fabulous wonderful strange and terrible creatures of the land and all this would be lost. Lastly, the wonder of the Osere, the generations of sacrifice and care, the cruel decimation of them and their continued hope for salvation.

Did it show interest in the Boughry?

Did it wonder at the sacrifice?

Was it entranced by the creatures of the land?

It did not know the animals of the world, they had not been here when the god had sat atop the temple and that made Venn wonder, just how long had it been? How long had they slept for?

Time beyond your understanding.

Despite all that Venn shared, despite all it saw, they knew the creature was unconvinced. It looked ahead and saw only ruin. It looked out and saw a world it did not understand, and did Venn feel an anger behind this confusion? A fury that what it wanted had not happened. That it did not wake to a perfect world where all problems were fixed, where everything that had been wrong, and ruined in the war, had been put right.

In that moment, Venn found something within themselves, something they had not expected. They reacted in a way that they would never have done had they stopped and thought about it, but there was no time for thought. Venn was tired, Venn had lost much, seen so many they loved and respected ground beneath the boot of the Rai and now this new god that sat in Tiltspire would destroy them all to open a hole in the world for it to escape through.

Anger.

"You left us!" the thought delivered like a blow. "You did not solve your problems, you did not find peace among yourselves. You started a war, you destroyed our world, then you went away. You put off the solution. You gave your destruction to us and hoped when you woke again everything would be better." Venn felt the god's attention on them, like a great fiery light, stronger and more powerful even than the light above. "Everything has gone wrong!" Venn, shouting it into this unplace between minds. "Where were you when we struggled and died? Sleeping? Where were your instructions? Where were the signs for us to follow? The world is lost, Ranya shows us paths but provides no destinations. The skeletons of the dead wake in the deepest parts of the forest to build towers for you without ever knowing why. The Boughry rend and pull people apart as they look for answers within them. And where are you who are the great architects of our land? I will tell you where you are. You are sleeping in the hope we will fix what you broke."

The heat of attention intensifying, but now Venn had started they could not stop.

"And because you have not woken to what you wanted, because once more there is struggle and you may be called upon to make a sacrifice to help those who have struggled in the wasteland you created. You want to take the easiest option. Well, I have felt how great your mind is, how you know so much more than I ever will. So if you are so great, you must see all that has gone wrong was built on the mound created when you buried whatever you have for a head in the soil. While you looked away from us while we fought with a land that could barely sustain us. You wonder why things went wrong? Why the people were not working to fix Crua? It is because they barely had enough left to survive on." The anger burned itself out. Left Venn small and cold and shivering in the mind of another. "You let me feel the strength of the partnership our peoples once had. Now we are alone, and we need your help and you will turn away from us once more."

The heat cooled.

Venn felt something brush against them, almost the comforting touch of another on their arm. Words in their mind.

Let me consider.

45

Udinny

$\int$omething in the process of collaring the Forestals changed them. The arrows shot at us were not loosed with the usual unerring skill of Tanhir's people. Many flew wide, others far ahead, others behind us and some dropped short.

But not all.

Fortunate for us that we rose on a marant, its wide body and slowly flapping wings protected us from the arrows that were on target. Good for us but not for the poor marant, it squealed and moaned as it flew, the sound it made as each arrow sunk deep into its flesh was piteous. It made me wish I had Venn's skill, that I could reach out with the cowl within me to ease the creature's pain but the cowl only acted when it judged I was in true danger, the sort that may put its continued existence in jeopardy. For whatever reason, and despite the terrible sounds the marant made, it did not see dropping out of the sky as an immediate danger.

So we rose, the marant even more quickly than I expected. It needed no goading from Ustiore, all it wanted to do was escape the pain coming from below and its jets roared and the wings shook as it reached for the air. Below us, the army of Zorir stretched out, the wooden plinth for their god in the centre, the soldiers, Rai and collared all around it in a circle and behind it the tail, wreathed in the smoke of cooking fires. Outside of a spire city I do not think I had ever seen so many people in one place.

To our side rose the walls of Jinneng, the richest city in all of Crua due to a Treefall generations ago. The walls were huge, built of mud bricks, sloping steeply up to a thick and tall wall of wood. The whole edifice was maybe the height of six or seven people standing on each other's shoulders, and punctuated with towers. In front of it there had been wooden huts and small houses, overspill from the city, but with the coming of the army they had been raised to stop them providing cover for attackers. Soldiers and Rai patrolled the tops of the walls and even from where we were, far above, they looked splendidly dressed. Jinneng was the richest county and their armour would be the best, their equipment, too.

They must know, just as we did, that it would not save them.

Behind the walls, rising far higher than the works of the people could ever hope to, was Jinnspire. Fully intact unlike some of the other spires, black and shiny like the carapace of an orit, eight smaller spires and a huge central one, before the central spire the clearing where the people of Jinneng would hold markets. Unlike the other spire cities Jinneng backed onto the forest, it sat in woodedge so that only half of it was on the plain, surrounded by grasslands that had either already been harvested or were partway through growing, not fruiting yet, making a golden waving carpet before the city walls.

The marant continued to rise in a tight circle, mewling and crying as more arrows hit home and then, when the arrows were rising but no longer had the power to hit us,

Ustiore leaned into the goads and the creature beneath us bucked and turned toward Jinneng.

"Must you be so hard on it?" said Tanhir. Clearly the noises it made upset her as much as they bothered me.

"Yes," said the Rai, "it feels wrong, I have ridden many of these. I think it has been hit somewhere important." As Ustiore spoke the marant let out another piteous noise and lurched forward in the air, almost throwing me from my seat. "Hold on," said Ustiore, "I do not know how long it will stay up." She leaned into the goads and the pulsing roar of the marant surrounded us as it gulped in air and pushed it out to propel itself forward. As it did I heard its jets falter. "It's weakening," said Ustiore, "I had hoped we would have longer."

"What?" said Tanhir. "Is it dying?"

"I think so," said Ustiore. She leaned into the goads again, pushing the creature toward Jinnspire, air whistling round our heads and tangling our hair.

"And what happens if it dies?" shouted Tanhir.

"Then all its muscles will relax, and we fall out of the sky," said Ustiore, then added, pushing harder on the goaders, "at least it will be a quick death." Tanhir did not reply, only held onto the handles of the saddle, her knuckles pale through her skin. She was terrified, this woman who had lived all her life in the heights of the Wyrdwood. She had probably seen the results of falls. Probably grew up fearing it.

Within me something moved, crackled along my nerves and reached out to touch me, to make a contact. We did not speak, we only shared. I passed across my understanding and my fear and my need.

I felt in return a desire to live, a deep and abiding desire to finish something, of something hugely important left undone. A knowing that with death there was more than the loss of life, but the loss of some great hope that had been born through death in the forest. I did not understand.

A hopelessness enshrouded me. Then I heard a whisper, a voice in my ear that was for me but not for me and the strangest thing was I could swear it was the voice of Issofur, of Furin's son.

"All is not lost, trust them."

I felt the need to lay hands upon the skin of the marant. At the same time a strengthening of the weak bond between the cowl inside and me.

The marant's skin was soft, slightly wet. A connection grew from the cowl within me to the creature. I groaned, felt its terrible pain. It knew, in its own way, that it was dying, but it would fight to live for whatever time it had left.

Which was not long.

A few more beats of its great heart sending blood pulsing from a hole in a huge vein beneath us that had been made by a spear in the first moments of our rising. I had never even seen the thrower, they were probably crushed beneath the hooves of thousands of crownheads. As the marant's great heart finally gave out, as its dying brain sent out a signal to its muscles – *all is over, our struggle is done, you can rest now* – I felt myself fully connect with it. Not the mind of the beast, the mind was gone, flown to wherever marant minds went on death, freed from the pain of its wounds. In that freedom I felt echoes of how miserable the lives of these creatures were.

No time for that.

If its muscles relaxed fully we were lost and would fall like a stone from the sky.

The cowl within me knew death intimately, the mechanics of it, what caused it, how it worked. But it was not of death, it did not bring death or even want it, the cowl only knew what could be done with bodies afterwards, from the slow breaking down of flesh, to the raising of the swarden, and it used that knowledge. As the muscles began to relax into death it spoke with them in the language of flesh, in words understood only by vein and bone and muscle and fat.

Not yet, it said in whispers of blood and sinew, *not yet*, in the dialect of dissolution and liquefaction. In reply, every muscle in the marant stiffened. Instead of falling, we began to glide. Our course already set and with no way to steer we headed for the walls of Jinnspire.

"We are not falling!" shouted Tanhir, though her voice was stricken, full of panic.

"I am keeping us up."

"Lean," shouted Ustiore, "lean to the left, we need to guide it."

"To where?" shouted Tanhir.

"The gates of Jinnspire. I doubt we will make it over the wall at the rate we are losing height." The Rai was right, the stiffening of the marant's muscles had stopped us falling but without the thrust of its jets we would never make the wall, and we were gathering speed as we headed toward the ground, faster and faster. No longer in danger of falling from the sky, but the rate at which we were gathering speed was likely to dash us against the ground and end us as surely as the fall.

"We need to slow!" shouted Ustiore as we cut through the air, the walls of Jinnspire growing. I saw figures on them, staring up at us. They must be wondering what was happening, if this was the beginning of an assault, some strange scheme they had never seen before.

"How do you slow this thing?" all I could do to get the words out. I was half in this world half lost in another, a strange grey in-between. I think, if I had not died before I would have been entirely lost, mesmerised by the strangeness of this not-here-not-there place, but I had died, and that served me well.

"We pull up," shouted Ustiore, "it arrests the creature's speed, but it does not answer the goads."

"It is dead," I said, and at the same time knowledge was

seeping into me through my connection to the cowl and through that the marant. Strange concepts I could not understand. I felt air flow across my body, not the howling wind of our descent, but controlled air, and I felt how to move my wings, how to control the up and the down with the thrust of jets. The jets, however, were lost to me, there were complexities and concepts within it that I would never master as I was not a marant. But the wings, they were not, I had some rudimentary control and I knew if I moved them in a certain way then we would level out, or point upwards and slow, also, we would stop losing height at such a rate and may even make it as far as the gate of Jinnspire rather than smashing into the earth somewhere between the city and the army behind us.

Of course how to move the wings, that was beyond me, but it did not matter. The cowl felt from me what was needed and it understood enough of the marant to move the wings, using the slowly fading instincts of the creature still caught in its flesh. Our hurtling flight slowed, we cut through the air but not at the same terrifying speed. We fell from the sky but much more slowly. We levelled out and I thought us safe. Only as we approached the ground did I realise how fast we were still moving. The land rushing by below us, the walls and gate of Jinnspire, huge, and growing with every moment.

"Brace!" shouted Ustiore, "brace yourselves, hang on for your lives!"

The cowl and I did all I could to arrest our advance, angling the wings to pull us up at the last moment, stealing speed away.

We were still going too fast. The moment my hands left its flesh it lost its solidity, became soft and malleable, its weight digging a furrow in the field, the sudden deceleration throwing me from it so I tumbled through the air, losing sight of Ustiore, losing sight of Tanhir, saw no sign of either but I barely knew myself at that moment. The impact stole all breath from me, the sudden dislocation from the marant hurt. Darkness closing in.

"Udinny! Monk!" The voice brought me back from the brink of unconsciousness, Tanhir looming over me. "Don't say you are dead after all that!" Pushing the darkness away.

"No," I sat up. "The Rai?" Tanhir shrugged and I heard a groan.

"I have broken my leg, I think."

"We must help her," I said, "and make for the gate of Jinnspire. Hope they will let us in."

"I do not think," said Tanhir, pulling me up, "letting us in is our worry, it is whether they let us live."

The gates of Jinnspire had opened, and from them came a whole trunk of soldiers commanded by one of their Rai, and they headed straight for us.

"Truly," I said, "it seems we jump out of the pot and right into the flame."

46

Saradis

Saradis stood before the cage looking at the woman within it. No pity in her, only the feeling of triumph that she came here to enjoy. Her armies closed on Jinnspire, her skyraft sailed for Woodhome and her god sat above its temple. Before her the Cowl-Rai, Nahac Du-Nahere, lay on the floor, her body twitching and an occasional barely perceptible moan leaving her mouth.

"End me," whispers on the air, so quiet as to be barely there but Saradis heard them, and she smiled.

"I will, Nahac, that is my promise to you." She was careful not to get too near the bars. Even in such a weak state she did not pretend the woman was not dangerous. "In fact, I have been preparing for that moment." Saradis sat, folding her dresses beneath her legs. "I have had a knife made, from the same wood that keeps you imprisoned. My god tells me this will end you, no miraculous healing from that." She stared at the twitching body. "It must irk you to know the gods you denied all your life, that you laughed at, even going as far as creating your own, are real. You laughed at my faith, but no longer, eh? In death, do you think all the gods you expunged from Crua will be waiting for you? Do you think instead of the Star Path you will find eternal torture? I do, I believe that what you feel now will be nothing compared to what Zorir will inflict on you." The woman on the floor did not react, which disappointed Saradis. What was the use of taunting someone when they were too insensible to be taunted? She stood, going to the cage in the corner and picking up a squealing histi, throwing it through the bars and as soon as it passed through: a whipcrack, so fast to be unseen, a ribbon of black power from Nahac snatched the creature from the air, sucking the life from it so quickly it barely had time to make a noise. Not enough life there to make Nahac a threat, but enough to wake her a little. Enough for Saradis to feel her barbs would now find provide some satisfaction.

"You were always so desirous of reports, of knowing how your campaigns were going. Well, let me tell you, dear Nahac. Let me explain to you what you have wrought and where we stand." She went back to sitting, the woman in the cage staring at her, red-rimmed eyes looking through bars of dirty hair. "Your brother is impaled upon the tower of Zorir, a plaything for the god. If he lives still, and I am not sure he does, he is wracked with an agony that makes yours look pathetic and weak. Is that the vengeance you always wanted? That he likely suffers in ways you could never even understand? Well, not understand yet. But will eventually." She picked up a piece of fruit, looked at it, inspecting it for imperfections before taking a bite. "Tell me, is the physical pain worse than the fact you failed to protect him, let me mislead you?" Nahac only groaned, Saradis shrugged. "The Rai, those who are not collared and adjunct of our beloved god, serve me from fear, a thing I know you would have greatly enjoyed." Another bite of the fruit, sweet juices ran down her chin. "My armies, own all the major cities, except Jinnspire, but we are currently camped outside it, and if they do not surrender it will be taken very soon." She leaned forward. "It is of course not really necessary to take the cities, but there would be questions if I did not attempt it, and we cannot do with too many questions. Not when we are so close." She wiped juice from her face. "Not that anyone could stop us now, eh?"

She waited but there was no reply from the woman on the floor, only the stare, a constant wavering implacable hatred aimed at her.

"My skyraft, packed to the gills with soldiers, makes its way to the Forestal city even as we speak. We will destroy the city, and we will take the trion from them." A smile on Saradis' face, a real smile. "It's all over then, the time will come and all this," she waved a hand, at the room, at the city and the land beyond the window at the back of it, "ceases to matter as it will be ashes. Zorir will burn it to the ground and the chosen will be reborn along the Star Path, with me at their head. Not so for you, I think, but do not worry about the fire. I will end you before that, you will never see my triumph. Never see the fire I tricked you into starting with your brother as the tinder." Saradis watched her, and for a moment she wondered if that was a mercy, if by killing the Cowl-Rai before the fire she was saving her from a final moment of utter despair. Maybe. But the truth was, and Saradis could happily admit this to herself, she had dreamed of killing the woman ever since she was made to bow before her, and as it would likely be her last pleasure of this life, she would not deny herself.

"I do not think," said Saradis, and she stood, "we will see each other much in the near future. I have enjoyed our regular talks, my updates for you, but the next time you see me, Nahac, I am confident it will be the last. It will be the eve of my victory, the moment of fiery triumph for Zorir. The end of your life."

No reply, only that stare, and Saradis laughed, threw

what was uneaten of her fruit through the bars, to land near the edge of the cage and left.

In the cage, the woman dragged herself forward toward the uneaten fruit, though she paid no interest in it. As she neared it withered and dried, the substance of her body taking whatever life was available, the stones in her head sparkling and sending shivers of agony through her. Sometimes, she thought herself mad, that this pain had broken her, but deep inside the woman remained as determined as she ever had been. She had become fixated on one thing, putting right her wrongs. Saradis may think she had won, that was true. And, true, she may have manipulated Nahac into betraying her brother, into forgetting the one thing that she had thought important as a child, "*Protect him*". But Nahac was strong-willed, she believed in herself. She wanted revenge, she wanted to make amends.

If she saved her brother, maybe she could have both.

Nahac reached the edge of the cage. The blueveined wood was painful for her to touch, and she could not break it, she knew that as she had tried and tried and tried, but Nahac had always been clever, always been a thinker. Even inside a cage of agony that did not desert her. She had made this cage when she realised control was leaving her, she had designed it and she had watched them build it. There had been no blueveined wood thick enough or tall enough to make the bars. So instead the carpenters had taken hundreds of bits, used powerful wood glues to stick them together which gave the bars their twists and thorns.

It also created weaknesses.

Nahac found her place, where she had been working with her fingers, repeatedly broken, bloodied and healed, and she began to pick at the glue to weaken this bar. The glue was stronger than her flesh, the broken bones of her fingertips were the best tool she had found. She readied herself to continue.

She was Nahac Du-Nahere and, yes, she had been tricked into betraying the only person she had ever been close to by a woman she had once trusted. But she was also Cowl-Rai without a cowl, and she had conquered a world by sheer force of her own will.

She would not give up.

47

Venn

They were retained. There was no other word for how they felt. The god had not released them back into the darkness of Crua's beneath, but they were no longer directly attached to the god. They simple drifted in an in-between place and something of that place dulled all feeling. They knew, deep within, that they were on the edge of panic. They did not know how much time had passed, how long they would be kept here or if they would ever be set free. Was the creature simply putting them aside while it went away, joined its fellows in the planned destruction of the world, in its translocation to another place?

Translocation? Where had that word come from. They had never heard it before and yet at the same time they knew exactly what it meant. It was the mechanism of the taffistones. The act of stepping from one place to another instantaneously and spinning around the word was a thousand million things that Venn knew they would never understand, glowing numbers and parts of numbers that twisted reality. Colourful images of vast and strange towers, blooming with the fruiting bodies of mushrooms that pulsed and changed and twisted. Without knowing the true meaning of any of these things Venn knew what they saw was the mechanism: part machine, part fungal. Beyond that a vast dark shadow, and within that lights, lights that were on some level wrong. They were far dimmer than they should be, each light should be a point of brightness, connected to a hundred other lights just as bright.

The knowledge felt like part of them, and the more they considered that, the more they had the oddest feeling that they were not just them. That as well as them, in this place there was an echo of Venn, a Venn that was he, a Venn that was her and a hundred thousand other Venns who had been every conceivable version of themselves. It sounded like insanity, but it also felt real. Within this place, they felt something akin to when they touched Ranya's web, and the more they thought on that the more they thought that was where they were, suspended in the web, waiting.

Turning back to those lights they found brighter lights, almost hidden among the dull smudges of the others, hanging on to fraying connections in an attempt to sustain themselves. Venn found themselves. That is me, they thought, and around me the Forestals and the Osere and the greater light is the god. From their own light ran a million threads reaching out, and the strangest feeling they were not simply one light, they were like a candle flame seen through tears, a single bright point echoed and refracted into many upon many upon many. Yet still, they were only one.

From their own light it was easy to find others, the gods, dotted through the root forest, both here and far away in the south, and more of the Osere, hiding. Venn knew it would not be hard to reach out, tell them to come here, to Frina and so they did. A simple brush of thought, a return thought of surprise and acceptance and movement. They found the Forestal city, floating in the ether above the gods of the root forest in the south. Within it, they knew Furin must be there, the Lens were bright lights, and moving quickly about another light, a different shade to one of the people. Issofur?

Venn.

North from Woodhome another familiar light, burning bright and strong. Udinny, with them Tanhir? The strangest thing, that Udinny's light was similar to theirs, blurry and refracted. Close to Udinny and Tanhir the dimmer light of many, many Rai. Then something confusing, more Rai, and the strange, barely there glow of what Venn recognised in an instant as the collared, moving south, too fast to be marching, though and in the forest.

And high, high up.

A skyraft.

Collared on a skyraft moving towards the Forestal city. Venn needed to escape this place. To tell Tall Sera of the threat. But they could not. They were stuck, held in Ranya's web.

For a moment, panic, then it subsided, leaving them calm once more. Watching the world, feeling like they should be here, should be doing this. Finding more lights far in the north, these as bright as the gods, but not the gods, and somehow tied to the land, more part of it but in a way Venn could not comprehend. They were of nature, but outside it. With them, three other lights, burning with their own light, and this neither the cowls of Forestals or the light of the Rai or the dim glow of the collared.

It was its own light, something new to Crua.

Or something very old?

And they also burned blurry. *Ont. Ania. Dassit.*

What did it mean?

All this was a wonder to Venn. The world they knew seen through a different lens, behind the glowing lights of the people they saw Ranya's web, and the sickness that infected it, was corrupting it and changing it and Venn knew this sickness was inimical to the whole land. Of course, what had created it did not care, for them the land was expendable, only interesting as a vehicle for its own plans. Venn felt a deep sadness. How they had grown up, how everyone had grown up, was not the life the people of Crua had been destined to live. The land was created by the gods to care for them, and through avarice and impatience both they and the gods had failed the land.

It had been failing ever since.

One more thing. One more.

Cahan. Where was Cahan? With that thought they were whirled across the net, looking down on the great, sickly glow of the creature that sat atop a tower in Tiltspire. And it was sick, infected by whatever it had created to take over the land, strong, incredibly strong, but what gave it that strength also twisted it, and near it, so dim as to be almost imperceptible, was Cahan. For just a second, the briefest moment, Venn let their awareness touch Cahan, felt his mind next to theirs. His gruffness, his determination to do what was right, and his pain. His terrible, almost unbearable pain.

"We will come."

A thought, a gift, and then they felt the baleful attention of the beast upon the tower and Venn withdrew, pulling their awareness back and the last thing they noticed was another light, almost next to Cahan, and somehow like Cahan. A blurry light different from the Forestals and the Osere around them.

The golden presence returned. The shimmering light of the god and behind it Venn felt the force of others like it. Frightening, powerful, and interested.

"We have thought." The words filled Venn's mind, and where before it had been only one voice now there were many, speaking through this one entity. "Not all are in agreement, some are gone, some believe in the fire, others have died in the darkness between then and now." Within the words a terrible sadness. "But enough among us remain for hope. A concept we have learned from your people in time past. "

"What happens now?"

"War returns to the world," came the voices, achingly sad, "it is inescapable. Before there was pity, and attempts at understanding. Now there cannot be. Those who would destroy others, can only be destroyed. " Behind the sadness, a hardness that scared Venn, the voice of creatures who had purpose, and were willing to do whatever it took. "We have committed. We have planned. "

"What do we do?"

"Here. " Images filled Venn's head. "The towers must rise. The flow of power be renewed, the spires filled with energy." Again, words that Venn filled in with their own understandings. "Anjiin will rise. iFTaL will be restored."

Venn's mind, filled with sparkling images filtered through what they knew and places they were aware of, people they were aware of. The Spirecrown of Jinneng county, the broken Spirecrown of Harn county, the great spire of Tilt county with the tower of the god before it. A torrent of information pouring into Venn, things they could not and did not understand.

Things they knew.

Udinny was out there, they mattered, were important and were in the right place already. Sorha, was here, a single pure burning light unlike any other, with Frina, waiting, they mattered, and there were others out there, being placed. A battle to be fought and in some ways it was the sort of battle Venn knew, in others, it was the sort of battle Venn could not even begin to understand.

Two things they were left with, one that dismayed them more than they could ever explain but they could not voice it. Like a secret hidden inside that filled them with fear but must remain secret.

The second was puzzling, that though as far as Venn knew the man was barely alive, all that was and could be in the future relied upon Cahan Du-Nahere. Relied upon those who had been and would be again which Venn did not understand. They tried to ask a question but too late.

They were released. Flushed back into the darkness of the beneath. Breathing hard, falling to their knees.

"Venn!" the hand of Frina on them, steadying them.

"How long?" It seemed an age, like they had been gone for weeks. "How long was I in there?"

"Moments only," Sorha, her white make-up glowing in the light from the pod.

"No, half a day at least," Frina helped them stand. "It must have been."

"The Rai tells the truth, Trion," said Tall Sera. "You touched the thing, the next you were falling to your knees." Venn looked around, Sorha, Frina, Tall Sera, the Forestals and Osere watching them.

"I have learned much," said Venn. "And what we must do is clear, in a way, while not being clear at all." They took a deep breath. "Tall Sera, Saradis' forces have taken a skyraft, they are steering it into the forest, toward Woodhome."

"Then I must—"

"Wait," said Venn, holding up a hand, "listen to everything I have to say before you make decisions. We must plan."

"My people," began Tall Sera.

"You have time," said Venn, "but please, listen." The Forestal blinked, then nodded.

"I suppose a few moments listening to you will not slow us much." He nodded and leaned on his bowstaff. In the glow of the pod he looked tired and worried.

Venn stood. "What is planned, by Saradis and her god,

is death to us all." They looked around, faint presences in the glow. "But we can stop them."

"How," said Tall Sera, "how is that possible? They have all the soldiers, all the equipment, all the power. Even if we beat them at Woodhome, there are still not enough Forestals to . . ."

"Listen, you will have questions, I know, and I may not have answers. I can only tell what may be." Venn looked around, felt every eye on them, every blind head turned toward them. "What I describe, will sound like it has a small chance of success, but it is the only one. All others lead to death, for everyone, and everything on Crua." Tall Sera had been about to say more but did not. Venn felt Sorha stand nearer to them.

"Speak then," she said.

"The god in Tiltspire, it seeks control of what was Iftal, I have no better way of explaining it. But the god here, it says Iftal can be reborn and control taken away from the god in Tilt."

"Why do they need us?" said Sorha. "Can these gods not just fight it out among themselves?"

"No," said Venn. "The one at Tiltspire, what it has done has made it strong, it calls on the power of Crua through Cahan, and even though it only has a small part of it, it is still more power than we can imagine." Words, pouring from them and yet no one had told them this. Still, they knew every one was correct, real, as if whispered in their ear by echoes of themselves. "To restore what was, we must take the spires in Harn and Jinneng. In the top of each is a room. Udinny must be in one, and they are already in Jinneng. In Harn is another, and matters of Harn are in hand. I am assured of this. Another force, must be ready at the central spire of great Anjiin. That is you, Frina, I have called your people to us. Sorha, you must go with them."

"I should come with you," said Sorha. "You will need protecting." Venn smiled, shook their head.

"No," they said, "I have a place, it is not here. I am not sure where it is. Not yet. For you there is a stone at the top of the temple in Anjiin." Knowledge unfolding, like snow falling upon them.

"How will I know it?" said Sorha.

"You will," said Venn, and there was such certainty there that she shrugged, accepted what was said.

"But who will protect you?" she said.

"And what of me?" said Tall Sera.

"To you," said Venn softly, "the hardest job of all. Saradis has committed her entire army, half to the siege of Jinnspire. Half to take Woodhome. You have to hold her attention so she does not recall them, or set them all on Jinnspire and overrun it entirely. Because if we do not control the right towers at the right moment, all is lost."

"Many of mine will die, Woodhome was not built to withstand a siege from above," said Tall Sera.

"I wish it could be another way," said Venn. "I truly do. But I am coming with you." That surprised them. "I think that will help."

"How?" Venn shrugged. They did not know, that was hidden from them.

Frina spoke, a long string of words, and Venn found, this time, there was no need for Sorha to translate. Venn nodded.

"Frina is right, the Betrayers are concentrated in Anjiin. It will be a hard fight for you and her people, Sorha."

Frina spoke again.

"I thank you for your sacrifice," said Venn and saw Tall Sera bow his head.

"If Frina is willing to risk what remains of her people, I can do no less," said Tall Sera.

"I must warn you all," added Venn, "the gods who oppose us have been freed, they roam across Anjiin and the land above." Chatter, among everyone. Venn waited, felt a brief squeeze on their arm, a thanks.

"Is there no good news?" said Tall Sera. "Boughry curse me I could do with some."

"Maybe a little good news," said Venn, and they felt themselves smiling. "We will have some help." From behind them came a ripping and tearing and the glow of the pod flickered and died. From it, all writhing tentacles and black, oily skin, came a god.

48
Share

Strange, to be swathed in the forest, to once more be alive and aware and to see and to hear and to feel no pain. Somewhere, in the back of his mind he knew she was Ont-Ania-Dassit, but he was also so much more. He was her, she was him they were them and they were of the forest. "The cloudtree passed through them, water flowed into his mouth sweet as nectar, food filled his stomach and though she had tasted nothing but ash since he had been burned they knew the taste of this food was as good, if not better, than anything he had ever eaten. This was contentment, this was what it was, she thought, to be an animal in the forest. To be part of it in a way they never had been before.

What, in turn, do I give to the forest? It gives to me, we give back as is the way of things throughout the world of Crua, or as it should be.

Dark thoughts of those who only took. Who stood at the top of the food chain, but did not respect their prey or return it to the land or even hunt for anything as basic as food. As they ate and drank and existed in the shell of the Forest Man she felt something else flowing into him, a thing two had never known but one did and she wondered at it, at this brightness in her mind that stretched out through us.

It feeds our cowl.

I do not have a cowl.

But still it feeds it.

It did, he did not really understand, this golden touch within her, this feeling of being able to stretch out and touch the forest, to be one with it, to be infused with a wild desire to nurture the forest, and to protect it.

Protect.

Three minds echoed the word.

Why are we this?

Why save me?

The Boughry do not save.

They saved Cahan.

They saved Udinny.

They saved the child Issofur.

They had purpose.

It made no sense, but she did not require sense as he nestled back onto the embrace of the tree, into the touch of the vines and the blanket of the leaves he knew the purpose of the forest was simply to be. Behind that, there was more, there was a desire for order and direction but they did not care about that, her life had been filled with order and purpose, let her enjoy the sensation of only being while she could.

They knew it would not last.

The forest, and the Boughry through it, were creatures of purpose, a purpose mostly forgotten, yes, a purpose blurred and broken by time and decay, but they moved with that purpose even when they themselves did not understand it. To be a Forest Man was to be given a window into the minds of the Boughry, to feel the yearning. What others thought malice was not at all. The Boughry were alone, incomplete, trapped in solitude and driven by a deep desire for completion, to be together. The breaking down of bodies was looking for some clue as to what had gone wrong, and how it could be fixed. But there were no answers to be found in blood and bone and sinew.

The loneliness had been their only companion for a hundred thousand lifetimes and he-she-they felt such sadness, a misery that moved on geological scale – and so pure. Like a child who could never please their father, like a girl who survived the destruction of their village, like a brother slipping away from life in your arms.

We were always meant for this?

No.

Maybe.

Yes.

So strange, the ebb and flow of different minds, different ideas and inside it all an odd familiarity, his-her-their familiarity. Had they been this before? What a strange thing to think. What an odd idea to have. She was not a tree, to lose their lives and die each year, only to be reborn again.

But such familiarity.

You had to learn to live again.

I did. He did.

Was it that?

He felt himself a palimpsest, a scroll written and rewritten until it began to make a sort of sense.

We are not.

No. They were not, though no less important for it. We are all pieces. We are the puzzle that has constantly been remaking itself. As they thought she felt it through the connection, an endlessly spinning, whirling desire, a bright wind of need to solve what could not be solved with everything that lived either a piece to be placed or an obstacle to be overcome. No way to tell which was which because something was missing, something so important and fundamental to the Boughry that every moment without it was an agony to them. Yet without that piece they could not be fixed, and they could not rebuild and they could not replace. They flailed, as blind as Ont had ever been, trapped within a paradox, desperate to fix what was missing, but needing what was missing to find it.

Lost.

All of them lost.

The Boughry. Ont, Ania, Dassit, the Rai, the Forestals, Cahan, and Udinny and all of them. Lost.

Like a bell ringing.

Like waking from a dream.

Like holding the hand of a brother you thought long dead.

Like your father taking you in your arms to offer comfort.

Like waking to the family you thought lost to fire.

A voice that was not a voice ringing through the forest. Touching every creature and plant and tree, waking Ranya's web which shivered across the land; its gossamer tendrils touching every single thing as if to check the land at that moment in time. A faintness, a whisper of voice they knew, the scent of being they were familiar with. Venn? But, no, so much bigger, so different from them and yet they were there.

A shudder in the air.

A cold breeze in the clearing.

Before them the Boughry came into being, great and terrible, tall and sharp with old branches and forest moss covering their bodies. Each, despite how willowy and diaphanous they appeared, emanating the strength felt when you stood in front of the trunk of a cloudtree. An immortality, a solidness that should defy even death. Though each of them knew that was not true, even the cloudtrees fell, so even the Boughry may die.

"Come to us."

They did, the great wooden bodies standing tall, vines sloughing away. The three expected to feel a loss of power when they were no longer connected to the huge tree, but they did not. They were overflowing with energy. What they had shared would feed them and water them for a long time to come, would give them the strength for what they needed to do.

What that was?

They did not know, they only knew there was a task and that they were here for it, that these bodies had been waiting for them. As one they walked forward, a spear of three with Ont at the tip before the triumvirate of the Boughry, the air full of expectance, of an unspoken need. They felt no fear, something had changed, something in the forest, in the land. Possibility hung in the air. Step after step across leaf litter and soil, Boughry towering over them.

"Carry us?"

The voice of the Boughry, but almost like a child speaking, like something that had long ago given up hope and now saw a chance, was almost afraid of the hope it gave them, frightened to acknowledge even its possibility. It was Ont who spoke, who stepped forward, huge arms held open, head raised to look up at the bare skulls of the Boughry.

"Of course," he said and in those words he spoke for them all. The Boughry floated forward, one for Ania. One for Ont. One for Dassit and each of those wooden bodies opened their arms, felt no fear or trepidation. "Come to us." And like the wooden golems the Boughry opened their arms, drifting across the forest floor until they loomed over the three who waited, and then, slowly, and in both what seemed only a heartbeat and to take an eon, they dissolved into the bodies before them, and neither Ont nor Ania nor Dassit felt any extra weight at taking on those huge creatures. They felt no malice or attempt to wrest control from them. They knew only that now they carried a passenger, and that their passenger had little more understanding of what was to come than they did. Only that this was a momentous decision for them, to leave the forest. The Boughry were of the forest, as much part of it as tree and ground and soil. To leave it was to let go of their power, to become so much less.

"We will protect you," said Dassit or Ont or Ania, and they were suffused with a sense of gratefulness, of thankfulness.

And enormity.

For the briefest flicker of an eye, while the Boughry folded themselves away into the creaking, sinewy bodies of the Forest Men, those within them saw through the Boughry's eyes.

Maybe.

They had no words for the way the Boughry sensed the world. They saw it all. They saw Crua from end to end. Its wondrousness, its terrible sickness. How near it was to breaking and felt the Boughry's awful guilt that they had failed in fixing it.

Dizzying.

Terrifying.

Then gone.

"What now?" asked Dassit/Ania/Ont.

Harn, came the reply and in the words was something else, something larger, greater than they understood. An image of Harnspire, a desire to reach for the top of it.

"Harnspire," said Ont.

"Yes," said Ania.

"No," said Dassit. "Jinnspire."

"For you, yes." Agreement, knowledge. "We have long walks ahead," said Ania.

"Then let us begin walking," said Ont. They did, moving through the forest, and as they walked they pulled behind them a flow of curious rootlings, gambolling and playing among the soaring cloudtrees. In among them watched a boy, who laughed, danced, flickered, and vanished.

49

Saradis

She sat upon her throne and looked upon emptiness.

Figures stood guard along the great hall, the collared, but she had stopped thinking of the collared as people. They were an adjunct of her god, the lucky ones who had been touched by Zorir and lived. Now they did the god's will, they were Zorir's will made form.

Still, she missed the supplicants, she missed the people who came to her and begged her judgement on their problems. Once she had found them annoying, all those small and foolish troubles: whose house blocked another's light, which merchant had taken another's patch in the market. She had found it all so tiresome at the time, strange that she missed it. Was it the people she missed? No, she was honest enough about who she was to admit that. It was the exercising of power. She had never thought she worked for her own power and it was only in the absence of it, on the eve of her victory when there was no longer a threat, no people to cow, no Rai to watch over as they schemed among themselves, did she realise how much she had enjoyed exercising her power.

She took a breath.

It did not matter. Power was a small thing when compared to the will of a god. When she walked the Star Path she would be rewarded, Zorir would remake the world and she would be at its head, the most loyal of the god's followers, high priest of all and her every whim would be a command. All those who had doubted her would burn, and those who had been sacrificed would be reborn and would be thankful to her, would owe their new lives to her. If she had to sit here alone now then so be it. She wondered if the Osere beneath would still exist in Zorir's new paradise?

She was shaken from her reverie, her dream of a better world and her hand steering it, by the tap of feet on the polished floor of the great corridor. Rare to hear a thing once so common.

This was no supplicant. It was the soldier Vir. She had dallied with him, out of boredom, and found the experience unsatisfying. Since then he had been over-familiar so she had sent him away to round up citizens to be used by Zorir, linked up the great blue roots of the god that ran through the city and the spire. She had found, oddly, the collared struggled with the job. Being near the thick roots confused them, they became listless and slow.

The people screamed and cried as they were taken, despite being told their sacrifice would be rewarded, which should have given them some comfort, but still they fought and tried to escape. Vir had little pity in him, he was good at the job.

Nevertheless, she disliked the way he looked at her now, and she doubted he would be one she chose to resurrect after the fire.

He paid no interest to the collared, just as they paid no interest to him, though he looked around the great corridor as if he had never visited before, taking in the flags – now tattered and torn: what use in keeping them maintained when she was so close to the end of all this? Eventually he stood before her. He did not bow or look the least intimidated.

"Vir," she said. He was not smiling, but he looked amused in his own way. "I did not request your presence."

"No, Skua-Rai, you did not." He shrugged. For a moment she thought to demand he bow, but did it really matter? Who was left to watch, to know? He was useful as few others remained to corral the citizens and if he refused to bow when she asked she would have to kill him. She waited but he did not say any more, only stood there, looking amused.

"Well, out with it then," she said.

"It's the food, Skua-Rai," he said.

"Food?" She had never given a thought to what the lower ranks ate.

"It's what we call the sacrifices down in the depths of the spire. Easier not to think of them as people if we call them food."

"Of course," she said. "And what is it about," she let her words hang in the hollow silence of the great corridor, "the food?"

"They're talking, Skua-Rai."

"We do not cut out their tongues, Tree Commander."

Vir sniffed, shrugged his shoulders.

"Maybe we should," he said, "they whine a lot before we set 'em up, but I'm not talking about the ones waiting to be fed to it," he nodded backwards, towards the great doors and Zorir's temple, such a casual blasphemy. Once she would have had him killed for that, but not now. She would never admit it to another but she found comfort in the few humans that were left. Even this one.

"And?" She hated this, and felt the man was purposefully drawing out what he was saying as if to bait her, enjoying his small hold over her.

"Well, they don't usually, I mean, they scream when their skin first touches the blue and that's the last we get

out of 'em apart from moaning. Usually." This time she
waited, let the silence grow between them, watched the
man shift from leg to leg until he decided to speak again.
"But just in the last few hours, a day maybe, they started
to speak, only they all say the same thing."

"And what is that, Tree Commander, Vir?"

"Harn," he said.

Did she feel shock, to hear that name once more? That
place far in the north that had been a thorn in her thumb,
the first showing of power of Cahan Du-Nahere and now
it should come up again. She closed her eyes. Trawling her
memory.

"The woman who once commanded you," she said, "she
was seen in Harn, and not too long ago. With a small force."
His demeanour changed, eyes narrowed.

"Dassit? Let me go up there," he said, "I know how she
thinks. If she's a threat, I'll be your best counter."

"Maybe," she said. Then turned to one of the collared.
"Call Laha," she said.

"You don't need that thing," said Vir.

"You do not tell me what I need. Your job is to deal with
the food, as you call it." She stared at him, focused her
entire being on this man and though he did not bow he
looked away, some of his surety stripped from him, an
awareness of his true place returning. She smiled, a small
thing, barely registering enough to crack the white of her
face make-up. Then they waited, in uncomfortable silence,
for Laha to appear. When he did he made no sound as he
walked up the corridor and, had she not known he was
coming and been watching for him, it would almost be as
if he appeared from nowhere. His skin was more blue than
white now, thick veins extended from the stones and
twisted around what flesh was visible, his clothes moved
as if the flesh beneath pulsed in time with the beat of his
heart.

She felt as if something inside her squirmed. She did

not want to think about him, about what he had become. Somewhere, deep within her, the tiniest doubt. A small light flaring but one that was quickly extinguished. No doubt, not now. Not when she was so close. Who was she to question the ways of a god?

Laha did not speak, but she did not expect him to. He very rarely spoke now.

"Laha," she said, the man looked at her, eyes entirely blue, and he did not blink. Something she found disconcerting. "Vir here tells me the sacrifices have begun to speak and—"

"Harn," his word was the creak of old branches, the wet snap of rotten bark peeling away from soaking wood.

"Yes," she said, and something fluttered within her. Alarm? Why should she be alarmed? Crua was hers, her armies roamed freely, only Jinnspire remained and she attacked that more to keep her army busy than for any other reason. Soon it would be hers, and at the same time she would take the Forestals' tree city and with that the trion Venn. Then it would be time for the great fire and glorious rebirth.

But Harn. What was it about that place?

"Harn," said Laha again and she noticed that Vir was very slowly moving away from him.

"Is it a danger?"

"They wake," barely words, more a noise she could just understand.

"They?" she sat straighter, her clothes twisting uncomfortably beneath her. "Who are they?"

"Others."

She did not know what to say, did not know what he could mean. She sat, staring at Laha as his clothes and the skin of his face moved almost imperceptibly. Letting herself relax a little, thinking through all she knew about Crua and coming to a conclusion that she did not like at all.

"Do you mean other gods?"

"Others," creaked Laha and she felt sweat trickle down her spine. She noticed Vir was watching her with interest.

"Are they a danger to us? To Zorir?" Laha cocked his head to one side, as if listening to a voice she did not hear and she felt a pang of jealousy.

"I will go to Harn."

"What about me," said Vir. "I'm sick of being stuck in the basement with a load of bodies." Was there anguish there? His façade cracking for just a moment? She was about to order him back to the dungeons and the rooms full of slowly dying people whispering of Harn when Laha spoke again.

"Jinnspire," said Laha, looking over at Vir. "Lead."

"You want him to lead the troops at Jinnspire?" She could not keep the incredulity from her voice. A grin on the soldier's face. Laha nodded. Vir was about to speak, about to say something, when Laha acted. One moment still, the next holding Vir in his grasp, the man forced to his knees and his head bent back. Vir struggled but there was little he could do against Laha.

"Be one," said Laha and he put a hand over Vir's face, fingers splayed and even Saradis could not hide her horror at what happened. Something crawled from his skin, writhing out of the end of Laha's fingers and burrowing into Vir. The man screamed, but not for long. Then Laha let go of him. Saradis expected Vir to fall but he did not. He stood, swaying slightly. He still had that half-grin but now something moved beneath his face.

"I understand," said Vir.

"Understand what?" said Saradis.

"A servant comes to Jinnspire," when he spoke, he did not give her his full attention, it was almost as if he were on some drug, only partly here, "I will serve the servants." Saradis sat back. She no longer understood what was happening. More and more she felt like her god had forgotten her, was bypassing her for others. She told herself they were only tools, that she was still the chosen one but how long had it been since she had felt the touch of Zorir? The pleasure that had her almost blacking out? Too long.

Was she forgotten, forsaken?

Then, because Zorir heard, of course they did, they were always there. A wave of pleasure hit, blotting out the world around her and filling the long echoing corridors of Tiltspire with cries of ecstasy.

50

Udinny

You would think that if you crash a flying creature in front of a city while trying to escape the army currently besieging it, then the army being besieged would presume you are their friends.

However, as I, Udinny, warrior of Ranya and pathfinder for the same god, can attest, this is not the case. You are actually received with very little friendship and lot of rather unnecessary roughness and unpleasant language. We were pulled, savagely, I would say, from the ground around the body of our poor marant. The great creature did not yet know it was dead and as rough hands were laid upon me I heard the bellows of its lungs, still stuttering and struggling for breath even though its spirit had long departed. I wondered if it suffered, and also if it was my fault as it was with the strength of the cowl within me that I had kept the poor creature in a semblance of life.

Maybe it was good I thought of that, as it meant I thought less about the grim-faced soldiers and Rai who were dragging us back toward the gates of Jinnspire while the armies of Zorir roared and ran at us, bringing up a great dust cloud in a doomed attempt to take us back before we were within the, admittedly questionable, safety of Jinnspire's walls.

They did not catch us. Tanhir, Rai Ustiore and I were pulled through a gap in the gates and they were shut behind us creating even more dust. In fact, dust was one of the few things Jinnspire had in abundance. As they dragged us on it was plain that Ustiore was badly hurt, one arm was at a strange angle and they could not put weight on one leg at all. Tanhir seemed to have fared better; she was scratched and bloodied but was well enough to make holding her a task until a spear was brought to her throat and she was told that if she did not stop struggling her struggle would be ended permanently. So she let herself be led. She did not look happy about it, though it would have been strange if she did. We had definitely flown out of the fire and into another fire, one that was maybe not burning quite as fiercely yet, but that was only a matter of time.

I had expected our arrival to garner a reaction from the people of Jinnspire. I had hoped, and I know this was rather wishful thinking, for our escape to be cheered, for us to be heroes coming to them after a brave escape from their enemies.

If I had been a little more truthful with myself I should have expected jeering or booing, maybe some rock throwing

Neither happened.

Instead we walked through the streets of Jinnspire in what was almost silence. The houses here were very grand, built on the money mined out of Treefall in the southern Wyrdwood. Even the houses near the walls were as good as anything you would find in Tiltspire, many storeyed, with shutters covering windows and tall pointed eaves. I say houses near the walls, there were not many left on the route we walked, the soldiers of Jinnspire were in the process of pulling them down, making a killing ground between the wall and where a second wall was being built.

Clearly they did not expect to be able to hold the main walls or the gate forever and were preparing for their loss. It would be brutal and vicious when the city fell, as last stands often were.

They led us through the second wall and then we saw the people of Jinnspire, ragged and half starved. They wore no make-up, as was common in the rest of Crua. Like many things in besieged cities it was probably in short supply. The people of the city were not willing to give up their habits so easily though, and they had caked their faces with dust and ash. They did not speak as we were escorted along the narrow streets toward the spire, they only watched from eyes surrounded by what looked like flaking, decayed skin. Fear was everywhere: you could taste it on the air. Fear and hopelessness. As we passed tall grand houses I saw some were marked with a red slash on their doors, a traditional marker for plague.

I had hoped Jinnspire may have the strength to hold against the armies of Zorir for long enough that something could save us, some miracle I did not yet know of, but it was clearly not the case. The city was already dying and the fighting had not even begun.

Our captors led us on past hundreds of silent, sad faces and into the spire, down the grand corridor that was still festooned with flags and slogans celebrating Chyi and the god's Cowl-Rai. I expected to come face to face with them. This was to be the place of the last stand of their god after all, but instead I found a Rai on the throne at the end of the long corridor. Despite her elaborate wooden armour, with great flaring shoulders of hardened forest mushroom and lines of glowing sigils painted across it, she looked tired as she gave out orders to those before her.

" . . . and begin the lottery," she was saying to a trunk commander, "every citizen gets a number between one and twenty, when the time comes numbers will be called as to who will sacrifice their strength for the Rai."

"The people will not like it," said the trunk commander. "Better that they give to us than we lose their strength to plague." She sat up a little straighter, tried to look more commanding but it was clearly an effort. "How goes the quarantine?"

"Well as can be expected," said the trunk commander, "there are still some who do not obey the new rules, we make examples of them." Now the Rai smiled, and I saw a brief joy on their face.

"I had wondered what the screams I heard were." The Rai glanced over the soldier's head and at us. "You may go." The trunk commander stood, nodded and turned. Like everyone I had seen here he also looked tired, beaten, and he barely spared us a glance. Our captors brought us forward and forced us to kneel before the Rai. She stood, the better to try and intimidate us.

"I am Rai Hastan Jin-Prassit, right hand of the Cowl-Rai of Chyi and would know what you are doing trying to infiltrate my city?" Clearly news of our arrival had flown ahead of us. As Rai Ustiore was in no condition to speak, too busy gasping in pain, and I was quite sure that Tanhir would only shout abuse at a Rai, I decided I would be our spokesperson and stood. Only to be pushed straight back down to my knees. "I asked a question," said Rai Hastan.

"I am Udinny, warrior of Ranya, and I am fleeing the forces of the Zorir."

She leaned forward, studying me and her face contorted as if confused. I noted she had no need to use ash and dust as she still had make-up to cover her face.

"Are you man or woman, Udinny, warrior of Ranya?"

"I am never quite sure myself, Rai." A moment, while she decided if I was playing with her or not, then she shrugged.

"Not that it matters, I can think of few reasons for someone to leave the armies of the blue and come here rather than as spies."

"We are not spies. I had hoped to speak with your Cowl-Rai. We bring important information." The Rai blinked, looked around as if to check who was listening before she spoke again.

"Our Cowl-Rai long ago gave up the weakness of flesh for the power of spirit." Ah, I thought, they are dead then. "I rule in their stead, I am their hand and you will answer my questions." She did not really sound commanding, or even superior in the way Rai usually did, only tired.

"Very well, Rai Hastan," I said, this time I did not try to stand. "I am here on the thinking that the enemy of my enemy is my friend." I looked around, neither the Rai nor the soldiers holding us looked particularly friendly. "I was a friend of Cahan Du-Nahere, who is the sworn enemy of Zorir, the god, risen in Tilt." I did not think Cahan would ever call himself that, but he was not here to tell me off and I would say whatever I felt most useful at this moment. "I am also allied with the Forestals of the Wyrdwood."

"Bandits," she said.

"They do not believe so, and they stand against Zorir so could become your allies." I should probably have asked before suggesting this but I was more concerned with staying alive than politeness. Still, I was careful not to look at Tanhir. "It does appear allies may be useful to you." The Rai smiled, or tried to, she was old enough that her face did not really lend itself to expression.

"I would not expect help from the forest, Udinny, warrior of Ranya," she said softly.

"Why?"

"The enemy have a skyraft, we saw it in the sky before the army came to sit outside Jinnspire's walls. I believed it was for us when I first saw it, but it did not come near, for which I am thankful. Instead it made its way over the forest. It may well be in Wyrdwood by now so I imagine your Forestals will have their own problems." I heard a quick, indrawn breath from Tanhir.

"Oh," I said. Because what more could I say? A skyraft assaulting Woodhome did not sound good at all.

"So, you see, you have little to offer me. And even if you are not spies, the slim chance you are outweighs any use you may have." She began to raise her hand, to give an order that I suspected would be terminal.

"Wait," I told her, "it is not only an army you are up against, you need to know there is more." The hand paused.

"Continue," she said.

"You must have noticed the great platform they are building?" Her eyes narrowed, she gave me a nod. "It is built for a god, a subordinate to Zorir, they are bringing a god here. It will sit upon the platform, and they will use it to assault your city." I saw something die in the Rai's eyes then, some hope, however small, she had of surviving.

"Then maybe we should simply open our gates and let them in. Throw ourselves upon the mercy of Saradis and hope she accepts us. An easy victory may even—"

"No", coming from behind where Rai Ustiore lay on the floor and said more sharply than I would have dared. The horror of being taken by her old comrades overwhelming the pain of her broken limbs. The hand holding me still dug into my shoulder. "You cannot give up, what they do to Rai is worse than death." Rai Hastan stared at her. "You must have seen the blue warriors? Their skin changed? They call it collaring, they make you slave to the god but all you are is lost. Your mind is gone. Why do you think I ran from an army that all have fallen before? Because death is better than being given over to the collar." I felt something change around me, the hand on my shoulder loosened. I looked around and it was not hard to see that the soldiers were weighing up this new information. Probably wondering if they were better off giving up their Rai to the enemy.

"They treat soldiers no better," I said. "You must have scouts, they will have seen the bodies left behind the tail of the army, those infected with bluevein?" A nod from the Rai but she watched her soldiers now, not us. "They do it on purpose. It is the fate of all who serve Zorir. You have to fight." The Rai blinked once more, then shrugged.

"You are probably right," she said. "I cannot have talk of this collaring getting out into the city, it will cause panic. You will be executed as spies. We will do it now, an execution will raise morale a little." She looked at her soldiers. "If I hear one word of what these traitors have said spoken in the city, each of you and your families will die as slowly and painfully as is possible, do you understand?"

"Yes, Rai," came back the call.

"Good, now take them to the square, someone go ahead and call out what is to happen. I don't want anyone missing out."

We were led away, down the corridor and out to the square before the giant taffistone in front of the great spire. Rai waited for us, and a crowd was slowly forming. I had hoped for some sort of miracle to save Jinnspire, and along with it save us, but clearly that was foolish. Our whole mad dash here had been wasted and in that dying town, waiting for the hammer of the army outside its walls to fall, it felt like miracles were in short supply.

Foolish Udinny, how quickly I forgot that my lady of the lost always watches her servants, and never forsakes them while there is still a path to be walked.

51

Cahan

They were losing.

He could not doubt it any more.

They were losing.

The forces of the enemy, he did not think of them as Rai any more, they were not Rai, not even people. What came at them was a horde of twisted, half-person things, tentacles for arms, screaming mouths for heads, blades for feet and twisted shimmering blue branches for legs. Every one different and every one the same in its monstrousness. They were easy enough to cut down, they fell to a single arrow or blade swipe no matter where it hit, but they had numbers and were inexhaustible. Ravening, furious, hungry.

I am with you.

That voice, that companion that drifted in and out of his mind. Only there when it was there and forgotten otherwise. Was it quieter now? Yes. It had been getting quieter by heartbeats for so long and so long and in the back of his mind there was a scream.

He was barely aware of it at first, but it was getting louder and louder and louder with every attack. Each attack the same fight, the same battle, the same fading of those shapes that fought with him and his surroundings.

The walls of Harn were no longer ragged from battle, not burned and scarred and scored and holed from Rai fire or catapults, they were exactly the same as they had been at the start of the fight – but faded.

When the enemy came again, that howling, roiling glowing mass of blue, shot through with tentacles, gaping maws, snapping beaks, he could see them through the wall. Could gauge their attack, their strength, direct his archers with ease and for now the fading walls held and the enemy crashed against them in a wave.

Though the village felt smaller. As if it not only faded but contracted. As if with every attack the area of the land that he controlled was less.

He controlled? What foolish thinking was that? He controlled nothing, the land and the forest were their own and belonged to no one, not even the Rai. He felt a comforting phantasmal presence twisting around his body to lie around his neck. It had a name but he could not find it in his mind, still the screaming quietened, but only a little.

Where was it coming from? He moved around the village, around Harn, between the huts and houses, passing between the phantoms of the villagers and all this was wrong and he knew it was wrong but at the same time . . .

I am with you.

This place had to be protected. Harn must be protected. He must protect it and where was that screaming coming from? It was louder with every step; until he stood in front of the longhouse. The entrance to it a black hole, a yawning mouth, and from there came the scream. A constant, thin, sound of agony. A distillation of pain and he knew that he looked at the centre of the village. The real heart of it, the last bastion, and when the enemy made their final push, when he eventually had no strength this was where he would fall back to. And then, whatever made that scream, what was in there making that terrible noise of pure pain, then that would be all that was left.

A horror that he could not remember. How much had he forgotten? What had happened here that filled him with so much terror?

There was the farm, and losing the farm and travelling into Wyrdwood and . . .? From then, only the battle and the feeling that this had all happened to him already, and would happen again. That felt normal when surely it could not be?

He turned, to face the screaming house, the dark portal to something terrible. If he had learned anything it was that fear must be faced, it could not be run from.

He stepped toward the hole, ready to be embraced by whatever it was that screamed inside there, whatever pain was waiting he would face it.

Step towards the pain.

"No."

A voice he recognised. Before him, figures, almost see-through, if he walked through them he was sure they would simply tear, they were no real barrier.

"No," they said again.

He narrowed his eyes, looked at these people before them. He knew them for a moment he had names: Furin, Udinny, Ont, with them a woman he did not know, she looked like a soldier of the red which made no sense, a couple of Forestals and most shocking of all, Sorha. Who he hated, who had tortured him and put him through so much. There was no hate within him now. He did not understand why and he did not question it. He only blinked, looked at this line of barely there people.

"I will face what I fear." He tried to walk forward but was met by Udinny, happy, smiling Udinny, glowing with the gold of Ranya.

"Not yet," she said. "Not yet."

Not yet.

"Something awaits me in there, Udinny," he said, "I must face it."

"The path is not yet fully walked, Cahan." For a moment he was at a loss. What could he say? How could he put across how lost he was? How futile this all felt? That he was fighting the same battle again and again and again. The light rose and fell. He fought in the day, he fought in the night. He saw those he had come to care about fall and die. He saw them resurrected and all the time the thin, quiet scream was there in the back of his mind, like an ache in a tooth and . . .

If it had been a tooth Cahan would have pulled it from his mouth bare-handed to be free of the pain. He looked up at the entrance to the longhouse.

"Someone is missing," he said. "There is a name on the edge of my lips and I cannot say it." He looked along the line. As he did, the figures began to fade, their names fading from his mind.

"They are coming," said the largest of the figures.

"Hold, Cahan Du-Nahere," said the small woman. "Hold."

He was about to reply when the shout came from the wall.

"They are coming," and it was time to fight again.

52

Venn

There was much Venn knew and much they did not. They stood in the darkness of the root forest as a god unfurled itself above them. The creature was huge, and even though Venn knew it to be benign it still carried with it a sense of power so strong that it bled out of them as a wave of awe and fear. Any one of the constantly moving tentacles could crush them, two could rip them apart and the beak, hidden within the writhing mass, could chew through even the strongest armour.

But it did not move against them, instead it waited – never quite still – while each and every one of those gathered stared up at it. Unasked questions hung in the still air, most of those questions would never be asked, fear quietened their mouths and Venn knew they must use this time. Put those around them onto the path that was set for them. Every path would be difficult, and they worried for all of those that they knew and had come to like and respect. Venn did not want to send them into danger, but saw no other way to save more lives than they could ever count. The path they followed had twisted and turned and now they were at the final juncture, a way that relied as much on hope and luck as skill, but at the end was, if not freedom, then at least a new world. A second chance.

The only alternative was to do nothing, and that was a dark path that ended in fire and death for all.

Venn took a deep breath, ran a hand through their hair and stood forward.

"The god," they called it that for want of any better word, even though they knew what was behind them was nothing of the sort, "has seen the world. They have shown me what Saradis and Zorir plan for us."

"And will you share that?" Venn did not want to, what would it bring but hopelessness, to know the truth? But in the back of their mind they felt something else, the golden touch of Ranya, a gentle and familiar presence. *Let them know what they fight for.* Of course they should know. To keep secrets was the way of the other side, of Saradis, of her god and her servants. "If Saradis and her god win, everything is over."

"We have seen the collared," said Tall Sera, "we know what awaits those who go to her."

"You will not be collared," said Venn, their voice monotone, and they felt every set of eyes, and every face of the Osere upon them. "You, I, the Osere, we will all be dead. Saradis' god does not wish for power or control. They want to burn Crua, everything and everyone upon it, and from the fire they will take an energy that will hurl them, and the gods that follow them, along the Star Path to the paradise at the end."

"Is that not where we all go when we die?" said a Forestal. "Maybe the gods go to prepare the place for us?"

"No," said Venn softly. "Do not even allow the thought they may work for you to enter your head. To them we are nothing but fuel. That is what you must understand. Those who follow these gods are fools, and Saradis, she is the greatest fool of all. They do not care for her, she is a tool to be used and when she has outlived her use they will throw her on the same fire as the rest of us."

"And what of that?" said Tall Sera, stepping forward and pointing at the vast, writhing creature above Venn. "How do you know that tells the truth?"

Venn paused: how could they explain it? That they had been one with the creature, shared in its mind. How to explain that was how the gods communicated. How it had once been for all of them. The cowl existed for that, as a way to communicate with the strange minds of the gods, the creatures and their constructions. They could not explain it, and there was always the possibility the god had lied, though Venn could not think of a reason for them to do so. They could have crushed Venn at any point, then killed all those gathered here.

"Ranya put me on this path," said Venn, looking at the figures in the shadows, around them the bright glow of the Osere. "She has not steered me wrong yet. We have walked the path this far, Tall Sera, you will not become lost in the forest now." The Forestal did not reply, not immediately. Venn heard the hiss of material as the man shrugged.

"Very well, explain what happens now, Trion."

"We must split up, with the strength of the god I can open the taffistone portal." Venn felt movement above them as the god shifted. "Sorha, you must accompany the god and the Osere to Harn-Below. Once there, you must take and raise the temple."

"Why?" said Sorha.

"You must both get to the top of Harnspire. Others are coming to Harn. From the Wyrdwood. They must reach the top as well. Once the temple of Harn is raised, the creature in Tilt will understand our plan. Its forces will fight all the harder."

"That's comforting," said Sorha, and though Venn could not see her face they could picture it, the twist of her mouth, the amusement in her eyes.

"Tiltspire is the centre," said Venn, "I do not pretend to understand it but the centre gives greater control. We must take two points before approaching Tilt. Harnspire which is you, Sorha. And Jinnspire, which is already underway."

"How?" said Tall Sera.

"Udinny, is there."

"And when we have Harnspire and Jinnspire?" said Sorha. "What then?"

"Then Tilt," said Venn softly, "where Cahan Du-Nahere is waiting."

"And what of Woodhome?" said Tall Sera. Venn heard a crack in his voice, a fear. All this way and his home was to be overlooked? "Do you care nothing for Woodhome, Venn?"

"Of course I care," said Venn. "That is why I will be going there with you and we will do what we can to save your city together."

"With me?" He heard the surprise in Tall Sera's voice.

"Why are you surprised?"

"I don't know," a tangle of confusion in the man's voice. "I just thought, now you talk with the gods then you would be . . ." His voice died away.

"Too busy for Woodhome?" said Venn softly. "No, you took me in, you took in our people when you did not have to. I will not leave you when you need me."

"Need you?" almost a laugh in Tall Sera's voice, almost sarcasm but in this dark place, the opposite of his own lofty, airy lands, a place that was not his environment, he could not quite reach the confidence needed for sarcasm. "Why would I need a trion that will not kill, when I go back to a war?"

"You need me for the taffistone if nothing else," said Venn. "And you will need the remainder of Harn to fight with you, even though you have been sidelining them, making them other."

"Because they have disobeyed me," hissed Tall Sera.

"Because they brought down the wrath of Tiltspire on Woodhome." Venn walked across the small clearing in the root forest, stood before Tall Sera, put out a hand, touched Tall Sera on the forearm. A gentle touch, barely there at all and less a touch really, more an affirmation of what they said. An understanding that the people of Harn had disobeyed him, had ignored what he said.

"The forces of Saradis," said Venn very quietly, "were always going to come and you know that. And if they did not come, then you may have continued to live in Woodhome for a while longer, enjoying your ignorance and your isolation, but it would not have saved you from the fire. This way, tall Sera, at least you get to face your enemy head-on." Tall Sera said nothing, did nothing. "Or would you rather stay ignorant until the moment you burn, and the cloudtrees come screaming down around you?" The silence held a little longer, the tension in the Forestals like the tension in a drawn bow. Then Tall Sera spoke.

"You know I would not," he said finally, and it was like letting out a long-held breath. "Is there really any hope?" Tall Sera sounded different. They wanted Venn to lend them a little of their conviction, or at least the conviction Tall Sera believed they had. "You say Cahan Du-Nahere is where he should be, but all we know tells us he is dead."

"There is always hope," said Venn. "The god has gifts for us." Venn turned, looking at those standing in the clearing, the Osere, the Forestals, Sorha. "Gifts for all of us. The Osere first." Venn felt the attention of the Osere upon them. "Come forward, Frina," they said, "do not be afraid. You have laboured long and paid a heavy price. Now your god will reward you and your people."

Frina came forward, slowly, like an animal trying to pass a predator. She spoke a few words as she came to stand before the god, one of the creatures she and her people had imprisoned, protected and served for thousands of generations.

"She is frightened," said Sorha softly. Then the creature spoke; words in the language of the Osere and if Venn had expected something monstrous, something as strange and alien as the creature itself, they were to be surprised. Instead the creature sang, the Osere language looping and twisting through the air, high and sweet and as it sang Sorha whispered, a halting translation.

"It says, don't be frightened. It thanks Frina for her work, for her sacrifice." As Sorha spoke the Osere leader staggered forward, head bowed until she was below the great body of the god. "It says it is not a god, just a being like us but different. It calls itself Wa'urd." Sorha paused for a moment as Frina knelt. "I am not sure if that is its name or its people."

"It would be good to know," said Venn softly.

Huge waving tentacles came down to surround Frina. Sorha let out a laugh.

"Of course," said Sorha, "it is the name of its people."

"How do you know that?" said Tall Sera.

"Because of where it is, where they are. Where we are." Venn felt all eyes turn to Sorha. "In the language of the Osere, the word for land is ud. We are in Osereud. Land of the Osere."

"I don't understand," said Tall Sera, and the creature's tentacles surrounded Frina, softly touched her, as if exploring the leader of the Osere. Then Venn laughed, not loud, not even that amused. Only an affirmation as the pieces locked into place.

"Over time," said Venn as they watched the Wa'urd, its tentacles moving gently over Frina, "words change. Meanings are lost and so we make them into something we understand."

"Do not talk in riddles," said Tall Sera.

"Ud has no meaning in our language, so it becomes something else."

"Wood," said Tall Sera softly as he grasped what was being said, "ud to wood. Wa'urd to wyrd."

"Exactly," they said. "Wyrdwood. Wa'urd Ud. The land of the Wa'urd."

Before more could be said, Frina spoke, a long stream of language, almost jubilant. Her people moved, each one laying their hands on the roots of the cloudtree and the clearing was flooded with golden light. It started in the cocoon of Wa'urd tentacles that surrounded Frina, leaking out between the gaps in the creatures' oily flesh and then moved, like a thinking, living thing. The light ignored the Forestals, it ignored Sorha and it ignored Venn. It followed lines across the floor until it found the cloudwood roots, moving up them to enclose the Osere in a shimmering light, as if a hundred thousand tiny flying creatures twisted and buzzed around them. The air filled with a high-pitched, whining hum that pierced the eardrums of all listening, made them want to raise their hands to cover their ears, though they could not. All were frozen in place.

Then it was gone. The tentacles withdrew from Frina in one sinuous, twisting motion.

The Osere leader remained kneeling, around her the golden particles began to fade and Frina lifted a hand, held it in front of her face. Spoke three words in her language, halting, slow. Then said them again, louder.

"What is she saying?" said Tall Sera.

"That she can see," said Sorha softly. Venn looked around, the other Osere were doing the same as Frina, stepping back from the roots and holding their hands in front of their faces. They still had no eyes, instead, along the blank bulge of their foreheads ran two lines of gold. The same three words that Frina had uttered echoed around the clearing. Then the song of the Wa'urd changed and it no longer sang in the language of the Osere, it sang out a name.

Sorha. Sorha, Sorha.

Again and again and for the first time Venn could ever remember the woman looked frozen by indecision, she did not step forward, she did not sneer or spit. Only stood, staring up at the huge creature before her.

Still.

Unable to move.

Scared.

53

Sorha

She saw a miracle happen, saw the creature give the Osere back their sight. They did not grow eyes as she had imagined they would. Instead, the Osere glowed, lines of gold running across their faces. She could feel a warmth from them, a gentle surprise and a growing hope that a time long promised to them had come.

How could they think anything else? Their gods had returned, they had been forgiven and their sight had been restored.

She wondered if they would become zealots now, afire with the realisation of prophecy. She hated the idea, she'd had enough of zealots. At the same time she thought it did not really matter. The forces arrayed against them were too much for any of them to survive. Maybe zealotry was what they needed.

She wanted none of it, expected none of it. All the time she had felt herself a bystander in the events of others, support to those who were seemingly chosen by gods or whatever these creatures were. She was not chosen, only dragged along in the wake of others.

Then she heard her name, floating through the air. Sung

in the strange lilting, golden voice of the Wa'urd and that fear, that feeling that had been growing in her took hold, froze her in place. What did it want with her? Did it know who she had been? That once she had stood with the enemy, and fought on their side? Did it know all the terrible things she had done?

Was this her end?

She did not want her end to come from those oily tentacles.

But it wanted her.

Her.

She did not want it.

She would fight and she would die for the Osere and for Cahan and to stop Saradis but she did not want this creature to touch her. She did not want it seeing who she was, who she had been.

Sorha.

Her name sung again, and again and little by little she found herself moving, not of her own volition, more like the song charmed her flesh into betraying her. Carried her toward the great writhing tangle of the Wa'urd until she found herself beneath it. Within the cocoon of its tentacles the ground was moving, strings of gold rising from it that were thin as nettle threads, waving as if caught in a breeze.

She did not want this. She could not stop it.

It embraced her, surrounded her, and she could no more fight it than she could fight the urge to breathe. The threads of gold grew around her, twisting and weaving, and the Wa'urd's tentacles came down until she was encased within black tentacles and glowing gold light. Within she was warm. She heard the song and for the first time in as long as she could remember she felt safe.

Sorha.

It saw all she had been. She felt no blame. Only sorrow.

Firstchild, so lost. We are sorry.

She did not understand.

It touched her, she felt it under her skin.

Felt something within her changing, a light that had been snuffed out growing once more. Her cowl. The creature was bringing her cowl back, what she had desperately desired for so long. But no. How could it not understand that she did not want that Sorha back? She fought it. Did not want it, she did not want to feed on others, to be constantly fighting her own terrible hunger.

Sorha. Sorha Firstchild. Untouched by the past. Sorha, Sorha, Sorha.

The song of the creature calmed her. She was safe within the golden cocoon. She opened her eyes and saw the beak of the creature above her. The song came from it, flowing from it, floating out of it. Surrounding her, moving through the fibres of the cocoon which melded with her body. In strange conversation with the cowl within, which was itself in conversation with the Wa'urd.

Healing.

Her tiredness ebbing away and the cowl, it was waking. But it was different. How? She did not know, she only knew it was. Without trying, without reaching out with her power she knew it was not the same as before. She was not the same as before. She felt no hunger, she felt no sudden and burning desire to take another life, she felt no need within her for cruelty.

Sorha, and in her name, in the song of it, a deeper meaning, one without words but that she understood.

What was broken has been fixed, not only the cowl, but herself. She had fixed herself, become something more than she had been, no longer a shallow thing living only for herself. In return, the Wa'urd had taken her cowl, and fixed it. Only now did she understand that what they did as Rai, how they took to make themselves more was not making them powerful, not really. It was diminishing them, making them less, hollowing them out. The tentacles of the Wa'urd withdrew and the cocoon faded away.

She found herself breathing, but breathing as if for the first time. Feeling the freshness of the air of Osereud, the moisture in it. A thousand scents she had never noticed before. All around her life, the Forestals and the Osere, subtly different from one another. Venn, like a torch in the darkness, a golden glowing light and the Wa'urd was no longer black, its inky being shot through with the same gold as everything else, and not just the people, but the roots and the land. Even far above her the sky ran with gold.

And blue. She saw that too, saw it everywhere, curling around the gold, smothering it in some places, in others only a delicate filigree, an unseen war going on within the substance of the land.

"Sorha?" said Venn.

"It has given me my cowl back."

The trion took a step back, and she felt a shiver of fear run through them, a quiver in the gold of their aura.

"Not like before," said Sorha. She found herself echoing what the Osere had done raising her hand in front of her face and looking at it. She was golden, the web of the cowl beneath her skin the same golden web that ran through everything else. "I see it now, Venn, I see Ranya's web. It is beautiful."

"Do you hunger?"

"No," she said softly. She thought of fire, of making a flame within her hand and she felt the gold within her move, felt it break from her. No, break was the wrong word, it moved through the skin of her feet, through infinitesimal gaps in her flesh and in her shoes and into the ground where it found the web of gold and connected her to it. What sprung into being was not fire, not something harsh and burning and acidic. It was gentle, a light for seeing and with a twist of thought she focused it, into something sharp, a weapon, then she let it go and it floated away into the darkness, slowing, fading and in this one action she felt a kind of joy – something entirely alien to her. Something new and wonderful. "Is this how it was meant to be?" Above her, the Wa'urd sang, and, yes, this was how it was meant to be, but also she knew that she was different in some way she did not understand. Different from the Forestals and the Osere, and even Venn.

She also found she understood the song now. She did not know how, and it was not a direct translation, more like the creature sang and someone whispered a meaning in her ear.

"Harn," she said, turning to Frina and slipping into the language of the Osere, "there are more gifts for us in Harn." Then she turned to Tall Sera, "It has something for you as well."

"What?" He did not step back but she could feel his desire to, his fear of the creature, and she could not blame him. She had felt it also, she still did. The Wa'urd was not an ally exactly, to her its motivations were impossible to understand. That and it was powerful, strong. Those writhing tentacles could rip her apart, rip anyone here part. For that reason and at the moment she also trusted it. The creature had no reason to lie to them. This ramshackle group was little threat to it.

The Wa'urd sang again and in response Sorha held out her hand. Above it that gentle light and through her connection to the land she felt the Wa'urd make a request, gentle, no force behind it, only a wish for her to let it touch the land through her. Behind that the knowledge it could probably force her to do this, but it would not. So she let it use her, felt its touch and its mind ripple through her. The light in her hand grew, changed, morphed into an image of a plant. Brown, woody fungal brackets and from it grew bushy and bright orange fruiting bodies. The fruit of the brackets oozed a clear liquid and flying creatures were trapped where the stalks had curled up around them. The air filled with a pleasant, sweet smell.

"Is this a joke," said Tall Sera.

"What do you mean," said Venn.

"How is that a gift? It is just crupsall, it grows everywhere, a weed, and it stings if you touch it." While Tall Sera was speaking, sneering in his confusion and his fear, Sorha felt the Wa'urd sorting through her mind. It was not an intrusion, or she did not feel it as that, it felt right, natural, normal and that confused her, but she did not have time for confusion. A sudden and vivid memory pressed upon her. In Osereud, but not here. She was in Anjiin, strapped to a travois in pain and her and Cahan were talking. He was telling her about a trip through the forest with the monk, Udinny. She wasn't really listening, didn't want to listen then, wanted to stew in hate and resentment. Why was this normally taciturn man talking to a woman he hated, who hated him. Had he been scared, lonely?

Then, as if something tightened on her head, as if someone grabbed her and forced her to look, to pay attention, his words flooded in and she understood.

"It's a poison," she said, "for the Rai. Cahan touched some and it nearly killed him."

"The Rai are not the only ones with cowls," said Tall Sera, "and I tell you it was not crupsall or every Forestal would be dead, it grows everywhere."

"I do not mean to offend," said Venn, "but you are hardly as powerful as Cahan, maybe that is why it does not hurt you so badly?"

"No," said Sorha and she watched the image in her hand fade away at the same time as the memory in her mind faded, "it is not about power, it is about corruption. The Rai, Cahan, the way we were made. The killing. It corrupts the cowl. The Wa'urd fixed me, I see now. And you, Tall Sera, your people, the Osere. You are not corrupted."

"And me?" said Venn.

"You are different. The blooming rooms, they are corruption. But you have not killed, and you have been . . ." she searched for the right word. "Touched by something powerful," she said.

"The Boughry," said Venn softly.

"But it is not about power, not power singular, the cowl is meant for us to work together. You, your people, the Wa'urd, Crua itself." She could see Tall Sera, see him grasping at her words for understanding.

"So this plant is a weapon?"

Sorha nodded. "A poison, smear it on your arrows, your blades. Cover your barricades with it."

"Will it affect the collared?" said Venn. "They are not Rai."

"Why would the Wa'urd show me otherwise?"

"Well," said Tall Sera, "then I will take this gift back to Woodhome." Tall Sera looked up at the creature. "What about one of them? If Saradis' people have more than one, we cannot fight them." Something in the song of the Wa'urd, some other thing that Sorha needed to tell them.

"It says," she told him, "more of its people will come, some to fight for you, some for them. But their focus will be on Harn, and Jinnspire, not your home. More than that, it says we can win. It says the people beat them before."

At that Tall Sera said nothing, only blinked, nodded his head and looked around.

"Then Woodhome awaits us, and Harn awaits the Osere. We should go."

They left, the group moving through the darkness led by Venn. Behind them came the vast dark presence of the Wa'urd, moving from root to root above them. The Osere walked more slowly, every single thing in this world was new to them, seen with the new senses as gifted by the Wa'urd and they wanted to stop, to touch and look upon all the things in their dark world that had surrounded them and they had been unable to see. No amount of coaxing could change that, no talk, no begging, even Frina was lost in this new world that was presented to her. The

Osere were not only fascinated with the world, but with each other, the colours of their skin, movement of hands and arms. Only the Wa'urd eventually stopped them, pulling their attention to it with a song and they bowed their heads. Then the slow forward procession turned into a fast walk, that to a jog and as they speeded up there was light, cast by the massive body of the Wa'urd and when they could all see they could all run and they did.

The Forestals moved with a grim inevitability. Venn ran with their face set, purpose filling them, but the Osere, they ran with joy, with wonder at their new world even though Sorha knew that out there in the darkness waited the end of most of them. Their time with the joy they felt would be short, but Sorha found herself gaining strength from them. They knew their time was short and they were determined to take the joy in what they had.

She could learn from that, she would learn from that. So she breathed deep as she ran, she took the air of this underground place into her lungs. She let herself smile at the almost childlike way the Osere were fascinated by everything, even though they did not have time to stop. She looked around herself at the root forest, at the shapes of it, the way the shadows thrown by the light of the Wa'urd danced and changed with their movement. Even the Wa'urd itself had a great beauty to it, though maybe one that was hard to understand for those who did not see it.

The taffistone, when they approached it, had changed: some reaction to the presence of the Wa'urd? Sorha did not know, but it pulsed with waves of golden light as if the stone had become liquid. Venn stopped before it, put their hands upon it and with her cowl Sorha felt Venn reaching out, trying to open the taffisnetwork, to find the trion of Woodhome. It was like a pressure on Sorha's mind, like the moment in Tilt before the great geysers exploded, a knowing something was about to happen.

But nothing did.

"They need more strength," said Tall Sera. The Forestals gathered around Venn, sharing their strength and then the Osere joined them and Sorha, for the first time, knew she could be part of this. She was not apart any more, she was not alone any more. She took a step forward until she stood by Frina. She did not know what to do. She was lost, confused. Could she even do this? Was she welcome or would she poison what they did?

She was scared, that awful emotion welling up again. What if when they touched they saw inside her. What if they saw her and rejected her?

What if she was left alone?

Then she felt a warmth, a hand on her hand and Frina was looking up at her with her golden eyes.

"Come," said the Osere and she squeezed Sorha's hand. "Need you," and there was nothing she could do then, nothing she could say. Cahan had needed her, but that was transactional, this was not. It was genuine, it was an invite and she took it. Her consciousness drawn out, her power joined with the Osere and the Forestals and Venn and she sensed them, knew they were there and knew something of all of them: worried, happy, surly, frightened, and a thousand mixtures of those emotions and at the head of it all a strength, like a spire rising above them. A sure determination and a beacon of light: Venn. Something else too, each and every one of them had echoes, variations of them, all except her.

Again.

A gathering, a letting go of the power within them without a single one of them being drained. Exhilarating, so different from the singular experience of being Rai. This was to be part of something larger and better and stronger. The taffisnetwork, Sorha could sense it like a maelstrom before them, twisting and changing, laced through with threads of blue. Broken, she thought, it is broken. Saradis' god could not take it for themselves through its twisted version of Ranya, so they had broken it.

Again.

Another gathering of strength, another push.

Not strong enough. The creature in Tilt could not push through, could not take over, but it took much less strength to break a thing than to use it.

Again.

They tried again, and now Sorha felt the creature in Tilt become aware, with every push she felt the blue filaments reach out for them, thorny creepers to ensnare them. Venn balancing their power now, no longer using it all to push against the damage done by the creature in Tiltspire, now they were also having to fend it off.

Sorha knew, and she thought if she knew then they all knew, they could not do it. The taffisnetwork was effectively closed to them.

Until a new presence joined them, lent its strength, a vast and golden star. Alarm, fear and anger. Not from those gathered here, but from the other end of those blue filaments as they were burned away by energy provided by the Wa'urd and directed by Venn. In the gap between the two powers Sorha felt how the network itself wanted to be fixed, it desired it.

The creature in Tiltspire fought them. It was stronger than the Wa'urd with them, and its strength was a poison rushing into the system, bringing with it the stink of sickness. Pushing them back. Twisted thorns and vines constricting them.

"Hold it, push!" Venn's voice.

They fought, but a losing battle, little by little they were forced backwards. The network a tunnel, collapsing around them.

"We are losing," the plaintive voice of an Osere. She felt the fury of the Forestals, their determination, but it was not enough.

Another presence. Dark. An icy, biting wind. The rustle of dead leaves. The crack of falling branches.

"Fight it!"

"No!" Venn's voice. "Let them in!"

The new presence sweeping in, adding their own strength and a fury to the fight. This power not destructive like the blue but old and dark, and mixed with something alive and familiar.

"The Boughry!" Did a shudder of fear pass around the group? If so it was quickly gone. With an almost audible pop the network opened up, the golden fire of the Wa'urd, the strength of the Osere and Forestals and the ancient and desperate need of the Boughry scouring away the bluevein.

Venn calling them into the network. Forestals sent to Woodhome. Sorha felt the loss of their strength as they rushed through the stone but the Boughry renewed their push. She felt Venn ready themselves to follow, pause.

"We can hold it," she said, and she could, she knew that, for as long as they needed to anyway.

Sorha felt Venn pass into the stone, turn to her.

"Look after the Osere, Sorha."

I will.

Then Venn was gone, through the stone and into Woodhome. A moment later the stone twitched, Sorha felt other stones opening, presences that were both familiar and strange passing through and then she was done. The network closed and Sorha was left with the Osere and the Wa'urd far above them.

"It will fight harder now," said Frina. "It knows the Wa'urd have woken." Sorha nodded, and they felt an echo, a shiver, as if of a furious scream from very far away.

54

Udinny

Having died already, and been brought back to life after dying, both in this world and in the world of the dead, I was in no hurry to die again.

I had expected there would be jeering and throwing things, the great delights of a crowd offered an execution, but there was none of it. The people of Jinnspire were tired and they were frightened. Too tired and frightened to even take joy in the death of an outsider, which was a rare way for the people of Crua to feel, in my experience.

Our Rai, Ustiore, was no help. She had used all she had in the mad rush for the marant. The landing had broken her body leaving her in a catatonic state while her cowl used all it had left to keep her and it alive. Which seemed to me to be a waste of its energy as we would all be extinguished quite soon. I suppose cowls must very much live in the moment, if they are aware of the moment. I have not given it much thought.

Tanhir was not looking at me, or Rai Ustiore, or the silent people who watched us as we stood on a stage erected before the giant taffistone. The Rai who had condemned us stood there, together with another, a man slightly taller than her. They wore finely carved armour with great bracket fungus shoulder guards and helmets carved with spearmaws. Behind them was a soldier, a big man with a large curved sword. I suspect his job was to behead Ustiore, and then the Rai would feed off us. Rai, no matter how desperate the situation might be, do not really like to take risks, and taking power from another of their kind is always a risk.

As for me, I had hoped to be able to access my own cowl, in fact, that was what I thought it best to bet on. My cowl, or rather the cowl of Fandrai, Cowl-Rai of Hirsal, Lord of Murder, had come through for me before when I was about to die. However, at the moment it seemed preoccupied with something else, something very strange.

The Rai had asked if I was male or female, which I thought an odd question, given the beard. But the beard was gone. I do not think it had simply vanished or fallen out overnight. It had not been a thing I had thought about, and never having had one before I had considered the gradual thinning of it simply a beard thing. Now it was gone entirely. More, there were swellings on my chest that I had ignored for as long as I could but there could be no doubt about what was happening now. I was becoming a woman again.

That was definitely not a beard thing.

It was the doing of my cowl, and though I would be far more comfortable being what I felt I truly was, this was maybe not the time for it. I would rather use the cowl's power in other ways, for myself, and Tanhir, and even our Rai who I had grown fond of, as much as one can for a Rai.

I heard movement behind me and wondered if my cowl would come to life, protect me.

It would not, of course.

I had learned its behaviour, and so far it had only acted when I was in immediate danger, which meant I was probably safe at that second. I wondered if it would act when Tanhir was threatened and realised I did not want to watch her die. Though whether we were executed here or not made little difference, I suppose. It would not be long before the forces of Zorir overran the city.

Funny, that I was worrying about Tanhir, who hated me. Or hated this body anyway. I wondered if she would hate me less if I became a woman.

The Rai behind me forced me to my knees. I would never get to find out if Tanhir would be more forgiving of the man who murdered her family if they were no longer a man. To my right she was also forced to her knees. I had expected her to be the type to fight, to go down kicking and screaming but she did not. She let them push her down, submitting meekly and I glanced up. A large crowd had gathered now. They were as meek as Tanhir.

Tired, I suppose. We were all tired.

"Don't move," hissed the Rai, "don't turn around, don't say a word and we will at least make this quick for you."

On the other side of Tanhir they were tying Rai Ustiore to a chair, one leg and one arm were bent at the wrong angle, and I could see the white gleam of bone sticking out of her thigh. The man with the sword was watching them and behind me I could hear the creak of the Rai's armour. They stood forward and started to speak to the crowd. Empty words, of resistance, of strength, of how these prisoners had been taken from under the noses of the army outside their city. How that proved the enemy's weakness and how their weakness would make Jinnspire's Rai strong. While the Rai droned on I tried to contact the cowl within me. It was there, I knew it. I had touched it before and it knew about me. It must have accepted me or why else change this body.

Cowl? Cowl are you there because I sorely need whatever power you can give me.

No answer, not even a vague feeling that it was aware

of me. Though I was aware of it, a shifting, shimmering thing beneath my skin, busy reworking me.

"Now," shouted the Rai, "for the people of Jinnspire we will take one of the enemy's Rai! We will weaken them further." She looked across at the swordsman and he lifted his sword.

It fell. Swift and unreal. One moment Ustiore was alive and then she was dead. A bleeding stump for a neck, her head unblinking on the floor.

"Next!" shouted the Rai, "We will strengthen ourselves with this one," she pointed at Tanhir, "and this one!" and she pointed at me. "Rai Gastar, step forward and strengthen yourself." The man stepped forward to stand directly behind Tanhir.

Cowl, I thought, if you are there then now would be the time to show yourself.

But there was no reply. No feeling of acknowledgement. Nothing. It was as though it did not hear me, as though we were people separated by a vast distance and my inability to contact the cowl within me would cost Tanhir her life. She looked across at me as the Rai placed a hand on her shoulder and for the first time since I had met her, there was no hatred and no suspicion in her gaze. Only a resignation that it had come to this. Maybe she was at peace because at least we would both die, and painfully. Maybe it helped that she would die first and still remembering her family. Perversely, I almost blurted out that I may not die. That the cowl within me may yet save me but I did not think it was the time, or that it was wise to alert those around me to what I was.

"I'm sorry," I said. She opened her mouth to say something but did not get the chance.

Something changed.

A sound, like the ripping of material cut through the air and the crowd, up until now so absolutely silent, let out a collective gasp.

Though my executioner stood by my shoulder and had ordered me not to move, I could not help myself. After all, what is a Udinny if a Udinny is not curious? I turned.

The sound I had heard was the great taffistone. Behind it, black and covered with creepers, rose Jinnspire. The stone opened and as it did I had a vision. My mind was torn away from this place to a darkness where a great eight-pointed star slowly span. The darkness faded away and now I saw the star, sat atop Jinnspire.

"Ranya," I said softly, and was filled with an overwhelming desire to be there, to make my way to the top of the spire. I would have stood. Would have ignored the Rai and run toward the spire despite that it would have brought me directly into conflict with them, that was how strong the pull was.

But, like every other person there, my attention was pulled to the taffistone. I saw swirling snow. I saw a forest clearing. I felt the terrible, baleful and powerful presence of the Boughry and something stepped through, passing from the dark cold place on the other side. It moved ponderously, heavily, as if struggling to power its mass forward. It was twice as tall as any of the people I had ever seen, even Cahan, and twice as wide as well. The appearance of the thing was of a huge mass of wood taking on the form of the people. Arms as thick as a person, legs the same but shorter in proportion to the body than was normal. And the face, something of that face struck me as familiar, no matter how strange that may sound.

I had seen such a thing before, but where? Scouring my mind. Travelling through my pasts until I was in Wyrdwood with Cahan. A figure sat at the base of a tree, wreathed in vines and unmoving.

"A Forest Man," I said.

It stood absolutely still at first. Then the great carved wooden head moved, looking at the Rai, at the crowds, then at Tanhir and lastly at me.

It spoke.

"Free them." The voice was not deep, but it was powerful. It was the bending of thick branches in the wind, it was the promise that leaves would return to bare branches after Least.

"Saradis' creature," hissed the Rai and she raised her hand, fire leaping across the space between us and the Forest Man.

The Forest Man cared nothing for fire, it ran off it the way water splashes off skin. Another gout of fire joined the first, this from the second Rai who had turned away from Tanhir. The Forest Man, almost lazily, raised an arm. Around its thick wrists were what looked like shackles, wooden circles and from them sprouted a ring of thorns. With a flick of its wrist, and a sound like a splitting log it launched the thorns, hitting the Rai nearest me in the head, knocking them backwards so they fell over my body. Then it turned and launched a second thorn, killing the second Rai. More Rai were coming, and soldiers with them, running towards us but they slowed as they approached. This was something new, something unknown.

The Forest Man stepped forward. The stage creaked under its weight.

"They did not need to die," it said. I did not feel like it spoke loudly but at the same time I was sure everyone here heard its words. "And no others need die today." Something in that voice, about the planes of its beardless face, even in the way it stood made me think, as strange and unlikely as it sounds, that I knew this creature. It was not the one I had seen with Cahan though, that one definitely had a beard.

And yet?

And yet and yet.

Something of it. I knew.

The Forest Man took another step forward, the stage creaked even more alarmingly. It looked to the man with the blade, then to the body of the Rai on the floor then to us.

"Unbind them," it said and it felt like a command that could not be disobeyed, a compulsion made into words and the man almost fell over himself to do as he was told. I think, faced with this huge and alien thing that had dispatched the Rai with such ease, the people of Jinnspire would have run if they had anywhere to run to, but an army waited outside their city and maybe they were so tired they had decided if they were to die then better to do it here, now. I felt myself cut free. Stood, rubbing my wrists as feeling, quite painfully, flooded back into my hands and feet. The Forest Man took another step forward, then, as if considering the noises the stage was making, stopped. Tanhir looked across at me, then at the Forest Man. I shrugged because even with this wonder before me my mind was drawn away. I felt pulled toward the top of Jinnspire where I had seen the glowing, writhing star. The Forest Man relaxed, I heard it as a hiss, I felt it as a thump that ran through the entire scaffold, I saw it as its arms and legs and body locking together, only the head still moving, looking over the crowd of townspeople, soldiers and Rai

"People of Jinnspire," it said, and again, I knew and did not know that voice, "I am come as the spirit of Wyrdwood. I am tree, and leaf and wind and water. I am the life of the land and I exist to continue that life. I am the warrior of the cloudtrees." Its voice getting louder with every word. It raised its arms. "I come here not to save this city, or its people, but to save all of Crua and all of its people." It looked around. "Saradis brings only destruction. But even now, great forces move against her. You must do your part and hold Jinnspire for the good of all."

There was no reply, no words, no shouts. No one disagreed, there was only quiet and in that quiet I could no longer hold back my compulsion.

"I have to get to the top of the spire," I said. "Ranya wills it."

"Not yet, Udinny Pathfinder," said the Forest Man. "We must hold here, but when the time comes I will take you up there myself." In that moment, I recognised the voice, and the face. It was and was not someone I already knew. Someone I had met in the Forestal city.

"Dassit?" I said, and I swear the wooden mouth of the Forest Man moved a little, it almost smiled.

"Almost," she replied. Nodded to me, then it began to come fully alive again, backing away from the rickety stage onto more solid ground. "Now come, there is a lot of work to be done."

55

Venn

The transition was violent, and it begot violence.

No easy move from one place to another, no single step. Neither was it the falling, twisting journey of Venn's last transition. This was a shock, a battle with the substance of Crua itself, the taffisways had been damaged, cracked, the blue veins of Zorir were everywhere, corrupting what they could not have, sucking away energy, taking from the land in ways seen and the unseen. Venn held the Forestals close to them, they extended their strength and felt the touch of each and every Forestal reaching out for them as they were buffeted back and forth by the winds of the ways.

As they fell, hurtling towards Woodhome, Venn felt more than Zorir in the taffisways. There were others. Wa'urd drawn to Zorir's cause. The ones who would burn this place for what they wished and as Venn felt their influence they also felt the power and strength of these creatures and knew, from their communion with the Wa'urd of Wyrdwood, how few stood with them, how many had chosen Zorir, and its promise of fire and the Star Path.

Venn felt a hopelessness fall upon them. What was

arrayed against them was huge, success was a dream, the fire was already kindling.

Why fight? Why put so many through pain and death if what was to come was inevitable?

Then they were no longer moving. They were no longer connected to the Forestals. They were falling and falling and falling into a ring of bright gold, eight waving tentacles that opened to take them up and the gold filled them and surrounded them and suffused them.

They knew what this was.

Ranya.

A word and a name said in awe. Ranya was Crua and they were part of Ranya. In their warmth they felt a reassurance. They felt a hope. They felt there was a real possibility and something took seed in the back of their mind. Something they knew was there but did not fully understand, did not fully see, all they knew was that they had a purpose and that they had hope and that they must do what they had done for so long. What Udinny had taught them to do.

Trust in Ranya, walk the path.

Then they were thrown from the stone and into light and noise and screaming and anger and fury. They saw one of the Forestals they had brought through the stone with them begin to stand and be cut down by an arrow.

An arrow?

How could that be?

A hand on their arm, pulling them up.

"Come, Venn," Tall Sera, looking down at them, "stay down."

"Arrows," all they could say.

"The collared," said Tall Sera, "it is true, they have taken some of ours." There was a shout and Venn turned. A huge shadow above them. Oddly familiar and yet wildly out of place. A skyraft. Ropes falling from it and soldiers and collared coming down them. Screams and shouts as arrows picked them off, bodies falling. Spearmaws, swooping down on the defending Forestals, collared on their backs directing them at groups of archers. Arrows and Rai fire rained down from above. Forestals loosing arrows at the soldiers and the spearmaws, then running for cover. Villagers of Harn, and other Forestals standing with shields and spears ready to meet the attack. A shout from above, a Rai at the edge of the skyraft pointing down.

"The leader! It is the leader! Target him!" Everything slowed for Venn, above they saw archers, Forestals wreathed in the blue growths of Zorir turning their bows towards Tall Sera. Rai bringing fire into being on their hands. A deluge about to rain down on them and, though it was targeted at Tall Sera, Venn knew they would be caught in it.

"Protect them." Rang out. And above them the shimmering Forestals' shield came into being, arrows bouncing from it, fire slipping away from it to land in the clearing, splashing against a Forestal's house and setting it alight, streamers of fire leaping up into the sky.

"Quickly!" a voice amid the chaos, "this way, to the higher levels, we cannot hold here for long." Something in Venn leapt at that voice, familiar, a friend: Furin! She was leading a squad of Forestals who, together with Brione of the Lens of the Trion, were holding the shields in place. "Quick!" she shouted again, "others need protection." They ran towards her and she shook her head, pointed them at a ramp twisting and turning up into the cloudtree. "That way!" she shouted.

"No," shouted Tall Sera, "we can fight!"

"We are not fighting," Furin pulled on his arm, "we are withdrawing."

"You do not tell me what to do, this is my forest! My home!"

"They are bringing the raft down!" shouted Furin, her face contorted, voice desperate. "They intend to crash the raft into Woodhome." Alarm on Tall Sera's face. "They aim here, where the taffistone is, so we cannot leave. I have moved the children and those who do not fight further into the tree."

"We must hold the . . ." began Tall Sera.

"No, we must protect," said Furin. Tall Sera was about to say more but another voice joined, imploring him to leave. Brione of the trion.

"Tall Sera, while we hold this shield, we are not protecting the children and their carers." A moment where he warred within himself. Then nodded, standing and shouting.

"Withdraw! Withdraw!" They were running, running through the battle and Venn saw how it tore at Tall Sera to run when all round him his people were fighting and dying. Gasmaws and spearmaws swooping. Arrows singing through the air. Shields shuddering into being and fire flowing over them and through it all they ran. Venn began to see a sort of order around them. It was not the chaos they had first thought. There was a pattern, groups of Forestals hitting, running, drawing soldiers away. Others holding them to keep pathways further up into the tree clear. Small groups working with saws to cut supports, ready to drop the pathways once everyone had escaped.

Chaos, but chaos with a clear plan. Venn followed Tall Sera as Furin pointed them at a steep ramp. He stopped to tell a Forestal about the crupsall poison, and to smear it on all their weapons. As they moved on, the wood below them began rocking and bouncing with the action of feet, the usual solidness of Woodhome removed by busy saws.

"Down!" Before them Forestals with drawn bows. Tall Sera went to one knee, Venn and those with them fleeing the taffistone courtyard did the same. Arrows whistling overhead. Venn turned their head. Seeing a group of soldiers and collared cut down by arrows. The soldiers fell, the collared, too, but unlike the soldiers many of them got back up. Another hail of arrows and then arrows began to fall from above, not as well aimed but some of the Forestal archers fell before a shield was called into existence.

"Quickly!" a shout from somewhere above, "the raft is coming down!"

"Furin!" shouted another voice, and as Venn and Tall Sera reached the top of the ramp they turned. Furin, with a small group of Forestals gathered around her. Some with bows, others with swords and shields. They were surrounded by the enemy.

"Bows," shouted Tall Sera, "cut her a path!" The archers at the top of the ramp changed their aim. Arrows sailing through the air and slicing into the soldiers and collared who were blocking Furin's retreat. As soon as the first flight had hit, the Forestals around Furin formed into a wedge, pushing toward the nearest ramp. "Loose again!" shouted Tall Sera, and even though arrows were falling from above he took no shelter, stood in defiance of them. Venn looked up, the massive skyraft was listing, the angle so severe they could see the deck from where they stood. Soldiers were hacking at the ropes holding the huge balloons above the roaring fires. Others hacking at the anchor ropes for the gasmaw nets below. As the huge raft was put under stress it was never built for it creaked and groaned. Every so often burning logs and embers would overspill from the fire pits, cascading down the deck in showers of sparks to vanish into the forest below, or crash against the decks of Woodhome.

A noise, louder than any other as something cracked in the skyraft, something important to its structure, and with a groan that reverberated through the air and shook the pinleaves of the cloudtrees, a sound Venn felt in their guts, the skyraft began to fall. It was so massive the fall appeared slow, stately, gentle even, but it was not. It came down quickly. The soldiers and collared who had been blocking Furin's way running to escape it. He thought Furin would die, that the raft would crush her. Venn watched in horror as the thick edge of the skyraft came down and down and down, and it seemed impossible that the tiny people could escape the massive wooden edges of the raft, then it slowed. Groaning to a stop. Suspended by one remaining balloon. On the dangerously tilted deck of the raft soldiers were hacking at ropes. Below, Furin and those surrounding her made the ramp and ran up to it. Once she reached the top she made a signal, raising her hand and waved and from beneath each ramp the cutting teams appeared, running to the top before severing the final supports, sending their ramps falling to the level below and trapping the troops of Zorir on the burning lower level. Tall Sera only stood, looking down on the wreckage of his town.

"I never thought I would see this," said Tall Sera. "I thought Woodhome would be a safe place for us."

"Nowhere is safe," said Venn. "We must head further up."

"Not yet," said Tall Sera. He looked over at the raft. "They are doing something. I would know what."

"Tall Sera." He turned to see Furin coming towards them, around her neck was Cahan Du-Nahere's garaur, Segur, and with one hand she scratched its ears. She did not smile, she looked drawn and tired. "I am glad you are back, your people need a leader."

"It appears to me they have one." He nodded at her and the group of Forestals that stood with her. For a moment Venn thought they heard a darkness in Tall Sera's voice, the edge of a threat.

"An unwilling one," said Furin, "who is glad to give back the responsibility." Brione of the Lens stood forward, tall, proud, sure of herself. They had put stripes across their make-up that Venn thought were blood.

"When the attacks first started, Tall Sera, you were not here", he nodded, "and we chose Furin to lead us because she has fought the Rai of Zorir before. She has proved herself one of us since." Venn watched Tall Sera, and in that second they saw what made him a good leader. The man had clashed with Furin, she had disobeyed him and his anger with her had been great, but he did not let it override his good sense. He nodded.

"You could not find a way that would save my city?" he said, but there was no anger, he was resigned to it.

"No," she said, "and you will lose more of it yet."

"What do you mean?" he said.

"The maws, they're harnessing them. That's how they got the raft through Wyrdwood."

"They pulled it?" Furin nodded.

"And I think now they will pull it across, so when it comes down it falls over two levels. Making a ramp for them to reach higher up." Tall Sera looked to her, then back at the massive raft and down at the hundreds of soldiers and collared below.

"Above here," said Tall Sera, "Woodhome is split, there is no travel between the higher levels without coming down which we cannot do. Our enemy will be able to bring its forces against us one area at a time, overwhelm us easily." He sounded lost.

"So we put everyone in one area," said Furin. "It will be crowded, but it is the only way to protect them."

"Why haven't you done this already?" said Tall Sera.

"Not everyone will listen to Furin," said Brione. "Some of the Lens do not approve of an outsider leading us, some people do not want to leave their homes and others simply believe the tree or the Boughry will protect them."

"And there is worse," said Furin, "when we try and move people to the higher levels, the Rai attack with spearmaws, cut bridges with people on them, fire their homes when they see movement. The riders wait and pick on those carrying children. Some they kill, some they carry off and collar."

"My people will die if we move them," said Tall Sera as

much to the air as those gathered round him, "but more people will die if we don't." He stood taller then, looked over at the listing, creaking, burning skyraft. "Take my words out, all of Woodhome is to go to the great eastern branch, we will fight from there, anyone who can hold a weapon will fight with us. Those we lose will be honoured."

"I wish Cahan was here," said Furin. "He understands war."

Venn stood, wishing they had something to add. They had felt so sure that this was the place they were needed but now they were here there was only war, only war and death and the need for arms and that was not them.

They felt a tug on their hand, looked down to see Issofur, Furin's child though more rootling than child now, skin lightly furred, body stooped, teeth sharp and eyes bright.

"It's time," they said. "He needs you now."

"Who?" said Venn and the child giggled, span in a circle. "You know."

In Venn's mind a golden seed planted by Ranya sprouted into an idea, one that terrified them, one that they did not want to admit was there but they could not deny. They could save a lot of lives here, if they acted, if they did what Ranya wanted. They took a deep breath. This was the path. It must be walked. Now was the time for action, even if that action would cost them. A long time ago Venn had sworn not to fight, and here and now they thought they saw a way to at least delay the deaths of the Forestals. They stepped forward.

"I think I know what I need to do," they said. All eyes turned to them.

56

Sorha

She ran and she ran and she rejoiced while she ran.

She was Rai again, she felt the inexhaustible strength, she felt the power flowing through her, she felt a connection to everything. She could feel the Osere, she could feel the vast bulk of the Wa'urd above and behind her as it moved through the root forest and everywhere was gold, lines of bright yellow pulsing and chasing through the land as they moved. She could run forever, she was sure of it.

She was Sorha, she was Rai.

And at the same time she was not Rai, not as she had been. The gnawing, constant hunger was not there, the desire to strike out, to hurt and to crush and to dominate was not there. The need to be first among those she was surrounded by was not there. In the presence of the Osere she did not feel a threat, did not feel the need to overcome them. Instead she felt that each of the Osere around her made her stronger. They were part of her and she was part of them. She thought to conjure fire, to bring it into being as a weapon to burn and to kill and though she knew the possibility was there, she did not. She thought to create water, a weapon to drown and turn into spears of ice, but she did not. Again, the possibility was there but somewhere in the back of her mind was the thought that to use her cowl in that way was to go back to being who she had been. She was something new now, someone renewed and with a purpose, though quite what that was she was unsure of. She was still a warrior, but a different kind of warrior. A new kind of warrior. She was new, and that word carried a resonance, all those around her were not new in a way she did not really understand. They had lived and lived again but she had not. She was fresh.

From within, she felt a warmth, an approval and an acknowledgement and she found herself aware of her cowl in a way she never had been before. It was not a tool to be used just as the Osere were not tools to be used. It was part of her, she was it and it was her and they were far stronger together than they were when she was forcing her will upon it. It was not an offensive tool but reactive. With every step she could feel that she and the cowl were binding closer and closer together, her reaction times becoming quicker, her awareness of what was around her reaching further.

It was this that saved her, and saved the Osere that ran with her.

She felt them before she saw them, the Betrayers hidden in the darkness. They had bows, they had spears and the Osere with her, lost in their excitement of the return of their sight, were not themselves, not silent in their movement.

"Down!" Her voice ringing out, making her a target and drawing attention from the Osere. She felt the Osere move. Felt their natural aptitude for silence reassert itself. Arrows and spears coming and Sorha could hear them push aside the air as they were launched. She moved. Dodging from one side to the other as arrows hissed past. A spear, falling and falling, aimed right at her chest and in the last moment she turned her body sideways, grabbed the haft of the spear and used its momentum to spin herself around and launch the spear back in the direction it had come. It travelled straight, faster than it had been thrown, and took one of the Betrayers in the chest. At the same time she spoke to the air, and it twisted the paths of arrows and spears away from the Osere. Then she was in among the Betrayers, her blade out. No need for a shield, speed was her shield. Cutting left and right, twisting and dancing, and if she had seen herself, she may have wondered at how closely she resembled the spinning, dancing Reborn warriors of Cahan Du-Nahere. The sound of her footsteps and the cries of the slain drew more and more of the Betrayers toward her. Dodging, cutting left and right. Thrusting. With every movement a death. No, not a death. A release. These were no longer Osere, they had lost what made them unique. They had been removed from the great cycle of Crua. Now they dangled like puppets, every step they made controlled by unseen tendrils of bluevein deep in the ground. Sorha felt Ranya's web touch her, a rhythm to which she danced and span, but where the Betrayers were controlled, she was not. She gave and the cowl and the land returned, what had the betrayed in its grip only took.

Still, there were many of them, their numbers making up for their lack of speed and initiative and those numbers threatened to overwhelm her.

Until the Osere came, she felt them join, they fought grimly, with no pleasure as these were their people, even if they were lost. At the same time they exalted, their sight gave them a huge advantage over the betrayed. No more fighting by being still, now they took the initiative, now they cut and thrust and dodged and moved. Sorha felt where they were. The Osere felt where she was and they fought as a unit, dancing and twisting around one another. All, in their way, Reborn.

Still the Betrayers came. More and more until the final combatant entered the fray. The Wa'urd they had freed from the tree. Like the Osere she felt it and it felt her. It knew where she was. She felt its power and its strength but it lacked the same sort of connection to the land she had, that the Osere had. It was, she thought as she deflected a spear and thrust her blade home, like her and the Osere were inside, and the Wa'urd watched from atop a spire. There was distance, and that was how the world should work, how it kept all safe. Or was meant to. She could feel it, and that feeling for a moment connected her to the entirety of Crua, and in the moment she was distracted a spear came in, aimed unerringly at her throat.

Then the spear was gone, her attacker plucked away by a tentacle of the Wa'urd, and the vast creature brought its strength to bear, spilling their attackers over the ground, smashing them into the floor. An onslaught, and as quickly as the battle was joined it was over. Only the Osere and Sorha remained. The Wa'urd vanished, thundering away through the root forest after their attackers.

"Harn," said Frina to her, and pointed. "Not far now." Sorha nodded. She did not know whether they spoke in Osere or the language of the people. It no longer mattered. As Frina spoke Sorha not only knew the direction to go, but she felt its nearness, the power running through the fractured and damaged buildings of Harn-Below-Harn.

She felt something else as well, the web of bluevein. Far thicker here and in the centre of it something waited for them. Something huge and powerful. Like the Wa'urd that accompanied them but at the same time not like it and it frightened her, set off that feeling in her stomach, the slight tremor of her hands that she had to bite down on because she knew if she let it overcome her then she would shiver and shake until she could no longer walk and if she stopped walking she would stop altogether.

The terror would consume her.

From within she felt a warmth, a glow that was entirely new to her and she did not know where it came from. She felt a presence by her, Frina. The Osere smiled, gave her a nod and as they ran she stretched out a hand and just lightly brushed Sorha's armour. A small, sympathetic gesture that said, "I understand", and it said more than that, it told her "they understood", all of the Osere that ran with her. They knew and shared her fear and not one of them was ready to give up. If anything, the opposite was true, Sorha could feel more of them coming: Osere who had been hiding, Osere who had been holding out and Osere who had simply given up were being drawn here to Harn-Below-Harn and though they feared they also felt a fierce joy. They were forgiven, no longer forsaken and the end of the long punishment was here. Sorha bathed in their joy and took strength from it, though she also felt a great sadness.

"You should never have been punished," her thought pushing out and among the Osere. They did not agree, she knew that, but at the same time they welcomed her kindness.

They ran on, into the maze of broken buildings and she felt herself pulled to a stop, not by terror this time, but by a nagging feeling there was something here. Something she needed, something they all needed.

Around her, Osere were slowing too, looking around with their golden eyes, surveying the notched and broken walls, placing hands against smooth surfaces as if they held secrets. Above them, their Wa'urd appeared once more, holding itself high, seven of its eight huge tentacles touching part of the ruins and the eighth hovered over Sorha. She felt it as much as saw, the whip-thin tip curling and twisting in the darkness as if waiting for her to do something. Around her, the Osere let out a quiet hum, and it had the cadence of a prayer, an entreaty and a solemnity, though a solemnity tinged with hope and joy. Sorha put out her hands, placed them against the wall and felt only disappointment.

Nothing.

She wore gauntlets, the outsides of heavy bark and the insides of supple, tanned gasmaw flesh. At the moment she was about to remove her hands from the wall she felt the cowl within her, and the extrusion of a hundred thousand incredibly fine cilia that passed through the substance of her gloves without any sign of damage. Then she was connected with the wall – with the Osere – with Crua and she knew the hum was not a prayer, it was the song of the land, it was the vibration of the massive energies passing through it. The tentacle of the Wa'urd lowered itself, touched the top of her helmet. Curled around the hard and shining wood, slipped over the rim designed to protect her neck and under it to find flesh. She did not know what to expect, and was aware that at any moment she could recoil from this. That she could pull away and the Wa'urd would not follow, not force its touch on her. Maybe it relayed this through the air or through the buildings of Harn-Below-Harn, she did not know, she only *knew*.

If not for that knowledge she was sure she would have withdrawn, no matter that Venn had already communed with this being, that she had been given her cowl back by it – Venn was special. She was only Sorha.

Be at peace, Sorha Firstborn, Rider for the Wa'urd.

With those words an onslaught. Memories, her memories but not her memories. For a moment she saw people she knew, then realised it was not them. It was shadows of them, hundreds, thousands of different versions of every face she had ever come across echoed here. They had existed so many times, and in a way each version still existed, suspended upon the web of Ranya. She had the distinct feeling this was the material of Crua striving to fix what was wrong with it using the only tools it had, the people, the creatures, the trees. She felt herself dizzy, seeing a hundred thousand version of Venn, of Cahan, of Dassit, of Ania, of Udinny and even Saradis: Rai Venn, Trion Cahan, Soldier Udinny, Monk Dassit, Villager Saradis, and each one striving for something but not knowing what, each one restless and lost, dying and being folded back into the great cycle of Crua until they eventually arrived at this place.

And then her.

She had no shadow.

She was new.

A single crystal-clear image. A priest? A woman who could almost be her but was not. She stood at the side of a Wa'urd upon their temple. The Wa'urd provided the will, and she provided the conduit. A partnership that had worked for aeons. An understanding forged in a ruined land, the knowledge that to give one side all the power was to invite corruption and war.

"But it happened anyway," she said, and as she did she felt the eyes of the temple priest on her. Felt Ranya's web stir as it recalled ancient events through her and through the Wa'urd.

Sure in our ways, we stopped trying to be better. With complacency came rot.

For a moment she felt all was hopeless. This had happened before, Cahan, Udinny, Venn, Dassit, Ania had fought battles like this one more than once, but Sorha pushed the feeling away. Life was a battle, just because you may lose was no reason to give in. She felt the approval of this long-dead priest, and of the Wa'urd.

Will you let the Wa'urd ride?

With that word, a meaning she could not quite grasp. An offer of a deeper connection with the creature above her.

Even now, she knew she could back away. That the choice was hers just as it had been that ancient priest's so long ago.

"Yes," she said. She felt the Wa'urd call to her cowl, felt the cowl respond and the cilia extend from her neck to touch the Wa'urd, the link between her and it and the building lighting up. Her world golden. Gold everywhere, the cascade of hidden power that was meant to make Crua a paradise, that the forces of Saradis would use to burn the entire land for their own purposes were responding to her. Through her the Wa'urd manipulated the fabric of the buildings, changing them. She wondered why they didn't need a trion and as she thought it immediately knew. They were all trion if they chose to be, they were all Rai, they were all Cowl-Rai, all these names and labels were foolish, invented later. Brought into being by a people who knew something was wrong but not what. Unintentionally pushing themselves and the land apart instead of coming together to save what was. The truth was each and every person was who they were and made wonderful by it, they contained multitudes.

The web of Ranya is torn.

And now, one last desperate attempt to fix it, and she had some important part to play. Sorha, the one who had not been before, Sorha Firstborn. The web was torn and through the Wa'urd she knew that Ranya needed her to help repair it.

Around her, the Osere were taking their hands from the walls, and in them they held spears, and swords, and bows with quivers of arrows and each and every one of them glowed along the edges with gold. Frina turned to her.

"We are saddened to arm."

She nodded, she knew that and was filled with a sense of longing for a world she had never known where weapons were not needed, but also filled with determination that she would do what she could to make this world better. She felt the touch of the Wa'urd leave her, the world darkening again but when she drew her hands away from the wall, she saw her gauntlets were now incised with whirling patterns and filigreed with gold. From her gauntlets the patterns ran across her armour, a subtle web of shining light, and she felt even faster, even stronger.

It was time now, she knew it just as she knew who she was. Sorha Firstborn may be what the Wa'urd named her. But it was not her, neither was she Sorha Mac-Hean as she had been born to. As Frina and her people readied themselves for battle she took a breath and spoke her name.

"I am Sorha of the Osere, the warriors of the Wa'urd. I am one of the chosen of Ranya."

57

Udinny

There was a moment, as I followed the Forest Man, or Dassit – I was not sure what name to give them, it, her – when I realised they had rather taken the people of Jinnspire for granted. Their speech had been impressive, especially as it was underlined by killing two of their Rai, but there were still more Rai out there, and soldiers, and the people of Jinnspire were scared and scared people were easily manipulated. I did not, for one moment, think the Rai of this city would simply let some giant wooden figure appear from nowhere and tell them what to do.

I was, of course, right.

"Who are you, to order this city?" The words came from another Rai, pushing through the crowds who watched in silence. "This is our city, our land and our people." The Rai stopped before the stage. "You may have killed two of our number, creature, but could you take us all on?" More Rai were appearing around the edges of the crowd. I am not used to Rai being brave unless they are sure of victory, but these Rai had their backs against the wall and probably saw no other option.

The Forest Man turned, took two steps until they stood

at the edge of the stage, which creaked quite alarmingly. They made no attempt to raise their arms, to point the weapons on their wrists at the Rai. Instead their face scanned along the crowd. I expected the Rai to storm up the stairs, to come upon us with fire and blade but they did not. Their bravery faltered. Silence fell over the clearing in front of Jinnspire.

"I am here," the voice of the Forest Man filled the air, "as the spirit of Wyrdwood. Saradis has woken forces she cannot control. A god is coming to assault your city." There was a collective gasp, a new level of fear running through the crowd. "The old enemies have returned, and they want only to destroy."

"So you have come to protect our city?" For a moment the Forest Man did not reply to the Rai, all that filled the air was the sigh of wind.

"We must protect the city," said the Forest Man eventually, "but if we cannot protect the city, we must hold the spire." The lead Rai stepped forward.

"Why should we believe whatever you are? Wyrdwood has never helped the cities of Crua."

The air around us changed, it shimmered and filled with the smell of leaf mould and mushroom. I heard the cries of orits, felt the strange elongated eyes of shyun, the forest children, upon me. A shiver passed across the crowd, even the Rai must have felt it. At the same time the Forest Man tipped back its head, opened its arms and the air screamed. Not loud, not even really audibly but you knew it was happening. You felt something rip in the fabric of the world, you felt it connect to the land below. I felt it as a prickle across my skin and pressure in my ears, a sensation, like all the air being sucked out of me, a sudden hollowness within and then the air turned cold and I felt the icy harshness of least pass across me and the crowd gathered before the stage as one of the Boughry of Wyrdwood appeared.

A collective gasp of fear from the crowd.

The Boughry hovered above the Forest Man, all sharp edges, cracked branch antlers reaching up from a long skull, arms tipped with fingers of thorny briar.

Power and fear radiating from it. The crowd stepped back, would have run but they were held in the icy grip of the Forest Noble.

"Wyrdwood has never cared for the cities," its voice harsh: ice falling from branches, creaking trunks snapping, "as the cities have never threatened it." The skull head twitched, changed position without ever moving. One moment looking forward, then sideways and backwards all at the same time. "But time changes. Wyrdwood is Crua. Crua is Wyrdwood." I had the oddest feeling that what was said was not the Boughry's words, but the Forest Man's said through the Boughry. As if they took its thoughts and made them something more palatable. I had been in contact with the Boughry myself, and not a moment of it had been pleasant, or as wordy. "If this spire falls, we all burn, the people, the Rai, even us, the Boughry, the Woodhewn Nobles of mighty Wyrdwood."

Even the Rai were cowed by the appearance of the creature hanging in the air above the Forest Man. Around them the crowd were kneeling, not one standing. Even the most well dressed and privileged were down on their knees, getting their expensive, colourful clothes covered in dust.

"Heed my servants," the words shuddered in the air. "Heed Dassit Forest Man, heed Udinny Pathfinder. Heed Tanhir Forestal. They will guide you."

Then it was gone and what was left was a crowd bowing down to us, to me. I had not expected this at the start of the day. The Rai still stood but the fight had gone from them, they knew they had lost. The people of Jinnspire had made a choice.

"What are your orders then," said the leader of the Rai, a sneer, though maybe that was fear. The Rai were not used to coming face to face with anything more powerful than them. I turned to Dassit, in her guise as Forest Man.

"I am no tactician," I said, "but you are. So tell me what is required and I will see it done if we can."

"Tanhir," said Dassit softly, and now I heard only her voice, familiar and friendly. "Are there any other Forestals here? Anyone who can use a bow?" She shook her head.

"No, and I do not have a bow. Mine was lost in the crash of the marant."

"The rich may have bows," I said. "When I was young, my family often kept trophies, the more forbidden the better." Tanhir nodded.

"Well, one bow is better than none," said Dassit. It was strange to hear the voice of the woman I had known from behind the wooden face of the Forest Man. She walked around the edge of the stage. Then jumped off, landing in a cloud of dust. From there she walked out to be among the people of Jinnspire. "Stand," she said. "Inside this wooden body, gifted to me by the forest to protect you, I am one of you." As she talked the people stood. It was strangely magical, to see how she awoke a sense of wonder among them. Up close she was a thing of wonder, a living microcosm of the forest, of wood and vine, and mushroom and leaf. "You, Rai," she pointed at the one who had spoken, "what is your name?"

"Rai Ganhoss," she said.

"Well, Rai Ganhoss, split your Rai. Those who can send fire the farthest, who are the most powerful. Put them on the walls. I want any who assault us to have to walk through flame to do so." The Rai nodded. "Then I want to build a second wall here, in front of the spire. Have some Rai bring down those houses." She pointed at the buildings ringing the spire square. The Rai nodded.

"We have a second wall," they said.

"Then make a third," then Dassit turned away. "All those who cannot fight, who are too old or too young, move

them into the spire. The rest, have them help make barricades, pile up anything that will hold the enemy."

"If they break through?" said Ganhoss.

"I will not be dishonest," said Dassit, "we are both
warriors and we know the truth. They will break through.
Tanhir, you are to organise our lines here." The Forestal
nodded.

"What of me?" I said.

"You are to stay back, Udinny Pathfinder. When the
time comes, you and I must be at the point of the spire."
In her words I felt a sense of relief. Not because I would
be out of the fighting, but because I would ascend the
spire and that desire was still within me, not burning as
hot, but still burning. Though, as ever, I also had questions.

"The time for what, Dassit?" The wooden face looked
at me, expressionless, and yet I still felt something from
it, confusion maybe.

"I do not know. I only know that when the time comes
the top of the spire is where we must be."

A horn sounded. The note clear and powerful, cutting
through the air and Dassit looked up, wooden pupilless
eyes somehow giving the impression of being fixed upon
the far wall of Jinnspire. "It has started," she said, "they
come." Then she was striding toward the wall and despite
her advice I did not hang back, I did not stay with Tanhir
who was busy organising the flaccid and beaten citizens
of Jinnspire into a militia of sorts. I followed in the footsteps of the Forest Man, watching the strange and
invigorating effect it had on everyone as it passed, as if it
dragged a great cloak of possibility behind it. The forest
had come to stand with them. Even the Rai seemed more
hopeful around it. I suppose it is easier to feel like you
may be on the winning side when a forest god turns up
in your city and tells you it is here to fight for it.

I was not so hopeful. I had travelled Wyrdwood, I knew
how the forest thought. It was slow and powerful but above

all it was ruthless. No, that was wrong. Ruthless was not the right word, maybe uncaring? No, that was not right either. Single-minded, that was the forest and the Boughry. To it our lives were nothing special, we were small and quick where it was huge and slow. I felt quite sure it had a goal, and to accomplish that goal it would sacrifice everyone in Jinnspire if it must.

But still, it was good to see the fleeting hope the Forest Man brought the people and the soldiers. I enjoyed their joy despite having misgivings of my own. Let the people enjoy what time they had.

Another thing I noticed, and whether it was my imagination or not I was not sure, not at first anyway, is that in the wake of the Forest Man the city became greener. Every crack grew a plant, or a moss or a mushroom. Soon it was unmistakable, a riot of greenery in Dassit's wake, and in among the green a hundred thousand other colours. In dark alleys I saw the sparkling eyes of rootlings, we passed a stick shrine of the shyun, the forest children. I heard a cackle that sent a shiver down my back, and made me think a skinfetch waited, in a high window I thought I glimpsed the skeletal form of a swarden. I wondered if these creatures were there in every city, hidden, or if the Forest Man had drawn them here.

Our walk to the wall became a parade, accompanied by the sounding of war horns and the people of the city, holding whatever they could to use as a weapon and it felt a strangely merry thing. Even when Dassit pronounced the original second wall badly placed and worse built, ordering it torn down, there was no resentment.

Below all this Ranya's web spoke to me, it felt like a cradle and my connection, I think due to the Forest Man, was stronger than ever. I felt the warmth within me that was the cowl of Fandrai, Cowl-Rai of Hirsal, and there was the briefest connection, a touch, a recognition from it. It knew I was there, as I knew it was there. My body was becoming progressively more Udinny and less Fandrai and as such the cowl became more me also.

The Forest Man scaled the wall of Jinnspire, one of the largest in all Crua. I followed, though not for me to scale a sheer wall the way it did. I had to make my way up rickety ladders and swaying scaffolds that led me away from the Forest Man. The top of the wall was thick enough for two people to stand on with their arms outstretched. Arrayed along it were soldiers, staring out over the plain of Jinneng. Trunk and branch commanders waited among their troops, easy to pick out because of their brighter armour, and Jinnspire's troops were bright. They sported mushroom juice paint of greens and reds, flags cracked over their heads in the breeze and between every trunk of soldiers stood one of their Rai.

They were grand looking, in a martial sense. Further down the wall I could where Dassit stood. Behind the wall the soldiers had erected catapults, to counter those that had been built on the plains by the besieging army.

Looking out over the plains, I knew that any hope the Forest Man had brought the city was false. Following the army, and being among it, had not given me a true idea of its size. Only from above could you see it. It filled the plains, there were thousands of soldiers and in among them were the collared and Rai. I counted six huge siege towers and over thirty catapults in the process of having their great arms wound back, ready to throw their rocks. But it was not those that caught my eye, that set my nerves jangling. It was something nearer, on the side of the wall where I stood. I did not know if Dassit could see what I saw from where she was. If she had taken into account in any plan she had to defend Jinnspire what I had discovered.

A mine.

Soldiers were busy coming in and out of a hole in the ground. Each holding a heavy bucket. I knew what they did: undermining the wall then firing the mine to burn out the supports. The collapse of the mine would bring down the wall. Dangerous for the miners, but likely to succeed far more quickly than the catapults, or an assault by ladders and siege towers if it was not stopped. Most likely that was all a feint to distract from the mine.

I heard a muttering pass along the lines on the wall like a cold wind. At first I thought it was because the soldiers had also noticed the mine, but it was not. One of the spear carriers near me was pointing at the army before us. The platform we had seen under construction was being lifted.

On it sat one of Saradis' gods.

I did not know if it was the same one that ruled in Tiltspire, in fact I felt sure it was not. I think something of the cowl within me told me that and, though it was hard to be sure from this distance, I thought it smaller. Was this a new god, come to take Jinnspire? It writhed upon its platform, as if it was impossible for it to stay still. From the army below I heard chanting and shouting and jubilation. The army had been quiet and its morale poor when we had travelled among them.

The arrival of a god had changed that.

Still, I could do nothing about that, but I could warn Dassit about the mine. I pushed my way along the wall, through the soldiers waiting patiently for the enemy to come to them. They laughed and joked nervously among themselves. The enemy's god had not quite offset the hope they felt in the arrival of the Forest Man, but they were nervous. Jokes were passed back and forth, and insults, but their voices wavered. Hope was thin on the walls of Jinnspire.

"Dassit," I shouted, "Dassit!" She turned. In the posture of the wooden figure I saw annoyance, anger.

"You are not meant to be here!"

"I have something important to tell you, I . . ." As I spoke she closed the distance between us and a massive, three-fingered wooden hand clamped down on my shoulder.

Something very strange happened as we touched. The world receded, there was only me and Dassit, as if I looked through the body of the Forest Man to the woman within.

"If it is about the mine, Udinny," she said softly, "I know it is there. But it is out of the Rai's range and there is little we can do without sending a force out through the gates, which would be foolish in the extreme."

"But the wall . . ." odd, I spoke but did not speak. We shared the conversation in utter privacy and I felt within her what was within me, a cowl, and behind her the looming, terrifying ruthless shadow of the Boughry that rode with her.

" . . . will fall. Nothing can stop that, Udinny," she said. "What is important is to hold Jinnspire long enough for the others to get into position."

"What others?"

"Venn, Ania, Ont and Sorha."

"They live?"

"Yes," something in me soared, "but if you die here, Udinny, all is lost." I felt her annoyance at me, I felt the desperation and behind it and I felt something from the Boughry, a longing that it had nursed over aeons to be something more than it was.

"Sorry," I said, and the word poured from me in a shower of tears. What a fool you have been, Udinny Pathfinder. "I will return to the spire."

"Good," she said, and I was back on the walls, just in time to hear the shout of a soldier.

"Down!" and the terrible thud of catapult arms hitting the crossbeams, sending their payloads whistling through the air toward the walls of Jinnspire.

58
Share

We stepped into the taffistone as three and stepped out as two.

He had known this was going to happen, and yet they had not. In the moment of stepping into the maelstrom she had thought of themselves as three, going onwards together. They were still three, but when they had stepped out of the other side of the stone, into the enveloping green of woodedge, she had not been surprised that one of their number was gone.

Jinnspire.

He understood why and where Dassit had gone to. It seemed the most obvious thing in the world as she stood beneath the light above, felt as if it was inevitable.

She is needed.

We are needed.

They turned, unaware and yet aware of how the wooden bodies were changing around them, how Ont's grew and thickened, how Ania's became more willowy and how, on the back of both of them, vines were binding and twisting together to make bows. In the far distance they felt the draw of their goal, the place they should be.

There.

Harnspire. The broken parts of the Spirecrown pained her, but the central spire called and he knew it was a call they could not deny even if she had a wish to, though they had no wish to. They were no longer what they had been, they were more. Ont was still Ont, he felt and knew that. Ania was still Ania, she felt and knew that. But they were expanded, strengthened and they had purpose now in a way they could not deny, had no wish to deny.

They are coming.

A sentence that contained so much.

They were going to Harnspire in readiness for the end. In the sky, marant and spearmaws circled, bringing troops from Tilt. Something cold and dark followed them, something as blue as blue could be. Deep below, like a hoard of orits boiling out of a nest, were more of the enemy, these blank as the collared, controlled and inhabited by the bluevein, by their enemy and the one who sought to stop the great correction. The one who saw only fire and had forsaken hope.

With them were vast presences, dark and terrifying even to Ont and Ania, who up until that moment had felt almost invulnerable in these new bodies. They carried the Boughry, but even the Boughry shuddered at the memory of the huge dark shadows that passed below them. Within was some ancient memory the Boughry knew was there, but could not reach. They knew only that they were danger, real danger.

Others were coming, not of the bluevein. At their head something golden, and glowing. Something new, and it filled them with hope and with knowledge. They must be protected. That they were in their own way as important to the task as the Boughry were. As he was. As she was. With them travelled sparks, like the stuttering flames that leapt from a fire and above them, another of the dark presences, but subtly different, still full of power, but not as full of foreboding as the others.

Harnspire calls.

Yes.

He began to walk, never wondering why she had not been transported right to the centre of Harnspire, never asking why they had not simply walked out of the great stone before the spire as now he was part of the forest and the forest simply did, it knew what it must do the same way the leaves of the tree knew to turn and to twist in search of light, the floatvines knew to fill their bladders with gas and rise high into the canopy, and the animals knew to hunt or to hide. In her own way he was as forest-struck as any other called to the Boughry, changed by the experience, never to be who they were again. They stood, waiting and feeling the influx of forces toward Harnspire, they stood still for long enough that small creatures landed on them, or twisted between their great legs, emerged from the greenery around them until, at some signal not seen or heard but felt, a simple knowing between them, they began to move. The creatures that had been around them fleeing noisily into woodedge as the Forest Men began her trek toward Harnspire, and in his wake they pulled a train of rootlings and shyun and swarden and all the creatures of the forest that were neither quite the people or quite animal. Each and every one felt a great purpose in the air, something they had been waiting for in every generation of their kind. A need that was imprinted on them by the trees and the forest.

So, with the Forest Men at their head, Wyrdwood went to war.

59

Sorha

Time and distance were not the same in Osereud.

She had always felt that, but only since she had been given the blessing of the Wa'urd, the knowledge of the past did she know it for a fact – while still not understanding the how of it. It did not matter, they ran and while she ran she felt the movement around them of their enemies. She knew their places, she knew their intention and their destination and she felt their utter determination. No, that was not true, they were not determined. They were singular in purpose but not singular in will, they had no will. The betrayed were more akin to animals than people but where animals acted from instinct the betrayed acted on the instruction of the Wa'urd in faraway Tiltspire, and its allies waking in the north and south.

But more than their will and their movement, she felt their numbers and that scared her. Running with her were maybe a hundred of the Osere.

The enemy numbered in the thousands. They surrounded the little group as they ran and Sorha expected to be engulfed, to have a wave of the betrayed break over them. They would fight, of course, and they would fight well and hard and strong, but it was not a fight they could win, not even with the Wa'urd that travelled with them. The enemy were simply too numerous.

But the wave never came.

The betrayed ran, as fast and as hard as her and the Osere, maybe even harder as what drove them cared nothing for such small things as physical weakness. Those of the betrayed who could not keep up were left behind. Sorha killed the first few she came across, lying like broken straw dolls in her way, or leaning folded up against a root or mushroom tower. After the first few she stopped as they were no threat. Those left behind were simply abandoned, they lived but nothing animated them, thrown aside like the toys of a child once they reached adulthood. The Wa'urd driving them had no use for them and withdrew, leaving nothing but flesh without direction. Maybe it still used their senses, maybe it heard her and the Osere as they ran past, but killing these sentinels would not change that. The enemy would still know they were there. So she ignored them.

The Osere did not, she felt the small lights of those broken lives blinking out behind her and when Frina, who ran beside her, slowed and stopped to snuff out another of those lights, Sorha stopped with her.

"Why?" she said. "They are no threat."

"Whatever they have become," said Frina, "they were us once, and I give them the kindness of a swift death." From then, as they ran, Sorha once more joined the Osere in freeing those who had been snared by the tendrils of the dark Wa'urd in Tiltspire. She stopped seeing them as her enemy, as the Betrayers, and began to see them as the lost. With every one she released she found herself muttering under her breath.

"Walk the Star Path, friend."

And they ran and they ran and they ran.

But they were not first to enter Harn-Below-Harn.

The Betrayers owned the city. Sorha could feel them. They were on every street, they were in every ruined building and they lined the way to the central temple. Behind them was the massive, brooding presence of a Wa'urd.

This is it, she thought. They have waited for us. They knew where we headed and had no need to fight us on the way when they could so easily set a trap. She held up her hand, stopping the Osere who followed. Went to one knee. The Osere did the same. She felt the closeness of their Wa'urd above them. A tentacle wormed its way down through the air, questing about until it found Sorha, another came and found Frina and Sorha experienced a communion, their cowls allowing them to speak to the Wa'urd, a medium through which they found one another.

Why have you stopped? The golden voice of the Wa'urd like a gale in their mind.

"The enemy beat us here," said Frina.

"They wait for us," said Sorha and she felt Frina's agreement like a warm touch on her skin, "it is a trap, they will fall upon us the moment we approach the central temple. We need a plan."

No.

A single word, and with it a flood of feeling, images, knowing. So much more than words could ever transfer. The temple ahead, entirely free of the Betrayers and their forces. They wanted the temple to be raised, to be brought up into Harn so they could use it. Sorha saw a clear image of a priest standing by the Wa'urd, a communion shared lifetimes ago. A golden light suffusing them, the temple rising to Harnspire.

"Why don't they do it, like in Tilt?"

Understanding settling on her like a weight. The knowledge of so many generations ago. They could not. The Betrayers could not be the go-between for the Wa'urd, and the Rai could not be the go-between for the Wa'urd either, because they had broken what they were. The cowls within the Rai corrupted, and the Betrayers corrupted by the sickness of the bluevein.

"That was why they needed the trion, Venn," she said into the air, "and they did not even know it." Sorha found herself laughing. If she had succeeded in forcing the trion to kill, all that time ago in the wood, everything would have fallen apart. The Wa'urd in Tiltspire would never be able to access the power it needed to burn the world without them. She found confusion settling on her, questions. How did the creature use Cahan to raise the temple in Tiltspire? Did they not need a trion? From Frina she knew there were none left among the Osere. More images, more information. The slow creep over hundreds of generations as the bluevein infested Osereud, concentrating in Anjiin on the land and the buildings under Tilt, corrupting the area, and even then it had needed a huge amount of power, needed Cahan and his strength to force itself upon Ranya's web and raise the temple.

That had left it weak. Cahan and the bluevein were not enough, would never be enough. It needed access to Ranya's web and for that it needed Venn, or, realised Sorha, someone like her.

More than that, it needed their agreement. Guards built into the material of Crua, the Wa'urd could not force the people. Cahan had been corrupted, had invited in the corruption. Consent was everything. So much falling into place about how Venn had been raised, Kirven trying to impress onto them obedience. At the same time, none of those doing the bidding of Zorir in Tiltspire had truly understood what was needed. Even now, without the trion's consent, the creature in Tilt would never be able to do what it wanted.

"Or if it had you," said Frina.

"I will die first," said Sorha.

Another set of thoughts, dark images of unpleasant

truths. Bodies wracked by pain, minds twisted by the torture of others. The truth that Sorha already knew, consent could be forced.

"Why that temple, why Tilt?" said Frina.

More images. From Tilt the entire land could be controlled. It was linked to every spire in Crua. But close in power was Harnspire. Secondary. From there, and with power fed from Jinnspire, Ranya's web could be restored. And when Ranya's web was restored, the power of the spires could rebuild great Iftal. When Iftal was restored the sickness would be purged, all made anew. So much more information; spinning numbers, skeletal images of Crua, lines of glowing power. Images of her, of Cahan, of Venn and Udinny and more. There were the Boughry, Ont, Ania and Dassit. Sorha understood none of it, and felt beneath it a current of great danger, of desperation. A knowledge that this had never been done before because it could go very wrong, so easily go out of control and destroy everything. Strength was needed to hold it all together, and that strength was rare. When the gale of information had finished she knew three things.

The temple must be raised, because it was the only way to enter Harn from here, and that they had to enter Harn because that was how you saved Crua and, even then, the chance to save themselves was balanced on a knife edge.

"And what of you?" she asked the Wa'urd, and it answered in her language.

I will do what I must. Did she imagine it or was there some sadness there? Some knowledge that it did not share.

"Then we should go." Sorha raised her voice so all of the Osere could hear. "We go now."

Frina pointed at the temple. "There, we go there," she spoke clearly, loudly. "We emerge into the world above. The path will be hard." Despite the words Sorha had never heard such joy in the Osere's voice. The reply of her people, when it came, was shouted by all of the Osere. In the darkness surrounded by the enemy they gave no thought to whether they were heard or not. They only called out with great joy in their voices. "We shall walk above!"

Sorha did not understand, they walked to their deaths she was sure of it. So many of the Betrayers surrounded them, and the moment they began to raise the temple they would fall upon them. How could they ever hope to hold?

"You are sad?" Frina's hand touched her elbow. She glanced at the Osere, skin bright with glowing colours, golden light shining across her forehead.

"I feel like I have only just found who I am, and what really matters to me." Frina nodded, her closeness had become a source of strength to Sorha. "There are so many of the enemy out there, Frina, I do not want to die now, I do not want to lose you and the Osere." Frina gave her hand a short squeeze.

"The Star Path awaits," she said, "no matter what happens, we shall meet again." Sorha gave a small nod.

"Maybe we will," but she knew it was not the case. Those Crua found useful, it used again. Was that to be her fate if she died? Endlessly coming back, never knowing who she had been? The Osere may walk the Star Path but Sorha was not sure she would. Fail, and she might join the rest, to start all over again. All lessons unlearned, all friendships forgotten.

If there was still a Crua to come back to.

She put those thoughts away and walked through Harn-Below-Harn. Frina walked by her and with Frina walked their people, standing close, speaking quietly. Who they were slowly becoming clear to Sorha now the language barrier had been removed. She knew not from what was said, but from what was *not* said, the underneath of the language, the small endearments and familiarities. Here was Frina's firstwife, secondhusband and thirdwife. Sorha nodded, understanding how Frina could take comfort from them, she was glad Frina had that. For Sorha there was only the oppressive feeling of the Betrayers who surrounded them, hidden in the darkness.

As they walked she saw more and more of them: they began to line the streets, they stood in the gaps of broken walls or on top of them. Everywhere they turned they were there.

The strangest thing was she did not feel threatened by them, despite that they could not see, Sorha thought that they watched was as good a description as any. Their blind heads following as Sorha and the Osere passed, the faint and sickly blue glow of their skin lighting the path to the temple. Did they think? Did they wonder? Did they feel any trepidation or fear? Did some hidden part of them know Frina and her people for what they had once been, and long for it?

She did not know. She could only wonder and watch as her and the Osere, and above them the Wa'urd, moved through the ruined city of Harn-Below-Harn until they reached the temple.

The temple of Harn-Below-Harn rose, huge and black, and on the top squatted another of the Wa'urd: this one had the same blue glow she had seen in the Betrayers. The steps, that ran up the centre of the temple to the top were lined by the Betrayers. These ones slightly different, the bluevein that infected them had grown to mimic the armour that Sorha wore, but where the wood of hers was smooth, theirs was pitted and ridged. Where her shoulder pieces were formed from bracket fungus, theirs were grown straight from the flesh.

None moved to attack. Sorha took the lead and the Osere followed. Their own Wa'urd passed overhead, a great, dark, heavy presence that filled the air with a perfume like cut boughs in Least. It stopped on the pinnacle alongside the other. They intertwined tentacles, some conversation going on, and for a moment Sorha thought they were betrayed.

That they had been led here only to be given over to the enemy. Then the air filled with a shriek, loud and harsh enough that it made Sorha and the Osere around her duck down and cover their ears.

Then the Wa'urd of Zorir left, and its soldiers with it. Sorha's gaze followed them as they left the temple to stand at the bottom. There were thousands of them. Silent massive groups, and each of the more fancifully arrayed Betrayers went to the head of a group. A gap, slowly appearing in their numbers for the Wa'urd, which squatted amid them.

Sorha took a deep breath and ascended the temple. Their Wa'urd now on a raised dais, by it another smaller dais. That was for her and she moved toward it, Frina by her side. A tentacle found her, found Frina.

Not yet

When?

Soon.

What if they come? She pointed at the Betrayers.

They will not. They also desire the temple raised.

"We have time," said Frina out loud, "we should use it to be together, to be with those who may walk the Star Path before this ends." She said it so softly, so gently, and her acceptance that many would die held no fear. Little by little the Osere split up into groups, twos, threes, fours, fives and sixes. Sorha watched Frina's firsts and second join her. Then the Osere turned to her.

"Are you alone?" said Frina. "Or are yours above? The man, Cahan?" A small laugh escaped Sorha, but with none of the bitterness she was used to feeling at hearing his name.

"No, not Cahan. He was the first step on a journey. A friend maybe." Frina tilted her head, listening, interested. "For most of my life, I have not understood what it is to be alone and now I do, I wish I did not." She looked out at the gathered Betrayers. "Especially tonight, if it even is night."

"You think it is your last?" She nodded. "Join us, then Sorha of the Osere."

"I don't need pity," a flash of her old anger. Frina did not rise to it, she only put out her hand.

"You would always have been welcomed among us, Sorha. Among the Osere one simply asks, we were wondering why you did not." For a heartbeat, Sorha did not know what to do. Then she knew she wanted this, but it frightened her. For someone to give themselves freely, and for her to know it was freely given, was entirely alien to her. Maybe it would fill the place within her that had always been empty. It frightened her. But she refused to be frightened. Sorha took Frina's hand.

"Then I am asking," she said.

60

Venn

A sound, unfamiliar and yet terrifying on an instinctual level, filled the air. A deep, basso moan as if some untenable strain was felt and Venn wondered if it was the spirit of the forest, sounding out its distress at what was happening. Seeing its people stream through the tree, guided by warriors with bows and spears into the high boughs of the cloudwood and into places that could be defended more easily. Sounds of pain, the cries of frightened children as first, second and third mothers and fathers hurried them upwards. The rasp of saws as wooden walkways were weakened and cut. The cries of the wounded and dying. The shouts of soldiers. The chittering of rootlings who had joined the defensive lines, the growl of garaurs and the hissing breeze-through-the-trees of the shyun, all similarly ready to fight. Warriors shouted orders, as the people of the cloudtree created defensive positions. The lens of the Forestals gathering together, those with the strongest cowls stood ready to protect the defenders from Rai fire and the arrows of their own people, taken by the collar.

But all of those sounds, were background to the low moan that shivered through Venn's flesh. It was only as they walked toward the front lines, accompanied by Furin, Issofur holding their hand, that they realised what it was they heard.

The great skyraft had finally come down, its deck at a crazy angle where it had been guided into a position to act as a ramp between the lower levels and the higher where the people of the tree city had retreated to. Fires burned all around it but the crew were unconcerned. In the upper levels the tree city was thick with paths making it harder for the Forestals to cut it off. Venn knew that the fighting here, when it came, would be fierce and bloody and that, though the Forestals had their bows, the enemy had the numbers and unlike the people of Woodhome the enemy cared nothing for its soldiers. They would simply throw them against the Forestals, soaking up arrows until there were none left to defend Woodhome with and then they would overrun the tree city. It was a war that could not be won and Venn knew it, Furin knew it, Tall Sera knew it and most likely every Forestal in the city knew it.

But no one spoke of giving up.

Venn wondered if the boy Issofur knew? If so he gave no sign, he danced before them, laughing and giggling as though everything he saw was new and wondrous and joyful.

No joy among the rest, all that could be bought here was time but Venn believed with time came hope. Any time won held within it myriad possibilities. Venn had walked Ranya's path for so long they had to believe there was a destination, and that the others, out there walking it now, would help them find it. That they, Venn, would help them find it.

Since Issofur had first taken Venn's hand a certainty

had been growing in them, one that was surely suicidal but one they were, at the same time, sure was right. They felt they had known this was their path since they had spoken with the god in Osereud, but that knowledge had faded afterwards, only returning with the touch of Issofur.

The great moan came again, so loud and powerful that it shook the tree and both Venn and Furin almost fell.

"What is that," said Furin, though she only had eyes for her child. Her worry a counterpoint to his joy. "Some new weapon they bring?" Venn reached out with their awareness, the glowing presence of the Forestals, the cold blue presence of the collared and the spots of life in among them of soldiers and the Rai. Next to the collared even the Rai felt healthy.

But it was the tree they felt most strongly.

The power of it throbbing in their mind. It was from the tree, the noise was coming from the tree and was caused by the tremendous stress upon its branch from the weight of the skyraft. Venn felt it like a toothache. A pain they could not ignore. The forces of Zorir were already arraying themselves on the listing skyraft. Soldiers with thick shields to the front and behind them a few ranks of collared archers. Rai behind them and behind the Rai more collared, more soldiers lined up to attack than Venn could count, more than the Forestals could hope to cope with.

"We stop here," said Furin.

"No," said Venn.

"Do not be foolish, they will kill you."

"They will not," said Venn softly and they smiled at Furin. "They want me, I will give myself to them."

"That is madness, Venn," hissed Furin. "At least if you stand with us here you can live for as long as we can hold them. If you give yourself up then . . ." Her voice tapered away.

"They will not hurt Venn," said Issofur, looking up at

his mother, though whether the boy recognised her as that was hard to tell now. "They want them."

"And many died to stop them taking them," said Tall Sera.

"Listen to him," hissed Furin, her eyes limpid with unshed tears, she could not look at her child, instead addressing Venn, "do not waste those lives. Do not waste yours." Venn looked down at the strangely silent army of Zorir.

"Hope," they said, "is never wasted."

"Venn . . ." began Tall Sera, and Furin could not look at them.

"This is my path," said Venn softly. "The hope of Crua rests upon me walking it." They spoke with such certainty that any argument Tall Sera or Furin had died in their mouths. Issofur giggled and Venn stood, raising their arms, raising their voice. "Who leads you?"

Nothing, no reply not at first. Then from the army came one of the Rai, beautifully carved armour banded with inlaid wood of many colours and painted with glowing mushroom juice.

"I do," she shouted. "Rai Sasan Bu-lack. Do you offer the surrender of this tree city, you must know it is lost?"

"Do not do this," hissed Furin but Venn ignored her.

"I wish to discuss terms." The rai laughed, odd to hear such genuine laughter from one of them.

"We are here to wipe out your nest of bandits and thieves, not to offer terms. But I will give them to you. Every warrior here will die, every other will be taken to Tilt and Zorir can decide their fate."

"No," said Venn.

"No?" more laughter. "What do you think you can offer me? Archers." They beckoned forward the collared archers and Venn felt Furin pull on their sleeve. Tall Sera strung his bow and a group of Forestals ran up to join him and Furin where they crouched behind a fallen branch.

"We must go before they kill us," whispered the Forestal leader.

"I am Venn!" they shouted. "The cowled trion! You have been looking for me. I imagine you were sent here to find me." The Rai stopped the advancing archers with a wave of their hand, and now the collared, all of them, were staring at Venn. "Agree to leave the people of Woodhome alone . . ."

"Venn, do not do this," hissed Furin.

" . . . and I will come with you to Tilt, willingly."

"We will take you anyway," said the Rai. "You have no power to bargain."

"Or maybe I will die in the fight," said Venn. The Rai stared up, licked their lips then looked back at the collared who stared blankly back. Venn could almost feel them weighing up what they wanted and what they knew the collared desired from them.

"Come down here, Trion, and we will talk terms."

"Venn," hissed Furin, "if you go down there, they will take you and attack anyway." Venn leaned in close.

"Not immediately, at least not until I am far away," they said, then turned to Tall Sera. "The raft is too heavy for this branch, when they attack, hold them here for as long as you can. The branch may give way." Tall Sera nodded, Venn felt a hand in his and looked down to see Issofur. Furin stared at the trion.

"Tell Issofur to stay," she said softly.

"I have to go," said the boy.

"Is there no other way?"

"No, mother," said the forest child, "but do not fear for me, I walk Ranya's path." Furin blinked, then bowed her head.

"Then I hope the path is clear for you." She almost choked on her words, misery thick in them but she did not try and stop either of them. The boy smiled, and pulled on Venn's hand, walking them to the edge of the platform and as they did something shot out of the crowd of Forestals watching them, long and furred it threw itself at Venn, circling their body until it lay around their neck.

"Go back, Segur," said Venn, "there is no safety for garaur with me." In answer the creature only dug in claws, held tighter to Venn's clothes. "Very well," said Venn and took some comfort from the warmth of the animal, "I will do all I can to protect you."

"And I you," said Issofur, looking up at them with eyes much older than a child's.

With that they took hold of a vine and climbed down, followed by Issofur. With the senses of their cowl they felt the weaknesses running through the branch, the stresses and strains that made the great tree moan.

The army before them was a heat, it boiled off them, unnatural and hotter even than the air of the southern Wyrdwood. On the same level and through the ever present gloom they could no longer see the army's numbers, but they felt them in this wave of febrile heat.

"Take the trion and bind them," said the Rai, "kill the creature that clings to it, and the child."

"No," Venn took a step forward, "you will not bind me. You will not hurt Segur or Issofur. I come willingly or not at all." The Rai laughed.

"You speak like you have a choice, Trion," said the Rai. "You think we do not know about you? The trion with a cowl, the only one that lived." Then the Rai stepped up to stand next to them, drawing their shining wooden blade. "We have you, and we will take you. I will kill the creature and the child if it is my wish," she took hold of Issofur's arm, "and I will let you watch while we wipe this filthy nest of forest god lovers from Crua. Then I will deliver you to Saradis myself."

"No," Venn said softly. "You will keep your word and leave the Forestals alone, you will not hurt my garaur or Issofur and you will take me to Saradis."

"Or what," said the Rai, "you will say harsh words? After all you have famously sworn not to kill."

"You are wrong," said Venn. "I never swore not to kill, I swore I would die before I killed another."

"So?" confusion a cloud over the Rai's face, her thin, dry and stretched skin shuddering as she tried to piece together what she was missing. Venn almost laughed, she never would. It was simply not in the make up of the Rai to consider what Venn was prepared to do in the service of others.

"You need me," said Venn. "Saradis needs me. So if you move against Woodhome, try to bind my hands, hurt Issofur or my garaur, then I will end my life and all this," Venn gestured toward the army, the collared, the broken skyraft, "will be for nothing."

"Difficult, to hurt yourself when you are bound," said the Rai and stepped back, pulling Issofur with them, a laugh beginning in her throat. As she did Venn began to let go of life, to push it away from themselves. Felt themselves weaken, felt the forest heat leaving their skin and the gloom of the air becoming thinner, paler.

"No!"

Life rushing back to them with a deep breath. The stifling heat, the smell of broken branches, opened bodies and charred wood. The Rai, no longer amused or confused. Their face showing something entirely alien to her kind; fear. She had felt what they were doing, known Venn was serious and even as the trion had faded they had felt the Rai's panic.

"You no longer doubt me then, Rai?" The look she gave in return was not kind, and there was fear there.

"I do doubt you," she said, "I think you play a game and you would not truly carry through your threat, but they," she looked behind her at the collared. In the moments Venn had been dislocated from the world the collared had come forward. They must have rushed, there were soldiers picking themselves up off the floor from where they had been knocked down. Each of the collared had weapons drawn, spears and swords shining. Behind them the collared Forestals were pointing arrows at the Rai.

"They do not doubt me," said Venn, and reached up to scratch between Segur's ears. Gave the Rai a smile and put out a hand to Issofur.

"The collared are no longer people," said the Rai softly, "they do not understand subtleties but that has worked for you I suppose." The Rai let go of the child and took a step back. "Keep your forest creatures then, and have your hands free. Know we will not move upon your precious forest city." The Rai lowered their voice, "But have no doubt within yourself, Trion, about what awaits you in Tilt. I have seen the god and if you are only collared and made to serve it you will count yourself lucky." She could not hide her own fear from Venn. "But I suspect the fate that awaits you is far worse." It took all Venn had not to give in to the terrible despair that rose within them because this Rai was only putting in to words what they already knew. That something terrible waited for them in Tilt. Then Segur chattered in their ear, a croak and chirp, and the small warm and furred hand of Issofur took theirs and the touch and the sound reminded Venn there was not only horror in Tilt, there was a friend; Cahan. They gave Segur a stroke, squeezed Issofur's hand.

"We should leave," said Venn, "it is a long walk to Tilt."

"Walk?" said the Rai, "oh no, you are far too precious to walk. Is that what you imagined? That your fate was many risings of the light away? That you could engineer some escape?" The Rai laughed again, and it made Venn shudder. The crowd of collared split to reveal a waiting marant, its once beautiful lines ugly with veins of blue and strange blooms which patterned its skin. "You will be in Tilt before the light has fallen and risen once." Venn blinked, took a deep breath and looked into the face of the Rai.

"The path is before me," they said and their voice did not waver or crack, "and I shall walk it without fear."

61

Udinny

Splintershot, howling through the air. Great balls of old wood lashed together and designed to explode into flying shards that decimated anyone in the vicinity of the impact area. I heard the whistle of flying splinters and the screams of the wounded. It froze me. I had never been in the middle of such a violence. The nearest I had ever been was the siege of Harn where Rai fire had been falling from above, and even that only right at the end. This was different, a constant lethal rain of weaponry.

"Run," the voice of Dassit, amplified by the great wooden body of the Forest Man.

I am no fool.

I ran.

Dassit ran with me, using the wooden body of the Forest Man to protect my fragile flesh as much as she could. At the same time the Rai of Jinnspire, spaced out along the wall, began to loose fire in defence of the city, destroying the splintershot, raining burning wood on the wall and the city below, but they could not get them all before they reached the walls. I kept as low as I could, trying to make the nearest stair while splinters flashed past, soldiers fell, screamed, died. Blood ran in rivulets across the wall and I left footprints behind me in painful scarlet.

Knocked to the floor by Dassit. As I fell I saw her smash splintershot out of the air with a great wooden hand. At the same time I heard a noise like nothing I had ever heard before, a groan, and the wall shuddered beneath my feet. The sound of shattering mud bricks and splintering wood filled the air. The noise of old, hard wood giving way under forces it was never meant to withstand. A moan, the death of something ancient and the wall beneath us shuddered. Shouts and panic all around.

"The wall! It's coming down!" A soldier, pointing along the wall and I scrambled round beneath the huge body of Dassit just in time to see an entire section of wall begin to tear itself away, taking screaming soldiers and Rai with it, crashing to the ground in a great cloud of dust.

A moment of silence.

Shock.

The defenders must have expected their wall to hold for much longer. A great roar went up from beyond the dust cloud. Rai shouting.

"Trunks four and eight, defend the breach!"

"Udinny," said Dassit, pulling me to my feet, "withdraw to the spire. Now." She pushed me toward a stair, what had once been securely attached to the wall was no longer and it had come loose, creaking and swaying in the clouds of dust. "Go!" Dassit pushed me, forcing me to jump onto the stairs, almost falling, grabbing hold and feeling my stomach lurch as the stairs swung out and away from the wall. Then I was climbing down them with all the speed I could, feeling them complain beneath me. To my right I saw two armies meet in the ruin of the wall, the crash of shields and the grunts and screams of the combatants. The enemy trying to push through the breach and the trunk and branch soldiers of Jinnspire trying to hold them. On the broken wall Jinnspire's Rai rained down fire and their soldiers threw whatever they could get their hands on. All the while the bombardment of the splintershot continued. Now they not only targeted the walls but the city behind it. I saw roofs explode, buildings collapsing in on themselves, whole branches of troops cut down.

An impact.

I was on the floor, with a huge crash Dassit landed by me.

"Keep going," she shouted over the din of the falling city. "Back to the spire." She glanced back as the defence of the breach collapsed. The enemy killing indiscriminately, their centre a group of collared Rai who moved without the fluidity I was used to Rai having, they just hacked and cut and stabbed all before them.

The collared cared nothing for themselves, if one fell then another took their place, the sheer implacability of them was terrifying. The defenders rallied, the centre closed up and for a moment I thought they would hold, that they would be enough. Fire landed in the centre of the collared, concentrated and strong from the Rai on the walls, their faces twisted in hate. They knew what awaited them if they were taken and were giving little thought to conserving their strength, maybe the cowls within them thought it better to die than to be controlled. The forces of Jinnspire gave another push. Cheers and shouts and screams as the enemy stepped back. Fire cutting the air, splintershot raining down.

It almost looked like they were winning.

Then the god appeared.

It crawled over the top of the wall, oily skin shining, blue lines on its skin flashing, tentacles as thick as old trees pulling it up the wall. It swept Jinnspire's Rai off the wall with one contemptuous flick of a tentacle. Its appearance brought terror, the walls emptied, men and women running to the broken stairs, jumping from the walls where they could not find a safe way down. The army defending Jinnspire broke and the attackers fell upon them. A rout became a massacre. Troops dashing past. The enemy on their heels. Roaring, screaming; the soldiers mad with bloodlust, the collared silent and implacable.

"Go," shouted Dassit, "the spire, go!" She raised her arms and from the thick rings around the wrists of the Forest Man shot clouds of darts into the attackers running toward us, killing everyone in the street. "Go!" We were running. Into the city as it fell, the soldiers of Zorir, after spending time under the watchful, oppressive eyes of the collared, were running riot, killing, looting and burning. It was this that saved me, and Dassit and many soldiers. The soldiers of Zorir were too distracted by what they could grab and the collared were too slow, too methodical and, thankfully, their god, after showing itself on the wall, had not followed them into the city. We joined a huge scrum, pushing to get into the hastily erected defences around the central spire. All but one of the buildings had been brought down, fences put up with spears and spikes sticking out. The remaining building teetered over the gap in the defences crowded with pushing and shouting soldiers.

The crowd split when they noticed the Forest Man approaching, and that allowed Dassit and me to pass through, Rai followed us, pushing their way past as the soldiers once more began to crowd the entrance. A guard on the top of the remaining house was staring out into the city. Watching as the enemy troops streamed in, columns of smoke growing where burning splintershot had landed or the invading troops had fired the city in an ongoing orgy of violence. Soldiers crowded into the square at the centre of the Spirecrown. I thought it odd, as I followed Forest Man Dassit to the stage in front of the spire where the Rai had assembled, that I saw so few civilians. Only a few hundred, up with the Rai and all dressed in their finery, though it was wilted and dust-covered.

I wondered if the people had already fled the city, and only those I had seen when I first came were left. It was only as I walked past the soldiers, huddled groups, sweating beneath cheap and rough wooden armour, that I realised I saw the people of the city. They were the soldiers who had fought around me, old and young, many far too young, swamped by the armour they wore, others far too old and barely able to stand beneath its weight. First and second and third mothers and fathers gathered in family groups. I wondered how many were mourning, how many were saying their last farewells before the enemy broke through the final defences.

I had been in many unpleasant situations as I walked the path of Ranya but the fall of this city was somehow the worst. Even worse than the siege of Harn because the people of Jinnspire had given up. I felt it on the air, I heard it in the panicked shouts of the growing crowd at the entrance to the makeshift stockade around the spire entrance. One of the Rai stepped forward.

"We have decided to surrender," they said as we approached.

"No," said Dassit. As she walked closer to them her form shimmered in the dry, hot air of Jinnspire. "We hold the spire at all costs." The Rai shook their head.

"The decision has been made, we will—" and Dassit killed them. It was a simple and quick action, she reached out with one great wooden hand and broke the Rai's neck with a twist. I don't think any of the crowd, and most of the great and good of Jinnspire gathered round the table noticed, not at first. But the other Rai did. One began to gather fire and Dassit killed them with a flick of her wrist, loosing a dart that sent them sprawling. I expected screaming and shouting but there was only silence from those gathered in the entrance of the great spire. Maybe they had been dulled by the constant war, maybe they had no hope left.

"Each and every one of you is needed to hold this spire. So I do not want to kill you all," said Dassit, "but I will if you talk of surrender. It is not an option." More silence. The Rai were measuring up their chances, certain death now or likely death later? One of the finely dressed civilians stepped forward.

"I was High Leoric of this city," he said, he was very old, "and truthfully I am ready to die to defend it." Then he looked past Dassit. "But I do not think they are," he pointed and we turned. The people of Jinnspire were gathering in their borrowed armour and weapons. "They have lost all hope, you cannot hold this place without hope." The Dassit Forest Man froze in place then nodded.

"Then I will give them hope," she said and turned, her great weight making the stage before the spire shake as she walked to the edge of it to stand before the crowd.

"We are beaten," shouted someone.

"No!" said Dassit, the word like a wall, an end. "You are not beaten because I am here." Her voice changed, became deeper, darker, the air filled with the scent of trees, and grassy mosses, above her the form of the Boughry shimmered into being. "Crua is a land of many gods, and the forces of Zorir have sought to crush them all, now I come, and with me is the spirit of the forest."

"You come too late, forest spirit!"

"No," they said, "I was not long ago like you and did not understand. Now I am of the forest, it is not like you, like I was. We are the bright lights that burn quickly, the forest is the ember that sleeps beneath the ashes. It takes time to wake, it may even appear dead, but like an ember it is a fire that is only waiting. And when it comes there is a great conflagration." Her voice booming out. "A sudden and white-hot fire that appears from nowhere and burns all before it. The wrath of the forest is like that flame." The wood of the Forest Man creaked as Dassit surveyed the people before her. "Do not be under any false pretences, the fight here will be hard, many will die while we buy time for the forest to truly awake. But the choice between the fight here, and to give up to those outside the wall is no choice at all. In this fight many die, but in surrender all die. The whole of Crua will be destroyed by the sickness of Zorir, it is a broken god. The forest sees, it looks through my eyes." She let her words settle in then spoke once more, amplifying her voice. "Rejoice, people of Jinnspire! For I am the herald of the forest! Wyrdwood is coming!"

I don't know what I expected, a sullen silence maybe? But that was not what I got, the crowd erupted, into a chant, "Wyrdwood is coming!", and I could not help wondering if maybe the Boughry, hovering above Dassit, had cast some glamour upon them as I felt no great hope, no rousing of passions within me. Maybe that was because I knew what Dassit had left out of her speech.

That the forest was utterly merciless.

The echoing chant was cut short by the call of a horn. A voice from the top of the teetering houses.

"They are coming! The enemy are coming!" Below the teetering house over the entrance there was still a huge crowd, fighting to get into the defended area.

Dassit paused for a moment, her entire body still, then with a hiss she let out a long breath and turned to the nearest Rai.

"Have them bring that house down, close the defences. Order those still trapped outside to hold for as long as they can." The Rai nodded, then ran to give the orders.

I stood, unable to speak. The crowd beneath the house did not disperse as orders were shouted. If anything they began to fight harder to get in. Then whatever supported the house was removed and the building crumbled, crushing all those caught beneath it and blocking the way in or out. I looked to the Forest Man, her face implacable. I wondered how much of the Dassit I remembered was left within the wooden body of the Forest Man, and how much of her was the will of Wyrdwood. She must have felt something from me. The face of the Forest Man turned and I saw anguish on its carved features.

"Udinny," she said, "if I appear without a heart to you, know sometimes in war there are no good decisions. All that matters is we hold this spire. Without it, all die."

And though I knew she was right, the screams of those crushed by the falling building echoed in my ears.

62
Sorha

They waited in the darkness. Sorha feeling a warmth within her like none she had ever known. She had taken many lovers when she was a Rai but never understood that "taken" was the truth of it. Those who had come to her had either done so because they thought she offered some opportunity they could exploit or because they had no choice but to do as she commanded. To be with others, who came willingly and wanted nothing from her, was different. To wake up rested among warm bodies who genuinely desired her presence would be a memory she treasured for the rest of her life.

Not that she expected to live much longer.

The steps of the temple below her, and around her, were thronging with the betrayed. Behind the ranks of the betrayed the brooding presence of a god, no, two of them, watching and waiting.

She felt a shudder run through her as a tentacle gently touched the back of her neck.

It is time.

An image of herself stood by the Wa'urd, a tentacle around her shoulders, the others piercing the dark substance of the temple. Her hands on a plinth raised from the black substance of the building. The temple raising toward Crua and her mind filled with images of fungal blooms, huge, on a scale she had never imagined. Running through it the cilia that touched every living thing in the land. *Ranya's web.*

A moment of wonder, a whole land that had been grown? How? What did it grow on? Questions filling her mind and then the image faded away and she was once more in the darkness, feeling the betrayed all around them.

"They will overrun us, the moment we begin to lift," she said.

They need us to reach the surface.

"Then they will overrun us."

Be ready.

She took a deep breath. Turned to Frina.

"It is time, when we reach the surface we will have to fight." Frina reached out a hand, laid it lightly on her arm. "We will be ready." Sorha nodded, found herself unable to speak. Unable to find what she should say, Frina gently touched her arm. "Go, Sorha, we have waited a long time for this. We are prepared." Sorha turned, ascended the step pyramid and stood by the Wa'urd. The creature waited on the dais, huge, round body on a plinth, the air around it smelling faintly of woody spices. Seven of its eight tentacles were sunk into the substance of the temple. By it rose two small protuberances, stopping at just the right height for her to stand between and place her hands on.

Another deep breath. The fear within rising. What would happen? Would she lose herself within Crua? How would she do this? She was no trion. She had seen Cahan raise the pyramid with Zorir, it had been agony for him.

She was not afraid of pain.

Not even afraid of losing herself, of ceasing to exist.

She was afraid for the Osere, afraid of losing what she had found among them and at the same time knew that it was not her decision to make. They had waited generations for this, they wanted this and she could not deny them. She reached out, put her hands on the plinths. Felt a connection. Golden light running through her and her cowl. Running through the temple, running through the Wa'urd. The memories of those long past who had stood here before her ready to guide, warm, welcoming. She waited for the Wa'urd to act. Crua was full of energy. For a moment she thought she could take it, use it to strike down the gathered betrayed and the bluevein-twisted Wa'urd. These energies were huge, terrifying. But the voices of the guides told her it was not possible, not for her at least. Within Crua there were paths, that was the only way she could understand it, paths like the ones that ran through the forests or over the plains, but these paths were for energies not for walking. The Wa'urd would be her guide as it knew the paths. She was the walker, the energy was controlled by her. To carve out new paths would take time, that or enormous strength she did not have. It needed someone like Cahan.

Ready?

She was.

Paths opening, the memories of those before brushing her mind. She took the energy. At first terrifying, then the voices, the memories within the pyramid surrounded her. There had been a first time for each one and they had come through it. They lent her a familiarity that echoed down the ages, part of her blood, of her flesh, part of every living thing in Crua. This was a thing she should always have felt but had denied herself, lost herself. The energy flowed through her, down the pathways shown by the Wa'urd and into the places it guided her to within the temple. When the temple at Tilt had been raised, violently, under the power of Cahan she had not really understood what happened, imaged a great piston pushing it up from below but that was not the truth of it. The truth of it was that

Crua was growing, the temple and the fabric of it was alive and the path was a memory of what it could be, had been and would be again. To feed it with power was to awaken that memory, and that memory invigorated the fabric of the land, the web of Ranya. It grew and pushed the temple higher and higher into the air. As it rose, she felt the betrayed stepping on to the winding stair that ran around the outside of the pillar. If she could change it, take it away, they would fall and their numbers would be cut in half, those still waiting to join the rest would have no way of following them. But she could not, she could see faint pathways that may allow that but at the same time knowing she lacked the power to alter the memory that made them.

When iFTaL is reborn you will not.

So she fed power into the temple, and as they rose the market square before Harnspire began to cycle open, light flooded down and she raised her head, bathed in it. Crua, as she thought of it, waited and she felt the entire land laid out around her, the sickness within it, the slow strangulation of bluevein.

Be ready.

The voice echoing through her. The betrayed surrounding them. The twisted Wa'urd scaling the outside of the tower as it rose. They had no need for the stairs their troops were swarming up. Somewhere, in the far distance, she could feel others. They were attached to here by the faintest of golden cilia, part of the web, all moving toward one goal: Udinny, Dassit, Ania, Ont, Venn, and somewhere very far away, barely there at all but still there, Cahan.

So few of them.

It all seemed so hopeless.

Only moments and they would lock in place before the spire of Harn. Only moments and the attack would start, a wave of those infected with the bluevein would break over them.

"I am ready," she said.

Peace.

A second of peace when she was balanced between the Wa'urd, the land and herself, all was as it should be. Then the cold air of Harn biting her skin, the brightness of the light above hurting her eyes. The city around her, unnaturally still, unnaturally empty.

Completely empty.

The people, gone.

"Ready!" Frina's voice. The Osere backing into a tight circle, spears and shields in the front line, the second line with their small bows. Further down the temple the betrayed, crowding the steps, boiling up from below like disturbed orits and not one of them made a sound. Sorha reached for her blade, ready to join the Osere, to die in a wave of violence and blood. The tentacle of the Wa'urd brushed her.

No, together.

Image: her, stood on top of the pyramid, golden tentacles radiated out from her and each one touched upon the Osere the way the Wa' urd touched upon her.

A compulsion. The spire, they had to get to the spire.

Sorha about to run, to find Frina and tell her to head for the spire. Lifting her hands from the plinth.

Image: her hand on the same plinth she had used to raise the temple. A word in her mind. Together.

She didn't understand, together was to be at the front, to be the leader, to bathe her weapon in blood. To feel the crack of splitting wooden armour beneath her weapon, the soft give as an edge found flesh.

Together.

The Betrayers closing. No anger or hate or fury in their faces. Only emptiness.

Her desire, everything in her saying join the Osere, die here with them under a wave of bluevein-sickened flesh.

But the Wa'urd wanted her here. Twin needs pulling at her, what she knew, and what she did not.

Clarity. Such a long journey, walking Ranya's path. And every turn had been toward something she had never expected.

She had walked the path.

She would be a fool to abandon it now.

She was not a fool.

Sorha slammed her hand back down on the plinth. Felt the cilia of the cowl extrude through her skin, through her gauntlets and into the temple. Felt the Wa'urd, like a weaver, pulling threads to create something new. Through the temple she found the Osere, their cowls bright in her mind and the golden power of the land was in her.

Contact.

Almost losing herself, almost falling to her knees and breaking the link. Death seen not through her eyes, but through the golden "eyes" of the Osere around her. She could make no sense of it. Too much for a mind only ever alone, only ever seeing through one set of senses. Then the Wa'urd was there. Its mind different, barely understandable to her, not even one mind. It was many minds in one, as if each of her fingers and toes and arms had its own conscience, that was to be Wa'urd. Singular, and yet distributed. A mind in the centre, a mind in the tentacles. Many working as one.

The Wa'urd could no more understand what it was to be one of the people than she could understand what it was to be Wa'urd, but it knew how to sort, how to create a sense of order from the chaos of so many senses. Fear running through Sorha, she had no experience of this. What if she destroyed these people she had come to love? What if she became like the bluevein, like Zorir, turning the Osere into puppets of her will.

No, it was not that.

This was a shared mind, each and every one of them unique

and alone and yet each and every one of them together. She was not a trunk commander, pointing her troops at a target and letting them fight alone. She was the trunk of the tree and they were the leaves, part of her, and yet themselves, each with their own purpose and will and each feeding into her awareness, sorted and made sense of by the Wa'urd.

They moved as one.

A blade about to strike one down was seen by all. They became a swift and efficient fighting machine. Arrows slipped through gaps in the shield wall no Osere would ever usually have risked. An Osere spear stopped by a Betrayer sword, leaving the spear wielder open to a thrust from the enemy but when that thrust came a shield was there. She saw all, she shared all. The enemy, they were a shadow of this togetherness, a dark dream of it.

"The spire."

Her words unspoken but said aloud to all. A plan forming between them. It was so obvious, they could easily hold here, the betrayed breaking against them until none remained. What had seemed impossible before felt inevitable now. The first wave of the betrayed was already falling apart and more could not get up from below quickly enough to become a true threat.

They would win.

They could win.

Then the city awoke.

What she had thought was dead was not dead at all. Every person in Harnspire, every man and woman and child, every first-, second- and thirdmother and -father had fallen to bluevein running rampant through the town. Not only them, but it had gathered up all the soldiers sent from Tilt. Something new had risen here, something bred from the power of the god in Tiltspire, something that ran as fast as a fever through the populace and, though it killed many, she could feel the places where bodies polluted the ground, it did not kill all and those left alive joined the Betrayers, they heard the call and they were coming.

A hoard so much greater than the betrayed, like leaves falling from trees in Harsh, great drifts of them running for the temple, holding spears, or swords or hammers or saws or anything that could be a weapon. Those that did not have weapons curled their hands into claws. Not even Sorha's new sight could protect her people from so many.

The spire.

The compulsion. The knowing.

All depended on her reaching the spire and in that was her downfall and that of the Osere. To get to the spire she must leave the control plinth. Then they would no longer be one great organism. They would no longer be the tree. They would be alone and the drift of Harnspire's collared would bury them.

As the first group of the collared reached them, joining with the betrayed, the lives of the Osere began to blink out. She felt each one as an absence, an ache like nothing she had felt before because through the link she knew each and every one of them, not just as a face, or a presence, but as a life. An utterly unique gathering of experiences and moments that were abruptly taken away in pain and in blood. Despair filled her. They were all going to be lost. There was nothing she could do. If they did not break for the spire now they would not have the numbers for even the smallest chance of cutting their way out, but, even then, in the cutting so many would be lost.

She readied herself.

No. Hold.

Why?

Wyrdwood is coming.

63

Saradis

It was over.

They had the trion. The fool had given themselves up in the mistaken belief that it would save their fellows. It would not, of course. She had not gone to all the trouble of taking a skyraft and having it dragged into the Wyrdwood just to let the Forestals go free. Not that anyone would escape the coming fire anyway, but it pleased Saradis to think the last moments of the Forestals, who had caused her so much trouble, would involve being hacked apart by the collared.

Vengeance owed to her.

As she walked through the great corridor she ignored the tattered flags, the flaking material of the spire, the great curling roots of bluevein that pierced the walls of the building. These were all glory in their own way; they may look like degradation, like disrepair and neglect, but she knew that was not the case. It was simply preparation. Zorir drying the land, making it tinder for the great fire. Soon she would be the right hand of a god in a new and glorious land.

First, though, there were scores to be settled. There were

those she would deny the fire to. Deny any chance of being reborn along the Star Path, the Forestals were in hand. Another waited behind the throne in her cage. Saradis had a special end planned for her, a very particular end. She could not forget Nahac, caged and filthy now, once making her beg before her. Forcing her to be nothing until she won over the woman's trust. She had made Nahac believe they were friends once, maybe they had been for a short while, but Saradis could never forget the truth. That this woman, this girl who had managed to carve out a revolution for herself, had not come from nothing. That she owed all she was to Saradis and that she refused to see this, refused to know her place, infuriated her.

Clanless. Nothing. A tool.

The last tool.

Cahan had been the other and he was finished. So now it was time for Saradis to end Nahac. At her waist she had the knife. She had worn it a long time. Laha made it for her, it was no ordinary knife, no knife to be used for eating. It had one purpose and one purpose only. Saradis opened the door to the cage room. Ready to see, to speak, to mock. Expecting to find Nahac on the floor of her cage, wracked by agonies.

She was not.

Instead, Nahac stood before her cage – out of her cage – one of the bars broken, her arms bleeding freely where she had pushed herself through a too thin gap and the wood of the cage had opened her flesh in cuts already beginning to heal as liquid, black power flickered around her. She smiled.

"I've been waiting for you, Saradis," she said. A flicker and she was across the room. Saradis' head between her hands. "The pain," said Nahac, "I'm going to show it to you, I'm going to let you feel it." She blinked, for a moment lost in a thought, and Saradis knew it had to be now. Slipped the knife from its scabbard. Then Nahac was back.

"I was meant to protect my brother, Saradis," she said, "and you turned me against him. Now he is dead. All you have left me is revenge."

For a moment Saradis could not breathe, expecting Nahac's power to reach out, to crush her, but it did not come. Nahac was waiting for her to say something.

"Revenge," said Saradis, "is a worthy emotion." She thrust the blade into Nahac's chest, at the same time pushing her backwards. The Cowl-Rai of Crua screamed as she staggered back, oily black threads of power extruding from her body but as quickly as they left they curled back in on themselves, twisting round the site of the knife wound, trying to heal what could not be healed.

"What have you done?" hissed Nahac and fell to her knees. "What have you done?"

"A bluevein knife," Saradis looked down on the woman, felt no pity, no great joy either. She was more curious than anything, watching as Nahac's power tried to heal her but failed and failed again. She could not even pull the blade from her chest, she was paralysed. Saradis smiled. "Laha made it," she said. "It will kill you, eventually, and you will feel every moment of it." She backed away, still unsure of whether Nahac had some way of lashing out but the knife was doing its job, the magic twisting around it, never touching it, Nahac twisting and writhing on the floor as agony powered through her body.

"If you can live long enough," said Saradis as she backed into the door, opened it, "look out of the window. You will see Zorir's fire coming. And if it comforts you, Nahac," she said, "know you could never have protected your brother, you could not even protect yourself."

64

Cahan

They were losing. Ghosts were everywhere.

He fought. It was not in him to give up on his people, but the walls of Harn were barely there now. Not destroyed, not burned or pulled down, the gates were not wide open allowing their attackers in, the walls and defences of Harn were not broken down by acts of war. They were faded, tired. He could see right through the curtain walls of Harn, past the pits they had dug for ranging their arrows, past the spikes dug into the earth and to Woodedge where the fires of the enemy burned, eerie blue against the glowing green of the trees.

Sometimes, he wondered what was happening, because this all felt so unreal. He missed being alone on his farm, though that had long been overrun by the enemy. He missed being alone in the darkness, watching the bright and colourful displays of the forest. It had been a long time since he had seen the night displays.

He could not even remember it being night.

It was always day and always the fight. Or always the eve of the fight. Or always the aftermath of the fight. There was only the fight and the enemy got stronger and his forces got weaker and he, and they, began to fade. He was surrounded by his people, though they no longer looked like people, He knew they had names but could not recall them. And they did not speak, not any more. They were forms, not people, they were the shape of people but they had no features, no clothes, no details, just a faint glow and each and every one was the same as the next.

He had the strangest feeling he had forgotten something. Something that had been instrumental in the defence of Harn. Something he had not wanted but that had impressed itself upon him, that had been a whirlwind among his enemies but he could not recall who or what that was.

All that lived here are here.

That echo in his mind, that other voice from within.

I will protect you.

But even that voice sounded tired now.

"They are coming." A voice familiar but the name had slipped from his mind. He turned. He could see the armies of the blue through the walls. A formless mass, a huge body of writhing tentacles, an army linked to a creature above that squatted over Wyrdwood, a thousand tentacles reaching out from it and each and every one ended in a soldier. The enemy would not win this time, just as they had not won before and before that and before that.

But they would push him back.

The walls would fade further and he would be forced toward the last stand, the longhouse that scared him more than the attacking army. There had been something in there, some memory that he had pushed away. Pain, it was pain and sacrifice and yet at the same time he felt it was empty. His head ached, his body screamed at him as though it were pierced by swords.

"They are coming," said the voice again, and it was his own voice flat and dead and barely even there. Outside the walls the hoard, coming on so quickly that in a blink they were within range.

"Loose!"

A cloud of spectral arrows cutting into the enemy. It would not be enough. It was never going to be enough. With every attack the enemy got stronger. With every attack his forces became weaker, became less. He was so tired, it was becoming hard to understand why he should lift his arm, bare his axes, loose the arrows.

Hold.

"Why?"

Wyrdwood is coming.

65

Udinny

If the run through the falling city had been terrible, the assault on the spire precinct was worse.

I had expected it to be like Harn, where attacks came and were repulsed and between we rested, but it was not. The enemy soldiers attacked the makeshift walls, many of which were little more than piles of rubble, and kept coming. No matter how hard the defenders fought, and they did, these children, these old women and these wounded men fought with the desperation of people with nothing left to lose – or maybe they were people with everything left to lose. Even the Rai of Jinnspire threw themselves into the defence, even the pampered and expensively dressed nobles of Jinnspire took up arms.

But the enemy kept coming and fought with their own desperation. Maybe for the soldiers of Zorir this was the end, this was the last battle. If they could just conquer Jinnspire the war would be over for them and it pushed them on. Or maybe it was because if any of them weakened, if any of them found themselves disheartened and frightened by the desperate blades they faced, if any of them turned and ran, then they ran to a wall of collared who would cut them down without thought.

There was nothing but the fight, for either side.

In the centre of the defences stood Dassit, and I stood with her and by me stood Tanhir. She had found a bow from somewhere, and arrows, to replace the ones she had lost in the crash of the marant. From the centre Dassit directed her forces, her voice unnaturally loud, amplified by the barrel chest of the Forest Man. She would not let me fight, even though I was quite vociferous in saying that I was Udinny Mac-Hereward, warrior of Ranya, she would hear none of it. Tanhir, she commanded to protect me at all costs. Which I am sure she hated as much as I hated being forced to watch while so many died.

"You are too important to risk," said Dassit. When I tried to join the fight her wooden hand stopped me.

If a gap appeared, or when the forces defending the spire square faltered, then Dassit would join them. Her great wooden body unstoppable, shrugging off sword and spear and smashing through the enemy, sending bodies flying through air filled with screams and shouts and the stink of death.

At the weakest places in the defences bodies gathered in drifts. I saw children in ill-fitting armour climbing up hills of the dead. I saw soldiers slipping on the guts of their own family members. I saw nobles, their fine clothes soaked in blood, give their lives to protect commoners. And just like Tanhir, and just like Dassit, I knew this place could not be held. The collared had joined the fight and they were too much. At least in fighting soldiers there was something real there, your own fear mirrored in the enemy, a version of your own hate facing you, something understandable. That made victory seem possible because you faced what you understood, and Dassit had told them all before the fight, "They are not as desperate as you, they will break."

But the collared, they would not break. They were no mirror of humanity, they were cold and implacable and uncaring and it was with their arrival that the rout began. The great strength of Dassit was of no use. Maybe if we had ten of the Forest Men we could have held. Maybe then. But we did not. We had one, and a Forestal and me and a ragged army of untrained civilians and all else were corpses or as good as. Horror filled me. So much death. Dassit was backing up, step by step toward the spire and I could hear her murmuring under her breath, or whatever a Forest man has for breath, "too soon, too soon."

Which, I must admit, did not appear to be a good thing.

I think it was desperation that had me reach within for the cowl of Fandrai, or my cowl, I suppose, as I was no longer Fandrai. Even my body was no longer his. I was a woman once more, changed by the cowl. Maybe because it had finished that work, desperately reshaping my body into the mental image of who I saw myself as, I found the cowl was not hiding any more, it was waiting for me.

It knew me.

It remembered Fandrai fondly, but it knew me now. It had taken all this time to explore who I was and know me and accept me. These were things I felt, and through the cowl I also felt Ranya's web. It was all around me, even here. A moment of peace. I felt the connection to the land and I shared my desperation with the cowl. My terror at the battle, at losing. I shared how we needed time.

Together, we reached out, touching the land, the cowl feeling for what it understood, for grasses and bare skeletons to pour its power into, but there was no grass in the centre of Jinnspire, though there were plenty of corpses.

It was at a loss.

I was not.

Swarden, I had seen the swarden, and how they used grasses for sinew, and if what occurred to me in that moment was dark then let it be dark, for this was the darkest and most desperate time. Dassit said we needed more time and I would buy it for us. I closed my eyes, let the cowl see what I saw, how its use of grass in the Wyrdwood was to replace something already existing in the flesh that clothed the bones of the dead. It took an eternity for it to understand, or maybe it was instant.

But the cowl did understand.

It extended out of me, thin strings that burst from my hands, feet and knees. I had not even realised I was on my hands and knees, the strings moved through the ground until they found Ranya's web, joining with it, taking power from it and using it to extrude out and through the city, finding corpses, touching the strands of the web within them. As it did it found the sinews that had once pulled on muscles and it saw in those bloody thongs the grass it knew.

Corpses exploding with light around the square. A certain and directed fire that flensed flesh from gleaming white bone and when that was done the sinew stayed, wending itself around bone still wet with blood, twisting and tightening and all through the city a new kind of soldier rose.

The blood swarden.

"What is happening," said Dassit as the hills of corpse before us dissolved in light and flesh, vast pools of blood flooding across the spire clearing. White skeletons standing knee deep in gore, taking up swords and spears.

"I am buying us time," I said, eyes closed, body full of heat.

The battlefield paused. Soldiers on both sides frozen in horror at what had risen.

I saw the world from where I crouched. I saw it through the eyes of my blood swarden and saw a world as not one of the people ever has. A place of burning golden lines: to them everything was made of this energy, it ran through and around it, created their world and within each and every one of them was a nagging, gnawing sense that these shapes were not right. Their other desire was to head upwards. I had thought of the swarden as warriors of the forest but the desire to fight in them was secondary to the desire to build, to reach upwards and create, though the why and the where and the when was lost to them. A huge gap in their minds, if they had a mind. A moment's more concentration and I knew they did not have a mind, not as I understood it: all they had was instinct and desire. The desire to build, the instinct to fight anything that tried to stop them and in the lull, while the troops of the enemy looked on – even the collared momentarily frozen by what had appeared before them – I pointed the blood swarden at the enemy.

"They will stop you building."

Once directed, they focused on the collared. I felt a loathing pass through them, a stuttered word.

"Corruption."

The blood swarden attacked, throwing themselves at the ranks of the enemy. They fought soldiers but their real fury was for the collared. The soldiers, caught between what must have been a nightmare come to life, and the collared who commanded them, broke and ran. Those who ran toward the collared were cut down by their own side, those caught by the blood swarden were cut down without thought and those who ran into the ranks of the defenders were ripped apart. The anger of Jinnspire knew no mercy and gave no quarter.

Whatever I had done, whatever my cowl had put in motion, no longer needed me. I could feel it waiting in the ground. Every corpse that fell was reborn in a flash of light and a gout of blood. Swarden smashed into the ranks of the collared, pushing them back to the gaps in the wall, killing and killing without stopping or tiring.

"We are beating them," said Tanhir, lowering her bow,

"the swarden fight with us, and we are beating them." She sounded full of wonder, and when she looked at me I did not see the same hate in her face I had seen before. Instead, I saw a kind of fear that I liked even less. "The Boughry work through you," she said. "May they not see me."

"The spire," Dassit's voice, quiet now even though it was usually loud enough to heard by all. "We need to make for the spire. We must go." There was desperation there, fear.

"Why?" said Tanhir, "this is our victory, we should . . ."

"The spire, Udinny," said Dassit and there was heartwood in her voice, "now." She began to back up and I followed her. Tanhir followed me with confusion on her face. The same confusion I felt. Why leave now? Why leave when an army of swarden was about to sweep the enemy away from the spire? When Jinnspire was about to be won back? When the battle was almost decided in our favour?

Because I was wrong.

An odd feeling at first, a disquiet within me, as if something on the edges of my senses was changing. Like a high-pitched ringing in my ears. Like the sense of pressure before the geysers erupted in Tilt. Like watching Rai pull fire to themselves.

Then the gods came.

Not just the one we had seen on the plinth that had been erected by the besieging army, but three of them. They smashed into the lines of blood swarden, tentacles bowling aside both swarden and collared. The power in them, the strength, was terrifying. They did not stop the swarden, the skeletons attacked the gods as mindlessly and determinedly as they had attacked the collared. Swarden massed around them, some grabbing tentacles, others hacking with sword or skewering with spears. One of the three gods began to falter, the weight of bones on it dragging it down. It shook itself, skeletons falling from it.

"The spire!" shouted Dassit, "to the spire!" and we were

not the only ones that heard her. Every Jinnspire soldier heard her, too and they broke from the battle and ran towards us. As the nearest god escaped the grasp of the swarden, Dassit raised a hand and loosed a storm of splinters into it. The creature staggered back and the swarden attacked with new ferocity, bringing it down, and it filled the air with a hideous screaming, like no sound I had ever heard before. As it fell I saw it was not black, its entire skin was threaded with veins of blue that ruptured as the swarden hacked it apart.

I wondered if its fellows would stop and help it but they did not, instead smashing their way through the swarden toward us, and then I was running and Tanhir was running and Dassit was running. We were first into the spire. Behind us soldiers were streaming in and along the great hallway. The gods slowed at the entrance, let through collared who began to cut away at the panicked soldiers and the people of the Jinnspire.

"Scatter!" shouted Dassit. Her great wooden head turned to me. "Up," she said, "we go up", and, pursued by collared and their gods, we began to climb.

66

Sorha

Noise and pressure. Blood, slick and slippery below her feet. So many feet. All moving in unison, a dance of blade and spear. Each knowing the movement of the next. A cage of sharp wood to keep them safe.

A pain, cutting through her side, welling up, but the pain was not hers, one of the Osere's, then the link was cut. Gone. Another Osere fallen, cutting themself off from her before death took them, they spared her that. A gift she did not feel she truly deserved as she was not in the fight, the Osere took the brunt of the attack. The blades of the betrayed, the pressure of the sickened soldiers and people of Harn – who even without weapons were more than enough – were a constant, a building strength that they could not fight with spear and sword. It was that which Sorha knew would beat them, the pressure that she could not fight no matter the skill of the Osere, no matter the link between them. The great press was too much and further out, on the plains of Harn, coming for them, was a god, no, two gods, maybe three.

They were lost, Sorha knew they were lost. The time to break from the temple for the spire had passed. They were surrounded by the betrayed and the collared people of Harn. There was no way out.

Hold. Wyrdwood is coming.

The voice of the Wa'urd in her head. But what could that mean? She had a momentary image of the cloudtrees uprooting themselves and coming to her aid. So ridiculous a thought in such a desperate place it almost made her laugh. Her sudden amusement spread through the link and the Osere, and they began to laugh as they fought and as they died.

A last gift from her to them.

Then she felt it.

Like the dam of a wetvine pool coming apart. A hint of gold on the edge of her consciousness. Something was at the gates of Harnspire, something was flowing through the streets. She could feel whatever it was linking with her as they approached, but these minds were not Osere, they were different, simpler, stranger, *greener*.

And there were *thousands* of them.

An army, at the front the shyun, the forest children slipping through darkened streets with poisoned spears that would kill with a touch, behind them rootlings, hundreds and hundreds of rootlings as furious and angry as they could be innocent and playful. Flanking them, marching behind them with minds she could neither touch, read nor understand, came an army of swarden, joints creaking, skull faces grinning, orits marched around them, gasmaw and spearmaw flew through the air, and leading this army of the Wyrdwood were two beings she did not understand at all. In some ways they felt more like the Wa'urd, like the gods of Wyrdwood, and in another they felt like people, familiar people, even.

"Wyrdwood is coming." She said it to herself more than anything, but she heard it from the mouths of the Osere who still remained. An echo of her voice, with all the wonder in it she felt. They knew, through her, the Osere knew what was coming though they did not understand in the way she did. She let them into her mind. Let them feel what she did, how the mass of approaching rootlings had a fury unlike anything else, how the shyun moved like shadows, killing without being seen, how the swarden were implacable and uncaring, and in those last moments, when they should have been overrun, the Osere fought even harder. They could not turn the attack, they should not even be able to hold it, but Sorha's hope was as powerful a weapon as any spear.

Then Wyrdwood came to them.

A mass of furious rootlings hit their attackers, spreading around them, stealing attention from the main attack. Shyun spears took down scores of bodies. Then the two beings Sorha almost thought she knew hit. They had circled around so they came in from the direction of the spire. Smashing into the hoard, great sweeps of huge arms sending the enemy flying through the air. She saw them now, great wooden people, many times taller than her, many times stronger and seemingly impervious to any weapon. Behind them, in a wedge, came a phalanx of swarden, and on all sides the swarden and the rootlings were cutting through those sickened by the bluevein. Any normal army would have broken at the onslaught, but what attacked here was not a normal army. They did not think for themselves and continued mindlessly coming on no matter how much damage was done to their ranks.

Be ready

The Wa'urd in her mind. An image. The great wooden people and the swarden, holding a corridor to the spire.

Be ready.

"We are ready."

Violence everywhere, the pressure growing, the air thick with blood and the sound of the rootlings screaming as they bit and scratched their way through an army.

Now.

"Now!" she screamed and let go of the link. All around her the Osere screaming. "Now!" They broke, turning and running into the corridor held for them by swarden, in front of them ran the wooden soldiers. *Forest Men* and, as she followed them, the Osere followed her.

"Hurry," the voice of a Forest Man, loud and strange and yet she knew it, "the gods are coming, you cannot fight them." They ran down the corridor of swarden and it closed up behind them to protect the rear. Following the great wooden Forest Men into the spire and she could still feel the pressure of the bluevein army behind her.

"Gods are coming," shouted the Forest Man, and one stopped either side of the entrance to the temple, letting her and the Osere pass.

"Our Wa'urd!" she shouted

"It holds," said the Forest Man, and Sorha looked back. Three Wa'urd were smashing through the army, past the temple, ignoring it entirely. On the top of it, Sorha's Wa'urd turned, then did the strangest thing: it ripped off one of its own tentacles and threw it toward them, to be caught by one of the Forest Men who wrapped it around their waist like a belt. Then the Wa'urd leapt from the temple, its remaining tentacles outstretched, and it landed on one of the three attackers, the two creatures rolling and shrieking, a high-pitched noise that hurt her ears. The Forest Men took great bows from their backs and began to loose glowing arrows at the other two Wa'urd, forcing them to dodge aside, leaping away from the path of the arrows, crushing the sickened people and the betrayed beneath their huge bodies, smashing through friend and foe alike to get to the spire. Coming forward at a terrible speed despite having to dodge the Forest Man's arrows. The Forest Man stepped back, put their shoulders to the great doors and as the Wa'urd ascended the stairs they slid them shut with a boom that reverberated through the entire tower. A moment later another boom as something huge threw itself against the massive black doors of the spire. The doors shuddered and a new sound filled the air. The screeching of the frustrated Wa'urd outside.

"It will not hold them long," said one of the Forest Men, the first, which was much taller than the second.

"They will climb," said the other. "We must go."

"We can fight still," said Frina. A cut on her face bled freely and the smaller of the two Forest Men reached out to touch her.

"You have fought well," they said, "but you cannot fight them. The fight is now ours, take your people and go low in the spire. The Wa'urd will not come there. Stay safe."

"No," Frina stepped forward. Sorha looked around, no more than seventy of the Osere still lived. "She is one of us," Frina pointed at Sorha, who almost wept at that moment, a great pain in her throat and her heart, "we protect ours."

"Frina," said Sorha, "you and your people have given me more than I could ever ask, not only in battle, but in life. It would break me to ask more of you, to see more of you die. Take your people to safety, stay with them." She could tell from the Osere's body language that she wanted to argue. "Please," said Sorha, "I am likely to fail in whatever is asked of me if I must worry for your safety also. Without me ever knowing, you opened a door, and through it you have walked into my heart. Save your people for me. Save yourself. You have given me many gifts, make this the last one." The Osere stood, entirely still, then nodded and grabbed Sorha, holding her tightly, arms wrapped around her. Her face crushed against Sorha's, her blood streaking Sorha's white face paint.

"Live," she said, "live and come back to us."

"I will do all I can to."

"Come," said the first Forest Man, "we must go up, the Wa'urd will already be climbing."

They ran, up stair after stair and as they ran Sorha became aware the spire was different from how she remembered it. She had been here when Venn's mother ruled, and like all spires it had been a disquieting place, the dimensions of it not human, though now she had seen the Wa'urd she understood why. The spire's interior was not only designed for creatures who walked on the ground, it was also for the Wa'urd, creatures who moved in three dimensions, that were as at home in the trees, or on the ceiling as they were on the ground. All the strange ledges and protuberances, all the spikes and ridges were there to aid reaching tentacles in climbing, the balconies without rails were for creatures that could climb up and down the outside of the spire with ease. The strange arches and spaces were easily passable by creatures who could change the shape of their bodies. This was the home of the Wa'urd, not just for the people.

Also, the spire had changed, the black material shot through with bluevein. In most places she saw only faint patches of it but in others there were veins as thick as her arm and a clear, viscous, sticky liquid bled from the walls around them, as if the material of the tower itself was wounded. The air smelled of bogs and rotting wood.

In other places the spire was green, plants growing from the wall, flowers filled the air with scent and banished the smell of rot.

"The tower fights its own battle," said the smaller Forest Man. "But it is losing." She pointed at a great vein of blue, around it plants and bushes had been growing, clearly at an accelerated pace, but they had died back and were now mostly brown and dead. Pools of stinking clear liquid shone on the floor, forcing Sorha to step carefully as it was slippery, and something in her was repulsed by the idea of falling into it, of getting it on her skin.

"Climb," said the taller Forest Man and it was then that she finally knew who it was, though not how that could be.

"Ont," she said as she walked up another flight of steep

black stairs between the two Forest Men. "You remind me of Ont, the monk."

"I was and am, and yet I am not."

"I am and was named Ania," said the other.

"How are you this?"

"The forest," said Ont, "it needed us and we answered, together with Dassit who stands with Udinny in far-off Jinnspire."

"Udinny lives?" Sorha found a strange sense of joy in that. Once she had found the little monk nothing but a figure of hate, but with her own change she had come to see people differently. For the monk to stay so light when the world was dark, well, that was a heroism all of its own.

"Yes," said the Ania Forest Man. "We will meet her at the top."

"Of this tower? But you said she is in Jinnspire."

"She is, and will be. But if we live we shall all be together."

"What does that mean?" Sorha felt like she had stepped into another world, one even stranger than Osereud far beneath her feet.

"I wish I knew." Sorha heard the voice of the Forestal in the voice of the Forest Man then, the sardonic lilt. "I only know we must take the Boughry to the top, and that you must be there, and we must be there."

"How will the Boughry get there?" In answer a shimmering from the Forest Men, and she saw the shadows of something old, ancient and twisted, encrusted with lichen, human formed but not human, appear over them. Then it vanished.

"You are Boughry now?"

"No, we carry them. We are still us, but we are partly them."

"Is this what Udinny calls Ranya's path?"

"Maybe," said Ont, and she heard amusement, "but I think that path was always wider than we knew. Ranya is part of it, but for long we have been walking in circles, never reaching the destination."

"You talk in riddles," Sorha was out of breath, struggling to keep up with the Forest Men as they climbed the stairs.

"We do not really understand ourselves. Only that . . ."

"The world was different once," said Sorha. The two Forest Men stopped.

"You know?"

"One of the Wa'urd, it showed me. I stood atop a temple with it, but it was not me, and it was not Crua as we knew it."

"We have all walked these paths before."

"Not me," said Sorha. "I saw through another's eyes. The Wa'urd called me firstborn." She felt a sadness fall upon her. "Is it dead? I saw the enemy attack it." The two Forest Men became very still.

"No," said Ania, "the attacker is dead, the swarden fell upon it. Though your Wa'urd will not fight again, it lives as we carry it with us." By her, Ont patted the tentacle wrapped around his thick waist. Sorha nodded, not really understanding, and she continued to push herself on up the stairs.

"How much further."

"Not far," said the Ont Forest Man and they stopped at a door that looked like it had not been opened in a hundred lifetimes. The ghosts of the Boughry appeared above the Forest Man, and sunk stick fingers into the weeping walls of the spire. The door cracked open. Daylight flooded through it. At the back of a huge gallery was an archway open to the air. In the centre of the gallery waited two Wa'urd, their black bodies threaded with bluevein and strange, fungal growths that glowed brightly, their bodies never still, tentacles waving in the air. Sorha was close enough to see how the suckers on their tentacles were ringed with sharp, blue spines, sliding in and out, weeping something that Sorha felt sure was venom.

But it was not the Wa'urd that drew Sorha's eye. It was the figure crouched between them that stood as they entered, his skin thick with veins of blue, eyes blue, swords in his hands.

"Laha," she said. He did not reply, instead his body twitched and both he and the Wa'urd came forward.

"We must pass through them," said Ania, drawing her bow.

"Yes," said Ont, "sometimes not far can also be a long journey."

Sorha nodded, drew her own blade and pointed it at Laha.

"You and I," she said.

He did not reply.

He came at her, fast.

67

Venn

Venn had been to Tiltspire when they were much younger, with their mother. That had been before the horror of the blooming rooms was forced on them. Before they had seen so much death, before they had known the truth of Crua.

Tiltspire had seemed like a magical place then. Huge curtain walls surrounding a city which spilled out past them, houses and huts falling over themselves and into the grasslands. Huge buildings within, built from wood and rock that rose into the air – far higher than anything else they had ever seen outside the spires, temples to forgotten gods. It was all for Chyi then, Venn thought, or maybe it was already Tarl-an-Gig, the memory was hazy in many ways, crystal-clear in others. The spires were what had amazed them the most, the crown of Harnspire was broken, three of the outer spires having fallen, but the crown of Tiltspire was intact, a huge central spire with eight smaller, but still massive, spires around it. It was bigger by far than Harnspire, taller and wider the way cloudtrees were bigger than normal trees. Within the crown the huge marketplace thronging with people, all busy buying and selling what was needed to live their lives beneath the huge black exclamations of power that were the spires. Before the main spire there was the array of taffistones, Rai always standing around them as if waiting for the citizens to make sacrifice.

The other memory of Tiltspire was of people everywhere. So many, more than Venn had ever seen before and different from the people of Harnspire. They walked taller, looked stronger and brighter and better fed.

Then there were the geysers, almost magical, launching water into the air in vast plumes that vanished into the sky, leaving only multi-coloured arcs that Venn remembered painting again and again and again as a child, taking pleasure in the many colours as they splashed them across the page. Venn had showed them to their mother, and she shrugged then threw them into the fire telling Venn that art was no pastime for someone of their standing.

Tiltspire was not as magical now, as they flew into it on the back of a bluevein-sick marant which wheezed horribly with each wingbeat, the air full of a stink like sodden mud and old grass.

Below they saw a different city.

The geysers remained, exploding into life as the marant approached. Was it Venn's imagination or did the plumes lack the usual height? Rather than vanishing into huge clouds, did most of the water fall back into the ground, flowing into cracks in the land that Venn was sure were more numerous, wider and longer than they had been before?

The massive walls of Tiltspire were cracked now, long, jagged black lines running up them and the riot of huts and houses that had once spilled from the city were gone, flattened in some places, dilapidated and falling apart in others. From the cracks in the wall grew spiderwebs of bluevein, twisting and writhing over the sheer sides. Above the walls flew gasmaws and spearmaws, on their backs the collared with spears in their hands. They sat upright on them in a way that looked unnatural and uncomfortable to Venn, though from the collared who accompanied them Venn was sure that they did not feel discomfort. They did not seem feel anything.

Tiltspire was a twisted city now, the great buildings that Venn had once marvelled at no longer stood straight, massive thick rootlike structures wound through the streets growing through houses, breaking walls, twisted around each other in tangles and there was no area of the city left untouched. Tiltspire was lost, the city no longer a city. Streets that had once thronged with life were now empty of it. Venn saw no one living as they passed over on the final approach. No people ran through alleys, no one climbed over bluevein roots in the streets, no one had set up market stalls. No children laughed, no adults looked up to observe the passing of the marant. Nothing, only the twisted glowing roots and all of those leading back to one place, the black temple before the great spire.

Even the spire was not untouched. As Venn and the marant moved in they thought the spires had become the focus of the bluevein, the thickest roots twisted around the outer towers, almost creating a wall, each and every spire pierced by multiple roots that ran around and up and into them. The great central spire was punctured by three massive roots that had twisted right around its heights, and these roots, unlike the others, pulsed brightly and regularly, like a heartbeat.

Venn did not see the creature that called itself Zorir, the god, until the marant lifted over the twisted wall of bluevein roots. The god was huge, swollen, distended and twisted, entirely unlike the sleek gods Venn had seen below Wyrdwood.

Zorir sat atop its black step pyramid and the thick roots that ran everywhere all terminated at it. The god's body was covered in huge irregular lumps, in fungal growths and dry-looking scales. As Venn watched one of the scales sloughed off, falling to the ground where it shattered into dust. Venn could feel its intention even from above, its malignancy. Whatever it had brought into being, whatever the bluevein was that it had created, had not been without price. The thing was sick.

The marant lost altitude, coming in to land and the air changed, became warm and moist like fever.

Venn felt Issofur's hand tighten around theirs. Looked down to see the child looking up, his eyes alien and faraway.

"This is where you are meant to be," he said. Venn had no reply, but he did not think Issofur expected one.

Below Zorir, hanging limp, impaled on a bluevein spike, was the body of Cahan. He looked dead, though Venn was sure he was not. The creature needed Cahan in the same way it needed Venn. What they were in some way unlocked the power the creature needed. So Cahan must be alive, and if Cahan was alive there was hope because, even here, in the midst of all this sickness, all this wrongness, Venn could feel the presence of Ranya. Venn felt sure the presence of Issofur meant they still walked Ranya's path. The boy was part of the forest, no longer of the people, he had become something else. A guide.

The marant began its final approach.

Waiting for them was a large group of people, standing before the taffistones that filled the plaza before the great spire. Rai and collared stood in rows and in front of them stood a woman clad in the thick and elaborate clothes of a ruler. For a second, a moment only, Venn thought they looked at their mother. A cold shock passing through them, then they were nearer and the illusion passed. This woman was taller, more gaunt. A cage of twigs enclosed her body, a great headdress towered above her. She had her face painted in white and the elaborate lists of her lineage crawled down her face, coloured lines painted over her eyes.

Saradis, Skua-Rai of Zorir. Architect of all their ruin. She watched with a smile on her face as the marant came in to land. It was not a good landing, not a soft one, and it jerked Venn in the saddle, knocked the breath from them. When they could breathe again they wished they could not.

The smell almost overwhelmed them.

Sickness.

Venn's mind transported back to the blooming rooms, too hot, too close, the stifling stink of rotting corpses, clouds of choking spores. The other trion dying in agony, screaming and—

"I said dismount." The voice cut through the memory. Shocked them back into the present. Issofur squeezed their hand.

Saradis, Skua-Rai of all Crua stood before the marant. Behind her the Rai and the collared and an alien landscape, bluevein everywhere, roots and webs and nets, things that looked like fungal blooms but the usual arcs or balls of their fruits never became complete, as if they had withered part way through growing. It was like a landscape drawn by a child who lacked concentration, who kept moving on to the next object before they finished the first, and even that they drew too quickly and without really observing what it was. A nightmare place. Even Saradis, when they looked at her, she did not look like a woman in her glory, she did not look like a woman pleased with her victory. The skin beneath her white make-up was dry and flaking, she stood straight, but Venn thought that was only because of the cage of blueveined twigs built into her clothing. The clothing itself was, up close, dirty and tattered. As Venn climbed down from the marant, legs shaky from lack of use – but not fear, Venn was not afraid any more – Saradis came to stand by them and the trion could smell her. The rank, bitter smell of someone who had not bathed for weeks, old sweat and ingrained dirt.

"I have waited a long time for you," she said. Venn did not reply. What could they say? She watched Issofur. The trion had the distinct impression Saradis expected something from them but the child only smiled at her. She stood a little closer and the smell of her enveloped them, she reached up, touched their face. "Have you ever thought about how much bloodshed could have been avoided, if you had only done what you were born for?" The words stung, because they echoed thoughts Venn had long held close. Could all this war have been avoided, could so many who were now dead still live if Venn had simply not run away all those years ago? "It doesn't matter, though, Trion," she said, "not now. I will even let you keep your little pets." Her eyes glanced at Issofur, then to Segur who held on to their shoulders. "The fire is coming, all will burn and be reborn along the Star Path." When she spoke, her eyes glittered and Venn saw the surety of the fanatic there, and the question they had tortured themselves with was answered. No, all those deaths could not have been avoided. The death was the point, the cruelty was the point. Venn thought of the little Cahan had said about his upbringing in the monastery and this woman and knew, without any doubt, that Saradis enjoyed the pain of others. "Look," she said and pointed behind Venn at the black temple, "glory in what I have wrought, a god brought into being." Venn turned, but they saw no glory in the creature on top of the step temple, in the writhing tentacles which split and split again as they left its body. It did not look balanced or natural. The creature looked sick in the same way Saradis looked sick.

"There is something wrong with your god, something wrong with you," said Venn, turning back to her. She frowned, her brows coming together, dry skin wrinkling and cracking. A clear liquid leaked from the crack, running down her cheek.

"Sacrifices have been made," she hissed, "for the glory

and the greater good of all. After the fire, when we have travelled the Star Path, all will be remade anew. What flesh clothes us here does not matter." She grabbed Venn's arm, painful, dragging them toward the step temple. Segur jumped from them and ran to nestle around the shoulders of Issofur. "Enough talk, it is time. This is the hour of my triumph, this is when my god will kindle the fire and all will be reborn."

"Stop." A single word, sounding like it came from one and also many throats. Saradis froze, still holding Venn's arm tightly. Then she turned, turning Venn at the same time. One of the collared, its body swelling with strange glowing growths, had stepped forward. Venn saw surprise on Saradis' face.

"You speak only when spoken to," she said, but the collared was not looking at her, its face was turned to Venn, eyes, which the trion felt sure saw nothing, locked on them while at the same time appearing not to focus on anything.

"Do you come willingly," it said in a croak, and behind it the whisper of a hundred other collared echoing the words. Venn felt sweat on their arm from Saradis' hand. They glanced back at the temple, at the creature on it. Could they really go willingly to that, knowing what it meant? That they were the key it wanted to access the power within Crua. Venn's eyes scanned down the temple, finding Cahan, hanging on a spike, attached to the god by a tentacle. Issofur squeezed their hand, as if to give comfort. Looked up at them.

"He needs you," they said softly.

"My people have already recommenced their attack on the Forestal city," hissed Saradis in their ear, "but I can stop it, even from here. Ask yourself whether you want those people's final moments to be spent screaming in terror while the blades fall, or whether they will be allowed a little peace with those they love before the end."

She lied, Venn knew that. She would not stop the attack

no matter what Venn did, but it did not matter. The trion had already made up their mind.

"I come willingly," they said, and what they saw on Saradis' face made them shudder: joy, triumph. She dragged them forward and Issofur let go, that small comfort left behind. She pushed Venn down so they knelt before the god, her hand tight, painful and sweaty around their arm.

"Now is the time!" she shouted, "now has come our triumph!" Venn watched her face as she spoke, saw how she faltered, glanced over her shoulder at the ranks of silent collared and cowed Rai. She had probably imagined this moment her entire life, imagined a speech made to an adoring crowd before her god. Instead she spoke her words to a silent city, corrupted by what she had brought into being and Venn wondered if she regretted it.

"Are you proud of all this?" said Venn. She glanced at them, her eyes wild, a heartbeat when Venn knew the truth. Somewhere, deep inside, she was just as frightened as they were.

"I will stand in paradise at the side of a god." She let go, stepped backwards. Venn turned away from her. Looked up at Zorir. A tentacle slithered down through the stinking air to hang in the air before them. It was split from another thicker tentacle and that from another and another until it met the bloated, lumpy body of the god. The tentacle shot forward, skewering Venn through the shoulder and although it was agony they did not cry out, not even when they were lifted in the air. Cahan was before them, a spike through his chest and to all intents and purposes he looked dead, but there must be life there, there had to be or Venn had thrown away their own life and so many more for nothing. They were spun through the air, seeing a dizzying vision of Tiltspire, diseased and broken. A moment, the briefest, briefest moment to think they had made a terrible mistake, misunderstood, then a spike exploded from Venn's chest, the tentacle withdrew and they were left hanging on the step temple next to Cahan. All they were aware of then was pain. That and the slowly growing power within Crua, the pressure of a god's mind upon their own. A voice that filled every part of them, crowding out their own mind.

Access iFTaL remnant. Begin emergency translocation.

We are lost, thought Venn, *we are lost*.

And then they thought nothing at all.

68

Udinnу

It may seem an odd thought to have when you are in the middle of a crisis, but all I could think of was that I am not built for climbing. Dassit, with her new and powerful wooden body, had no such trouble. She led me up and up through Jinnspire and, if she tired, she did not show it. But me?

I tired. I tired a lot.

I did my best to distract myself from the aches in my knees and hips and in muscles I had previously been unaware of having by wondering how high we had gone, trying to gauge it by the receding sounds of battle. Dassit had used her great strength to shut the main doors of the spire, entombing everyone who had managed to retreat into the place within it, but many were still trapped outside.

I hoped the blood swarden would protect them.

The interior of Jinnspire was not like other spires, it was far better looked after. The riches of the city were on display everywhere: tapestries, ceramics and glass lined every wall, the many balconies and openings on the side of the spires had been walled up, most using shining cloudtree wood that was incredibly hard. The walls did not have the strange noisome look of other spires, or have the upsetting geometry that was not of the people as they had been plastered and built over, the tunnels reduced to more acceptable dimensions and painted white to catch any light that came in through the slits and small gaps in the walls. On many of the walls were murals of Rai worshipping Chyi, taking sacrifice at the taffistones, fighting and winning wars, bathing in fire and water.

Those murals nearly killed me.

In desperate need of a rest I stopped, studying one of them: a Rai, standing before another figure who I suspect was the Skua-Rai of Chyi, from them spread a million golden threads and I was wondering if in some way they were aware of Ranya's web. If they sensed it without ever realising what it was or how important the web was to the land. So lost was I in the contemplation of the mural that I did not notice a shadow pass the window, something huge that scuttled past with obscene speed given its size. I did not hear the scraping of tentacles on the outside of the building, so quick and so rhythmic – scrit scrit scrit scrit. Neither did I notice it stop and start again, more slowly, more stealthily. When I did realise that the light shining on the mural had vanished, when I saw the oily, blue-veined skin at the thin window it was too late. A tentacle, thick as my body, shot through the gap and wrapped itself around me, lifting me before I could even cry out.

It is exceedingly fortunate for me that Dassit was no lover of art. As the tentacle began to squeeze the life out of me, as I would squeeze water from a wetvine, she appeared, great wooden hands taking hold of the creature. I expected her to try and pull it off me, but she did not. Instead, with a huge effort, I could see wooden muscles bunching beneath wooden armour, she ripped the tentacle from the body it was attached to. A terrible scream from outside, as much fury as pain, blue and black ichor spraying from the end of the tentacle, burning the mural where it touched it and filling the air with the stink of rotting vegetation as I was loosed from its grasp. When I was free, scuttling away from the vile thing, Dassit threw it down the corridor where it continued to writhe and curl upon itself as if it had a mind of its own.

"Come," she said, "and keep away from the windows."

"I did not know they could climb," I told her. "Though I suppose, with all those arms they will be good at it." As I spoke Dassit cocked her head.

"What is it?"

"They are in, below, we must make haste."

"What if that creature you hurt is waiting for us, above?" Dassit shook her massive head.

"Jinnspire is not like the others," she said, her voice so odd, recognisably Dassit but much deeper, "all entrances are blocked, even the marant pads at the top. The monks of Chyi were paranoid about being attacked."

"Not paranoia if it actually happens," I said, and was rewarded with a laugh.

"I suppose not," she said and made a cradle of her arm. "Climb onto me, I do not tire, the forest sustains me." I sat in the crook of her arm feeling very much like a child. "We must make speed, we must reach the top before they reach us."

"What is at the top?"

"A chance," she said, and then we were running. No time now to look at murals, to inspect flags or tapestries, but no tiredness in my legs or pain in my knees and hips. As we ran our enemies followed. Something of the collared meant they did not tire either, and when I reached out with my cowl I felt them. Those who had escaped the blood swarden were gaining on us, and at their head was one of the gods, moving ahead of them. Its intent, its desire, to catch us felt like a wound in Ranya's web. As if in answer Dassit went even faster, up and up and up, until we reached an area where the spire was no longer plastered, the walls their original black, strange outcroppings all over them. "We are nearly there," she said. Behind us a shriek, the god, angry, tentacles propelling it down the corridors at even greater speeds. Ahead of us doors, and beyond them a plinth, a thing I had never seen before.

The god here, on our level, coming nearer and nearer. Then Dassit skidded to a stop. Dropping me, sending me tumbling across the floor, so she could use her great arms. While I was righting myself she was pushing on a heavy door, slamming it shut behind us just as the god reached it and the creature screamed in frustration at being stopped. Then began to throw itself at the door.

Boom

Boom

Boom

"Will it hold?" I said.

"For a while."

It was joined by another crash from behind us. We turned to look at what had once been a balcony, long ago boarded up. Something was tearing at the wood, smashing angry tentacles against it.

"Will that hold?"

"For a while," said Dassit again. As if in answer, there was a groan of splintering wood and light spilled in from a corner of the balcony. The Forest Man drew a huge wooden blade from her side as tentacles worked their way in, trying to pull off more of the wood, but whoever had done the work had done it well and the creature could not. There was a moment of silence. Then a tentacle, elongated, pushing through the gap and worked its way in. Held within it a figure. The god withdrew its appendage, gradually exposing a body and I wondered what atrocity it was showing us.

The body moved, pushed itself to all fours and stood.

I knew this man, or had known him once. He was

changed now, like the collared but subtly different. Bluevein had worked its way around his body but his eyes were clear, his movements though, they were not right. Too quick, too jerky, as though he were filled with an energy that was almost too much for his body to contain. He smiled at us.

"Vir," said Dassit, "what have they done to you?"

"No worse than what they've done to you, Dassit," he said. "I travelled a long way to see you, thought the battle was over when I first arrived." He drew his sword.

"They intend to kill us all, Vir, your masters." Vir smiled and nodded.

"Aye, and those of us lucky enough to be chosen will rise again at the end of the Star Path."

"So they tell you."

"No," he said, and he stepped forward, all at once very much one of the people and not some uncanny creature of bluevein. "I have seen through their eyes. Crua and all on it will burn and the chosen, we will leap upon the fire and be washed along the Star Path to wake in paradise. It is not too late for you, Dassit." His eyes slid over to me. "Kill the monk. Join us, we can be together like we were once before."

For a moment I was afraid, then Dassit shook her great wooden head.

"I think not." She stepped forward, closer to him and as she did his face darkened, the blue running through his body becoming deeper and brighter.

"You have already lost, Dassit," he said, "only one of you has to die and all is lost." As he spoke those words I had the distinct impression he did not know what they meant. "Cahan is already gone, we have the trion, that is two gone. You fight a pointless battle." My heart fell to hear Cahan and Venn were lost. The pain within like nothing else I had felt. For a moment, Dassit did not speak and I wondered if she was also grieving.

"If what you say is true," she said eventually, "then why are you here? Why are your gods throwing themselves so desperately against the doors of this place?" My grief lifted a little. "Maybe Cahan and Venn are not as lost as you think? Maybe they," she pointed back towards the door, the air still full of the rhythmic boom boom boom of the creature trying to gain entry, "know that we still have hope."

"Kill the monk," said Vir, "and gain paradise with me, Dassit."

"Kill her yourself," she said and stepped in front of me. I wanted to help, but at the same time I had the feeling there was something deeply personal at play here. Something that I would not be welcome to interfere in, and I would definitely, despite the fact I was one of the greatest warriors of Ranya, be in the way.

"Always wondered who was better," said Vir.

"Time to find out," said Dassit.

They fought.

Hard and vicious. She was stronger, but he was quicker. His mission may be to kill me, and had he not been so focused on the Forest Man, I suspect he could have killed me three or four times over, but whatever was between them took all his attention. Dassit's great sword swept around and he dodged, going over or under to score a hit on her, his blade raking the Forest Man – though it did little damage. Not at first anyway. But bit by bit, as he dodged her sweeps, her punches, as he ran around the edge of the room to avoid a shower of spines shot from Dassit's wrists, I saw he was wearing her down. She was slowing. He forced her to come lumbering after him, then danced away. Every time she failed to land a hit he did not. The wood of her armour leaked sap. Her movements began to show frustration and, little by little, Vir was gaining the upper hand, and all the time as they fought gods smashed themselves against the doors of the room.

Boom

Boom

Boom

Vir attacked again, getting inside her guard and Dassit staggered back as he landed another hit, forcing her down on one knee. As she pushed herself up, she overbalanced, falling backwards, having to use her sword and one flailing arm to stay upright.

Vir struck. Leaping into the air and driving his blade down and through the breastplate of the Forest Man, Dassit falling backwards and crashing to the floor with him standing on her body.

Everything still for a moment.

Dassit's breath coming in great wheezes, the clear sap dripping from her body polluted with the red of blood.

"I always knew I was better than you," he said, looking down at her.

"And I always said your over-confidence will get you killed," she replied. Her great wooden hands came up, one grabbed his chest, the other his hips, and with grunt she ripped him apart, throwing the halves of his body to opposite sides of the room. Then she rolled over, pushed herself onto all fours and crawled over to the plinth in the centre of the room, sitting with her back against it, the wooden face focused on me. Vir's blade still sticking out of her chest.

"He was better than me, you know." A cough, such a strange thing for the great wooden body to do. "I think, I think . . ." her voice began to fade away.

"Dassit!" I was at her side.

"Hope . . . he lied . . . about them needing us all." Above her a shadow was growing, terrifying, or it should have been as I recognised it as one of the Boughry. Instead of fear I felt a yearning from it. A great desire for something, a great sense of loss, and I knew that whatever *it* may be, they needed Dassit. "Thought the land . . . would heal me . . ." she coughed, "but . . . no land in here." I put my hands on her, and plunged my mind within myself to find the cowl. I wanted it to heal her but I could not. The cowl in me did not understand healing, it only understood death, and rot. Even if I had understood healing I do not think I could have done anything for her, she was not one of the people any more. She was part Dassit, part Forest Man, and part Boughry too. I could feel the Boughry's desperation, something remained of the link I had once had with it and what it wanted was time. I needed to buy us time.

I did not understand life, my cowl understood only death.

Maybe if I could not keep Dassit alive, then I could at least stop her dying. An image, I think from the Boughry, of how she had cradled me to carry me up the stairs. Could I cradle her? Could I hold her spirit within my own? This the cowl understood, it knew the moments at the end of life, understood what I wanted and cilia extruded from me into the Forest Man. The great wooden body was slowly giving up its own energies in an effort to preserve Dassit within it. The Boughry was there too, and it knew the Forest Man in a way I never could. I let it guide me, I let it show me what could be shut down in the Forest Man, what was not needed, what was beyond saving. In turn I let the cowl move through me and, as ever when I was desperate, it rose to the occasion. Together, Boughry, cowl and Udinny, warrior of Ranya, became a glowing light, a spinning star and within our light we held Dassit's spirit. We shared our life with hers.

It hurt.

To hold her, something must be given and all I had was my life. The power of Ranya was within the spire, there but not there, and I could not reach it. If I could, somehow, then I felt sure all would be well but without it death was slowly creeping over us.

"What now?" I said to the air.

"We wait," said Dassit.

I wondered what for.

Or whether she meant death, or simply meant the inevitable moment when the gods broke through the door to finish what Vir had started.

69

Sorha

Laha came at her fast. A whirlwind of violence, of sharp blades, lightning kicks, headbutts and flailing elbows. All of him a weapon, even his skin sharp with extrusions of blue crystal. She stepped back and stepped back. He did not think of defending himself, his entire focus was on attack. When she struck him, when her blade scored his unarmoured, unnaturally grey skin, he did not bleed and the flesh healed almost immediately.

She bled.

She bruised.

Blood ran freely from a cut on her forehead where an elbow, crusted with blue rock, had caught her, fortunate for her that the helmet she wore deflected most of the power of the hit but still she found her head swimming, and it was the cowl within her that saved her, defending her as she fought to keep control and Laha pressed the advantage, twin blades whirring. Even with the cowl assisting her he scored hits, and beneath her finely carved wooden armour her flesh was bruised, and that armour was not so finely carved any more. He hit hard enough to chip and crack it.

Yet, even during this fight, this struggle against an opponent that felt almost overwhelming, she was noting what was going on around her. She fought a man, a changed man but a man all the same. The Forest Men fought gods. At the beginning they had each had time to fire one glowing arrow. Ont's hit one of the creatures square, making it scream and smashing it backwards in the hall, but the god facing Ania was quicker, dodging out of the path of the arrow. The way it moved was inhuman and made her shudder. Compared to them Laha moved as if in slow motion. By the time he had taken two steps the first god had closed with Ania. She did something with a hand and fired splinters into its body, making it scream but not stopping it. A furious ball of scything tentacles and clacking beak smashing into her, the Forest Man and the god crashing to the floor. To her right, the second god hit Ont, a mirror of the first, but it was maybe a little slower, one of its tentacles dragging behind it, limp and useless. Then it barrelled Ont to the floor and she saw no more because Laha was on her again and all she could do was protect herself.

It was a disappointment, in a way. The few times they had come into contact she had never liked Laha and he had never liked her. Maybe she would have felt better if there had been some venom in him. If she had felt this was a personal fight, but she did not. His relentless attack had no animosity for her in particular, just a furious drive to end a threat, and because he didn't defend, only attacked, she was being beaten. Put into a position where she could not attack, only defend, and she would lose if that was all she did, but he was too quick for her. Never still. Always leaving her off-balance. Never where she expected him to be. All her life she had attacked and now, when it really mattered, she could not. It was stolen from her and little by little Laha's furious energy was wearing her down, sapping the strength of both her and her cowl.

Outside the spire she had been full of energy, felt in

touch with Ranya's web, but here, in the spire, she did not. She could almost sense the power around her, but not touch it.

Her strength was running out, it was finite and Laha's did not seem to be. But she still fought, and around them fought gods and Forest Men, a titanic, angry battle that rolled around the room so not only was she concentrating on Laha, she was watching them. Tentacles would lash out towards her, the fight would roll her way and she would have to duck and dive, the air full of the screams of the gods and the grunts of Forest Men, wrapped in black tentacles that extruded long, blue spikes to tear at them. In turn the Forest Men tore back, the wood of their bodies changing, spikes growing where tentacles held them, hands becoming claws. Showers of splinters firing from wrists. Of the two, it seemed in the glances she gave them, that Ont was doing best, the wound taken by the god he fought was holding it back. Ania on the other hand was struggling, her god unwounded, furious and powerful.

Then Laha was back on her, his blades beating on her shield until her arm was numb. It was all she could do to fend him off and with every blow she weakened. A crash as Ania was driven to the floor again, the god rearing over her, four tentacles holding her down, four hardening into sharp spears. Ania brought up her arms, slapping away attacks, but she only had two hands, it had four tentacles. In desperation, Sorha threw herself at Laha, going on the attack, ducking and dodging but, again, he was like water. So quick as to be almost untouchable and what came back from him was threefold. Anything she could do, he beat her back, eyes glinting.

She could not win. And if she fell then it doomed everyone, the Osere included, and in that moment she hit upon a desperate plan. The only plan, the only possibility, the only way to go that could save those who had come to mean so much to her.

How much life was left in her?

Enough?

She did not know.

It would be or it would not be.

She dropped the shield, lifted her arms.

No hesitation on Laha's part. No joy in his triumph as he drove his blades into her chest. For a moment it was only a sound, the crack of her wooden breastplate. Then a pressure on her chest. Then pain, agony. Laha's face close to hers. Staring at her. Feeling nothing.

"Sorha," he said, her name long and drawn out into a hiss.

"Laha," she said, and she pushed all of her remaining will into the hand holding her sword, feeling the cowl within her lean into her strength, give its own power to her. "I just needed you to be still." Her blade whistled through the air, cut through Laha's neck without even a sensation of slowing as it hit the bones of his spine. Sending his head spinning and the stump that was left did not even bleed, the flesh dry and desiccated.

She fell to her knees. The blades sticking out of her chest no longer hurt. To her left a god was on Ania and she had ceased to fight back, the hardened tentacles stabbing and stabbing into the Forest Man. To her right the opposite, Ont, ripping apart a god with his great wooden hands. He threw the halves of the creature aside, and then turned, jumping on the back of the god attacking Ania and his fury was terrible to behold, though Sorha watched it through a haze, the world slowly fading. Huge hands pummelled the creature, ripped away tentacles, and it screamed and screeched but he did not stop until it made no more sound at all. Then Ont leaned over Ania, and Sorha heard her speak.

"Finished, Ont," she said softly, "it has been a long journey, I do not regret it. I am only sorry we have failed."

"No," he said softly and he put his great hands on the

wooden body which leaked blood and a strange, clear viscous liquid. "When I fell, when I was sorely wounded, you would not let me lie down and die, you would not leave me. I will not leave you now. My back is strong, I can carry us all." Strong he may be, but Sorha could see the marks of the fight upon his wooden body, cracks in the armour, plates torn away, the same clear liquid and blood that ran from Ania running down his arms and legs.

"Let me carry you," said Ont, and Ania nodded, and it looked to Sorha like she died, all volition left her Forest Man, all sense of life vanished from it and once more it was only a wooden statue. Then the air shimmered, and above it floated a figure of stick arms and branch-headed nightmares, one of the Boughry. In its arms it held a frail body, though not a real body, a spirit. Ania's spirit. On the back of Ont's Forest Man something opened with a hiss. The Boughry and the spirit of Ania were taken into the remaining Forest Man. The huge wooden body shuddered under this new burden, tried to stand, failed. Tried again, pushing itself up with what seemed a titanic effort then it lumbered over to Sorha.

"Go," she said, "I am done, finished."

"They need us all," said Ont and he used one hand to pull the blades from her chest. She did not even feel pain, only the gradual darkening of the world.

"Too late," she said.

"We will lend you our strength," said Ont, and she felt the touch of the Forest Man, felt the connection to Ranya's web she was lacking, though it was only the web within Ont that she touched. She felt the others there, too, the passengers, two Boughry and Ania. She felt how sorely Ont was tested, how little energy the Forest Man had left to share.

"I do not know how to be a spirit," said Sorha.

"Then you must walk in flesh," he said, and shared what he had with her cowl which fixed enough of her body so she could stand and then, together, they could stagger on through Harnspire, up and up, with every step they felt death coming closer. No enemy was needed now as time was on their heels and could not be escaped.

Eventually, they reached the top of the spire where a dais waited, one that drew Sorha to it.

"What now?" she said and something in her legs gave way. She found herself lying against the dais.

"We wait," said Ont, and the wooden body crashed to the floor by her.

"For what?" thought Sorha.

70
Cahan

He took a step backward.

They had lost.

Harn was lost.

The walls around the village faded into nothing, the houses of the village. Gone. No fire, no wreckage, no corpses lying on the ground, no enemy soldiers rejoicing in victory, only a roiling blue mass flowing over the ground and from it came thick tentacles that dragged it forward. It surrounded Harn; not only on each side but also above it, blocking out and consuming everything until all that remained was Cahan, and one building. The longhouse of Harn's Leoric, the one that contained pain and fear and guilt.

That building frightened him more than the oncoming tide of blue, even though he knew once the blue overtook him all that was Cahan Du-Nahere would be gone, diluted within the mass, lost forever. No Star Path for him, no falling into the web of Ranya.

And still, part of him preferred the idea of dissolution to entering the longhouse.

Why?

You know.

So much pain in there. So much pain waiting for him. So much guilt.

He took a step backwards.

There was death in there. So much death. So many, many deaths. Deaths he caused. Deaths that were on him as so many others had been. He had tried, done his best to avoid the darkness he had been raised to. Done his best to help others and it had not been enough, no matter which way he turned he had walked into the darkness. He had been conditioned for it. No matter his desires, his actions had brought on the fall of Crua, every turn he had made, every path he had taken the wrong one, and in that longhouse. What was in that longhouse? He did not remember but he knew he did not want it.

He took a step back.

Almost at the entrance to the building, its eaves hung heavy with pain, dripped with the same blood that was on his hands. His reckoning waited in there. He knew it, could not face it.

He was beaten and somewhere deep within Cahan believed that was right; he should have been beaten in Harn all that time ago. If he had died there then so much blood that was spilled upon the land would not have been. Maybe those he cared for would have lived longer.

But you would never have known them, learned to care for them. Fought for them.

The blue came on, and he was ready, he was tired. He was frightened of the longhouse behind him and the blue offered annihilation, it would be a blessing.

No.

He took a step back.

The blue oncoming, writhing boiling, dragging itself on, hungry for him.

He felt a touch.

Unexpected. Soft. Surprising.

Something took his hand and he looked down. A boy,

a small boy, looking up, smiling at him with too sharp teeth and bright, bright eyes. He knew this boy. Unlike the rest of the ghosts of Harn, this one was not faceless and formless. He was solid and real. A name floated into his mind.

"Issofur?" said Cahan.

"You offered your life to the forest once, Cahan Du-Nahere," said the boy and Cahan felt he spoke to the boy, and not the boy. There was something else behind him, or with him or in him. "Even before that, you walked Wyrdwood as a child. The forest has always been with you. In you as it is in me. As you once told my mother, those who are foreststruck are never the same."

"Furin," he said and there was a warm point, a single bright light. He had felt for her. She had given him so much.

"As she needed you then," the boy squeezed his hand, his bright eyes flashed, "she needs you now. Woodhome is about to fall and she will fall with it."

"Why tell me that?" Was this some final cruelty of the Boughry? To taunt him with the fate of those he loved before he was lost to the final attack. "I cannot escape this place."

"Your cowl has held you within a dream, kept you safe, but even it tires, Cahan Du-Nahere." Another gentle squeeze. "You must go in there," Issofur pointed at the longhouse. "The way out is in there."

The longhouse, no, it held so much more: the weight of guilt, the drip of blood, the bitter stink of failure.

"I cannot. Something awaits me in there. Something terrible happened to me in there."

Issofur smiled, his face open with all the wonder and innocence of a child, but behind those bright eyes shone the ancient wisdom of the forest.

"No, Cahan," said Issofur, "in there you were given a gift."

"A gift?" He looked at the dark entrance to the long-house, and felt sure that waiting within was pain and agony and death. "There is only death. I have brought only death." He tried to pull away but the small hand on his would not let him. It had all the strength of a cloudtree.

"Once, as a child you acted. Not in thought, but in fear and it was an act beyond your control, moulded by the cruelty of others, that it has haunted you proves you are not what you believe." The boy's voice felt like a blade in him. "In the longhouse, you received a gift."

"I caused so much death."

"Come," said Issofur, pulling on his hand, "come, Cahan Du-Nahere, Cowl-Rai of Crua, one of the chosen of Ranya, come and meet those who wait and fulfil your destiny."

"I . . ." words failed him.

"And if what is in there you cannot abide," said the boy, "then what comes will take us all, and you will worry no more." Issofur pulled, with all the strength of a determined child, with all the determination of an immortal forest.

"I . . ."

"Can you not sense what is missing from this place, Cahan Du-Nahere?"

"I . . ."

"Who is missing?"

Something in his mind, they had been missing, had always been missing. There were people here but they were not people. Only shades without names.

"I let everyone down."

"They await you," the boy pointed at the longhouse, "in there."

"But . . ."

"They need you."

"I killed so many, I caused so much death. They will not want me."

"You will only know the truth if you face them, Cahan Du-Nahere."

He looked behind, looked above, the blue slowly encroaching, oblivion calling. It offered the loss of guilt and fear. He almost heard a whisper, a voice but not a voice. *An end to your struggle.*

A squeeze of his hand. The open face of Issofur looking up at him, pointing at the building.

"You saved me once, Cahan Du-Nahere, now let me save you."

And in that, a decision made. An entreaty he could not deny.

He closed his eyes.

Despite his fear, despite everything he felt, the guilt, the truth that he had only ever let down those who had relied on him, he took one step forward.

Two.

Three.

Through the door, fighting the desire to turn and to run.

He could not.

Issofur vanished as he passed the threshold. The inside of the longhouse was familiar. The smoke from a fire, one that was never large enough to ward off the cold of Harn. The delicious smell of broth cooking over the fire and on a stool by it a figure, spooning out a bowl of broth.

He did not speak, not at first, did not know what to say. The figure was different from the villagers he had fought with and different from Issofur who had brought him through the door. Even clothed in shadow it was more real than any of them.

"Cahan," said the figure and looked up, holding out the broth. Their painted face familiar, though changed by age and by knowledge. Memories flooding back.

"Venn!" The trion nodded as he spoke their name. "What are you doing here?" Such a foolish, mundane question in such a place as this.

"The same as you, Cahan Du-Nahere," they said as he

took the broth from them. "I am dying." Venn opened their cloak to show the bare chest beneath and the great sucking wound in the centre of it. Cahan looked down, finding his own chest bare, finding the same great wound in his flesh.

"How?" He felt no pain, only shock.

"Sit," said Venn.

"No time," said Cahan, "the enemy has taken Harn and . . ."

"We have all the time we need, and no time at all," said Venn. "You and I are suspended between life and death by the corrupted god that sits atop the temple in Tiltspire."

"Why?"

"It needs us. It needs your strength, it has part of it through the bluevein in your body but not enough for what it wants to do. It needs me to provide a link to Crua that you can channel. Even now it makes connections between my body and Ranya's web. My consent allows it."

"Then we do not have time," said Cahan.

"In here we do, out there," Venn pointed at the door, "we do not."

"Why?" Venn shrugged then laughed softly.

"Our land is broken and has been so for time beyond time. We are an attempt to fix it, and it has been trying to fix itself for so long. We have been trying to fix it for so long."

"We have?"

"You, me, Udinny, Dassit, Ont and Ania, and many others." Those names, flooding into his mind, faces and acts and emotion attached to each and every one of them. "We are born and die and we are born again, but everything in Crua is broken. The way we feed cowls twists them, twists us." Cahan knew that, deep inside, he knew it. Remembered the plaintive voice within him before he had made his first kill. The voice begging him not to. "The land has been creating, in the depths of Wyrdwood, cowls of great strength to fix itself."

"Like me?" Venn nodded at his words.

"But then Cowl-Rai are forced to kill, twisted, and never become what they should be. The power the land needs to fix itself. To unite all cowls in this great task."

"You have never killed, Venn." The trion shook their head.

"No, but my cowl is born of generations of cowls from the Rai, that I do not kill has strengthened it. But I am still only a pathway, not a power."

"And the others?"

"Each an attempt to fix the land, I think. I do not really understand it. Whatever we are, we are important and needed. Drawn to each other again and again and again in life after life. But just as the land needs you to fix itself, the corrupted god wants you to burn everything and escape what it believes is a broken place."

"Why do I still live, if a god has me?"

"Your cowl," said Venn and they took up a bowl of broth for themselves. "I think it made this place, to keep who you are safe from the ravages of bluevein, from the siege of the god on your mind. You have held this place because there was nowhere else for you to go." Cahan nodded and Venn smiled at him. "That is not the case any more, Cahan." Venn stood. "What was it Udinny said? That we must walk the path, and trust in Ranya?" Cahan nodded confused, not really understanding. "Well, I am become the path, Cahan, and you and I have much work to do. But first we must escape Harn."

"If we have failed so many times, why even try again?" Out of the shadows of the back of the room came the boy, Issofur.

"Something has changed, someone who is new became caught up in the desire to fix the land," he said. "But you must escape this place, or you will become the tool of the corrupted and all is lost. You must reach the others."

"How? We are surrounded. I can feel the power out

there, the creature is too strong. You said yourself we are dying." As he spoke he felt a presence behind him, turned to see Issofur. Somehow he had moved without Cahan seeing and now he stood by the door.

"I will show you the way," he said softly.

"The enemy are too strong," Cahan shook his head, "even when the village was full I could only just hold them off."

"All you had then were ghosts and memories." Venn pulled their brightly coloured cloak tight, covering the wound in their chest. "What you need are warriors, Cahan."

"Who?"

"There were those I could not heal because my cowl could not see them, and I think to it they were not real. This place, this sanctum for your mind, is created by your cowl, and to it they do not really exist either, so there is no hint of them here." Venn smiled. "But they made a promise, they exist to fight for the Cowl-Rai, and if you call them, they will come to you."

"How can I call those who I do not remember?"

"They swore to protect you, Cahan. Do you not remember someone swearing to protect you?"

He searched his mind. Found a memory, an ancient one, two children being taken from their parents. One to be a power, the other trained to be a warrior who would protect them. A voice, her voice. "*We will always have one another.*" A stab of pain as he remembered her name. Nahac. His protector. His sister. But she was dead. Pain. But he heard another voice as he remembered the name, not that of his sister. "*Call my name and we will come.*"

"Warriors," he said, and spoke the name out loud. "Nahac."

Deep in the Forest

In far-off Tiltspire
  Two figures still as statue
  Broken and reborn and broken again
  Heard their name
  Opened their eyes
  And were gone.

71

Harn-Not-Harn

They appeared in the longhouse in a place that was not Harn. Two grey figures, solid in a way nothing but Venn had been until that point. Yellow wool wrapped their armour, making them bright slashes in the gloom, the grey face of one Reborn looking around, the other as silent and still as she ever was. With their appearance came memories, knowledge.

"This is not Crua, we are not in Wyrdwood," said the Reborn.

"No," said Cahan, "but I am in need of your help. Venn and I must escape this place, the enemy that stands against us is terrible and strong."

"We have promised ourselves to your cause," she said. As she spoke he saw something new about her, something that could not be seen in the true world, was lost in the teeming life of Crua, but here, where nothing truly lived, he saw a single golden thread attached to the head of each of the Reborn. It hung in the air like the finest strand of wool or a nettile string, drifting with an unseen breeze and through it flowed the power that brought the Reborn back to life, no matter how terrible their injuries.

"I also made you a promise," said Cahan, "to free you from the eternal life forced upon you and I will fulfil it now." He reached out a hand to the glowing line above the Reborn that had taken his sister's name, and with a twist of his hand he broke the thread. "Your death here will be final. I will ask nothing more of you." She stared at him, and did he imagine it or was there more life in those eyes than he had ever seen before. Then she turned to her sister, the second Reborn.

"Our last fight, sister of the spear, firstwife and friend," she said softly. "It pains me that I cannot look upon your face or hear your voice one last time, but take comfort from my touch." The nameless Reborn put out a hand, placed it on Nahac's armour, over her heart as Cahan reached out to sever the cord.

"Wait!" said Venn. They stepped forward, twisted their hand above the nameless Reborn's head, twirling the almost invisible thread around it and closing their eyes. The golden string glowed more brightly for just a moment, then Venn let go, stepped back and let Cahan snap the string. "I heal," said Venn softly. They sounded a little out of breath, a little more tired than they had before.

"She cannot be healed," said Nahac.

"And you thought you could not die," said Venn, "but the rules are different here." Nahac looked to the other Reborn. At first she did nothing then, hesitantly, she raised her hands, placed them either side of her helmet and very slowly lifted it. Beneath, her face rebuilt itself from the terrible wound that had taken her life. Some blunt weapon that had caved her skull in, then the two warriors looked upon each other, seeing who they were before they were returned from death for what must have been the first time in countless years.

"Avianaha," the once silent Reborn spoke as if speech was new to her. "Firstwife and sister of the spear. Look upon me, and know if it pleases Our Lady of Violent Blooms then it pleases me to die this day with you." Then the woman who Cahan knew as Nahac, tears on her face, nodded.

"Theanaraha," she said softly. "Firstwife and sister of the spear. Look upon me, and know if it pleases Our Lady of Violent Blooms then it pleases me to die this day with you." Then the two warriors replaced their helmets and pulled down their visors, turned to Cahan and when they spoke they spoke in unison.

"We are ready."

It will not be enough, thought Cahan, and a sense of hopelessness overcame him. They were fine warriors, but the force that waited outside was more than the four of them could fight. It was overwhelming, it was everywhere. Venn did not know, they had not been fighting the enemy for what felt like lifetimes. Issofur may be the forest but he had not felt the slowly gathering strength. They would not be enough – maybe if Cahan had all the strength of his cowl, maybe if the Boughry were here.

He took a deep breath.

If he were to die here then at least one good thing had been done. He had freed the Reborn from their torture, their time upon the land had been ended, and with an extra gift from Venn, which Cahan thought may be even more valuable to them than death.

"It is time," said Issofur.

Cahan nodded, stood before the door of the longhouse. He felt the pressure of the god outside, Tarl-an-Gig, Zorir, the one who would bring the fire for Saradis. He felt hopeless, they would not escape. They were not enough. Better to die trying, though. He felt Venn behind him and thought at least he would die with a friend.

Then.

Deep in the Forest

In far-off Tiltspire
  A dying woman
  Full of regret for mistakes made
  Heard her name
  Opened her eyes
  And was gone.

72

Harn-Not-Harn

third presence appeared in the longhouse. The Reborn
drew weapons.

What appeared, what came. It was unasked for, unexpected.

Another child.

A young girl.

To Venn who watched in confusion as this apparition
came into being, she had the unmistakable cast of Cahan
– an echo of his looks, a familial resemblance.

For Cahan, there was only shock, confusion and then
sadness, because who stood before him could not be
standing before him.

"Sister," he said, and in his voice was more sorrow than
had ever come upon him before, "have I called you here
from the Star Path?" A terrible guilt washing over him, to
have torn her from the next life to where only annihilation
waited.

"Brother," she looked up, and though she had the face
and body of a child, she had the eyes and voice of someone
much older. "I have not walked the Star Path, not yet, and
never did. I let Saradis turn me against you. I learned to

hate in a way you never could. I took all she taught in the monastery, and all my anger, and raised an army who called me Cowl-Rai." Words like a blow. Like being impaled on the temple all over again. Like hearing news of her death all over again.

"So," the word caught in his throat, "now you have come to do the bidding of your dark god?"

"No," the rasp in her voice one of sorrow, "you were my little brother. She made me believe you were weak, that I was your only strength. That you were less and I was cheated from my birthright. She did it too well, I ran away because I believed I should have been chosen, not you." The girl looked up, her eyes limpid with unshed tears. "But it has haunted me, who I became, what I did." She let out a long breath. "What I did not do."

"What do you mean?"

"I should have protected you. I was your older sister, maybe if I had done that, if I had stood with you as I should have, then you would not be here now." She looked around. "She has killed me, Saradis, she ended me with a knife of twisted wood and on the edge of death I heard you call my name. I felt your desperation and what I did not do then, I will do now. I will protect you, little brother."

"How?"

"Saradis enslaved me to her god, made me a part of it to give me power." She raised her head, her skin changed, throbbed until it was thick with veins of blue and lines of black, her voice now that of a grown woman, full of pain and fury. "But her god also strengthens me, Cahan." She raised a hand and from it came black whips, tentacles of fizzing power playing around her arm. "So let us leave this place, have your warriors take up arms. I will use what Saradis made me against her." With every word, the child changed, becoming something else, something dark and terrible. "I am part of this place. I am fed by it and yet I am not collared to be a slave. Under the canopy of my power let us cut a way out, and if it costs me my life so be it, but I will protect you, little brother, as I always should have."

He could not speak, could not understand. At once overcome by her great betrayal, that she had never died and had almost caused his death, and yet, warmed within that at the last she had come. He only wanted what he had always wanted of her. Not for her to protect him, but simply for her to be there.

"I do not expect forgiveness, Cahan," she said.

"And yet you have it, sister," he tried to smile but it was not a thing he had ever been good at. The emotions whirling within him he had no way to express and he turned away, back to the door, falling back on a familiar gruffness as each word threatened to choke him. "Come then, let us take a walk. It is time to leave here", he drew the axes from his sides, "if we can."

They stepped out of the longhouse. Each understanding the long path of their lives may end here, each expecting it and each strangely light of step despite it. Somehow they were complete in a way they had never been before.

Outside, Harn was gone and they found a landscape that was completely alien, like none Cahan had ever seen. It was not Crua, and not Osereud. This place was not light or dark but blue, a sickly, creeping blue and running through it was a single, wide, muddy path. At the end of it a small silhouette. Waiting.

"Issofur," said Venn.

On the path they fell into a formation, as if long practised. The Reborn at the front, then Cahan, Venn and behind them Cahan's sister, Nahac. Nothing happened at first. They simply walked. Cahan felt that what waited for them wanted to make sure they were away from the longhouse, so they could not run back to it. He could feel the cowl within him, how desperately it wanted to go back. How it believed it was the only place of safety.

You have looked after me, cowl, he thought, now trust me that we must at least try for freedom.

His thoughts calmed it, he felt it change within him. The longhouse faded away. His muscles swelled, his vision became sharper and what little the cowl had left it gave to him.

The attack started without warning, no roar of anger, no gradual oncoming enemy. The last battle of Cahan Du-Nahere was joined in a rush of blue as fast and strong as a falling tree, unstoppable, heavy. He was seized by a certainty there would be no fight, there would only be a sudden crushing defeat. Instead of raising his axes Cahan raised his arms, as if they could protect him.

"No!"

A shriek that cut through the weight of the onrushing blue. His sister, Nahac, rising into the air, her small body buffeted by an unseen wind. From her extruded black light, twisting and spinning into a cage about Cahan, Venn and the Reborn, holding off the weight of their attacker and he saw the terrible toll of this on her face, heard it in the long, single scream that came from her mouth.

But she gave them time, Cahan could feel the fury of the creature Saradis called a god, and also its confusion. It recognised in his sister that what fought it was also part of it and that gave it pause. Ahead he saw the path they walked was no longer just mud, but a glowing golden filigree of lines so delicate it seemed impossible that it could support them.

"We walk the path," shouted Venn and pointed ahead. In the distance, looking so very far away, Cahan could make out the familiar silhouette of Issofur and above the child a circle, with eight glowing lines that waved above him. "Ranya," shouted Venn, "Ranya awaits us!"

They ran, and Zorir overcame its confusion. Tentacles, snaked through the bars of Nahac's cage to attack, searching for those within. The razor-tipped tentacles were met by the warriors of Our Lady of Violent Blooms. The Reborn became a whirlwind of spinning spears and flashing blades, slashing and stabbing and all the time they moved forward. Cutting about themselves, making a path. The star in the distance and the silhouette of Issofur, growing.

But with every step toward the star the cage about them shrank. The tentacles grew more and more vicious, thicker and stronger.

When the end came, it came quickly.

The Reborn fell first. One skewered by a tentacle through her midriff, her body stilled, weapons falling from her hands. Her sister, lover, firstwife, saw it and was overcome, because this time it was true loss, a true end. In her momentary pause the tentacles of the creature found her, ripped her apart and then Cahan was fighting for his life, his axes flashing, left and right, making space for him and for Venn.

From behind him he heard the scream of his sister begin to falter.

He looked back to see her writhing, a blue tentacle through her chest. As he saw her, she saw him, smiled.

"Run!" her voice an echo, and then it was as if she gathered all she had left and threw it at Cahan and Venn, the cage surrounding them, twisting and turning into a ball that held them and bounced along the pathway while she was left behind, reduced to nothingness by the power of a god.

They were close, the burning star before them surrounding a black hole, a way out. Only a few steps away but the cage around them was disintegrating without Nahac to hold it together. All that remained was Cahan and Venn. Cahan dropped his axes. Instead of defending himself he pushed Venn as hard as he could toward the hole. Hoping they at least would make it out. They at least would live.

A blue tentacle, sharp as triumph, darting toward his face.

Issofur, saying a name, one familiar to Cahan, forgotten until the syllables were on the air, creating.

And from around Cahan's neck, a sinuous shape detached itself and launched through the air, sharp teeth biting through the tentacle, but another and another quickly appeared and ripped apart the garaur, reducing it to a cloud of golden dust.

"Segur!" the memory of his garaur coming hard and fast as the creature died, dissipating into the blue air. Tentacles began to choke him, to invade his body. Taking him over, the pain as sure and real as the grief he felt for the animal.

But the dust of Segur's body did not vanish, did not dissipate, instead it danced a spiral around the blue tentacles that held him and reformed, golden and lithe, before vanishing toward the black hole.

In those last choking moments Cahan had a little happiness. At least the garaur had escaped. And Venn? Had Venn?

From the darkness, a point of light, a golden hand in the air before him.

Was this the hand of a god, welcoming him to the Star Path? How could it be, the blue would take all of him. He reached out, faltering, suffocating, took the hand. After all he had nothing to lose.

"I have you, Cahan!" Issofur's voice.

Connection.

73

Congregation

Udinny

The door before us was splintering, thick black tentacles writhing as they pushed through. This was our end, we had fought a noble fight against insurmountable odds and we had done better than I, or anyone, could ever have expected. Dassit, in the body of the great Forest Man, was trying to get up, trying to make one last effort to defend us. Great wooden hands sliding on the blood and sap that pooled around her damaged body. It was galling, I suppose, to have come so close. To have got so near and yet to know you could not succeed.

"No, Dassit," I said, leaning back against the plinth. "Rest yourself. I think we are at the end of the path." I put my hand upon her great wooden body.

Connection.

Sorha

Broken and bleeding, both her and the great wooden thing that housed Ont, and Ania and two of the Boughry. They had fought, and fought and fought. She had never given up and, if she was to die now, bleeding out her life on the floor of the spire, then at least she had saved the Osere.

"You fought well, Ont, Ania," she said, each word barely a grunt, her life ebbing away with every breath.

"And you," replied the Forest Man. Its exhalation the gentle tap of dying leaves falling in a quiet forest. The wooden construct lifted a great hand, held it out toward her. Sorha lifted her own hand, bloodied, two fingers broken, skin filthy with the dirt of battle. She could not hold the Forest Man's massive hand, only managing to wrap her fingers around one of the Forest Man's.

Connection.

74

Connection

They stood atop the temple in ancient Anjiin.

Three Boughry
   Cahan Du-Nahere
   Venn
   Udinny called Pathfinder
   Ont, of Harn
   Ania, of the Forestals
   Sorha Firstborn, who called herself of the Osere.
   A Wa'urd fragment.

If it was dark they did not see it. The landscape before them was one of gold, of lines of power that ran across temples, under and through walls and around them and each and every one of them could feel its strength, its need.

"Well, this is strange," said Udinny.

"Are we dead?" said Sorha.

"No," said Udinny, "I have been dead and it was not like this."

"Then why are we here?" said Ont.

"And where is this?" said Ania.

"Ancient Anjiin," said Udinny, "I came here when I was dead."

"I have been here, too," said Cahan softly.

"And I," said Sorha, looking around at the others before adding, "I was not dead."

"Nor I," said Cahan. He watched as the Boughry floated over to the edge of the temple, their skull heads orientated on the three great towers, so tall they almost reached the roof far above.

"These are towers of Iftal," said Venn. "Once they were eight."

"Why are we here," said Cahan, "if we even are here?"

He got no reply from Sorha, the Boughry spoke, voices riding over them, like great wooden bells, like cracking flags, like the trunks of trees shattered by ice.

"What once was broken must be remade."

"I don't understand," said Sorha

"The path is Ranya's," said Ont softly, "we only walk it."

The Boughry had not moved. They remained with their skull heads fixed on the towers. Cahan felt helpless, he had been brought here for a reason but he still did not understand.

It was Venn who moved first, to the centre of the great pyramid, and rising up from it came three poles, one like a seat, the two flanking it flat and stopping where the hands could easily be placed upon them. Venn held what looked like a Wa'urd tentacle in their hands and lay it upon the seat, then crossed to the plinth on the left. Cahan felt himself drawn to the one on the right. One moment he was standing with the others. Then he was in front of the plinth.

"What do I do?" He felt like he should know but did not, and he blamed it on grief, his sense of confusion about all that had happened, how so many had died and at the last his sister. Found, and lost again just as quickly. So many dead and now he stood here, useless, confused. Only a clanless forester. A forester who had lost everything.

"Put your hands on the plinth, Cahan," said Venn. He did: what else could he do?

Awareness.

Flooding into him, unbearable at first, golden light, nothing but golden light.

Control it.

Venn's voice but not Venn's voice.

You need me.

The cowl inside him. So long he had fought it. Then it had saved him. Now he felt as if it burned beneath his skin, as if it wanted to take control of him. He could not, he could not . . .

Work with it, Cahan. It is part of you, like your arms, or your legs.

He couldn't. He was scared. More scared than he ever had been. He could feel the Boughry on the edge of his mind, feel their desire, and they terrified him. He could feel his cowl, its need to rise up, and it terrified him. He could feel the fragment of the Wa'urd, its mind strange and unknowable.

This was like the corrupted god, trying to consume him. No.

He felt the others as well, gathered here for him, by him, and a new fear rose. Of letting them down. They had come so far, done so much. He didn't know what to do. All he had ever wanted was to protect people. All he had ever done was fail.

No.

The voice of Venn and not Venn. So much more.

Alone you fail. Together we shall not. *Join with the cowl.* Join with me. *Join with us.*

So many voices. Behind them all something bright and golden – but incomplete.

The Wa'urd is with us.

For just one second, the gold vanished, he saw a burning circle with eight arms, three bright, five not, and it filled him with wonder. He felt the entire city of Anjiin around him, within it the sickness of the blue vein. There were people, broken by it, and gods, twisted by it. All coming this way. He felt this pattern repeated, throughout Crua above him, he thought himself small, almost non-existent and yet he glowed like the light above among them.

As he saw them, they saw him, or at least the gods and those infected with bluevein did. They were coming for him, they were coming for all of them.

Behind them he felt a presence he knew and feared. The god in Tiltspire, it was starting the fire. How? It needed him. It needed Venn. More knowledge seeping into him. His mind was here, Venn's was here, but they were physically on the temple. It had access through their bodies.

All feeling vanished and he was lost again. Adrift in the golden light, buffeted by such power as he had never believed possible. He was just one man. Too much was happening.

You need me: The Cowl.

You need me: Venn.

You need me: Ont.

You need me: Dassit.

You need me: Ania.

And we need you: Udinny.

We need you.

How was he hearing them? Was he hearing them? It felt like echoes of them, but not echoes of them. Nothing made sense. A sudden searing pain through his chest. He was dying. He was burning.

The twisted gods are coming, Cahan.

Time is limited.

Despair. He was not strong enough, he had never been strong enough. His only true victory had been at Harn, and that given to him by the sacrifice of others. He only brought death.

He could feel the god in Tiltspire, felt its fury. Feel how its allies were adding their power, finding places within Crua to join with it. Networks of bluevein syphoning off power. Others were here, physically, climbing the temple to try and stop them, to destroy the columns and the seat. Either way they would soon overwhelm him.

It was all too much.

He was only one man.

And he understood.

Only one man.

He finally understood.

Not only one man.

He was no lone hero here to save his world. He was one of many. It was like sticks. One on its own easy to snap. A bundle together so much stronger. One archer alone, nothing, a hundred together could stop an army.

Not about him. Never about him. He was strong but brittle. He needed others and they were here. He was never meant to be the one to use all this power that he could gather to him, he was the one to share it.

He let go, let the cowl meld with him. Let it link him to Crua.

Connection.

He gasped. The power was unbelievable, huge, everywhere. Filling him, drawn to him and he felt panic rising up. Too much, he needed an outlet, it would burn him to nothing here on this temple and he would be lost. Dead. Had to share. How?

Take my hand.

Venn! He felt like someone drowning offered a rope and he grasped hold of Venn. Held tight to them.

Control it, Cahan. Not too much.

He did not know how.

You need me.

The cowl, his cowl. He let go, let it know what he wanted, and the golden light began to fade as together they held the power in check. He still felt the enormous pressure behind it, and he knew he could not hold it for long.

He was burning, burning inside. Burning on the temple in Tiltspire. Burning here. Burning. Venn's voice. Cool.

Now, feed it to me.

How confident Venn was, how much they had grown.

Together, Cahan, we are almost what was once. What should be all of us.

He let some of the power escape, it wanted to escape and almost had a mind of its own, what started as a trickle wanted to be a torrent. Agony ran through him, and urgency, as he slowed it even more. Fire, every nerve ending alive.

Keep going, Cahan.

From him, the power went to Venn and Venn took it, the conduit. Through Venn he felt the presence of one of the gods, but not like the one on Tiltspire. This one was smaller, diminished. The fragment on the seat. Within it a map, an instruction. The trion was reading it, using it, passing the power from Cahan to the waiting Boughry who raised their stick arms as if in worship. He heard the echo of their thoughts.

Iftal, to be remade!

iFTaL remade

The ground below Cahan began to glow, the same golden glow that ran in lines all around them. The corrupted gods climbing the temple slowed, as if they were caught in sap, reaching tentacles held before they could snatch up those on tip of the pyramid who were both here and not here. Somewhere behind them he felt other gods, those untouched by the bluevein, moving with purpose through the ancient city.

The Boughry took his power, and from the temple each of them extended a bridge of light that rolled out across the expanse between each Boughry and the three huge towers.

Contact.

The Boughry floated across the gaps. Every moment an agony to Cahan, his body burning, beads of sweat were hot coals running down his skin. The Boughry reached the towers, falling into them, becoming them. Something snapped, like a vine stretched beyond its strength, the light bridges vanished and left behind solid streamers of pure power, filling the air with a hum. Filling Cahan.

Connection.

Burning him.

It has started, Iftal will be reborn here.

And the weight upon Cahan became less, not a lot less, but the power that boiled through him became shared, part of it siphoned away by the Boughry's towers.

Are you ready?

Yes, was it Venn speaking still? Or more than Venn?

More, Cahan. Let me have more.

He opened the gates within himself. Power flowing from him to Venn, from Venn to the Boughry towers.

Re-establish.

Pain, almost impossible to bear as he drew power, he felt the cilia of the cowl expanding in his feet and hands, usually so small as to be barely discernible, now like great cables funnelling through him. His body buffeted by unseen winds, hair and beard a lambent halo around his head as he took on more and more energy, handling it, passing it to Venn in a form that was safe for the trion to use and manipulate as instructed by the Wa'urd. Power pulsing back and forth between the towers and the trion.

Five more golden pathways, growing out from the top of the temple. More power, pulled screaming from him. Growing up from the ground of Anjiin frameworks of gold, ghostly towers, memories of what was, and once more eight towers rose around the temple. In the mind of Cahan names for each rang out.

Ont, Dassit, Ania, Venn, Udinny.

The points of an eight-pointed star, and him the centre, the burning circle of Ranya that linked them all.

Three left first. He felt them, Ont, walking across the golden path. Joining with the skeletal tower, a moment of wonder as the world opened up for the monk. The snap and release of the light bridge vanishing and a streamer of power replacing it. Then Dassit. Then Ania. Then he felt the touch of Udinny on his mind. Playful, amused, elated.

"This is what my swarden were building. This is the path I have always walked, Cahan. Ranya, the Boughry and us. We are the parts needed to fix Broken Iftal." Then she was gone, the snap and release. He felt Venn detach from him. A thought left behind.

My turn.

They walked across the final bridge and to their tower. Snap and release.

Gone, but not gone. There, with the others, separate and together, filled with wonder and joy at the possibilities now open to them. But Cahan knew the servants of Zorir were coming. Slowed, yes, but not stopped. The fire was still burning.

And what of me? he thought. But in thinking it, he knew. The pain of holding the power was gone. Now he felt only a pleasant warmth. A feeling as if this had always been. This was his place, the others, they were the facets, the arms of Iftal. He was the centre. Not scared any more, the huge amount of power below him no longer burned, it twisted and changed and moved through him and to the towers as they needed it.

It needs us.

Yes. It needed him. It needed his cowl. But something was still missing.

His mind reached out, one figure left on the top of the

temple. Sorha, looking around, all those with her gone, all that was left was her and the Fragment of the Wa'urd, a single tentacle. She looked lost.

"What of me?" she said. "Why am I here, Cahan? There is no tower for me."

He did not know, and could not have said if he did as his flesh was melting away, into the glowing power of the pyramid. He was becoming Cahan and more than Cahan. A facet of great Iftal, a part of something more and at the last a knowledge filled him. What needed done with this land, this place.

Sorha stood alone before the golden chair on top of the glowing temple, lost, alone and believing herself abandoned. Surrounded by the creatures of Zorir, moving almost imperceptibly to take her. Above, the temple of Zorir and the god that sat atop it, still drawing power, vying with Cahan for the energies of Crua. Lacking his mind, but using his body.

Somebody had to stop them.

Sorha felt her body, far away, slowly dying. Then it was pulled across Crua, rebuilt around her mind and she stood atop the temple. Real in a way she had not been until that moment. The fragment of the Wa'urd floated up and wrapped itself around the top of the seat. She felt a compulsion that drew her toward the chair and the Wa'urd around it. She heard voices; the Boughry, Cahan, Udinny, Venn, Ania, Ont, Dassit, all of them beating against her mind.

"Take your place, first Priest of Wyrdwood."

75

Crua

Fear ruled Crua for those few who had escaped the depredations of Zorir. For the soldiers, advancing behind shields with the collared at their backs, for the people hiding in derelict towns, woods and the long grasses of the plains. Their fear only deepened when the light above, the constant of their lives, blinked out of existence. Then, when the land shook and threw them to the ground, they shook and moaned and held one another, sure the land was about to open up and swallow them or disgorge Osere to claim their spirits. When the sky split and showed them a second sky, as full of tiny points of light as the forest at night, they did not know what this meant. They only knew fear and had only known fear for so long that they stared up, numb to this new terror.

In Tilt, Saradis, so sure of her victory, so pleased with herself, found her soul swelling with joy as the geysers of Tilt exploded and the land cracked around them. This must be it, the fire. She felt it, she had watched as Zorir drew power, screaming and writhing on the temple. Below her god the bodies of Cahan and Venn danced like puppets before they ignited. She felt the heat of them dying even from where she stood before the spire.

She felt only joy when a second temple rose. It consumed Tilt, massive old houses falling into the yawning gorge created by it. This temple was far, far larger than the one Zorir sat on. Soon it was towering above it. Here was the end. This must be last sign of Zorir, the bringer of fire.

Only when she saw what was on top of the temple did the smallest amount of worry enter her mind.

There was someone there.

A woman.

As the huge temple locked into place the woman lit up. She was surrounded by a golden halo of power. Below her, on the steps of the temple, Saradis saw more of the gods, her gods, an army of them and she exulted in them. Until she saw they did not move, they were frozen in position.

The world shook, a tremor ran through Crua so powerful she feared the great spire would come down on her. Zorir writhed and screamed and began to burn and she should have been pleased, because Zorir was fire, but this felt wrong, deep within her she felt this was wrong.

"No," she said.

"It is time." The voice that spoke was unfamiliar to her and she looked down. A child, the forest child who had come with Venn, was looking up at her.

"The fire is here?" she said, her voice so soft, so quiet. The child shook his head.

"No," said Issofur. "Wyrdwood has come."

She looked down at the child, at this strange creature of the hated wood and in that moment realised she had lost. All her dreams, all her work, somehow the fact that this child stood before her meant it was all undone. Zorir burned, not to bring the fire, but because the dream was ended. For a moment, she did not know what to do, then spite and hate welled up within her. If nothing else she would rid Crua of this hateful thing before her and she drew the knife from her belt

From beneath her came a spear of wood, the tip of a

great tree. It fractured the stone, spearing through Saradis and carried her up, twisting and reaching for the sky, taking her body up into the air while on the temple her god screamed and writhed and died.

76

First Priest of Wyrdwood

She felt the touch of the Wa'urd, the same one she had met in Osereud, but greatly diminished now though it was ready to grow again. This time to grow with her, they would grow together.

There was much to do, she knew there was much to do and together Sorha and the Wa'urd reached out for Iftal, found the facet Udinny and requested energy, to build and to fix.

In Wyrdwood, north and south Udinny spoke and the land of Crua opened its shield to the vastness beyond, the great cloudtrees unfurled their leaves and drank in the power that flowed to them, fed it into the ground below where it was gathered by Ranya's web, overseen by the towers of Ont and Venn who pulled on the old knowledge of the Boughry and moment by moment the web became stronger. The power flowing into her temple grew and it was managed and regulated by Cahan.

Atop the temple, she, Sorha, first Priest of Wyrdwood, communed with the Wa'urd. She let power flow into the Boughry, let the energy fill them and fix them and they remembered what once was. Power flowed through Crua, fallen spires rebuilt themselves in moments, rising from the ground as if time worked backwards. She commanded her temple rise.

Sorha found the Osere, found every one of them where they hid in the spires, or in Osereud, and she spoke gently to them, sending them to temples and spires, she pushed them towards taffistones. She found those who were not too far gone in bluevein and she healed them, then she found all of the sick and the wounded of Crua and Osereud and healed them too.

She brought Frina, and her first, and second husbands and wives to her. A people with unspoiled cowls, not twisted by the work of the Rai, who had proved their devotion through long and thankless years. Here was a priesthood in waiting, a kinder way to live beckoning.

She heard the voice of Iftal, and it was the voice of many she had known and there was no sadness in their transformation. They and she rejoiced in their new place, in their ability to make their land a better place.

Corruption detected. Purge corruption?

"Yes," she said and she felt for Ania. Together they reached out into the land with the power of Iftal, burning the bluevein from Crua.

In Woodhome, an army on the verge of victory fell to the floor.

In Tiltspire, a god writhed and screamed as the fire it had dreamed of burst from it and ran along the thick bluevein roots that covered the city of Tilt and consumed all that was within it, leaving only the spires and two great black temples.

Ont whispered of the forests to her. She felt the legions of swarden, compelled to try and build spires they would never be able to create and she told them they could sleep now. She found the skinfetches, let them know they could stop trying to be the people, and let them sleep also. She found the rootlings and the shyun and found they were happy, a part of the land, and she let them be.

Dassit whispered of the cold in the north and the heat in the south and how it brought them war, again and again, and Sorha found an ancient mechanism that controlled the gentle sway to and fro of Crua around the axis of Tilt. Something that always should have been, to create a rhythm of seasons, and Sorha made it work once more. She found the breaks and crevasses throughout Crua and knitted the land together and all the time she felt the presence of those who had been her companions, felt their approval.

Ont told her of his grove, and the taffistone within and how the network should allow any of the people to roam across the land and go where they will. Sorha burned the bluevein from the network, rewove the web around it and made it usable by all. Cahan pulled her eye to the east and west, the Slowlands, and she knew it had a purpose, great generators that held the people to the land. That it had been used to torture so many and contained so many tortured souls was an affront to her so she freed them to once more become part of Crua, ready to be reborn.

Udinny showed her Ranya's web, and held within it the minds of all those who had fallen in battle, who had the bluevein forced upon them, and Sorha knew that through Udinny each would be reborn, made anew.

Then Udinny pulled her further into the web and showed her a mind, a woman, lost and in pain. Through the web she heard a name and with the name came meaning. Nahac, sister to Cahan, and torment followed her, memories of what she had done, who she had been and how through her Saradis had brought about such destruction. She felt Cahan's sorrow and removed Nahac's pain, her memories of what she had done and returned her mind to the web. Before she could turn away, Udinny showed her another mind and Sorha recoiled. She knew this mind, the fury and horror held within in it. Saradis.

It was in Sorha's power to destroy the woman, remove her entirely, and that was her first instinct but at the last moment she did not. There was something within Saradis she recognised, something hidden deep within the people she had been. She dived into her mind, peeling back layers of time, and found a surprise. Here was the priestess who had spoken to her from ancient Anjiin when the Wa'urd showed her Crua as it once was. In that instance she also saw how Saradis had been twisted. How she had been one of those born again and again to fix the world, always searching for what she had once been. Always knowing deep down she should sit by the Wa'urd and change the world for her people. Instead of hate, Sorha felt pity and, rather than destroy her, she peeled away the layers of lives, the memories of what she had once been and then released her mind into the web. She was sure she felt a sense of approval from Udinny.

Lastly, there was Venn, who sat closest to the Wa'urd of all those who had become Iftal. But Venn did not look to Crua, they looked out, and away from it. Stared through a darkness filled with myriad glowing dots and toward one particular point. She felt a longing from Venn, and when she turned her mind toward this point it engendered within her such a feeling of need, a desire to be there, she almost wept. There was a safe place, somewhere she wanted to be. She felt the Wa'urd gathering, leaving their pods, connecting with Ranya and Iftal, and she felt the tremendous power within Crua. Venn laughed, and shared with her the numbers that the Wa'urd conjured up, the numbers of movement and place and distance and time. They danced through her mind, creating lines in the sky, showed her where to go and she woke ancient Anjiin, she released the power of Crua. In the north, great energies were set free, huge mountains of fire that had been cold for so long lit up and they *pushed*, once more setting the land upon the Star Path.

Sorha took her hands from the plinths, stepped down from the dais and left the Wa'urd fragment behind her.

Waiting for her were the Osere. Frina stepped up and took her hand. Behind her, one of the old gods was climbing the pyramid and there was no threat from it. She knew it came to help.

"Are we safe?" said Frina.

"There is a long way to go," said Sorha, "but, yes, we are safe."

"And what now?" said the Osere.

"We will make a better world, but first there is something I must do."

Frina nodded, let go of her hand and stepped back.

"We will be here when you return, Sorha, Priest of Wyrdwood."

Epilogue

The army that had attacked Woodhome was gone. Dead. Those infected with bluevein had simply fallen where they stood. The rest had either surrendered or quickly been overcome, and now the Forestals celebrated. The sound of music and dancing filled the tree city of Woodhome. All were happy to escape a death they had come to believe was inevitable.

All except Furin.

She had nothing. Cahan was not coming back, she knew that, felt it deep within her, and Issofur was gone along with Venn. She sat before the taffistone, trying to block out the sound of the celebrations, trying not to hate them for their joy, and she felt the call of the void beyond the platforms of Woodhome. One step and all her pain would be done. She did not notice the opening of the stone. Nor the figures who stepped through it.

"Furin." She looked up. Recognised the Rai woman, Sorha. How could she still live when so many others were gone? Good people, people who . . .

Her thought remained unfinished, her mind overcome with emotion. Standing by the Rai woman was her son,

Issofur. But not how he had been, not the foreststruck, furred child who was bright of eye and sharp of tooth. This was her son as he had been, just a boy once more.

"I had a strange dream, firstmother," said Issofur. He sounded tired. "I travelled all over the land, and was often frightened. Then I was alone in a strange city and this lady came to find me." Furin could not speak. Could not think.

"Go to your firstmother, Issofur," said Sorha, "she needs you." Then he was in her arms, and she was burying her face in his hair. Lost in the smell of him, the feel of him. She did not notice Sorha, a smile on her face, slip away through the taffistone.

meet the author

RJ BARKER lives in Leeds with his wife, son and "a collection of questionable taxidermy." He grew up reading whatever he could get his hands on, and having played in a rock band before deciding he was a rubbish musician, RJ returned to his first love, fiction, to find he is rather better at that. As well as his debut epic fantasy series, the Wounded Kingdom trilogy (*Age of Assassins*, *Blood of Assassins* and *King of Assassins*), RJ has written short stories and historical scripts which have been performed across the country. He has the sort of flowing locks any cavalier would be proud of. RJ's novel *The Bone Ships* was the winner of the British Fantasy Society's Best Fantasy Novel, aka the Robert Holdstock Award.

Find out more about RJ Barker and other Orbit authors by registering for the free monthly newsletter at orbitbooks.net.

orbit

Follow us: